Praise for THE HOUSE OF DUST

'In a series of highly original books set a couple of decades in the future, Paul Johnston has created a portrait of the post-Enlightenment city-state of Edinburgh . . . the books are always entertaining, in part because of the unsquashably rebellious personality of Johnston's maverick sleuth, Quint Dalrymple, and the sardonic humour which enlivens the narrative . . . another fine example of great storytelling'

Sunday Telegraph

'Johnston's plotting is consummate and his characterisation deft. He is also a very funny political satirist so that although *The House of Dust* is set in the future he is, of course, commenting on Scotland and England today. Very enjoyable'

Observer

'Johnston has cleverly developed a series . . . multiplying his options for Swiftian satire by moving his cussed sleuth around the former United Kingdom'

The Sunday Times

Praise for THE BLOOD TREE

'Johnston introduces some welcome new characters and a change of scenery by sending his quirky investigator, Quintilian Dalrymple, outside the city state of post-Enlightenment Edinburgh to its hated rival, Glasgow . . . this futuristic series is still refreshingly original and entertaining'

Sunday Telegraph

'Quint Dalrymple [is] a testy, tenacious detective . . . a smart move to shift much of the novel to Glasgow'

The Sunday Times

'The platonic dystopia of Enlightenment Edinburgh is perfect for blending crime stories and satire . . . a pacy read and all the required elements are there: villains are unmasked, loose ends are tied up, and like revenge, justice is served cold'

The Scotsman

'An engaging protagonist . . . an imaginative and enjoyable read and the futuristic setting is well worth a visit'

Manchester Evening News

Praise for WATER OF DEATH

'An acclaimed crime series . . . Johnston brings an intelligent perspective to the dark excitement of the thriller'

Nicholas Blincoe, *Observer*

'Both prescient and illuminating'

Ian Rankin, *Daily Telegraph*

'Johnston's vision is shot through with the bleakest of black humour, never losing sight of the humanity of his characters. This series is getting better all the time'

Val McDermid, *Manchester Evening News*

'A thoroughly enjoyable tale'

Sunday Telegraph

'Trendily dystopian'

Glasgow Herald

'Not only a cracking thriller (with a hugely shocking climax), but a timely one. Johnston's vision of the future is highly entertaining'

Ham & High

'Sardonic wit, brilliant concept and a strong plot'

Birmingham Post

Praise for THE BONE YARD

'A sly satire and gruesome thriller'

Mike Ripley, *Daily Telegraph*

'Impressive follow-up to the award-winning *Body Politic* . . . Johnston's conceit with Edinburgh is brilliant and there's a mordant Scots wit . . . stylish'

Guardian

'First-rate crime fiction with an original twist'

Sunday Telegraph

'A powerful, fantastical thriller'

Mail on Sunday

'An ingenious and chilling thriller that has the added bonus of being a sardonic political satire'

The Sunday Times

Praise for BODY POLITIC

'A hugely entertaining fantasy . . . engagingly imagined'

The Times

'Think of Plato's Republic with a body count'

The Sunday Times

'An intricate web . . . Johnston is a Fawkes among plotters . . . Quint's career looks set to blossom'

Observer

'Fascinating and thought-provoking'

Val McDermid, *Manchester Evening News*

'A thrilling hunt-the-psycho novel with countless twists . . . accomplished . . . offers real proof of the vigour and class of current Scottish crimewriting'

Ian Rankin, *Scotland on Sunday*

'Imaginative . . . remarkable . . . shows that crime fiction can be not only thrilling but intellectually exciting as well'

The Economist

Also by Paul Johnston

Body Politic
The Bone Yard
Water of Death
The Blood Tree

About the author

Paul Johnston was born in 1957 in Edinburgh, where he lived before going to Oxford University. He now divides his time between the UK and a small Greek island. He is the author of four previous novels, *Body Politic*, winner of the John Creasey Memorial Dagger for best first crime novel, *The Bone Yard*, *Water of Death* and *The Blood Tree*. You can visit his website at www.paul-johnston.co.uk

The House of Dust

Paul Johnston

NEW ENGLISH LIBRARY
Hodder & Stoughton

First published in Great Britain in 2001
by Hodder and Stoughton
A division of Hodder Headline

A New English Library paperback

2 4 6 8 10 9 7 5 3 1

All characters in this publication are fictitious
and any resemblance to real persons, living or dead,
is purely coincidental.

A CIP catalogue record for this title
is available from the British Library

ISBN 0 340 76613 1

Typeset in Melior by Hewer Text Ltd, Edinburgh
Printed and bound in Great Britain by
Mackays of Chatham plc, Chatham, Kent

Hodder and Stoughton
A division of Hodder Headline
338 Euston Road
London NW1 3BH

In memory of
Margaret Johnston
(1926–1996)

Belated but heartfelt thanks to:
Philippa Pride, editor *sans pareil*,
and to
Ronald Johnston, master mariner, storyteller and reader.

THE HOUSE OF DUST

Life goes by like a dream. The nightmare only begins when your brain slips out of gear and you realise that everything is turning to dust.

I can remember when spring was a non-event in Edinburgh. We used to go straight from the damp chill of winter to summer's deceitful blue skies, and the wind's well-honed knives never took more than a day off at a time. Things are different now. April 2028 was even warmer than previous years. People started parading around in clothing that revealed far too much, juxtaposing the skin and bone of undernourished locals with tourist flab. In June the Big Heat that results from global warming would kick in and the city would turn into a giant Turkish bath, though not in the air-conditioned hotels occupied by our honoured guests.

Except, come June, the tour companies might well have voted with their feet and left us to enjoy the sweat season on our own. The ruling Council of City Guardians has been losing the fight against the youth gangs in the suburbs for over a year. These days groups of Edinburgh's generation excess even mount raids into the central zone, divesting foreigners of currency, clothing and consciousness – not necessarily in that order. The headbangers in the City Guard, no strangers to extreme violence themselves, have had more than their hands full.

Which is why the guardians, fearful that their main source of income is about to go drier than the Water of Leith in August, have been working on a plan to put even more of a squeeze on their subjects. The appearance of the first swallows – they arrive earlier every year – coincided with the completion of the city's new corrective facility: it was intended to turn the Council's "perfect city" into a fully operational prison-state. Personally I've never been a supporter of banging people up, but no one asked my opinion. After all, I'm only an investigator. What do I know about crime and the causes of crime?

So every night the city resounds to the frantic rush of youthful feet and the slap of truncheons on flesh. Special squads of extra-hefty guardsmen and women were formed to deal with the gangs late last year, but the so-called "beaters" end up beaten more often than not.

The problem for me in recent months has been one of commitment. When I was a kid I loved Edinburgh for its breathtaking vistas and its glorious if blood-lathered history. Even after my home city set itself up as an independent state twenty-five years ago, I stayed on the scene. The Council's extreme policies were better than the mayhem we'd lived through when the UK was ripped to pieces in the drugs wars, and its high-minded Platonic ideals at least meant that people were treated with a reasonable degree of fairness. But I've had about as much as I can take of the present regime's iron fist. I've even been considering slipping over the border and heading for Glasgow – at least there's a semblance of democracy there.

To hell with spring. I go along with Merline Johnson. Back in the 1930s she sang about the blues being everywhere. I've always had a tendency to pessimism, but it took the fatal shooting of a guardian and a journey to the underworld to make me realise just how right the old diva was.

CHAPTER ONE

The windows to my bedroom were barred – thick, rusty steel implanted in the worn stone – and the walls were damp with condensation. I couldn't see much out of the grimy glass, but I knew the flats across the street were also decorated with heavy metal fixtures. When the Housing Directorate started erecting the bars last year, it was claimed they were to protect citizens from incoming scumbags – though how the youth gangs' members were supposed to climb three storeys of vertical granite was never explained. Everyone knows what the guardians have really been up to and that's turning us all into prisoners.

There was a tap on the window, then another. It was a small bird, a blue tit. It peered in at me, motionless, then twitched its head and disappeared in a blur of feathers. I felt the smile die on my lips and turned away. The birds are as free as it gets in Enlightenment Edinburgh – if they can avoid the kids armed with slings who trade the tiny avian corpses for stale bread from the hotels. Apparently there are tourists who regard songbirds as a delicacy.

"You're going to wet the bed, Quint." Katharine took the mug from my hand and sat down on the bed. Watery sunshine was making an attempt to filter through the dirty glass.

I shook my head at her dispiritedly.

"What is it?" She ran a hand over her spiky brown hair and held her piercing green eyes on mine.

"It?" I said, playing for time.

She shook her head in irritation. "Come on, Quint. I'm not an idiot. More mornings than not since I've been coming back to this cesspit you call home, you wake up like a long-distance sleepwalker. Obviously something's getting to you."

I took the mug back from her and swallowed the last of what the Supply Directorate solemnly swears is coffee. "Shit." I wiped my mouth with my hand. "What do they put in this stuff?"

Katharine smiled. "I think you've answered your own question." She held her eyes on me. "So are you going to tell me what's disturbing your slumbers or not?" She waited for a reply. "Apparently not," she said, getting up from the bed and heading for the door. "I'm off to the drop-in centre. At least the people down there converse."

"Hold on," I said, stretching out to grab her arm. "Sorry. I don't . . . I don't really know what it is." I glanced out of the window again. There was no sign of the blue tit. "This place is going down the bloody tubes, Katharine, and we're just sitting around watching."

"Speak for yourself," she said, her tone caustic. "I'm doing the best I can for the city's confused kids." She shook her arm out of my grip. "Anyway," she continued, "what about us? Haven't you got anything out of us being together again?"

I bit my lower lip. "Us? What does 'us' mean? After the nightmare case in Glasgow back in '26 you lost yourself in Welfare Directorate business. I hardly ever saw you. You stopped coming round here, you moved down to Leith to be closer to your work. And then you turned up out of the blue a couple of weeks ago. I mean, I hadn't even laid eyes on you for months—" I broke off and gave her a blank stare. "If you ask me, 'us' isn't worth a flying fuck, Katharine."

She glared at me, then the lines on her face slackened. "A flying fuck," she repeated. "I don't think I've ever had one of those." She sat down on the bed again.

I pushed her away gently, feeling slightly less suicidal. I've never been good in the mornings. "Well you're not getting one now, citizen. I've got a report to make to the public order guardian in under an hour."

Katharine looked at me then shook her head. "You'd better not keep the old bastard waiting then." She got up and headed to the wardrobe. "I presume you'll be needing these."

"Here, watch it!" I yelled as a black sweatshirt and trousers were thrown over me.

She waited till I shifted the garments off my head. "And I guess you'll be needing these."

Supply Directorate underwear and socks that were beginning to show their age hit me in the face.

"Breakfast in two minutes," Katharine said, marching out of the bedroom. "Dearest."

I splashed water from the sink over my face and got dressed. At least Katharine hadn't thrown my steel toe-capped boots at me. I reckoned that two days' stubble would irritate the guardian intensely so I left it untouched by my blunt razor blade. I needed a new one but I wouldn't get a voucher till next week.

"You look lovely," Katharine said, inclining her head towards the kitchen table as I went into the main room. "Though your hair could do with a mow."

I normally keep my head with less than an inch of grey matter on it. I hadn't had time to hit the barber recently and it was double length now.

"What's this?" I asked, examining the crusty object on the table.

"A barracks bagel, would you believe?" Katharine said. "Someone must have done a deal with a foreign supplier. Twenty tons of last year's bakery products for five hundred holidays in Edinburgh or the like."

"Anything to keep the tour operators sweet." I bit into the bagel and immediately wished I hadn't. "What's inside this?"

"Prune and date, I think. Nice, isn't it?"

I grimaced as I swallowed and headed for the door. Even by Edinburgh standards it had not been a breakfast of champions.

"Wait a minute," Katharine said. "Haven't you forgotten something?"

I patted my pockets and felt keys, mobile phone, notebook and cosh – the last object essential these days given the city's lunatic fringe. "Don't think so."

She came towards me, her slim form and strong legs crossing the confined room quickly. "Tonight, Quint," she said, enunciating as if to a backward child. "Are we doing anything tonight?"

"Ah." I gave her an awkward smile. "Tonight's a bit of a problem. You see, it's the Council's party for the Oxford delegation and—"

"What?" Suddenly Katharine's face was set hard. "I thought you said you weren't going to that freak show."

"Em . . . true enough, I wasn't going to."

"So what's made you change your mind?" Katharine demanded. "Surely you don't want to stand around exchanging chit-chat with those repressive shitebags, do you?" She glared at me. "The Corrections Department is going to ruin this city and it's all because of those supposed geniuses from Oxford." Her eyes were wide open and her chest had begun to heave. "Prison won't solve any of Edinburgh's problems and you know it."

"Yes, Katharine," I said as patiently as I could manage. "I know that. I've been against the reintroduction of incarceration all along. I was only invited to the reception so the Council could rub my nose in the new prison."

She was still staring at me, her lips pursed. "Why are you giving the guardians the chance then?"

I shrugged. "I'm a glutton for punishment." I raised my eyes to hers. "And I also want to find out exactly what's going on between the Council and the Oxford delegation. You never know how useful that might be in the future."

"Oh." Katharine's expression softened. "Okay. As long as you don't turn into a supporter of imprisonment. I'd never forgive you, Quint."

"I know you wouldn't," I replied, smiling cautiously. "See you here afterwards?"

She shook her head. "No. I'm doing an overnight shift at the centre. Tomorrow evening?"

"You're on." I leaned forward to kiss her.

She let my lips touch hers for a second then pushed me away. "Give them hell," she said under her breath.

"Give who hell?" I asked as I turned towards the door.

"Everyone," she said. "But especially the bastards who want to lock young people up. They should try a few years in solitary themselves."

I wasn't going to argue with that. Katharine knew much more about life inside than I did.

I could have called for a guard vehicle to pick me up but, since the Supply Directorate had finally come up with a new front wheel for my antediluvian bicycle, I decided to get some exercise. The citizen rush hour was long past so I had the streets to myself apart from the clapped-out, diesel-spewing buses and the tourist taxis; no private cars have been seen in the city since the original Council outlawed them twenty-plus years ago, along with cigarettes, computers, television and private telephones. It had turned into about as good a spring morning as we get in Edinburgh and, as I headed up Lauriston Place towards the infirmary in the weak sunshine, I could hear the school kids rioting in the Meadows. Structured play, of course – or so the education guardian claimed. I suspected the poor wee buggers were really getting combat training so they could get home in one piece every afternoon.

Panting from the gradient, I passed the city's main hospital on my right and swung round towards George IV Bridge. As I was approaching a pair of dull-eyed guardsmen in grey uniforms – the body armour and helmets they wore being evidence of the youth gangs' ability to do serious damage – a high-pitched, mechanical scream almost canted me over into the gutter. After what seemed like a very long time, the noise reduced to a steady whine that was almost bearable.

I looked up to see the senior of the two guardsmen mouthing a phrase that would have earned him a day licking the latrines; the Council requires auxiliaries, even the muscular ones, to observe a strict language code.

"Bloody right," I agreed, putting my right foot back on the pedal.

The younger guardsman stepped forward, hand on his steel-filled truncheon. He obviously fancied taking his angst out on an over-familiar local.

"Let him be," the older man said. His accent was the soft lilt of a Highlander; although most of them go to Glasgow to escape the marauders, a few prefer Edinburgh's hair-shirt and haggis regime. "Morning, Citizen

Dalrymple. Arse-juddering machines, aren't they?" He stared up at the dark blue aircraft with cutback wings that was coming down slowly on the roof of the pale brown museum building.

"Aye," I agreed, reading the badge on his tunic. "You're right, Knox 87." Auxiliaries are known by barracks name and number rather than their own names, at least in public. This one had probably seen me at some crime scene or in the pages of the *Edinburgh Guardian*. "Who would have thought the top of what used to be the Museum of Scotland would end up as a miniature airport?"

"Progress is a wonderful thing, is it not?" Knox 87 said. His ironic tone drew a shocked look from his youthful companion.

"The New Oxford helijet is an amazing machine," the junior guardsman said. "Vertical take-off and landing capabilities, fifty luxury seats and a cargo capacity of over thirty tons. There are twenty-two in service and—"

"I thought I told you to stop reading those dirty aeroplane magazines, Raeburn 543," the senior man said sternly, giving me a wink. "Take care of yourself, citizen." He led his scandalised subordinate away.

I peered back up at the museum roof. Transparent anti-blast panels had been built out over the streets to protect innocent bystanders like me. We weren't provided with earplugs though. I shook my head in an attempt to regain full hearing. The New Oxford helijet. It was as good a symbol as any for the influence on the Council that the southern city had built up over the last year. Who did they think they were, these academics? First they get a contract to oversee the construction of Edinburgh's first operating prison for ten years, then they insist on having a landing pad built for their poxy aircraft as near the central zone as possible. And do the guardians lie down and open their legs? You're bloody right they do.

I continued up the road and flashed ID at the checkpoint beyond the main archive. Ordinary citizens are only allowed into the tourist zone to work and technically I'm still of that rank, having been demoted for refusing orders back in 2015. But the Public Order Directorate has been using me as a freelance senior investigator for years so I'm allowed to move around unhindered, at least in theory.

As I squeezed through a group of Indian tourists on Castlehill, I forced myself to concentrate on the report I was about to make. Lister 25 was Edinburgh's chief toxicologist. He'd worked with me on some of my biggest cases. More interesting as far as I was concerned, he was a closet blues freak, a devotee of Robert Johnson – which wasn't bad considering the Council banned the blues decades ago because of what it saw as the music's subversive nature. A senior auxiliary like Lister 25 would have been for the high jump over the North Bridge if he'd ever been caught listening to the old master.

But even more interesting right now was the fact that the city's number one chemist had disappeared twelve days back. Without leaving a trace.

I crossed over the narrow drawbridge leading to the castle gatehouse and asked the guardswoman on sentry duty where the public order guardian was. Lately, Hamilton had acquired the habit of roaming around his domain like a lost sheep and not answering his mobile. I was directed to the command centre in what used to be the Great Hall. On the way up the winding cobbled road I couldn't miss different shots of the panorama over

Edinburgh's northern sector. Beyond the shops, marijuana cafés and gambling tents in the central zone – tourist access only – the suburbs where ordinary citizens live stretched away to the Firth of Forth, windows glinting in the sunshine. It looked like a picture of urban serenity; unless you knew how dangerous the youth gangs had made the streets the further you went from the city centre.

In the restored medieval hall with its hammerbeam roof I got a surprise. It must have been a month since I last visited the Council's security headquarters, but in that time a bank of new, ultra-modern computers had been installed. The detailed wall maps of each part of the city had been replaced in certain central locations by interlinked screen panels that gave virtual displays of streets and even individual buildings. As I watched in astonishment, one panel zoomed in on the greyhound track at Easter Road. I heard a dispatcher directing a guard vehicle to the perpetrator of a mugging who was hiding in the groundsman's shed.

"Impressive, don't you think, Dalrymple?"

I turned to the public order guardian. He was looking pleased, no doubt because he'd managed to sneak up on me. "What's all this, Lewis? Don't tell me the Council's finally entered the twenty-first century?" Till now the city's leaders had always done all they could to restrict the use of computers; they wanted to control the flow of information, but all they did was land themselves with a huge, paper-driven bureaucracy that no one could handle – not even an archive rat like me.

"Trust you to carp," the guardian said, shaking his head. "I'd have thought technology like this would make your job easier." Although he was in his late seventies, Lewis Hamilton was still an imposing figure, his white hair and beard giving him the look of an Old Testament patriarch. Unfortunately, in recent times his staff have paid about as much attention to him as they do to the Holy Writ: auxiliaries are required to be atheists.

I nodded. "It probably would." I watched a heavily built middle-aged woman move towards us. "If I were given a free rein."

Hamilton caught the sharpness in my voice. "We'd all like one of those, Dalrymple," he said sotto voce. "Ah, Raeburn 124, everything in hand?" He was trying to sound like he was in command but I didn't buy it. Neither did his deputy.

"Oh yes, guardian," she said, a tight smile cutting across her fleshy face. "Everything is very much in hand." Raeburn 124 – known throughout the City Guard as "the Mist" both because she'd appeared out of the blue at the top of the directorate tree and because she came down everywhere to put a serious dampener on things – glanced at me with ill-disguised disapproval. "Citizen Dalrymple," she said, aiming her small eyes at a point several inches to the left of me. "To what do we owe the pleasure?"

I smiled malevolently. "I've no idea what gets you going, but I own up to whisky and the blues."

The deputy guardian moved her eyes off me and tried not to spit. She had a reputation among her subordinates for enforcing standards of discipline that Stalin would have been proud of. I was an independent operator – inasmuch as such a being exists in Enlightenment Edinburgh – so she couldn't lay down the law to me. I got the feeling that kept her awake at night.

"I don't imagine we'll be continuing this diverting exchange at the reception tonight, citizen," the Mist said, smoothing down her mousy hair. She was in charge of the Corrections Department within the directorate and had been overseeing the implementation of the Council's incarceration policy, as well as the refurbishment of the prison building. "Your opposition to imprisonment is on record."

I registered the snub. "That's why you sent me an invite, no doubt." I shifted my upper body into the line of her gaze. "Thanks very much. I'm looking forward to the event." Raeburn 124's face was impassive, but I could see that her fingertips were jammed into the palms of her hands. "And to the inauguration of the New Bridewell facility the day after tomorrow."

"You'll be very welcome at both," she said, the thin smile on her lips again. "Make sure you don't get locked up in the Bridewell in the meantime." She nodded to Hamilton. "Guardian."

He watched her lumber across to the computer bank. "Bloody woman," he muttered. "She'll be the ruin of this directorate." He turned to the door. "Come on, man," he said over his shoulder. "You've got a report to make."

I followed him into the courtyard. It was a close call whether the guardian or his deputy was the bigger pain to deal with.

"All right, let's hear it," Lewis said impatiently. He was sitting at his desk in his quarters in what used to be the Governor's House, the creases in his guard uniform sharper than a butcher's knife. "Where's that bloody chemist got to?"

I made a show of pulling out my notebook and flicking through its pages, even though I didn't have a lot to say.

"You haven't got anywhere, have you?" the guardian said with unusual perspicacity.

"Em, no, not really," I said, putting my notes down.

"Lister 25 was last seen by his staff in the laboratories in King's Buildings twelve days ago, on 25 March. I've interviewed all of them and no one seems to have noticed anything unusual in his behaviour leading up to his disappearance." I shrugged. "Of course, being chief toxicologist he had plenty on his plate, especially considering the quality of food served up to ordinary citizens—"

"Spare me the social outrage, Dalrymple," Hamilton said, his shoulders slumping.

In the past I would have laid on some more ironic observations, but baiting him wasn't what it used to be. The fact was that Lewis was yesterday's man. The Council was full of young, go-ahead guardians now and he'd lost his grip on what used to be the single most powerful directorate. Public order was effectively handled by his deputy, who'd been transferred from the Welfare Directorate when her former boss became senior guardian six months back. It didn't help that Lewis Hamilton had been caught with less than pristine hands after a major investigation in 2026. He was lucky he was still in a job, but the changes in the command centre made me wonder how long he'd keep the keys to these quarters.

"All right," I said. "There have been no sightings of Lister 25 anywhere in the city since he vanished. I've collated all barracks, city line and Fisheries Guard reports."

Hamilton sat up. "You think he may have deserted?"

"It had to be a possibility, Lewis."

"One of the city's most eminent and experienced scientists?" the guardian said, having a stab at outrage himself. "Why would he—" He broke off. "You said it *had* to be a possibility, past tense. You mean you don't think it realistically is one?"

"Nope."

"Why not?"

"First, there's his record: Lister 25's never shown any sign of disloyalty to the Council. Second, there's the fact that he seems to have taken no personal effects with him. All his standard auxiliary-issue clothing is still in his rooms above the lab, apart from what he would have been wearing. All his lab coats are accounted for too."

"He'd hardly have walked off wearing a white coat, would he?" Hamilton scoffed.

I let that go. "Third, none of his work appears to be missing. All files, materials and computer disks are present. Though the disks could have been copied, of course. And fourth—"

"All right, Dalrymple, you've made your point."

I raised my hand. "This is the most convincing bit," I said. "And fourth, he doesn't seem to have taken any of his blues cassettes with him."

The guardian sank further into his chair. "What?" he asked faintly. He was looking as depressed as a headmaster presented with incontrovertible proof that his star pupil is responsible for the life-size drawings of matron on the chapel roof.

I knew this was going to be hard for him to accept but it was what made me certain. "Look, Lewis, the old scientist is a blues freak like me. I came across his stash of Robert Johnson recordings when I was investigating the Electric Blues case in 2022."

The guardian stared at me dumbly.

"The thing is, he lived for his music, he used to listen to the blues every night. There's no way he'd have walked away without at least some of his cassettes."

Hamilton was about to say something fierce but he

held back. "Very well. The indications are that Lister 25 didn't desert. Could he have been abducted?"

I turned my hands up non-committally. "Doesn't strike me as very likely. Someone would have seen him being led away. Security at the labs is tight."

"Do you know what he was working on?"

I nodded. "He was overseeing several experiments and procedures: a tourist company complaint about the sewers under the Waverley Hotel, food poisoning in Corstorphine, something nasty in Brewery No. 1 in Fountainbridge . . ." I flicked pages again. "Oh, and something about soil contamination. He was working on that himself. None of his staff knew anything about it, but his assistant saw samples of soil at his work station. They aren't there any more."

Hamilton stirred. "Soil from where?" he asked.

"Some of the city farms, I suppose. Though none of them have owned up to anything out of the ordinary." I shrugged, then put my notebook on my knee and pushed myself back in the uncomfortable chair that visitors to the guardian's office were forced to use. He seemed to have sunk into himself and I let the silence run on, thinking about the city's chief chemist. I'd worked with him pretty often and I liked him. He was a strange old guy with a worrying tendency to pout at you when he was speaking; he also had the most pachydermic skin I've ever seen on a human face. Maybe he'd shambled off to some hideaway like an elephant that knows its time is near.

Eventually Hamilton came back to earth. "So, Dalrymple, what am I to tell the Council about the toxicologist?"

"Tell them what I told you," I replied. "He's gone, we don't know where or why. Have the file stamped 'Level Two Active' and maintain the all-barracks alert. What else can we do?"

The guardian peered at me and shook his head. "Not exactly your finest hour, is it?"

I got up and headed for the door. "It won't exactly be yours at the Council meeting either, Lewis," I said with more vehemence than he deserved.

He stood up, legs braced like a boxer about to swing a punch. "Are you really going to the Oxford reception, Dalrymple?" he demanded. "You're just doing it to irritate Raeburn 124, aren't you?"

"Among others," I said, turning back towards him. "Anyone who thinks that we'll improve things by locking up young people needs their head examining. That means I'll be up against everyone there tonight."

Hamilton got up and walked stiffly to the window. "Of course it does, man. Don't you see? We've got to change things. We'll have a revolt on our hands if we don't."

"You'd have liked to implement the incarceration policy yourself, wouldn't you, Lewis?" He might have been yesterday's man but he wasn't completely out of tune with the other guardians.

He nodded. "I make no secret of that. I don't know why we had to invite those arrogant intellectuals from New Oxford to tell us what to do."

Neither did I, but I intended to put some feelers out at the reception. "New Oxford?" I said. "Until a year ago I didn't even know there was anything left of old Oxford. The Council always said that the whole of England had been devastated in the drugs wars. Then again, we were always told that Glasgow was a hotbed of anarchy as well."

The guardian flashed an angry glance at me. "That's what the Council itself thought."

I turned away again. "See, Lewis, that's what you get when you restrict the flow of information. You cut yourself off from the good ideas as well as the bad ones. Take the helijet. Think what fun you could have had dropping bombs on the suburbs with one of those." I waited for a response but none was forthcoming.

That was the second time the guardian had let me get away with taking the piss. He must have been sickening for something.

I was halfway across the esplanade, picking my way through the ranks of rusty maroon guard Land-Rovers and pick-ups, when a familiar voice assaulted my ears.

"Over here, Quint!"

I looked round and saw the hefty figure of Hume 253 emerging from an ancient Transit. He dragged a handcuffed young man out and pushed him up against the vehicle's side panelling with a fair amount of force.

I went over to the northern side of the open area by the statue of a guardswoman at attention. "Morning, Davie. What have you got here?"

"'What' is right," the big man replied. "This wee shitebag was caught in a female citizen's room in a retirement home in Willowbrae." He slammed the youth against the Transit again. "With her food and clothing vouchers in one hand and the other up her skirt."

I examined the kid. He was about five feet six and skinny, which made him look like a midget against Davie's bulk. That wasn't stopping him giving his captor the eye, a non-stop litany of obscenities streaming from his blood-caked lips. He was wearing gear that must have come from the black market: Japanese combat top and trousers, top-of-the-range Bolivian trainers and a pair of ugly orange shades. There was a bright yellow tattoo of a waterfall on his left forearm, showing that he was part of the Portobello Pish. Not a gang to mess with.

"What's your name, pal?" I asked.

"Fuck your hole and fuck your sister's and fuck your—" He broke off as Davie planted an elbow in his belly. He continued mouthing words but no sound came out.

"His name's Pete 'Mad Mouse' Craig, Quint." Davie looked round. "Guardsman!" he shouted to one of his subordinates. "Get this piece of slime down to the dungeons. There's a rehabilitation squad wanting a word with him." The City Guard was still coy about what went on when youth gang members were caught.

"Your guts are on the slab," the kid gasped, glaring at Davie with cold blue eyes. "Your balls are—" He dropped to the ground as he was straight-armed by the guardsman who'd arrived on the scene.

We watched as the young lowlife was dragged away to the bowels of the castle.

"I suppose he'll end up in the New Bridewell now," Davie said, going round to the front of the Transit. "Fancy a bite?"

I joined him and watched as he spread out a mammoth packed lunch on the driver's seat. There were wholemeal barracks rolls filled with bacon – a lot better than the citizen-issue equivalent on both counts – and cartons of broth, as well as what the bakers call doughnuts and auxiliaries call cannonballs. In the time it took me to finish one roll, Davie had dealt with most of the rest.

"Still in love with your food, I see."

He raised his shoulders. "What else have I got to live for?" A smile spread slowly across his bearded face.

I grinned back at him. "Apart from the attentions of a posse of guardswomen, the inter-barracks rugby championship, and the friendship of the city's finest investigator."

He swallowed soup and frowned. "You think I like putting the boot into the city's scum, Quint? That's all they've let me do since I was sidelined." Davie had got caught up in the same case that led to Hamilton being fingered. He hadn't done anything to be ashamed of, but he'd left the city without permission and serving guard personnel aren't allowed to get away with that kind of indiscipline. The fact that he's close to me and has acted as my assistant on numerous investigations has made him plenty of enemies too.

"You don't have to arrest the buggers yourself, Davie," I said. "You're still a guard commander. You can stand back and let the beaters do their work."

The smile was back on his face. "I prefer the hands-on approach," he said, brushing crumbs from his grey tunic. "That's the difference between genuine public order professionals and jumped-up criminologists."

I discarded a cannonball after one bite and watched as Davie took custody of it. "You wouldn't be referring to our honoured guests from Oxford, would you?"

He nodded, struggling to clear his mouth. "And the Mist that's settled over the castle." He shook his head. "We're fighting a losing battle, Quint. The gangs are getting the better of us – you know that."

"That's why the prison's about to open."

"Prison my arse," he said. "What bloody difference will that make?"

I looked away across the sun-dappled city and ran a hand over the stubble on my face. "What bloody difference indeed, my friend?"

CHAPTER TWO

"Wake up, old man."

My father's head came up slowly. He was sitting in an armchair, the lower half of his body wrapped in a tartan blanket and a large bound book on his knees. The only light in the room came from a reading lamp on the rickety table beside him.

"Is that you, failure?" he asked, screwing up his eyes. "What are you doing here? It isn't Sunday."

"Glad to see you're keeping your wits about you, Hector," I said, smiling as I spoke the name he'd insisted I address him by since I was a kid. I took the chair from his desk and sat down in front of him. "You're right. It's Wednesday. I just needed another blast of your wit and wisdom."

"Watch it, laddie." My father was over eighty and pretty frail after a series of heart attacks, but he could still put himself about. He peered at me. "Why are you dressed up like a Christmas tree?"

I looked down at the red, green and white tartan waistcoat I'd found in the depths of a discarded clothing depot in Tollcross. "I'm going to a Council reception. I thought I should look my best."

The old man examined my black suit – the only one I possess – then raised his eyes to my face. "You didn't think of taking that field of stubble off your face?"

I grinned. "I wouldn't want the guardians to think I was conforming." Ordinary male citizens – including demoted auxiliaries like me – are not permitted facial hair.

I glanced around my father's room. Although he was a founder member of the Edinburgh Enlightenment and had served as a guardian, he'd been assigned to a standard retirement home. The house was all right – it was a large former merchant's villa in the northern suburb of Trinity – but Hector had got used to a modicum of privacy when he occupied the only room on the third floor. When his health worsened he was moved to the ground floor, where the chatter and splutter of his fellow inmates did nothing to improve his temper. He spent his waking hours buried in Latin tomes that he must have read a hundred times when he was a professor of rhetoric in pre-independence times.

"Reception?" Hector demanded, his sunken eyes glistening. "What are the bloody guardians wasting the city's resources on now?" Since he fell out with his colleagues and resigned years ago, my father had been one of their most vehement critics – not that anyone except me has noticed.

"It's to do with the prison that's about to be inaugurated," I said. "The Council's hosting an event for the Oxford experts who worked on it."

"Oxford experts!" The old man's tone was scathing. "What did they need them for? There are enough self-appointed experts in this city as it is."

"True enough," I agreed. "I wonder what's in it for Oxford – or New Oxford as they apparently call it now. Edinburgh hasn't exactly got a surplus of funds to hand over to them. It's a bit of a puzzle."

Hector was studying me, his gnarled hands resting on

the blanket. "That's not by any chance why you're gracing them with your presence, is it, Quintilian?"

I winced as he used my full name. Fortunately he was the only person who did. "That and the fact that the best malts will be on offer, no alcohol vouchers required."

"I can read you like a book." My father laughed then shook his head. "It'll end in tears. Incarcerating young people always does."

We'd had this discussion often in recent months. Despite his time on the original hardline Council, Hector had always been concerned about the dangers of excessive authority.

"I suppose the guardians had to do something," I said with a shrug. "Youth crime is a major problem these days and the foreign tour companies have been putting the squeeze on them to improve safety."

"Don't play the devil's advocate with me, lad," the old man said. "The tourists have already been afforded plenty of inducements. Free whisky, hot and cold running tarts – what the hell's the city coming to?" He coughed then started wheezing alarmingly.

I felt my stomach somersault. I'd been a helpless witness of his first heart attack.

"Water," he gasped, waving his hand shakily.

I dashed to the bedside table and poured him a glassful. I watched as he gulped it down.

"That's better," Hector said after a minute. He glanced up at me with a mischievous smile. "Did I give you a fright, Quintilian?"

"Yes, you bloody did," I said, scowling at him. "It would be just like you to drop dead in front of me."

He croaked out a laugh. "I'm not finished yet." He handed me back the glass. "How's that girlfriend of yours?"

"Girlfriend?" I repeated. That term would have really impressed Katharine. "We're not really—" I broke off, struggling to describe the stop-start relationship that had been going on for eight years. It seemed to have been rekindled again in the last couple of weeks, but I didn't have much idea why Katharine had suddenly reappeared.

"Not really what?" the old man demanded. "Haven't you learned to express yourself at your age?"

I shook my head. "No, I haven't. Happy?"

The satisfied look that spread across the parchment of his face demonstrated that he was. In fact, he got on well enough with Katharine. Despite the fact that he was a misogynist of gargantuan proportions, she'd never laid into him. She reserved her fire for me.

"And Davie? How's he getting on?"

"Okay," I said, bending down to pick up the book that had dropped to the floor when Hector had his coughing fit. "He isn't happy about being shunted sideways, but he's probably the only person in the city who approves of the rise in crime. It's given him plenty of opportunities for what he calls hands-on public order work."

"His hands on the bootboys' private—"

"Quite." I handed over the leather-bound volume. "*The Dialogues of Plato*?" I said, managing to decipher the Greek. On my fifth birthday the old man decided that the best way for me to spend my spare time was learning dead languages. My lengthy rebellion against that order started when I was five years and one day old. "Why aren't you up to your elbows in Latin as usual?"

He tapped his head and winked. "The Latin's all up here. Permanent resident."

"Juvenal on your mind? Worrying."

"Nothing as worrying as what you fill yours with, Quintilian. Murders and mutilations and—"

"All right, I accept I'm a picture of depravity." I looked at him, eyes wide open. "You still haven't told me why you're reading Plato. Not turning back into a fan of the old fascist, are you?" The Edinburgh Enlightenment had based their city-state on ideas derived and extrapolated from the ancient philosopher's *Republic* and *Laws*.

Hector shook his head. "It's not Plato that fascinates me these days, it's his protagonist Socrates. I've been reading the *Phaedo*. It's hard to understand how someone as rational and rigorous as Socrates can believe in something as woolly as reincarnation." He looked at me, the set of his face softer. "But he does. And he dies well because he believes that, in some form or other, he's coming back."

I got up and returned my chair to the desk, the corners of my eyes suddenly damp. It wasn't only the calm assurance of the old man's voice that was affecting me. My former lover Caro – dead for thirteen years – had flown up before me, her dark hair glistening with the sheen it always had after she'd washed it, her eyes soft brown and her lips parted. Then I blinked and she was gone.

"I'd better get moving," I said, nodding to Hector.

"Aye, don't let those Oxford buggers get a head start with the whisky."

"Goodnight, old man," I said, tugging the blanket up so it covered his chest.

"Goodnight, failure," he replied with a hoarse laugh.

I walked out of the retirement home and into the twilight. I wished I had the ancient Athenian's faith in eternal rebirth. If I had, I might have been able to let Caro go more easily – as well as prepare myself more adequately for the full stop that I knew was soon going to be applied to my father's life.

* * *

I turned the corner and walked down to the bus stop on East Trinity Road. It was coming up to half past seven and I knew there would be a bus along any minute to pick up citizens who worked in the tourist bars and restaurants in the central zone. As I headed towards the small cluster of people I heard a voice raised in anger.

"Yer vouchers, ya cunts! Gie us yer fuckin' vouchers!"

I slowed my pace but kept walking towards them, slipping my right hand into my coat pocket.

"Awright, here you are!" a woman cried, the last word turning into a long-drawn-out sob.

"Take them and leave us alone," said another voice, male and unsteady. "Please!"

I stopped and looked at the group. It was almost dark and though the streetlamps had come on, their light wasn't yet bright. I thought I could see a pair of young men wearing cut-off coats and trousers turned up to beneath the knees: standard youth gang get-up. I considered calling Davie on my mobile then decided I could handle them on my own. That was my first mistake.

"You two!" I shouted. "Stay where you are!" I walked quickly towards the bus stop as five heads turned in my direction: two middle-aged women, one with a scarf round her hair, an elderly man whose cheekbones looked like they were about to break through the skin of his face, and a pair of pimply, shaven-headed youths. One of them had a red lightning flash tattooed on his left cheek.

"Who said we were goin' anywhere, shite?" Flash stepped forwards and jabbed the point of a stick at me. I reckoned it was a sharpened broom handle, the weapon of choice for your standard headbanger.

The other bootboy looked less courageous. He moved behind the innocent bystanders and stared at me, his jaw slack.

"Eh, shite?" the first guy said.

"Put it down," I said, making sure my voice didn't waver. "It'll be better for you if you do."

"Fuck you, pal," he said, running his eyes over me and grinning broadly to reveal shiny yellow teeth; some of the gangs apply metallic paint. "What are you, anyway? Undercover slime?" He stamped his boots on the pavement. "I like steppin' in youse."

"Put the stick down," I repeated. "Last chance."

"Last chance for you, fucker." Flash lunged at me, his weapon aimed at my throat.

I stepped aside and brought my cosh down hard on the youth's forearm. The unmistakable sound of cracking bone rang out.

The stick fell to the pavement, rapidly followed by its owner. He started squealing in agony.

I left him where he was and moved towards the others. They were all motionless, the other gang member included.

Then the timorous one shouted, "Nae surrender, Gus," at his prone pal.

I turned my head for a second. In an instant the shouter was away, his heavy footwear pounding down the asphalt. There was no chance of my forty-four-year-old legs getting near him so I didn't bother giving chase. I went back to Flash and dragged him to his feet.

"You bust ma arm," he said in disbelief, his bravado completely gone. "You bust ma fuckin' arm."

"Stop whining," I said, trying to get my heart rate down.

The man at the bus stop looked at the two women, then turned to me. "You didn't have to do that," he said. "He isn't much more than a child."

"Aye," one of the women put in. "Ma Kenny's about the same age as him."

"Terrible," the other woman said. "The violence in this city nowadays is a disgrace."

"What?" I gasped. "They were robbing you. This scumbag tried to skewer me."

The elderly man was shaking his head. "It was your own fault. You threatened him." He stepped up to me. "Who are you? Show us some identification, please."

"Oh, for Christ's sake," I said, glaring at him and the women. "I was trying to help."

"Aye, well, you needn't have bothered," the woman in the scarf said. "The wee tike that ran off had all our vouchers."

I groaned then raised a finger at Flash who'd let out what sounded like a laugh.

"I want to see some identification," the man insisted. "You can't just attack people in the street." He gave me a stern look. "Nor can you take the Lord's name in vain."

"It was self-defence," I said, shaking my head. "Have you ever heard of that?"

"The gospel teaches us to turn the other cheek," he said piously. Typical. I'd run into one of Edinburgh's few remaining Christians.

"I suppose you'll be wanting me to let him go next," I said, watching as the three victims shuffled their feet and looked away. Then the penny dropped. "Oh, I get it. You know this specimen, don't you? He's a local and he knows where you live."

They all nodded.

"Can ye no' be lenient wi' him?" asked the bareheaded woman. "It'll be better for all of us . . ."

I glanced at Flash. His face was still screwed up in agony, but his eyes were pools of viciousness that were focused on the three citizens. Bloody hell. I didn't fancy letting the little barbarian hoof it; he'd be back on the streets as soon as his plaster was off. On the other hand, I still wasn't keen on calling the guard. Davie would cover for me but since the Mist descended over the castle and cramped Hamilton's style, I'd been trying to keep a low profile. Although I was still officially chief special investigator and my anomalous position as a DM in the directorate was tolerated, I had less room for manoeuvre than I used to.

So I let Flash go. From the end of the road I was treated to a detailed breakdown of what he'd do to my internal organs when he caught up with me. That – and the atmosphere of frosty disapproval created by the three citizens before the bus arrived twenty minutes late – really put me in the mood for an evening in the company of the city's great and good.

The City Guard had slung a chain across Waterloo Place beyond the east end of Princes Street. What appeared to be an army of uniformed personnel was looking alert and checking everyone's papers. Even though the guardswoman who stopped me seemed to know who I was, she insisted on seeing my authorisation.

I walked up the slope and got an eyeful of the new prison. I didn't have any choice. The whole area on the crag above what used to be Waverley station in the days before the Council did away with railways was lit up like a bonfire. Filters over the floodlights were turning the high walls of the buildings maroon, the city's pet colour. White searchlights were roving across the stone surfaces, even though the first prisoner hadn't yet been admitted, let alone managed to escape. Passing the Old Calton Burial Ground, I realised that it was enclosed behind the razor wire that festooned the whole area. It seemed that even Edinburgh's venerable dead were going to have to do time.

A line of guard vehicles swept past me, slowing as they reached the New Bridewell's main accommodation block. The scaffolding that had been over the building for months had now been removed. It used to be St Andrew's House, a grandiose edifice with a pillared façade that housed the Secretary of State's office and then the Scottish Executive when Scotland still existed as a component of the United Kingdom – until the drugs wars did away with the concept of stable nations. The busts over the mullions high above street level represented, among other ideals, education and health. I had a feeling those weren't the moving forces behind the Council's incarceration policy.

"Quint!"

I looked to the left and saw Davie waving at me from a parked Land-Rover. "Don't tell me they've got you on sentry duty, guardsman?" I said, heading towards him.

"Screw you, pal," he replied. "Believe it or not, I'm in charge of security in this sector tonight."

I glanced round at the swarms of auxiliaries in unusually pristine uniforms. "You've got enough personnel to help you out."

"Aye. Nothing but the best for our friends from the south."

I leaned against his door. "I'm surprised they put a reprobate like you on this detail."

He laughed. "The Mist wanted to give the job to one of her tame monkeys, but Hamilton insisted it went to – I quote – a commander with proven public order skills."

"Looks like you're back on the fast track, Davie."

"Nah," he said. "That argument's the only one the chief

has won recently. His deputy's got her podgy fingers in every other pie." He looked past me. "See what I mean?"

A large Jeep drove slowly by, its occupants all gazing at the prison's maroon and white walls.

"I don't see Hamilton in the pleasure wagon," I said.

"That's the point," Davie said. "The Council's taken it away from him. On the Mist's recommendation, so I heard. The poor old sod has to use one of these wrecks like the rest of us now."

Things were definitely looking bad for the guardian. The Jeep was a gift to the Council from a multinational company that the guardians had collectively brown-nosed, but Hamilton had been treating it as his personal wheels for years.

"See you later, big man," I said. "Try not to beat up too many locals." The words were out of my mouth before I remembered I'd been guilty of exactly that offence less than an hour before.

In its wisdom the Council had chosen the Corrections Department as the venue for the reception. I reckoned that was another of the Mist's recommendations, considering she was in charge of that particular department. In fact, it was a good location if you wanted to impress people, which seemed to be the guardians' predominant aim. In pre-Enlightenment times the replica of a Doric temple had been the Royal High School; as it dated from 1829, it could be said to form some kind of link between the original Edinburgh Enlightenment of Hume, Smith and Adam and the pale reflection produced by my father and his colleagues. The buildings had been designed as part of the acropolis that was meant to turn the city into the Athens of the North. The uncompleted Parthenon on top of the Calton Hill above was a juicy and still relevant metaphor for the substantial gap between ambition and reality.

After showing ID again, I went up the steps and reached the main entrance that was behind a row of columns. A large banner had been hung above the ornate door, informing guests that the Corrections Department of the Public Order Directorate cordially welcomed them. No doubt the first inmates of the prison would get just as cordial a welcome.

Hamilton and his deputy were standing inside the door, the guardian looking uncomfortable in an Enlightenment tartan kilt and the Mist filling out a long skirt of the same material. The sash over her white blouse was tight and less than flattering.

"Get out of the way, citizen," she said sharply. "Now!"

"Charming," I said, pulling out my invitation and waving it at her.

"Step aside, man," Hamilton said in a firm whisper.

I looked round and saw a group of individuals in dark clothes heading up the steps from the Jeep. "Sorry," I said, giving the Mist an ironic smile. "Wouldn't want the likes of me to get in the way of the VIPs, would we?"

"Correct," she said.

I moved and stood at the edge of the hall to watch the New Oxford delegation make their entry. I stifled a laugh as Hamilton shouldered his way in front of his deputy and took centre stage.

"Good evening, Administrator Raphael," I heard him address a tall, statuesque woman with silver-grey hair. I guessed she was in her early fifties. She was in pretty good shape, though the loose black trouser suit with the high neck that she was wearing didn't give much away. I picked up an aura of power immediately, power cut with a hint of mystery. This was a woman who knew how to handle herself.

"Public order guardian," she said, her voice clear and unaccented. "How pleasant to see you." The coolness of her tone and the way she continued rapidly to the Mist made it clear where her priorities lay.

Hamilton's deputy turned her back and shielded the guest from me, so I couldn't hear the words they exchanged. They seemed to be on close terms, the Oxford woman's hand resting on Raeburn 124's fleshy arm.

I glanced back at Lewis Hamilton. The three remaining members of the Oxford group were all male academics; they were wearing long black robes over their immaculate suits. They were also equipped with small flat silver gadgets hanging on fine chains round their necks. The striking thing about the trio in gowns was the ethnic mix. Between them they had the features of a great swathe of the earth's population. In succession the public order guardian greeted Professor Yamaguchi, a short, smiling Japanese; Doctor Verzeni, a youngish man with dark curly hair and what sounded like an Italian accent; and, last but not least, a gloomy, bearded figure by the name of Professor Raskolnikov. I wanted to have a word with the latter, but now wasn't the time – the Mist had quickly ushered the administrator and her entourage out of the entrance hall.

I followed them down to the sunken reception room which used to be the old school's assembly hall. In the 1970s it had been converted into a debating chamber for the devolved Scottish assembly that failed to materialise after the mishandled referendum. When Scotland's short-lived fling with national government finally took off in the late 1990s, the executive turned its back on the pre-prepared chamber and spent millions on a custom-built heap at the bottom of the Royal Mile. The original building remained unused until the Council decided it needed to reinstitute the Corrections Department. That process involved tearing out all the benches and microphones and creating an open space for auxiliaries to play with their papers and filing cabinets. Tonight those had been shoved to the side and the long room with its original coffered ceiling and the balcony that ran all the way round the pit looked resplendent – despite the preponderance of maroon paint and wall charts detailing the achievements of the department and its advisers over the last year.

A throng of guardians and senior auxiliaries soon gathered around the group from Oxford. Waiters and waitresses were circulating with glasses of whisky on trays and platters of smoked salmon. The staff were clad in what were apparently convict uniforms from all over the world: white suits with arrows on them, blue denim shirts and trousers, heavy tunics with badges in some Far Eastern language. As I was shaking my head at those examples of Public Order Directorate wit, I caught sight of an array of metal objects at the edge of the hall. On closer inspection they turned out to be prison equipment: leg-irons, handcuffs, straitjackets – there was even a ball and chain.

"Don't worry, Quint. That gear isn't going to be used in the New Bridewell."

I turned to find the medical guardian by my side. "How can you be so sure, Sophia?" I bent down. "Well, well, look who's here. Shouldn't you be in bed, Maisie?"

The little girl stared at me seriously then stuck her tongue out.

"Maisie," Sophia said softly. "That's not nice." She smoothed the red hair back from her daughter's forehead and straightened up. "Stop that, Quint. You're no help at all."

I put my own tongue away and smiled as Maisie burst out laughing. "Sorry, couldn't resist it," I said. "She's a sweet kid."

"I know." Sophia suddenly looked flustered.

"What's the matter?" I asked.

"I don't know if I should have brought her along to this event," she replied, tugging at a crease in her sash. "She's only fourteen months. The noise might scare her."

I watched as Maisie tottered towards the ball and chain. "She seems to be coping." I glanced at Sophia. "Are you? I mean, with looking after her as well as performing the duties of a guardian." Sophia was a single mother, the first guardian to give birth in office.

She pursed her lips to show me that she thought the question was out of order, then nodded. "I get help from the Welfare Directorate. We manage. She's pretty easy, though now she's started to walk . . ." She leaned across and gently took her daughter's arm.

A hand bell was rung from the centre of the balcony and everyone looked up. The chattering dwindled away.

"Ladies and gentlemen," announced a pompous male auxiliary in a kilt, "pray silence for the senior guardian of Enlightenment Edinburgh."

I grabbed a glass of single malt from a passing convict, watching as Sophia closed her eyes for a moment and twitched her head. It was good to see that inter-Council rivalry was still alive and well. When the guardians went through a phase of being more user-friendly a few years back, the City Regulations were changed to permit the senior guardian – effectively the president – only one month in the job; it rotated between the fifteen guardians, to remove the opportunity for empire-building.

More recently, mainly because of the increase in crime, the senior guardian is elected by his or her colleagues for a term lasting one year. The former welfare guardian had been in power for six months and it was said that he was keen on an extension. This would require a change in the regulations and there were rumours that Council members were being offered sweeteners: hyper-expensive suits from independent Milan, watches from the Swiss colony of Mallorca, the kind of goods their rank was supposed to despise. But how the hell would the city coffers run to bribes like that?

The head honcho stepped to the rail, gold chain round his neck. "Honoured Oxonian guests . . ." He paused to allow a burst of applause to be led enthusiastically by Hamilton's deputy. "Guardians, senior auxiliaries and other invited representatives."

I suppose I was one of the last group, not that I was representing anyone except the Demoted Auxiliaries' Malt Whisky Appreciation Society.

"The day after tomorrow the magnificent New Bridewell facility will be inaugurated." The senior guardian stopped again and let the Mist smack her palms again. "This will mark the realisation of the first part of the Council's ambitious incarceration policy. We believe that the imprisonment of criminals is an essential component in the drive towards the eradication of crime."

I looked around the crowd, most of whom were paying avid attention, and wondered how many of them remembered the original Council's proud boast that crime had been eradicated from Edinburgh. Admittedly it took them over ten years of fighting the drugs gangs to achieve that end – and, like all boasts, it didn't tell the whole story. Still, for a few years, there was very little serious crime in the city. The guardians had even been able to close the last prison on Cramond Island. And now we were in for another dose of incarceration. Call me a pessimist, but I had to see that as a mark of the Council's failure. So we had work, welfare, housing, education and sustenance for all. But we also had a climate of disaffection among citizens that the reintroduction of imprisonment was hardly going to alleviate.

The senior guardian, real name Lachlan Lessels, was young, earnest and bespectacled. He ran through the objectives of the prison: discipline, compassion and reintegration into society. Why was it I got the feeling that the first of those was going to be the main feature of the New Bridewell? Then he turned his reedy voice to praising the expertise of the Oxford academics and their great experience in carceral matters. This propensity for skilful arse-licking had got him the nickname of Slick. Before I could consider what that implied about the university city, he invited Administrator Raphael to address the multitude.

As the imperious woman left her gown-clad colleagues and approached the edge of the balcony, stopping on the way to shake the senior guardian's hand, I looked around the crowd again. Hamilton was in the pit with the rest of us, his jaw jutting out aggressively, while his deputy was up on the higher level with the nobs. Beyond him I caught sight of a crumpled figure in a wheelchair. Billy Geddes. I might have known the city's financial genius would be on the case.

"Many thanks, senior guardian," the administrator said, her voice ringing out across the chamber. She was obviously well versed in holding the floor. "I'll be brief. The Hebdomadal Council – New Oxford's ruling body – is delighted to have been able to provide expert guidance in the implementation of the incarceration policy so courageously embarked upon by the Council of City Guardians in Edinburgh."

If that was her idea of brief, I was glad I didn't have to attend many meetings chaired by her.

"We believe that control and authority must be applied rigorously in twenty-first-century society," Raphael continued. "And we believe that education is the root of progress and the cement of social cohesion." She looked round her listeners. "To that end we are pleased to offer places at the University of New Oxford for fifty of Edinburgh's most promising students."

There was a pause as the crowd tried to ascertain whether that surprise announcement was to the taste of the Council. When the senior guardian applauded vigorously, the noise level increased several-fold.

Sophia gathered up her daughter and turned towards the exit. "Too much," she said. I wasn't sure whether she was referring to the racket, Slick's performance or the administrator's offer.

I mouthed goodbye at Maisie. Again the little lass stared at me, then her face broke into a wide smile. It seemed I'd made at least one friend during the evening.

Fortunately the speeches didn't last much longer. I went in search of whisky, food and entertainment. I found the first two easily enough then looked around for the third. Billy Geddes was deep in conversation with one of the Oxford academics so I headed over.

"Evening, Billy," I said, butting in.

The man in the gown stood up from the wheelchair and gave me a cold stare. It was the bearded professor called Raskolnikov.

I introduced myself when Billy declined to answer.

"And what is your purpose, Mr Quint Dalrymple?" the

Russian asked, strong evidence of Russian vowels in his delivery.

"*Citizen* Quint Dalrymple," my former school and university friend corrected. "That's the term we use to designate non-auxiliaries."

"That's right, *Citizen* Geddes," I said, grinning at him maliciously. "Or have they made you an auxiliary again?" Billy and I had a lot of history, much of it revolving around my frequent discoveries of his involvement in secret scams. One such discovery had led to his demotion. The absence of a barracks badge on his suit showed that the Council had refrained from reinstating him – so far.

"Citizen Dalrymple is an investigator," Billy said sourly, his eyes staying off me. "He works for the Public Order Directorate. When he feels like it."

"Really?" The professor's heavy features became slightly more animated. "And what do you investigate?"

I looked at him. "Murders, mainly."

"How interesting. You must tell me about them."

I didn't like the way he was licking his chapped lips so I cut to what I wanted to know. "Tell me, is Raskolnikov your real name, professor? Or is it some kind of nom de guerre?"

His eyes flashed. "Very good, citizen. You've obviously read *Crime and Punishment*."

I nodded. "But Raskolnikov was the criminal. It seems a strange name for an expert on incarceration." I caught sight of something glinting on his wrist and looked closer.

The Russian laughed, not very humorously. "The criminal in question achieved redemption," he said in a firm voice.

"Tell me," I said, "what's that?" I pointed towards the object that had caught my eye. It was some kind of metallic plate, under an inch in diameter, and it seemed to be implanted into the skin.

"That is none of your business, my friend," the professor said and turned on his heel.

"Oh very good, Quint," Billy said. "Very good – putting the knife into one of the city's most important guests."

Before I could answer he'd wheeled round and shoved himself away.

I was on my own so I grabbed another whisky. What else can you do?

The reception finished about eleven. I wandered off, hoping I could get a lift from Davie. He was still tied up with the security rosters and it was a warm night, so I walked back to my flat. The bars and cafés along Princes Street were still packed with tourists, the dire music they were playing interspersed with raucous shouts which provoked no interest from the guard personnel on duty: tourists can behave as they please.

I stopped for a quick one in a hotel bar where they knew me, and by the time I got home the curfew had kicked in. I stumbled upstairs in the dark – the curfew means no electricity in citizen areas – and lit a candle. I'd just dropped my trousers when my mobile rang. After a struggle to find it, I hit the button.

"Quint? Davie." His voice was clipped. "Where are you?"

"About to get into bed. What is it?"

"Something weird," he said breathlessly.

"Oh shit."

"Aye. You know that administrator woman from Oxford?"

"Raphael? Not personally, but I saw her at the reception tonight."

"Well, a sentry heard a scream from her rooms." He was enunciating carefully now. "When he went to investigate he found a severed arm in the bath."

That sobered me up.

CHAPTER THREE

I ran down the stairs in the dark, my fingertips keeping contact with the rough paint on the walls, and jumped into the guard Land-Rover that Davie had sent round. As the female auxiliary floored the accelerator and headed for the castle, I went through what I'd set up. The Oxford administrator and her entourage were staying in Ramsay Garden at the eastern end of the esplanade. I'd sent Davie there to make sure that nothing was touched, and to put a marker down; it would be harder for the Mist or any other meddler to throw us off the case if he was on the scene early.

We came out of the darkened citizen area and into the central zone, the castle ahead of us lit up like a fireship that had run aground on a rocky promontory. The young guardswoman steered the vehicle across the deserted junction at Tollcross towards Lauriston Place, missing a heavy bollard by no more than an inch.

I gasped. "And people complain about my driving."

A tight smile appeared on the auxiliary's lips but she didn't speak.

My mobile buzzed.

"Yes, Davie."

"How did you know it was? . . . oh forget it." Edinburgh mobiles, as basic as they come, don't display the caller's number but I knew it would be him. "The scene-of-crime squad's on site."

"Okay, hold them back till I arrive." I glanced at the driver. "When will that be, guardswoman?"

"In four minutes," she replied.

"Shit," I said, gripping the arm-rest with my spare hand. "Any time now, Davie. Have you informed the Medical Directorate?"

"Aye."

"Lined up all the sentries who were on duty?"

"Aye."

"Any of your senior officers present?"

"Oh aye."

"Oh bugger." I'd been hoping to get a free run at the outset of what sounded like a seriously unusual case.

Davie signed off and I braced myself with both hands as we roared past the infirmary. Which brought my mind back to the object of the enquiry with a jolt. Why the hell had some sick bastard amputated an arm and left it in Administrator Raphael's bath?

The guardswoman pulled up at the checkpoint on the esplanade and waved for it to be raised.

"No worries," I said, my door already open. "It's been a lot of fun but I'll walk from here, thanks."

An even broader smile split her freckled face. "Have a good night, citizen."

"That'll be right," I said, slamming the door. "Remind me never to get in your dodgem again."

Davie emerged from a door nearby. "Quick, Quint," he said. "The Mist's trying to take over."

"Uh-huh. What does she know about apotemnophilia?"

"Eh?"

"Limb removal," I explained. "Often for sexual gratification."

"You're jumping to conclusions, aren't you?"

"Maybe." I glanced up at the harled white wall in front of me. The topsy-turvy complex of houses and flats known as Ramsay Garden had been started in the eighteenth century and it looked like something out of a Middle European fairy tale. There were projecting towers, patches of red ashlar and carved animals all over the place. It had originally been built to attract university professors to the Old Town. Something similar to that was going on now: the Council uses the accommodation for visiting VIPs and the delegation of Oxford experts had been put up in it.

Davie nodded to the guard personnel inside the heavy studded door and they let me through. Scene-of-crime personnel in white overalls had congregated in the hallway.

"Where are we going?" I asked.

"Second floor," Davie replied. "The woman's flat has a view of the castle."

I looked round at him. "You weren't responsible for security here, I hope?"

Davie shook his head emphatically. "No chance. Only at the reception."

"Just as well."

We reached the second floor and walked down, or rather through, a luxurious thick pile carpet – maroon, of course. At the far end there was a gaggle of figures in dark clothes.

"Coming through, gentlemen," I said when we reached them.

"Ah, Mr . . . excuse me, Citizen Dalrymple." Professor Raskolnikov's eyes shone above his long beard. "The investigator. Are you going to investigate this outrage?"

"I'm hoping to." I looked at the Russian and his colleagues. "Did any of you see or hear anything?"

They all shook their heads.

"Nothing," said Doctor Verzeni.

"Nothing except the administrator's scream." The permanent smile on Professor Yamaguchi's dry lips struck me as incongruous. "And the pounding of boots." He glanced at Davie's hobnailed guard-issue footwear.

"I want you all to return to your rooms," I said. "We'll take full statements from you later."

The academics departed reluctantly, deep in conversation.

The door to flat 2C – a.k.a. The Joseph Bell Rooms according to the ornate silver plaque at eye height – was opened the instant I knocked. I got quite a shock when I saw the pale-faced person inside.

"Andrew Duart," I said.

The man with the goatee and the high-grade pin-striped suit nodded seriously. "The great Quintilian Dalrymple. I was wondering when you'd turn up."

I stepped past him and saw Administrator Raphael, Lewis Hamilton and his deputy at the far end of the lavishly furnished room.

"What's the first secretary of Glasgow doing in the city that regards the west of Scotland as the Great Satan?" I asked.

He gave a dry laugh. "That's in the past. We're all friends now." He glanced at Raphael. "I just wanted to reassure the administrator. She was pretty shaken up."

"Know her, do you?"

"Oh yes. My city has a lot of contacts with New Oxford."

I saw Hamilton coming towards us out of the corner of my eye. "Are you staying here?" I asked the Glaswegian.

He nodded. "Came across in the evening."

"Go back to your room, please," I said, moving away. "I'll be wanting a word later on." I headed for the public order guardian, trying hard to come to terms with Duart's presence in Edinburgh. Apparently the Council had suddenly turned into a coven of devil-worshippers.

"I'm glad you're here, Dalrymple," Hamilton said, the skin above his beard glowing red. "That idiot deputy of mine has been trying to run things. I've told her you're in charge and that's all there is to it."

"Right. Thanks, Lewis. I want Davie in on it too."

The guardian nodded. "Very well." He glanced round at the administrator. "You understand the sensitivity of this investigation, don't you?" he said in a low voice. "I've already had the senior guardian on my back. As far as he's concerned, relations with New Oxford are of paramount importance." It didn't sound like Lewis Hamilton went along with that, but his position in the Council was precarious. "Find the lunatic who put the arm in the bath and find him quickly."

"Okay." I turned to Davie. "Let the scene-of-crime squad loose here, but not in the bathroom yet. I hope they find at least some fingerprints that haven't been obscured by people who shouldn't have been allowed access." I looked back at Hamilton. "Such as Andrew Duart. What the hell's he doing here?"

The guardian shrugged. "He's been invited to the prison opening ceremony. Don't ask me why."

I moved towards the two women, clocking the flat silver gadget that was hanging round the visitor's neck. "I'm relying on you to keep your deputy out of my hair, Lewis."

He smiled grimly. "My pleasure." He strode up to the Mist and tapped her on the shoulder. "Come on, Raeburn 124. The professionals are here."

The stocky woman turned and surveyed me with distaste. "Am I to understand that Citizen Dalrymple is investigating this case, guardian?" She shot me a withering glare. "He hasn't been able to locate the chief toxicologist yet. What makes you think he'll be able to find someone with one arm?"

"Out," Hamilton hissed. "Or I'll have you in the dungeons for insubordination before you can whistle."

The Mist's composure took a hit. She wasn't used to Hamilton asserting himself. "Em . . . surely a female auxiliary should be present when the administrator's statement is taken. I'd be happy to—"

"Out," Hamilton repeated, this time louder.

She wasn't happy but she went with him.

I flashed Administrator Raphael a brief smile. "Sorry about that. Demarcation dispute."

She gave the same look of self-control tinged with alarm that she'd been directing at the Mist. "And you are?"

I realised that Hamilton had hung me out to dry. "The name's Dalrymple." I often tell people to call me Quint but in her case I didn't bother – an air of formality came off the administrator like a very subtle, very expensive perfume. "Chief special investigator."

My title seemed to reassure her. I thought it might. "Raphael," she said, extending her hand and squeezing mine with surprising force. It was no surprise that she kept her first name to herself. "I direct New Oxford's liaison programmes, including the one we have developed with the Council." She gave an almost imperceptible nod. "But then you know that already. I saw you at the reception."

And I thought her head was up in the clouds – or rather down in the mist – of incarceration policy. "We'll take a statement shortly," I said, "but perhaps you could tell me what happened after the reception."

The administrator led me to a long settee covered in fabric displaying the titles of works by Sir Walter Scott. I watched as she sat down on *Old Mortality* and beckoned to me to join her.

"I won't, thank you," I said. "I need to see the contents of your bath."

She closed her eyes for a moment.

"You were brought back from the Corrections Department building at what time?"

"Before I give you that information," Raphael said in a cool voice, "you may like to know that I had a bath before the reception. I can assure you that, apart from my own, there were no arms in it then."

Touché. I should have asked her that.

"I returned at eleven fifteen," she continued, sitting back and crossing one long leg over the other. "I bade my colleagues goodnight and let myself in here. I went straight to the bathroom . . ." She gave me a forbidding look. "Call of nature. As soon as I turned the light on, I saw it." Her head twitched, the grey hair swinging in front of her face. That only added to the weird vibes I was getting from her, authority combined with an almost sensual physicality.

"And what was your reaction?"

Raphael looked at me and for a moment she almost seemed to lose her grip – which had been the point of my question. Then she ran a hand through her hair and regained control. "My reaction? I screamed. Only once." She shook her head angrily. "Stupid. I've seen worse."

Had she? I wondered about that briefly.

"Then the front door burst open and one of your colleagues thundered in like a mad bull."

"Technically, not one of my colleagues. I'm a citizen, not an auxiliary."

She regarded me with studied indifference. "I see. Well, citizen, I suggest that, without further delay, you view the object in my bath."

I nodded. "By the way, how do I address you?"

She put her hands together and I noticed that she had the same metallic implant in her wrist as I'd noticed in Raskolnikov's. "You have a choice. Either madam . . ."

"I don't think so."

"Or administrator."

Ask a stupid question.

The bathroom, with doors off both the main room and the master – or rather, administrator – bedroom, was palatial. There were twin sinks with what I hoped for the sake of the Finance Directorate's scant reserves weren't solid gold fittings, antique mirrors, a bidet and, along the far wall, a Victorian bath standing on dragon's feet or the like. I ran my eye over the white tiles that covered all the vertical surfaces and immediately realised that something was missing – blood. Stepping over the black and white chequered floor tiles, I reached the porcelain monstrosity and bent down to look at the limb that was lying lengthways, palm down, at the bottom. It wasn't long before the stump of my right forefinger – an old injury from my time in the Public Order Directorate – began to tingle in sympathy. The middle finger had been removed beneath the bottom joint and there was no sign of it anywhere.

"How very odd."

Sophia's voice made me jump.

"Shit. Don't creep up on people like that." I wasn't too surprised that she'd made an appearance. She would have been informed by her directorate dispatcher and it wasn't the first time she'd acted personally in major enquiries.

She was already engrossed in her preliminary examination, speaking in a low voice into a dictation machine. The words "humerus", "axilla", "biceps" and "severed" were to the fore.

I let the medical guardian complete what she was doing and carried out my own examination. The limb, from the right side, had been taken off about an inch beneath the armpit. As far as I could tell, a very sharp instrument had been used: the surface of the traumatised area in the upper arm was remarkably smooth, the skin, tendon and bone cleanly cut. And again, there was no blood, showing clearly that the amputation had been carried out elsewhere. The skin was pallid all over and the amount of dark hair as well as the size and the heavy muscle development in the upper arm suggested it came from a male. The fingers were dirty, the nails bitten to the quick and a couple of them blackened. The wound on the stump of the missing finger was different, much less smooth than the arm surface.

"What do you reckon?" I asked. "I don't suppose some medical student could have stolen it from the infirmary."

Sophia gave me an icy glare then nodded to her directorate photographer and his scene-of-crime squad minder to step forward. She moved aside to let them shoot.

"I'll have my staff check the pathology department, but it's out of the question."

"Okay, okay," I said, raising my hands to placate her.

"The skin and muscle condition leads me to think that the arm came from a young man – probably not more than twenty-five, possibly only nineteen to twenty. Hypostasis and other indicators suggest that the limb was removed between four and six hours ago; it's difficult to be precise. What intrigues me most, though, is the area of amputation. The trauma is very clean, very regular. A well-honed, extremely smooth blade, I assume. But that isn't all." She stepped closer to me. "It's almost as if the wound's been cauterised, though there's no obvious mark of burning. The exposed nerves and tendons have been completely sealed." She shook her head. "I've never seen anything like it."

"What about the finger?" I asked. "That looks more like a cut from a standard knife."

Sophia nodded. "Single, non-serrated blade." She glanced at me. "And before you say it, yes, it could have been done by an auxiliary knife."

I smiled. She knew that I had a long-standing habit of suspecting the Council's lackeys.

The photographers moved back.

"We're done on this side," one of them said.

"Let's turn it over then," Sophia said, pulling on transparent gloves. She leaned forward and lifted the arm up and over. "Ah-ha. Look at this, Quint."

"Well, well. This should help us find the victim." I took out my magnifying glass and held it over the tattoo that ran the length of the inner forearm. "The guy this came from is one of the Leith Lancers." A nine-inch spear had been applied in red ink. It pierced a heart bearing the letters "L.L." and the motto "Fuck the Guardians" in black.

"Scum," Sophia said, so vehemently that the Medical Directorate photographer almost dropped his camera.

I nodded. "They're about as vicious a gang of head-bangers as the perfect city's produced." I raised my hand to silence her objections. "But they're keen on drinking stolen booze until they're legless. Why the hell has one of them ended up armless?"

That wasn't even the half of it. What I now needed to look into was how the severed limb got into the city's top-security VIP accommodation. Davie and I spent a couple of hours supervising the taking of statements and, in the cases of guard personnel, the virtual interrogation of potential witnesses; strongarm tactics, so to speak, are par for the course with auxiliaries who are under suspicion, even of nothing worse than incompetence.

Except there didn't seem to be any witnesses. Sentries had been on duty on every landing, as well as in the entrance hall and on the main esplanade checkpoint, at all times. None of them had seen any suspicious individuals, not least any carrying a long, fleshy object. The only people to have been allowed access to this part of the building after the other occupants went to the reception were the Glasgow leader Andrew Duart and his assistant. They'd arrived at eight thirty-one p.m. The scene-of-crime squad was gradually extending its activities to the hallways and other flats in the block. So far they'd found no obvious traces of the intruder: no spots of blood, no sign of breaking and entering, no missing digit. They'd been dusting for fingerprints but those they'd found and checked all came from guard and cleaning staff.

Around four a.m. Davie and I sat down to compare notes in the empty apartment next to the administrator's. There were eight in this block: four occupied by the Oxford delegation and one each by Duart and his sidekick, leaving two vacant.

"Not much to go on," the big man said dispiritedly.

"None of the sentries reports anything out of the ordinary. All the human and vehicular traffic logged entering and leaving the castle area has been accounted for."

"Human and vehicular traffic?" I said ironically. The City Guard has a robotic language of its own.

"You know what I mean," he muttered.

I looked at my notes. "The three Oxford academics are no help either. They weren't here during the evening, and their rooms are clean and secure." Professor Raskolnikov had tried to pick my brains about the investigation but I deflected his questions.

"Which leaves the guys from Glasgow," Davie said, his brow furrowed. "What do you think they're doing over here?"

"Attending the prison opening, I reckon."

"No, I mean why have they even been allowed into the city? Remember the hassle we got after we'd been over there." There was bitterness in his voice. "As far as some of my superiors are concerned, I've been a pariah ever since."

I nodded and led him out into the corridor. "You're not the only one." I grinned at him. "Let's go and take it out on Duart and his monkey."

Davie was right behind me. "Hold me back," he said with grim satisfaction.

The two Glaswegians had been accommodated on the first floor. I sent Davie to talk to the assistant so we could compare stories afterwards. He pounded on the door with regulation guard diplomacy.

I gave Andrew Duart's door a slightly more restrained knock. After a minute I heard the chain being drawn back.

"Quint Dalrymple," the first secretary said, rubbing

his eyes. He was wearing an expensive-looking silk dressing-gown with a pink and black Charles Rennie Mackintosh design. He peered at his heavy gold watch. "Don't tell me. You want to have that word now."

"Correct."

He let me in and took me over to the lounge area. His accommodation wasn't quite as vast as Raphael's, but it would still have put up half a dozen citizen families. Before he sat down, Duart took a couple of pills from his pocket and swallowed them, washing them down with liquid from an insulated flask.

"Glasgow water," he said apologetically. "I don't trust the stuff you people drink."

"Are you all right?" I asked.

He looked at me. "Oh, you mean the pills. Migraine. I had a terrible one earlier in the evening."

I'd thought his face beneath what I was sure was dyed black hair looked unnaturally pale. "Is that why you didn't go to the reception?"

He peered at me curiously. "How do you know I was invited?"

I shrugged. "You told me you'd been invited to the prison inauguration. It's a reasonable conclusion that you were on the guest list for tonight as well."

"You're right," he conceded, smoothing his hair back. "I couldn't see straight and the idea of going to a party brought me out in even more of a sweat than I was already experiencing."

I glanced at my notes. "Yet you were logged arriving here at eight thirty-one. That was an hour after the reception began." I held him in my gaze. "Something go wrong with your travel arrangements?"

Duart looked straight back at me. "Yes, as a matter of fact we did have a problem. Or rather the helijet did.

There was a delay while they cleaned a seagull out of a turbine."

"You came in a helijet? One of those Oxford contraptions?"

He nodded, a faint smile on his lips. "Don't look so amazed, Quint. Glasgow and New Oxford have many joint interests. The Hebdomadal Council is sometimes gracious enough to afford me the use of its aircraft."

I stored that away for future consideration. "So you stayed here all evening nursing your migraine?"

"Indeed. I was past the worst when I heard the administrator's scream." He shook his head. "Pretty disgusting thing to find in your bath."

I was watching him closely again. "You haven't had any similar cases in Glasgow, have you?"

He knew immediately what I was getting at. In 2026 the trip I'd taken to his city had involved plenty of mutilation. Not to mention murder.

"No, my friend," he replied firmly. "The Major Crime Squad has been relatively underemployed since you honoured us with your presence."

"How about the guilty parties?"

"Safely locked up in Barlinnie."

I sincerely hoped he was being straight with me. The people behind those killings were capable of anything.

We chewed the fat for a bit longer but that didn't get me anywhere. I was pretty sure Duart was being straight with me about his lack of involvement in events on the floor above.

The first secretary looked at his watch again. "Are we done, Quint? I need some sleep." He gave me a cautionary look. "I have a meeting with the senior guardian at nine o'clock."

I got to my feet. "I wish you joy of it, Andrew." First

names were the way in Glasgow – something to do with equality and fraternity.

"What's this all about, for the love of God?" he asked. "Could the arm in the bath just be some kind of a sick joke?"

I opened the door and glanced back at him. "I doubt the donor's laughing."

Back in the vacant flat upstairs Davie and I checked their statements. Duart's secretary said the same as his boss and, since no one missing an arm had turned up inside the building and neither of them had been seen leaving the complex, we moved on to other concerns. We'd covered several procedural issues with the command centre when there was a tap on the door.

"It's open," I shouted.

Doctor Verzeni appeared, his thick hair ruffled. "Citizen Dalrymple," he said, tripping over the consonantal clusters in my name. "Administrator Raphael would like to see you."

"Right. Give me five minutes."

The doctor stayed where he was. "I don't think you understand," he said slowly. "We do not keep the administrator waiting." The menace in his tone made me look up from my notes.

"Look, pal—" Davie began, breaking off when he saw me shake my head.

"I want to keep her sweet," I said under my breath. The look on his face told me what he thought of that. "Finish off making arrangements, will you?"

Verzeni led me back into the Bell Rooms and I began the long walk to the lounge furniture. As I got nearer the plush Walter Scott sofa a frisson of surprise ran up my spine. The administrator was talking to herself.

She wrapped things up as I reached the end of the room, the only words that I heard being something like "imperative that camera locates subject soonest". It was only when she touched the silver appendage round her neck that I got a hint of what she'd been doing.

Raphael registered the direction of my gaze. "This is my nostrum," she said, raising her hand to her chest again.

"Your what?"

"My nostrum. It is what we call our personal computer cum communication device." She beckoned me to come closer and tilted the device towards me. Something she did with her finger made a tiny screen filled with letters and digits appear. Another movement on the rear brought up a selection of icons. "It's also voice-operated," the administrator explained. "My own voice is the only one that activates this particular unit, of course."

"Of course," I said, thinking of the new equipment I'd seen in the command centre. Even if it was Bronze Age compared with this. "Who were you talking to?"

She opened her eyes wide at me in admonition. "That is none of your concern, Citizen Dalrymple." Then her expression slackened. "Not that I have anything to hide. I was talking to my colleagues in New Oxford."

"Telling them how uncivilised we are in Edinburgh?"

She shook her head. "I wouldn't say that." She shot a glance at the bathroom door. "Though I could have done without the object in my bath." She turned to me. "Sit down and tell me what you're doing about that."

I ran through the sparse fruits of my enquiries then moved on to the preliminary examination of the arm.

Raphael raised her hand. "I've already spoken to the medical guardian about that," she said. "I gather she's intrigued by the nature of the trauma."

I nodded, suddenly aware that the administrator was less calm and collected than she'd been earlier. She'd laid one hand on top of the other on the upper of her crossed legs, the implant in her wrist glinting, and the slight tremor in the fingers attracted my attention. Maybe the shock was kicking in now, though she told me that she'd seen worse. And why had she spoken directly to Sophia? That suggested she was very curious about the severed arm. Or perhaps she'd had some bad news from the dreaming spires.

"However," Raphael continued, "she has come to no conclusion about the instrument used to produce such wounding." She glanced at me. "How about you, citizen? What do you think? I'm told you have extensive experience of mutilated bodies."

"That's not something I'm proud of," I said, irritated by her neutral tone. "For what it's worth I've never seen such a clean and surgical job, at least on the arm." I held up the stump of my right forefinger but Raphael gave no reaction. "The finger stump trauma is more standard." I decided to turn the heat up. "Have you had any experience of mutilation?"

"Certainly not," she said, giving me a steady look. "I'm a university administrator, not a surgeon." Her hauteur would have persuaded most people to take her words at face value. "I ask you again, citizen: what are you doing to find the responsible party?"

"My colleague is finalising things with the City Guard command centre as we speak. An all-barracks search for the amputee has been instituted. He'll either be dead or in a serious condition by now. Either way, we'll find him. The tattoo shows that he's in a youth gang that we know well. The guard has already started bringing his fellow members in for questioning."

Raphael raised a hand. "You haven't told me how the responsible party gained access to this place." Again a tremor ran across her fingers. "Is it safe for me to close my eyes even for a second?"

"Don't worry," I said, suddenly feeling sorry for her; she was far from home, in a city where she probably imagined that violence of the kind she'd encountered was commonplace. "This is the most secure accommodation block in Edinburgh, especially now."

She looked at me closely then nodded. "Thank you for that at least." She got up and moved away. "I will try to get some sleep now. I have a series of meetings with guardians and senior auxiliaries throughout the day."

That made me think of Andrew Duart. "I gather you know the first secretary of Glasgow."

She nodded, her face giving nothing away.

"He was wondering if this whole thing might just be some kind of prank."

"I think not, citizen," Raphael said.

I thought not too.

Dawn was breaking, grey with no more than an unreliable promise that the sun might make an appearance, as Davie and I headed across the esplanade to the castle. If I hadn't recently become accustomed to all-night investigations caused by the city's youth and to Katharine appearing in the small hours, I'd have felt more in need of my bed. As it was, I reckoned my batteries – unlike those you get in exchange for Supply Directorate vouchers – had a few more hours in them.

An old but highly polished black taxi pulled up ahead of us, blocking the drawbridge.

"Shit," I said in a low voice.

"Ditto," added Davie.

The senior guardian, a.k.a. the welfare guardian, Lachlan Lessels and Slick, jumped out and stood waiting for us, his arm in the tweed jacket worn by his rank resting on the vehicle's door. For some reason Edinburgh's top dog had dispensed with the Land-Rover normally used by guardians and taken possession of a restored cab. He'd also done away with his chauffeur and insisted on driving himself, even to official functions. It's easy enough when you don't have to worry about finding a parking space.

"Citizen," he said, eyeing me beadily through his thick, round glasses. He didn't favour Davie with ocular contact. "Proceed, commander. This is private."

Davie strode away with a spring in his step. The last thing he wanted was an early morning conference with the city's number one slimebag.

"It's rather cold," the senior guardian said. "Let's take advantage of my vehicle." A machine was just about all I could imagine him taking advantage of. Despite a wandering eye and a prurient tongue, Lachlan Lessels was as close to asexual as it gets.

I joined him in the back of the cab and glanced at my steamed-up watch. "I'm a bit pushed for time, guardian," I said.

"You can spare me a few moments, Dalrymple," he said, licking his finger and removing a spot from his green corduroy trousers. He looked round at me. "Let me make myself very clear." His voice was reedy but the tone was sharp. "I and certain carefully chosen colleagues have worked hard to build up Edinburgh's relations with New Oxford over the last year. The Hebdomadal Council has been extremely co-operative and extremely generous."

The way he stressed the last word made it clear what was driving the Council's relationship with the southern city. Money is underneath everything in Edinburgh – money and sewers. It's just that there are more of the latter than the former here. What did New Oxford expect to get out of Edinburgh?

"This appalling business with the severed arm must be resolved with maximum speed and minimum disruption, do you understand?" The senior guardian shook his head. "It's pure insanity. I want the madman who did this caught today, do you hear? Today!"

He was doing a reasonable impression of a moonstruck specimen himself.

"There's very little to go on," I pointed out. "We're trying to—"

"I know exactly what you're doing," he interrupted. "I've spoken to Administrator Raphael and to the public order guardian – not that he was much use." He turned on me again. "No excuses, Dalrymple. Find the lunatic today." His lips formed into an ugly rictus. "If you fail, you'll be among the first prisoners in the New Bridewell. Point taken?"

He'd screwed up. Being a lifelong atheist I don't go in for articles of faith, but there's one I always observe: never let a member of the Council get the better of you.

"Point taken, senior guardian," I said with fake deference. "But there's something I have to bring to your attention."

"And what is that?" he demanded.

"Well," I replied, looking past him towards the hills of Fife which had just been illuminated by a shaft of milky sunlight. "I know how the individual with the arm gained access to Ramsay Garden without attracting the sentries' attention."

His eyes bulged. "Really? How?"

"By wearing a guard uniform."

That put an extra layer of grease on his forehead.

CHAPTER FOUR

The upshot of my conversation with the senior guardian was an emergency meeting in Lewis Hamilton's office. Slick himself was unable to attend as the Oxford delegation was waiting for him, but he made it very clear that the sentries were to be dragged over all available coals. He also specified that the Mist was to attend the meeting – to maintain some degree of objectivity, as he put it. To act as his listening device was what he meant.

Hamilton stood behind his desk, the pens and pencils arrayed with military precision as usual, and glowered at his deputy. "Well, Raeburn 124, make yourself useful. Ask my secretary to send in coffee."

It was a cheap shot but she took it, only the slight colouring of her heavy cheeks showing what she thought of her superior's management style.

"What the hell do you think you're up to, Dalrymple?" the public order guardian demanded as the Mist went to the door. "How dare you accuse my directorate of involvement in this crime?"

"Calm down, Lewis," I said, glancing at Davie. He didn't look impressed either. "I didn't accuse guard personnel of anything." I felt Raeburn 124's fleshy presence at my side again; she hadn't taken long to put in her order. "All I suggested was that whoever took the arm into Ramsay Garden was wearing a guard uniform, not that he or she was one of your people."

Hamilton's face took on a slightly less aggressive appearance. "Why didn't you make that clear to the senior guardian then?"

I shrugged. "He drew his own conclusions." Everyone in the room knew that Slick would jump at any opportunity to put the knife into Hamilton's directorate.

The Mist was interested in something else. "You said 'he or she', citizen. You don't seriously think that a woman was responsible for removing and transporting the arm, do you?"

I looked into the pale blue eyes that shone from her round face. "It wouldn't be the first time a female criminal has run riot in Edinburgh."

That reference to one of the city's worst cases of serial violence since independence shut her up.

"So you're saying that someone – male or female – may have impersonated a member of the guard?" Davie said.

I nodded. "It has to be a strong possibility." I pointed to the sheaf of statements he had under his arm. "None of the sentries on the esplanade checkpoint reported seeing any unauthorised individuals." I looked at Hamilton and his deputy. "But they're not required to log their fellow guard personnel, are they?"

Raeburn 124, not long in the Public Order Directorate, made a face that showed her boss what she thought of that piece of procedure.

"But none of them reported seeing anyone even trying to enter Ramsay Garden, auxiliary or not," Davie insisted. "I asked that."

Hamilton's grey-suited female secretary bustled in, deposited a tray on his desk and bustled out again.

I let the others get stuck into the coffee – it had an

aroma that promised trouble. "Fair enough," I said. "But the point is, would they have noticed this particular one of the many guard personnel who pass the checkpoint on the esplanade?"

Hamilton gulped from a cup, the twisting of his lips showing that the mess-hall coffee was even nastier than usual. "Maybe not, but how did he" – he glanced at the Mist – "or *she* get into the accommodation block? There was no sign of illicit entry, was there?"

Davie shook his head. "The scene-of-crime squad is still checking, but there's nothing in the vicinity of the stair we're interested in."

The guardian looked at me triumphantly. "You see, Dalrymple? There's no way the miscreant could have got past the sentry on the door; he logged everyone who went in or out, auxiliaries included."

It was always like this: guardians and auxiliaries couldn't countenance incompetence among their ranks, let alone disloyalty or improbity. I never had that problem.

"What about the rota?" I asked innocently.

"What about the rota?" countered Hamilton, the glare he directed at his deputy warning her to keep out of the discussion.

She jumped in regardless. "Could the mystery person have slipped in when the guard was changing?"

Davie scratched his chin through the growth of beard. "Unlikely. I could ask the watch supervisors again."

"What's the point?" I asked. "They're hardly going to change their accounts and land themselves in the shit."

The guardian's face was suffused. "My people do not behave—"

"Spare us the sermon, Lewis," I interrupted. "You and I both know that there's often a delay of a few minutes between the time the sentry going off duty after a two-hour stint signs off in the guardhouse and the replacement takes up position."

"There is not!" Hamilton roared.

I looked to Davie for support. "Em . . . yes, there can be such a gap, guardian. People are desperate for a hot drink or a leak."

Raeburn 124 was enjoying the exchange. "I think I'd better institute an enquiry into sentry practice, don't you, guardian?" she said, trying to keep her lips in a straight line.

I raised my hand before Lewis could do another lion impersonation. "This raises a couple of important points. First, the arm-bearer must have had an intimate knowledge of guard procedures in order to have timed his or her arrival and departure so perfectly."

They had to accept that.

"And second, there's the question of the uniform. How was it obtained?" City Guard apparel is produced and stored in secure premises, separate from citizen-issue clothes. It's always been subject to stringent checks, and auxiliaries who lose garments face instant demotion; in the early days of the Council, drugs gangs used to steal uniforms and use them to cause even greater chaos.

"We're back where we started then, aren't we, citizen?" the Mist said. "You think the guilty party is a member of the guard."

I gave the guardian an emollient look. "Not necessarily. The uniform could have been taken from a serving auxiliary." I turned to Davie. "Any of your people gone missing recently?"

He shook his head. "You know how strict the procedures are on absenteeism."

Before I could respond to that, telephonic hell broke

loose. As well as all four of our mobiles going off, Hamilton's desk phone emitted a piercing shriek.

"What the . . ." the guardian gasped.

I stepped towards the window with my mobile to my ear and, as I surveyed the first leaves coming through on the trees in Princes Street Gardens, managed to make out that the body of a male citizen with one arm missing had just been found in Leith.

We all left the office at speed, boots clattering down the cobbles towards the esplanade. Davie and I left Hamilton and the Mist far behind.

"Don't wait," I said as we reached the nearest Land-Rover. "Lewis and his deputy can sort out their own transport."

Davie bundled the startled guard driver out and took the wheel.

As we headed for the checkpoint – alert sentries raising the barrier rapidly in response to Davie's gestures – we passed the VIP accommodation block. Outside the door I saw Administrator Raphael and her entourage moving towards the ceremonial Jeep. They were surrounded by a flock of guard personnel which was being handled, of all people, by the senior guardian. The three academics were keeping close to Raphael and she almost seemed to be keeping her head down. What did she think was going to happen to her in a city where the only firearms are those issued to guards on the city line and border posts? Maybe she was worried about dive-bombing seagulls.

Davie drove down the Royal Mile; for all the original Council's republican fervour, the street leading to the now ruined palace retains its name to make the tourists happy. He kept his hand on the horn to ensure the city's visitors stuck to the pavements. Most of them were more interested in the tacky souvenirs and cut-price woollens than in a rust-devoured guard vehicle.

"Hold tight!" Davie yelled as he took a left on to the North Bridge, the worn remoulds sending us into a skid that seemed terminal for much longer than was comfortable.

"Thanks a lot, big man," I said, my heart pounding like a bass drum.

"Think nothing of it," he said with a laugh. "Now sit back and enjoy the view."

I did what he recommended, struggling to get my breathing under control. There was plenty to see as we traversed the great triple-arched bridge linking the Old Town with the New. The gardens and the neo-classical galleries to the west were more pleasing to the eye, but my gaze was irresistibly drawn to the castellated walls to the north-east. There it was: the New Bridewell, the jewel in the new Enlightenment Edinburgh's crown. The fortifications of the original prison reared up from the bare rock face in an unbroken chain over three hundred yards long. The obelisk in the former burial ground – now topped out with transmitter aerials and discs – pointed towards the sky at the left. To the rear the Nelson Monument on top of the Calton Hill mirrored its effect, and the circular watchtowers were almost lost in the bulk of the central block. As we got nearer I could see the razor wire that had been erected on top of the old defences. The mob that stormed the Bastille would have got nowhere with this monstrosity.

"Where's the Council going to find the prisoners to fill its new toy?" I asked.

Davie grinned. "Where we're going now."

"Aye," I said, nodding. "There's no shortage of gang-bangers down in Leith these days."

"And there's even a gangbanger with one arm," he said. "Maybe it's a new form of initiation ceremony."

That sent a shiver up my spine.

We were in the depths of the citizen residential area near the docks. Davie had taken a left turn off Constitution Street and immediately lost his bearings. The narrow lanes were deserted, the locals at work or school. Some of them had optimistically hung their washing on the wires above the road – no tumble dryers outside the tourist zone in this city – but the sun's weak April rays were unlikely to do much good in the confines of the buildings.

"Where is it we're headed?" I asked.

"Socrates Lane," Davie said, grabbing the road map. "Should be somewhere around here."

"Socrates Lane?" I said. "Spot the name imposed by the Council." I wound my window down and checked out the place. I soon realised that it wasn't as deserted as I'd thought. There was movement behind the grubby net curtains over the upper windows on both sides.

"We are not alone," I said. The back streets near the port were a notorious haunt of youth gangs and black-marketeers.

Davie chucked the atlas on to my lap and let off the handbrake. "Don't worry. They won't attack a guard vehicle in broad daylight."

There was a light rattling on the Land-Rover's roof.

Davie slammed on the brakes and stuck his head out of the window. "Here!" he shouted. "I'll pull it off if I catch you!"

I decided against putting my own head outside. "Someone having a wettie?"

"Aye," Davie grunted. "I saw the little scumbag. He couldn't have been more than ten."

"They recruit young these days," I said. "Maybe he's in the Portobello Pish."

"Ha." Davie hung a left and pulled up behind a couple of barracks patrol vans.

I made a quick survey of the upper flats before I got out. No sign of any more piss-artists.

A female auxiliary with an unusually healthy complexion came over from a gaggle of solemn barracks personnel. "Hello, Citizen Dalrymple. Remember me?"

I glanced at the badge on her tunic. "Baltic 04. Oh aye. We checked out the spirits bond a couple of years back, didn't we?"

She nodded. "When some lunatic poisoned the whisky." She pointed to a doorway. "He's up there," she added, her voice suddenly trembling.

"Bad one?" Davie asked over my shoulder.

Baltic 04 nodded, her eyes down.

"All right," I said, "you stay out here. The public order guardian and his deputy will be arriving any minute now with the scene-of-crime squad and the medical team. Keep them on the street till I tell you otherwise." I waited till she looked up again. "Your people haven't touched anything, have they?"

She shook her head. "It's the left-hand flat on the second floor. I went in on my own after we got the tip-off. And I was wearing gloves, citizen."

I looked at her heavy boots. "Let's hope you didn't trample over any vital traces." I touched her arm. "I'm sure you were careful, Baltic 04. Have you got a murder bag?"

"On the front seat of the leading van," the auxiliary said. "Em, citizen? How shall I keep the guardian out?"

I was handed a protective suit by a solemn auxiliary. "Tell him I'm on the job," I said.

"Aye," Davie muttered. "That would put anyone off."

The stairwell we were ascending was completely covered in gang graffiti. Even the worn steps had been given coats of luminous paint, words and crude pictures applied in black ink. On the walls there were vertical red lances every few feet.

"Bingo," I said, remembering the tattoo on the severed arm. "This is a Leith Lancers base."

Davie nudged open a door that was attached by only one hinge and looked around. "Unoccupied, I'm glad to see."

"I'm hoping it stays that way, though the guard presence should have scared them off for a while."

"And as soon as the Mist comes down, they'll vanish for the duration," Davie said with a grim smile.

I kept going, stepping over a fairly recent heap of human excrement, till I reached the landing on the second floor. The doors to both flats were open and the reek made me choke.

"Christ, how do people live here?"

Davie shrugged. "They don't. They have other places where they kip. This is what they call a kicking hole, where they bring the ones they want to teach a lesson to. Members of other gangs, ordinary citizens who rat on them to us, you know how they operate."

I walked into the flat and almost fell into a wide hole where the floorboards had been smashed open. These walls had been decorated in the same way as the stairwell, the centrepiece above the shattered fireplace being a drawing of a figure in guardian-issue clothes looking remarkably like Lewis Hamilton. There were at least a dozen lances protruding from his torso. St Sebastian had it easy by comparison.

"The bog, Quint," Davie said, his eyes wide as he turned towards me. "Jesus, that's too much."

I went past him and looked through the doorway. At first I thought the walls of the confined room had been decorated like all the other surfaces in the tenement, admittedly with even more red than elsewhere. Then I realised that the white tiles, though layered with grease and muck, had not been coated with paint. The covering was dried blood.

"Fuck," Davie said, staring into the bathroom despite himself. "I don't believe this."

I looked at the floor and pointed. "Footprints. Some of them are probably from our friend downstairs but we might get lucky." I stepped round the ribbed markings on the bloodstained boards, my feet unsteady in the protective bootees I'd pulled on outside the front door.

The room was about ten feet by eight, the small window in the left wall covered by uneven planks. All that remained of the sink and lavatory were blackened holes in the surfaces. There was no bath – the water restrictions during the Big Heat had led to all remaining baths being removed from citizen residences – and the shower base was three inches deep in shit. I glanced up and saw that the ceiling was also criss-crossed by long sprays of congealed red. The guy I assumed they'd come from was lying along the right-hand wall. His head was resting on the raised surround of the shower base and his hair was smeared with its contents.

"Fuck is right, Davie," I said, trying to breathe only through my mouth. Then I kneeled down beside the one-armed corpse.

The lower part was dressed in standard youth gang gear: citizen-issue trousers turned up to beneath the knee, heavy boots. I remembered the yob with the red flash on his cheek I'd encountered at the bus stop. This guy was taller, his legs stretched out and close together. I moved my eyes reluctantly to the torso. It was naked, the victim's motionless chest scrawny and spattered with muck. I looked closer. The spots on the pallid skin were dry faecal matter, not blood. I glanced up at the ceiling again and wondered how fresh the blood up there was. Maybe the victim had been mutilated elsewhere.

I steeled myself to lean over the upper part. The young man's face was almost at ease, the muscles slack, eyes closed and the mouth shaped into an incongruous smile. I felt in my pocket for my magnifying glass and held it over the stump of his right arm.

"It looks like a perfect match." Her voice was muffled by a surgical mask that she'd sensibly donned.

I wrenched my neck as I twisted round. "Jesus, Sophia, stop doing that. I almost had a heart attack."

"Sorry." She looked about the room. "What a hell-hole," she said, shaking her head. "I suppose it's an appropriate location for a sick attack like this." She nudged me to one side. "Let's have a look then." She bent down and examined the wound. After a minute she straightened up. "Yes, I'm almost certain the arm in Ramsay Garden came from this victim."

"*Almost* certain?" I demanded. "How many other recently severed arms are you engaged in identifying?"

"None," she said tartly. "But I won't be a hundred per cent sure till I have the body and the limb on the slab together."

"From what I can see, there's no blood on the floor underneath the stump," I said, trying to make sense of the scene. "I reckon he might have been dumped here after death."

Sophia leaned forward again. "Possibly. It really is quite extraordinary. The stump is completely sealed, as was the arm. Cauterisation of some sort but, again, there's no sign of scorching." She stepped back and started talking into her dictation machine.

I watched and listened, trying to follow what she was saying but rapidly getting lost in the medical terminology. Then Sophia's eyes opened wide and the cassette recorder dropped to the floor with a crack.

"Oh no, Quint!" she gasped. "Oh no!"

I looked to the front and felt the hairs on the back of my neck go as rigid as porcupine spines. "What the—?" I broke off and watched what was happening in front of me.

The corpse with one arm had come back to life. Eyes half open, the young man scrabbled on the filthy floorboards with the fingers of his remaining hand, let out a cracked groan and then lapsed back into unconsciousness.

"He's in shock," Sophia said, hitting buttons on her mobile.

I knew exactly how he felt.

"I should have checked for a pulse," Sophia said, her face pale.

We were back on the street, an ambulance having just taken the comatose youth to the infirmary.

"So should I," I said. "So should Baltic 04. But the guy looked deader than a dodo. I didn't see any sign of breathing."

She nodded. "I know. I'll be running tests. He's most likely in deep post-traumatic shock." Her brow beneath the white-blonde hair was deeply lined. "There should have been some chest movement though." She stripped off her protective suit and moved towards her Land-Rover. "Let me know what you find at the locus," she said. "I'm going to supervise this intriguing patient."

"Don't let him die on you," I called after her. She made an unguardian-like gesture with her hand.

Davie came up holding a clipboard. "That was a surprise."

"This case seems to be full of them. What have you got?"

"Nothing much so far. We're tracking down residents and canvassing for witnesses. Oh, and there's an all-barracks alert out for anyone who looks like a Leith Lancer."

I walked to the vehicle we'd arrived in. "I need a wash and something to drink. I've still got the taste of that shithole in my mouth."

He followed me. "The guardian's set up base-camp in Baltic Barracks. He's expecting you there."

"Great." I opened the Land-Rover door then took in the surroundings of Socrates Lane again. Broken windows, litter in the gutters, drainpipes hanging at crazy angles from stone blackened by the smoke from coal fires. "Jesus, Davie, this must be the worst street in the city."

He started the engine and laughed. "Aye, it's almost as bad as the Fisheries Guard mess-hall down the road."

"Close call," I said, nodding. I'd spent a horribly drunken night on a horribly filthy floor with the crew of a patrol ship during the whisky investigation in 2025. The crew and their crazy captain had subsequently sailed off into the wide blue yonder. The latter wore an eye patch and had a dunt in his skull from a crowbar. "I wonder where Dirty Harry and his pirates ended up, Davie?"

"Wherever it is, I wouldn't fancy being in the vicinity,"

he said, shaking his head as he pulled out of the street. "Harry'd have felt at home here though."

"No, he wouldn't." My thoughts were still full of the flat where we'd found the victim. "Not even a psycho drugs gang boss could survive in these tenements." I stared out at the grey granite walls. "But the Council expects ordinary citizens to manage."

Davie looked like he wanted to argue but he didn't bother. There wasn't much he could say.

Baltic Barracks was only a hundred yards from the junction, a solid building that used to be a spirits bond; the small, heavily barred windows had made it easy to defend during the drugs wars. No tourists ever come to Leith these days, so the guard depot and the main street it's on have had minimal maintenance.

Baltic 04 was in the entrance hall. "Thank Christ," she said, taking her life in her hands by using a religious reference proscribed for auxiliaries. "The guardian and the Mi— His deputy have been making everyone's life—"

"All right," I said, wading in before she was overheard. "You did a good job keeping them off my back at the scene." I gave her an ironic smile. "Pity you didn't notice the victim was still with us."

The auxiliary's face fell. "Sorry about that, citizen."

"Don't worry about it too much. I made the same mistake. Where are they?"

"In the ops room." Baltic 04 pointed down the corridor. "Forgive me if I don't join you." She headed off rapidly in the opposite direction.

"Come on, Davie," I said. "Time to perform some more operations."

That took up the whole afternoon.

* * *

"I don't understand why these adolescents won't talk." The Mist turned away from the pair of sullen lads, irritation bringing dots of sweat to her face.

"Because they think all auxiliaries are poison," I said, watching as the younger of the only Leith Lancers the guard had so far managed to pick up sniggered contemptuously. I was wasting my breath trying to get them on my side. I'd already had a go at breaking them down individually without any guard personnel present. They regarded me as poison too, my DM status notwithstanding. They wouldn't even confirm their names. We knew one of them was called Jax – the name was tattooed on his neck – but that was about it. They'd been found in a ruin on the other side of the Water of Leith so they probably didn't know what had happened in the tenement in Socrates Lane. Even a photo of the victim sent down from the infirmary provoked the big zero as regards reactions. The rest of the gang members were obviously keeping their heads as far down as they could.

"Very well," Hamilton's deputy said to the barracks commander. "Lock them up. In separate cells. No food or drink."

I watched as the youths were led away, the leg irons they'd been fitted with clanking as they walked to the door with studied jauntiness.

The public order guardian got up stiffly from a mess table. "This is getting us nowhere. We have no idea of the victim's identity and it doesn't look like he's going to be much help in the immediate future."

Sophia had called several times. The one-armed guy was stable but still unconscious. There was a question of brain damage, though there were no visible wounds to his skull. It had been confirmed beyond all reasonable doubt that the arm in the administrator's bath came from the Leither.

I swallowed the last of my barracks coffee and got a mouthful of gritty dregs. "Anything more on the tip-off?" I asked Davie.

He shook his head. "The guard haven't been able to find anyone who'll own up to seeing who used the public phone in Easter Road." The Council restricts telephones to one on every street and the exchange had been able to trace the number of the phone used to tell Baltic Barracks about the one-armed man.

"I'm still guessing it was a Leith Lancer who made the call," I said. The barracks operator was only able to say that the voice had been male and the accent coarse. "Someone out there knew about the attack. It may just have been a witness who wanted to get help to the boy."

"The scene-of-crime squad is still following up traces and prints, but so far there's nothing that points to the assailant's or the victim's identity," Davie said. "The missing finger hasn't turned up either."

The Mist was standing under the opaque glass at the edge of the basement mess ceiling; the heavy boots of auxiliaries on the pavement above were passing regularly. "And the Housing Directorate's list of residents in Socrates Lane tells us only that the tenement's been unoccupied for five years," she said.

"Damn," Hamilton said, shaking his head. "The senior guardian's not going to like this."

His deputy turned and gave him a mocking smile. "No, he's not, is he?"

I glanced at her and raised my eyebrows. "What are you complaining about?" I said, finding myself in the unusual situation of standing up for Lewis. "We've found the source of the arm. What more does he want?" I realised too late that I'd given her an open goal.

The Mist directed her heavy features at me. "What more, citizen? A perpetrator? A motive? A weapon?"

I was spared further humiliation by the door to our rear bursting open.

"Quint? What happened in Socrates Lane?"

"Katharine?" I said, taken aback by her dishevelled state. "What is it?"

Hamilton stared as she approached us, her black coat hanging loosely over her arm. "What is she doing in a barracks, Dalrymple?" Ordinary citizens are only allowed entry to auxiliary locations when they're under arrest. Lewis had forgotten that Katharine had an "ask no questions", an undercover operative's authorisation that I got for her years back.

"This youth gang member who was attacked," Katharine said, ignoring the guardian and his number two. Her words were coming out in a rush. "I think I know who he is."

That got everybody's attention.

"So tell me exactly how you got on to this," I said, turning to look at Katharine. We were sitting shoulder to shoulder in the front of the Land-Rover that Davie was driving at full speed towards the infirmary.

She shrugged. "I've been in the drop-in centre in Ferry Road since yesterday evening. The usual stream of desperate kids, most of them more frightened than aggressive. I tried to give them what advice I could." She shook her head. "There was even one poor lad, Gus was his name, who'd had his wrist broken. He wouldn't tell me how."

I managed to stop my jaw from dropping.

"He was worried about going to the infirmary but I

eventually managed to pack him off there this afternoon. Anyway, some boys I've known for a couple of months came in to play table tennis. It was one of them who'd heard a rumour about one of the L.L.s being attacked in Socrates Lane."

"What was his name?" I asked.

"Oh no," Katharine said firmly. "I'm not landing him in it. He wasn't involved, I'm sure of it."

I nudged her gently. "Not your source. You said you could identify the victim."

"Wait till I see him; if it's who I think it is, I've met him a couple of times." She gave me a tight smile. "Then, if you and the medical guardian ask nicely, maybe I'll tell you his name."

I looked ahead as the monuments on the Calton Hill came into sight at the top of Leith Walk. And wondered if Katharine would ever let me forget the torrid relationship that Sophia and I had during the Big Heat of 2025.

We stood outside the intensive care unit and watched the nurses hovering over the guy with one arm. Tubes and wires hooked his motionless frame to several machines. Katharine was in with him, swathed in surgical robes.

This time I glanced round before Sophia reached me. "Anything new?" I asked.

She regarded Katharine with glacial eyes then nodded. "I'll tell you after Citizen Kirkwood does what she has to do."

The seal on the door hissed as it opened to let Katharine pass.

"It's him all right," she said, pulling her mask down. "George Faulds. They call him Dead Dod."

Davie shook his head as he wrote down the name, then went off to run a check.

"What else do you know about him?" Sophia demanded.

Katharine shot me a glance. "Ask me politely, guardian," she said in an arch voice.

Sophia hit me with her eyes too – I was everybody's punch bag. "Oh, for goodness' sake. Citizen Kirkwood," she said mechanically, "please tell us what else you know about this George Faulds."

"That's better." Katharine handed the robes she'd been removing to the guardian. "Not much, as it happens. I've only seen him a few times in the centre. He has a reputation for being a loner. And he has quite a temper. He once broke a snooker cue over his knee when he missed a shot." She shrugged. "At least it wasn't somebody else's knee."

"He's definitely a Leith Lancer?" I asked. There have been cases of kids, desperate to join the gangs, doing their own tattoos. They usually end up with broken heads, but not severed arms.

Katharine nodded. "Oh aye. A Lancer and proud of it." She looked at me. "What happened to him, Quint? It looks like he's lost an arm."

Sophia passed the robes to a nursing auxiliary and turned away. "That information is classified," she said.

I put a hand on her shoulder. "Katharine's helped us, Sophia. She works with these kids. She's entitled to know."

The guardian wasn't convinced, but finally she gave in and took us to her office. "There are some strange aspects to this case," she said, sitting down at her desk and opening a grey folder. "First of all, the patient doesn't appear to have lost much blood."

"What?" I said. "He had an arm severed."

"Oh, you noticed?" Sophia said ironically. "There's no arguing with the test results, Quint. Second, the preliminary analysis shows an as yet unidentified chemical compound in his veins."

"What kind of substance?" Katharine asked. "Sometimes those kids pick up new designer drugs from smugglers."

"It may be something of that sort," Sophia agreed. She gave me a stern look. "Unfortunately the city's chief toxicologist has been missing for a fortnight so we're not well equipped to identify the compound. His department's doing the best it can."

I sat down heavily, suddenly aware of the fact that I hadn't slept last night. "Could it have something to do with the state he's been in?"

Sophia nodded. "Quite possibly. The assailant may have put him under before severing the arm. The reduction in heart rate and oxygen intake may have caused permanent brain damage – it's too early to say."

"So we may not get a description of his attacker from him," I said. "Great."

Sophia put the file down slowly. "And I'm still no clearer about what was used to sever the arm. The surfaces are smooth but not as clean as a heavy blade such as a cleaver would produce. And the sealing, cauterisation, whatever – I can't make sense of it." She looked at me desperately. "I don't suppose the scene-of-crime squad has found anything suggestive?"

I gave a hollow laugh. "That would be too easy, Sophia. The finger is still missing as well, by the way."

"In that case the lunatic who took this arm off is still

out there," she said, her face pale. "With the means to do it again."

The conversation ended.

Katharine and I headed to the exit in silence. Not for long. As we were crossing the reception area, a voice rang out.

"Here, Katharine!"

I looked to my left and saw a figure with his forearm in plaster approaching. I recognised him immediately. Oh shit.

"Hello, Gus," Katharine said. "How's your—?" She broke off as the youth with the red flash on his cheek gave me a fearful stare.

"This is the bastard who broke my fuckin' wrist," Gus yelled, his voice breaking. "Dinnae let him near me."

The look I got from Katharine would have made William Wallace wet himself.

CHAPTER FIVE

"So now you're beating up kids, Quint."

Katharine had managed to contain herself until we reached the middle of the infirmary courtyard. Then she planted herself in front of me and set to.

"He's a gangbanger," I said, knowing already that this was an argument I wasn't going to win. "He and his pal were stealing citizens' vouchers."

"And that gave you the right to break his wrist?" she shouted, her eyes wide. "Christ, you're no better than one of the guard's beaters."

I tried to step round her but she moved to cut me off. "The beaters go looking for trouble," I said, avoiding her gaze. "I came across the robbery by chance."

Katharine jabbed her finger into my chest. "My hero," she said sarcastically. "Edinburgh's knight in a shining donkey jacket. Has it ever occurred to you that the city's young people need sympathy and help?" She shook her head. "What good is more violence?"

I stared at a pair of guard drivers who were leaning against their vehicles' doors and watching us avidly. "Your wee pal Gus went for me with a sharpened stick, Katharine," I hissed. "What should I have done? Invite him round for tea and scones?"

That only enraged her more. "For God's sake, Quint, I thought you were different from the rest of the lunatics in the Public Order Directorate." She was leaning towards me, her lips wet and her chin flecked with spittle. "But you aren't, are you?" She turned on her heel. "Away and inaugurate the prison with your fascist friends."

I watched her storm through the gateway and disappear in the twilight.

The guardsmen by the Land-Rovers nodded at me, their bearded faces creased in mocking smiles.

"Had you on the run there, didn't she, citizen?" one of them said.

I was on the point of laying into him when I remembered Katharine's reproof – and restricted myself to giving him and his mate the benefit of my middle finger.

Three hours in the castle did nothing to improve my mood. Davie and I found a small unused room across the yard from the command centre and co-ordinated the investigation from there. Hamilton and the Mist kept appearing and disturbing us, but at least the confined space prevented them setting up permanent residence.

"Do you want that roll?" Davie asked, eyeing the sole survivor of what had originally been a heaped plate supplied by the castle mess.

"One slice of reconstituted mutton per lifetime is enough for me, thanks."

He leaned forward and snaffled the wholemeal bap. Shortly afterwards he spoke some words I couldn't decipher.

"Didn't they teach you not to eat with your mouth full on the auxiliary training programme?"

He glowered at me and swallowed. "What do you want to do now?" he said, enunciating like the jackasses who read the news on *Radio Free City* – the Information Directorate thinks listeners enjoy being talked down to.

"Oh, right." I gave him a derisory smile. "What do I want to do now? I want to get to my bed, big man. There's not exactly much going on here."

Davie looked at the notes he'd made. "Dead Dod's file didn't tell us much we couldn't guess."

"Persistent truancy, a spell in a Youth Detention Centre for stealing clothing vouchers from his granddad, failure to attend a whole series of work placements," I read from my notebook.

Davie nodded. "Plus numerous sightings with known members of the Leith Lancers."

"And none of the few we've caught are telling us anything about Dod or about what happened to him."

"Do you reckon they know who attacked him?" he asked, draining the last of his barracks tea from a chipped City Guard mug.

I shrugged. "Maybe not. Dead Dod seems to have been a bit of a loner. Which would have made him a perfect target for the assailant."

"So," Davie said, throwing down his pencil, "no witnesses from Socrates Lane, no statement from the victim – who's still comatose from whatever hyper-strength drug was pumped into him – and nothing useful from the scene-of-crime squad. Hell of a day's work, eh?"

There was a knock on the door and a statuesque guardswoman came in. "Report from the scene-of-crime squad, commander," she said, handing Davie a maroon folder and giving him a smile that was warmer than the occasion required.

"Friend of yours?" I asked as the door closed behind her.

"Oh aye," he said, grinning. "I'm a great believer in maintaining close relationships with my team."

"Primarily the female members of your team."

He'd raised a hand. "Hang on. It looks like I spoke too soon. The SOCS has lifted some footprints from the locus."

"I'm not surprised. There was enough muck on the floors in there."

His face darkened. "No good, though. They can't match the prints with anything in their archive."

I went round to his side of the table and checked the facsimile of the print. "What, this shoe or boot is unknown to them?"

He ran his finger down the report. "That's what they say."

I leaned back against the table, hearing the wood squeak on the bare flagstones. "Interesting. This might be more useful than you think."

"What do you mean?"

"I mean that the footwear would appear to have been produced outside Edinburgh." I rubbed my hand across my forehead, feeling a headache beginning to set in. That made me think of the man who said he had a migraine yesterday evening. "How about Glasgow?"

Davie looked up at me, one eye screwed up. "Andrew Duart and his bum chum? Nah, don't be stupid, Quint. They were inside Ramsay Garden all night and I bet they've been in meetings all day. Shall I check?"

I nodded. "Aye. But I wasn't thinking of those particular individuals. If the Council's decided the west coast isn't the nest of vipers it used to be, perhaps there are other specimens on the loose."

Davie was looking even more doubtful. "And how do you think you'll be able to track them down? There haven't been any passes issued to non-tourist aliens in the last few days. I looked at the register when I was setting up the security for the reception."

He was right. If it was a foreigner who'd cut off Dead Dod's arm, he or she was likely to have entered the city illegally.

"Course, there's no shortage of tourists," Davie added. "You want me to institute a census of our honoured guests' shoes?"

I shook my head. "Forget it. You know the Tourism Directorate would never allow that." I walked round to the other side of the table and made a note in my book. "Anyway, whoever attacked the kid in Socrates Lane and left the arm in the administrator's bath had local knowledge."

"Yeah, I suppose so." Davie grinned. "Pity. I was going to point the finger – so to speak – at another group of visitors to Edinburgh."

"Who?"

He looked over his shoulder and reassured himself that no one else had slipped in. "The Oxford delegation."

"What?"

He raised his shoulders dispiritedly. "I know, I'm clutching at straws. There's something about those people that puts my back up. Why are they here? We don't need a prison, let alone one designed by a bunch of crazy professors."

"What kind of investigation technique is that, guardsman?" I demanded, demoting him to the rank he'd had when I first met him; I still felt more comfortable with it than commander. "Something about them puts your back up?"

"Aye," he said combatively, "take the piss if you like, but I know you feel the same way. And I know you're not a fan of the New Bridewell."

According to Katharine he was wrong on both counts.

* * *

At midnight, when there was nothing new to report, we signed off with Hamilton and his deputy. We were informed that the senior guardian was unimpressed by the lack of progress, but that the Oxford delegation was at least glad that the arm's owner had been discovered. The Mist said that Administrator Raphael was particularly concerned and had been in touch with Sophia several times about the victim. The inauguration was to go ahead, though Raphael had asked for additional security; apparently she was worried that the perpetrator might try to disrupt it, though she'd given no explanation of that fear.

Davie drove me back to Gilmore Place and I climbed the stairs to my flat slowly, the effect of forty-plus hours without sleep numbing me as effectively as a pint of hemlock. Before I turned in I made a couple of calls, stabbing my finger on the buttons of my mobile by the light of a guttering candle. Neither got me anywhere. Sophia advised that the one-armed man was still deep in his chemically assisted slumbers and that the Toxicology Department was still no nearer identifying the substance in his system. And Katharine's mobile had been turned off, so I couldn't tell where she was or whether she'd calmed down: experience told me it was way too early for that.

So I took a couple of large grey Supply Directorate aspirins and collapsed into bed, too exhausted to take off more than the outer layer of clothing. I berated myself momentarily for having forgotten all about Lister 25, the missing chief toxicologist, then sank into oblivion.

We were standing in groups in the exercise yard of the prison, waiting for the circus to begin. It was a bright, cool day, the only clouds a ripple of cirrus high above;

they looked like the exhalations of a giant winged creature that had overflown Edinburgh and decided it could have a better time elsewhere. I glanced at my watch and saw through the permanent condensation that it was a quarter to eleven. Fifteen minutes to kick-off.

Tackety boots clattered on the paving-stones inside the heavy gate as members of the Public Order Directorate pipe band moved their lower limbs surreptitiously to keep the circulation going. The area enclosed by the walls with their new wire excrescences was about eighty yards square, on a mound rising from the north to fall on the south and covered in grey gravel. Apart from the obelisk and the round structure on the west side, the yard was empty of stone structures. All the tombstones, funerary monuments, statues and miniature temples to the souls of the departed had departed, no doubt bulldozed away. The Corrections Department's requirement for a prisoners' exercise area was more pressing than that of conserving one of the city's prime historical sites. I wondered if they'd taken the bones out of the ground too, then decided it was unlikely: the symbolism of doomed prisoners tramping round on human remains would have been irresistible to the Mist and her friends.

I heard the gravel crunch to my right.

"Do you think the old philosopher would approve of what's been done to his mausoleum?" Billy Geddes gave a hungry laugh. "Neat, isn't it?"

I let my eyes follow his shrivelled arm in the direction of the rotunda that had originally been erected in honour of Edinburgh's native thinker David Hume. It used to be an open, uncapped space – appropriate for a man of ideas – but now the structure had been transformed into what looked disturbingly like a naval gun-turret. A mobile glass canopy had been placed on top, with a protruding steel extension that enabled a sentry to oversee the entire yard. As I watched, a group of VIPs that included Raphael and her brainboxes were shown the canopy in operation. The guardswoman on top was gripping the handrail almost as tightly as she was gripping her snub-nosed machine-pistol. It was a model I hadn't seen before in the city.

"I think the sainted D.H. would have been sceptical as to the building's benefits," I said.

"Ha-ha," Billy said. "Anyway, I thought Hume was an atheist. Who'd canonise him?" He was dressed in a charcoal-grey suit that definitely hadn't come from a Supply Directorate store, but the expensive material couldn't do much to hide the twisted, emaciated legs in his wheelchair. "What the hell are you doing here, Quint? They haven't got you on security detail, have they?"

"Sod off." I looked round at the numerous guard personnel in the former burial ground. There was enough security here to satisfy an American President, not that the disunited states of America bother with one of those any more: the chief executives of the major global corporations pull all the strings. "I'm flying the flag for liberal values."

"Mind you don't end up with a guardswoman on your head like David Hume."

"A guardswoman with a new toy." I glanced down at my former friend. "You haven't been indulging in a spot of arms dealing, have you?"

Billy grinned at me, his eyes the liveliest part of him. "Maybe. What's your problem, pal?"

"My problem," I said, leaning over the wheelchair, "is that things are getting out of control here." Then I ran my eyes round the walls and watchtower of the New Bridewell and realised I was talking rubbish. "Or rather, there's suddenly too *much* control in this supposedly benevolent dictatorship. Since when have firearms been allowed in the central zone?"

Billy shrugged. "As soon as the Council went ahead with the incarceration policy, that became inevitable. You can't expect a prison to operate without fully equipped warders."

"Let me guess," I said, staring into his grey eyes. "You did a deal with New Oxford for the weapons."

He gave a harsh laugh. "The Council did a deal with New Oxford for much more than a few high-tech guns, I can tell you."

I wasn't very surprised. "And how exactly is the cash-strapped Finance Directorate managing to pay for that?"

I think he would have told me – Billy Geddes had never been shy about blowing his own bassoon – but we were interrupted.

"What's going on here?" The senior guardian was wearing a black suit that was even more sumptuous than Billy's, the only concession to his rank being a maroon and white Council tie. He was also wearing a Grade A disapproving look. "Confidential information is not to be disclosed to Citizen Dalrymple." He opened his eyes wide at Billy, the thick round lenses of his glasses giving him the appearance of a fish – one that ate flesh rather than seaweed. "Is that understood?"

Billy Geddes nodded sullenly. His eyes flashed as the headman stalked off to join the Oxford group. "Understood, Slick," he said under his breath.

I spotted Andrew Duart talking to the Mist and decided to rescue him. Hamilton's deputy made her excuses when I arrived and went to find someone who was more deeply in love with the concept of imprisonment.

"I understand you've made some progress with the case of the arm in the administrator's bath, Quint." The Glaswegian was also dressed to the nines but, unlike the Edinburgh dignitaries, he could carry haute couture off. In the sunshine his hair and goatee beard had an even darker lustre than before: he'd been at the bottle again.

I nodded and glanced down at his shoes. From above it was impossible to tell the pattern of the soles; not that I seriously imagined he'd been in the tenement in Leith – his feet were much smaller than the prints that had been found. "Some progress, yes," I said, taking a leaf from Slick's book: no disclosure is good disclosure.

The first secretary of Glasgow smiled. "Don't worry. Administrator Raphael's kept me fully informed."

"Has she now?" I glanced across at the Oxford party. They were standing close to the obelisk, being addressed by the senior guardian. Raphael was in her high-necked black suit. She looked as regal as ever, but the way her eyes kept flicking in all directions made me curious. "The business with the arm seems to have given the administrator quite a turn," I said.

Duart raised an eyebrow. "Do you think so? She's a very controlled person, Quint. I don't think she'll let it distract her."

I watched as Lewis Hamilton joined the group at the foot of the vertical stone needle. He responded to the words Raphael directed at him with an expansive gesture that took in the guard personnel on the walls and towers all around, and on the ridge of the Calton Hill to the rear. It wasn't hard to guess what he was saying: something along the lines of "Don't worry, we've covered every angle." But what was it that the administrator was nervous about? As I watched, she turned away and raised the device that hung round her neck. Then she spoke into it briefly. I wondered who was on the other end; and what she was talking about.

Davie came up when Duart went into conference with his assistant.

"Anything new, big man?" I asked.

He shook his head. "Still no witnesses coming forward. The Leith Lancers we picked up this morning are keeping their gobs tightly shut."

"Nothing else from the scene-of-crime squad?"

"Nope. And the victim's still out cold." He looked round at his colleagues. "I'm bloody glad I'm not in charge of security for this jaunt. There are enough guard units outside to rerun the Battle of Bannockburn."

"Let's hope the youth gangs don't do too much damage in other parts of the city while they're on parade here."

He nodded, his expression grim.

"Of course," I continued, "the mass of uniformed guard personnel might be just the cover our arm-remover needs if I'm right about him or her having guard clothing."

Davie laughed. "That won't be enough. The Mist has got a hand-picked squad of senior auxiliaries checking everyone's ID every few minutes."

"She's running the show then, is she?"

"Aye." Davie's tone showed what he thought of that.

"We're bound to be okay then," I said. "As long as a real sea mist doesn't roll in from the Forth and get in everyone's eyes."

There wasn't much chance of that. Visibility in all directions was perfect. I could even see the guard-post on the Lion's Head, the summit of Arthur's Seat. The armoured glass of its narrow windows was glinting in the sunlight.

It certainly was the perfect day for an open-air ceremony.

A few minutes before eleven, guests and local nobs began to gather around a wooden dais that had been placed between the obelisk and the east wall. I pulled out my mobile and tried Katharine again. Still no answer, either from her mobile or from her office in the welfare centre. She was probably making a home visit to the poor woman whose son's wrist had been broken.

I froze as something grabbed my left calf.

"Man," said a small voice.

"Maisie. Hello." I bent down and gently disengaged the toddler's arms. "What are you doing here?"

She gave me a shy smile. "Man," she repeated.

"I've been making sure she can tell the difference," Sophia said drily.

I looked up and took in the medical guardian. She was wearing the standard tweed jacket and corduroy trousers her rank wears – no dressing up at Slick's behest for her. "Bit young, isn't she?" I said with a smile.

She led her daughter towards a space next to Lewis Hamilton. "You can never be too careful, Quint."

I was about to give her my views on gender-biased indoctrination, but the public order guardian's frown shut me up.

"Get into line, Dalrymple," he said in a hoarse whisper. He'd obviously been giving his larynx a hard time – defending his directorate to the senior guardian, I guessed.

What he meant by "into line" was behind him, on the opposite side of the dais from Slick and the Mist. I wasn't complaining.

"Everything ready to roll, Lewis?" I asked in a low voice.

"Don't ask me," he said, shaking his head. "That bloody deputy of mine has taken over the entire planning and execution of this event."

"Interesting terminology," I said, glancing up at the fortified towers of the former Governor's House. I wouldn't have put it past the Mist to have installed a gallows or similar mechanism in the new prison, despite the Council's official opposition to capital punishment. I wondered how long it would be until state-approved murder got a clause in the City Regulations.

Hamilton looked round at me, his cheeks red above the heavy white beard. "Do you realise that I haven't even been invited to make a speech?" He looked like he wanted to spit rather than orate. "I'm the public order guardian and I'm not allowed to have anything to do with my directorate's biggest project in years."

I almost felt sorry for the old curmudgeon. "Take it easy, Lewis," I said. "You're well out of it. The incarceration policy stinks."

Sophia turned and glared at me. "Be quiet, Quint," she hissed. "There are more effective ways of bringing about change. If you don't want to be here then go away."

I was about to tell her where to go when I caught sight of Maisie's face. The little girl was holding her mother's hand tightly, the expression under her maroon woollen hat a picture. She had her lips pursed like an angry schoolmistress and she was moving her eyebrows up and down. I couldn't resist smiling at her.

Then the speeches started and my mood swung back to thunderous.

* * *

It could have been worse. The senior guardian gave an address that sang the praises of the incarceration policy, of the new-look, distinctly non-user-friendly Corrections Department and its senior officials – I thought for a moment that he might have a hankering for the Mist, but decided that not even Slick could be that desperate – and of the "invaluable expertise provided by New Oxford". If he'd been hoping to improve his standing with the Oxford administrator, he was on a hiding to nowhere. Although her eyes were still more mobile than those of the sentry on the David Hume memorial turret, she wasn't favouring the senior guardian with any attention. It looked like she had other things on her mind.

Then the Mist got her chance to impress. She hoisted her heavy frame on to the platform and surveyed the crowd like a magician about to produce a rabbit from a guard beret. Then she pointed to her left, towards a raised gangway that had been built between the mass of the main prison building and the exercise yard.

"Send down the first prisoners!" she ordered, the sound system amplifying her voice well beyond the pain threshold.

Everybody watched as a sorry collection of individuals in luminous yellow overalls walked slowly down towards us. At first I thought they were auxiliaries dressed up as inmates, then I recognised some of them. They were all young men, most of them with dark bruising on their faces.

"Christ," I muttered, looking round at Davie in the row behind. "Those are the Leith Lancers the guard's been questioning."

He nodded, looking over my shoulder.

I turned back and was confronted by Hamilton's angry features. "Did you authorise the transfer of those citizens to the New Bridewell, Dalrymple?" he demanded.

"Of course not. Did you?"

Hamilton shook his head. "Certainly not. It must have been that—"

I didn't catch what he said when he turned his head in the direction of his deputy, which was a pity – it was obviously choice.

"These prisoners are the first to learn the cost of criminal activity," the Mist continued, her voice even shriller now. "The New Bridewell will soon be renowned for the discipline it imposes. We owe such discipline to our citizens and" – she broke off and bowed obsequiously to a group of foreign tour company representatives – "and to our honoured paying guests."

There followed a description of the rigours awaiting the poor sods on the walkway: reveille at five a.m., compulsory cold baths, compulsory social responsibility lessons, eight-hour work details and the like. None of the youth gang members looked keen but they were keeping their mouths shut. I was sure they'd already had a practical lesson in the length, breadth and weight of the billyclubs carried by the warders to their rear.

After what seemed an eternity – during which I counted the seagulls landing on and taking off from the roof of the Waverley Hotel to the west and gave up after a hundred – Raeburn 124 ran out of propaganda and looked encouragingly at Administrator Raphael.

"And finally, I extend Edinburgh's thanks and gratitude to the members of the New Oxford delegation for their guidance in this vital project." I caught sight of Billy Geddes's face as the Mist said those words. His lips were twisted in a sardonic smile. He knew as well as I did that very few of the Council's subjects were keen on the prison.

"I now call upon the leader of that delegation to address us," Hamilton's deputy concluded.

The way that Raphael fixed her eyes on the Mist gave me the distinct impression that she was not happy. She stood firm amid her begowned colleagues and almost glowered. I wondered if she'd been taken by surprise. Perhaps she'd said earlier that she wouldn't give a speech, but was now unable to refuse the offer in public. She set her lips in a tight line, shot a last irate glance at Raeburn 124 and started walking.

To my astonishment she headed straight for Lewis Hamilton and grabbed him firmly by the arm.

"Come, guardian," Raphael said in firm tones, "you and I will both say a few words."

Hamilton stood up straight, his chest in the guardian-issue dark suit poking out like a soldier on a parade ground. "Delighted, administrator," he said, removing her hand from his arm with a grimace of what looked like pain. "After you." He glanced over her shoulder at me, his features triumphant

Raphael nodded and set off towards the platform.

It was then that everything went into slow motion. Suddenly my senses seemed to be operating in a different dimension. I could hear perfectly – hear the raucous screams of the gulls and the dull grind of the buses on the North Bridge. I even picked up the strangled squeal from the set of bagpipes that a negligent guard bandsman let slip. And I could smell the new paint on the walkway above, as well as the dust coating the recently laid aggregate. But all the movements I saw – the wind in Sophia's hair, the Corrections Department flag fluttering on the pole behind the dais, the flick of Raphael's black woollen coat tail – were reduced in speed so they were gradual and agonising as if, without warning, the atmosphere around us had somehow become viscous.

The first thing that happened was that Maisie slipped her hand out of her mother's grasp and tottered after Hamilton, her stubby legs in the bright blue suit struggling against the thick layer of gravel. By this time the guardian was level with Administrator Raphael. He stopped and stood at attention next to her. Then both of them caught sight of the little girl, their eyes directed downwards. And then Maisie stumbled and fell forwards. I could hear the sharp intake of breath from numerous spectators as well as an involuntary gasp from Sophia.

Raphael and Hamilton were way ahead of her. They both leaned over rapidly, arms outstretched to break the toddler's fall. I watched as one end of the multicoloured scarf Sophia had wrapped round her daughter's tiny neck flew up like a playful foal's mane. Then the administrator, her reactions a lot faster than the guardian's, had caught Maisie, the outside of her hands brushing the stones as she received the full weight of the child.

But by that time no one was looking at Raphael and Maisie any longer. At the same moment that the two females came together without disturbing the gravel too much, Lewis Hamilton continued the movement that he'd started when he saw the wee girl trip. With a crash that my heightened senses clearly registered, he hit the ground flat out.

It was only when I pushed through the line of VIPs ahead of me that I began to make any sense of the sounds my ears had picked up before Lewis went down. First there had been a high-pitched whine that seemed to lower in tone as it got louder. It had been followed almost immediately by a solid clap that made me think of a large fish slapping against the gunwale of a boat. The result was that an inch-wide hole suddenly blossomed in the rear left shoulder of the public order guardian's jacket.

Pandemonium was an understatement for what subsequently broke loose in the prison compound's former bone yard.

CHAPTER SIX

"Mu-mmy!"

The cry of the toddler, emphasis and rising intonation on the second syllable, cut through the raised adult voices. Administrator Raphael set her down and moved away.

I looked up from Lewis Hamilton's prone form to see Davie lift Maisie up and hold her so that she could see her mother. She immediately stopped wailing and studied the scene, a serious expression on her wet face.

Sophia was on her knees, manoeuvring the guardian's head to the side and checking the airway. "Turn him on to his side!" she said urgently.

I took hold of Lewis's left shoulder.

"Here. I'll help you." Andrew Duart was by my side, the knees of his expensive suit buried in the gravel.

We pulled the inert body round gently, aware of the wound in the upper back.

"Give us some air!" Sophia shouted.

The crowd moved back slowly. I glanced up and, through a gap, saw the senior guardian talking in a very animated fashion to Administrator Raphael. Raskolnikov, Verzeni and Yamaguchi had formed a protective huddle around her. She gave the impression of being in control, but her face was ashen and her restless eyes showed how agitated she was. As I watched, the Oxford group was ushered away by Slick, a posse of guard personnel in attendance.

"He isn't breathing," Sophia said, raising her head from Hamilton's face. "Roll him on to his back."

I got to my feet as she started pressing on his chest, assisted by an ambulance-man who had just arrived on the scene.

Duart turned to me. "He's not going to make it."

I let Sophia get on with the procedure but I knew he was right. Lewis had already left us, his normally rigid frame loose and his eyes glazed. In the cruel sunlight he suddenly looked his age, the air of authority that he used to project nothing more than a fleeting memory.

As Sophia straightened up and shook her head slowly, I said a silent farewell to the public order guardian. Lewis had been my boss before I was demoted and he'd given me a hard ride ever since; he'd even turned out to be as untrustworthy as everyone else who held power in the so-called "perfect city", but at least he'd always tried to distinguish right from wrong.

Which was more than could be said for the bastard who'd shot him in the back.

We left Medical Directorate personnel to deal with the body and got out of the prison yard. Maisie was in her mother's arms, her body limp. She understood well enough that something momentous had happened in front of her.

"Are you taking her home now?" I asked. "She's far too young for all this."

Sophia's eyes flashed ice blue. "I didn't expect someone to take a pot shot during the ceremony, Quint." She walked towards her vehicle. "Anyway," she said over her shoulder, "this is the reality of life in Edinburgh now. There's no point in hiding her from it."

"Jesus, Sophia, she's one year—"

"Back off, Quint." Sophia's voice was firm. "It's not your concern." She started strapping Maisie into the child-seat in the official Land-Rover.

"All right, all right." I stepped closer. "What was the cause of death?" I asked quietly.

She glanced round. "Can't you wait for the post-mortem? I'll be doing it shortly."

"I have a feeling I'll be too busy to attend," I said. That was true enough, but I also had no desire to watch Lewis being cut open on the mortuary table. "Was it the bullet?"

Sophia waved a small teddy under Maisie's nose and waited till she gurgled approval. "Did you notice anything strange about the wound, Quint?"

I nodded. "It produced a minimal amount of blood."

"Quite so." Sophia's face was stern. She'd switched from mother to medical guardian in the time it took her to straighten her back. "That can happen with high-velocity shells. But there was no exit wound, so I don't think we're necessarily dealing with one of those."

"No exit wound means that the bullet's still inside him. We can get the ballistics experts to check it out."

Sophia had a hungry expression on her pale face now. "I'll be extremely interested to examine that bullet," she said.

"So will I," I said as she got into the vehicle. "So will I."

Davie came down the steps and past the sentries on the gate of the exercise yard, his expression even more sombre as he joined me by the kerb.

"What now?" I asked.

He glanced over his shoulder. "We're off the case," he said. "The Mist says she's running it."

I saw red for a few seconds then beckoned to him. "Come on, we're going to sort this out."

He put a hand on my arm. "Hang on, Quint. It isn't safe up there."

I started walking. "Whoever put that slug in Lewis is long gone, my friend."

Raeburn 124 didn't seem to think so. She'd taken refuge in the sentry post and was making sure she was flat up against the circular wall of the old philosopher's mausoleum. The sun was blazing through the glass roof and the guardswoman on the gantry was tapping her foot nervously.

I went round the bank of screens and computer terminals manned by a pair of guardsmen in the centre of the building and put my face up to the Mist's. "We can have this conversation in front of your people or in the open air, deputy guardian," I said in a low voice. "You choose."

She preferred showing herself to the sniper to losing face with her subordinates.

"I've already told Hume 253," she said, looking disapprovingly at Davie; he was examining the ground over by the obelisk with his notebook out. "I'm taking personal charge of the investigation into my predecessor's death." She led me to the southern wall of the former burial ground.

"Your predecessor?" I said. "Have you been promoted already?"

The Mist's heavy features took on a pink tinge. "Well, not yet. But I fully expect—"

"Jesus Christ," I said, leaning towards her. "Haven't you got a shred of respect for Lewis Hamilton? He's only been dead a few minutes and you've already taken over his desk."

Raeburn 124 drew herself up and gave me a cold look. "The directorate's work goes on, citizen. Especially at a critical time like this."

"You're bloody right it does," I said, returning her stare with interest. "And if you think you're shutting Davie and me out of the investigation, you can forget it. I worked with Hamilton ever since I joined the directorate in 2007 and I'm not letting some fucker get away with killing him."

The Mist smiled emptily. "You didn't exactly give the guardian your complete support at all times, did you, citizen?"

"That's nothing to do with you," I said. "I'm going after whoever shot Lewis and you can't do anything about it."

She pulled out her mobile. "Just watch me, Dalrymple."

I put my hand in my pocket, came out with my authorisation and held it under her nose. "You can read, can't you? It says that I'm empowered to act without Council, auxiliary or citizen interference." I'd been given those powers during a particularly bad case of corruption involving senior auxiliaries back in 2020.

The Mist stilled the movement of her thick fingers over the keypad. "That authorisation can be revoked easily enough." I reckoned she would be pulling her friend the senior guardian's chain the next time she saw him.

"Only by the full Council," I countered. "That was the agreement. Until you manage to convince all the guardians to go along with you, I'm taking the case." I turned away, pointing to Davie as I went. "And he's working it with me. Keep out of our way."

Her ironic reply followed me across the yard. "Enjoy it while you can."

I resisted the temptation to give her the finger – but only just.

"What do you reckon then?" Davie was squatting beside the pegs that marked where Lewis Hamilton's body had lain.

I stood up and gazed southwards, shielding my eyes with my hand. There was a wide open space between the lower outcrop of the Calton Hill we were standing on and the buildings of the Old Town, most of it filled with the vast Supply Directorate depot over what used to be the station and the railway lines. "I reckon we're in the wrong place." I started towards the gate. "Where have you got the search squads looking?"

"Everywhere," he said, catching me up. "The Waverley, the Observatory Hotel on the Calton—"

"Your geometry's rubbish, guardsman. The shot came from the south." I looked over the prison wire towards the pair of high buildings at the far end of the North Bridge. "Are you looking in that pile?" I asked, pointing towards what the Tourism Directorate had imaginatively named the Old Town Hotel.

"Aye," he said, nodding. "A squad just went in there."

"How about the knocking shop across the road from it?"

Davie beckoned to the driver in the nearest Land-Rover to get out. "The Skin Zone? Guard personnel should be there by now too. There were spotters in all those places for the inauguration, you know. None of them saw any sign of a sniper."

I stared at him as I got into the guard vehicle. "Spotters? What do you mean?"

"Apparently the Mist put guard personnel on all elevated points around the burial ground."

"Did she now?" I wondered about that as I put on my seat belt. It was almost as if Hamilton's deputy were expecting a shot to be fired. "Let's get up there sharpish."

He nodded and slammed the vehicle into gear. We careered towards the checkpoint, the sentries hoisting it when they saw who was at the wheel – Davie's reputation for speed was second to none in the city.

Tourists outside the gaming hall in the former central post office at the end of Princes Street stared at us, jaws slack and hands grabbing for each other.

"They probably think we're late for our lunch," Davie said, feeding the wheel rapidly between his hands and making the left turn on to the North Bridge with a couple of inches to spare. He glanced at me. "You think the shooter took the guardian out from the Skin Zone? There haven't been any reports of gunfire. It would have been a hell of a shot, Quint."

I had the street atlas open on my lap. "Around three hundred yards."

"Nobody heard it either, so the shooter must have been using a silencer." He shook his head. "A hell of a shot is right."

I watched as the tall buildings that formed a gateway to medieval Edinburgh loomed before us, the hotel on the left augmented by a couple of figures in guard uniform on the roof. On the right stood one of the city's premier brothels. The Skin Zone was reserved for the most affluent tourists, its luxurious premises housed in what had originally been the home of Scotland's national newspaper until the old building had been flogged off and turned into a hotel during the last, short-lived Edinburgh boom before the Scottish Parliament imploded. Although the multi-storeyed edifice with its foundations far below the level of the bridge had been completed at the beginning of the twentieth century, the effect of the façade's tall windows and turrets was more medieval than Edwardian.

"Why are you so interested in the Zone?" Davie asked as he pulled up outside the building. "Surely the shot could just as easily have come from the hotel."

"Call it intuition," I said, opening my door.

"Call it an unhealthy interest in female citizens of the night," he said.

I stood on the pavement and looked up at the dark grey, dressed stone walls. A large white banner with the establishment's name in wavy red letters had been hung from the upper-floor windows. The hot metal of the newspaper's time had been replaced by hot flesh – another victory for the Tourism Directorate.

Davie nodded to the guardsman on the door and pushed it open. We were halfway across the entrance hall – marble columns, thick pile carpets and hazy photographs of half-dressed women – when we heard shouting from the staircase and exchanged suspicious glances.

"No, no, no!" said a high-pitched male voice. "You do not have the authority." The accent was foreign, I guessed Middle Eastern.

"Then I must call my superior," came the neutral tones of a female auxiliary.

"Don't bother," Davie called. "Your superior's here."

We met them at the foot of the stairs. The complainant was dressed in what looked to my untutored eye to be a very expensive cream-coloured suit, his shirt collar open to reveal a heavy growth of chest hair. He was peering at the nondescript guardswoman with extreme antagonism, dark eyes glaring above a hooked nose; the guy looked like a caricature of an Arab in the braindead British movies I couldn't avoid when I was a kid.

"Ah, Hume 253," she said, relief flooding into her voice. "This gentleman, Mr . . ."

She glanced down at her notebook.

"Aldebran Mohammed," the foreigner said. He whipped a business card from his pocket and held it up to us like a talisman.

"Senior Customer Service Executive, Aldebran Travel, PO Box 83006, Republic of Central Arabia," Davie read out.

"Mr . . ." Napier 208, the guardswoman, either couldn't cope with the name or couldn't be bothered to try. "The gentleman has a client on the top floor. He refuses my team access to the room."

"Yes, it is very private," the tourist representative said. "My client . . ." His voice dropped to a whisper. "My client is a government minister."

"Really?" I said with a slack smile.

"Yes, really. I can tell you that he knows the senior guardian." The Arab nodded. "Everything fine now?"

I smiled again. "Very fine." I turned to the guardswoman. "Napier 208, you are authorised to use all means at your disposal – including your auxiliary knife – to keep this gentleman out of our hair." I walked past them. "Good to meet you, Mr Aldebran," I said, receiving no acknowledgement. He was probably already formulating the abuse his client would direct at Slick. Great.

We left them to it, taking the next three flights of stairs at a run which hurt my legs more than Davie's – he worked out in the castle gym most evenings. On the way we passed several disgruntled tourists heading for the exit. A female Prostitution Services Department worker cast a weary eye over us then went back to darning a Supply Directorate fishnet stocking.

"Where was the spotter located in this building?" I asked Davie as we approached the top landing.

"The roof," he grunted. "The command centre reported he called in after the shooting, said he saw nothing."

I slowed as I reached a wide window giving a spectacular vista of northern Edinburgh, the firth and the wastelands of Fife beyond. "Where is he now?"

Davie glanced at me. "I don't know. Still up there, I suppose."

I raised an eyebrow at him.

"Shall I find out?"

I stepped towards the velvet-covered door halfway down the hallway. There was only one room on this floor. "Let's check on the Minister for Screwing first." I put my ear against the door but couldn't pick up any sounds. So I made my own, laying on a heavy pounding that would have impressed the drummer in an electric blues band.

Nothing.

"Mr Minister?" I shouted.

Still nothing.

"Oh shit," I said, turning to Davie. He'd already moved back as far as he could. "It's all yours, big man."

He dropped his shoulder and ran into the door. It never stood a chance.

It didn't look like the overweight man on the bed or the woman draped across his legs had either.

"What happened here?" Davie had pulled open the heavy curtains to let in the light. The windows gave a perfect view of the New Bridewell and its exercise yard. The armoured turret of the Hume mausoleum was glinting in the sunlight.

I stood beside the wide bed and tried to work out if the body count had gone up. The naked female was on her front, her head hanging over the edge of the bed, long blonde hair touching the carpet. I took her wrist and felt for a pulse, then kneeled down and checked for breathing. Nothing that I could detect, though there was no sign of injury anywhere on her pallid skin.

"This guy's been abusing his body in a big way," Davie said, peering at the corpulent form that was taking up much of the bed. The Arab was lying with his arms outstretched in what was almost the crucifix position. The only small things about him were his genitalia.

I nodded. "The question is, what stopped him abusing this female citizen's body? He doesn't appear to have sustained any injuries. Can you get a pulse?"

After a few moments Davie shook his head. "No chest movement either."

Then I remembered the one-armed youth gang member in Leith. He'd appeared to be stone dead as well. "Call the Medical Directorate. We may have another couple of deep sleepers on our hands. You'd better get the scene-of-crime squad over as well." I cast an eye round the opulent chamber. "Not that I can see much for them to go on."

While Davie was making the calls I went over to the window, pulling on a pair of protective gloves. I examined the window frame with my magnifying glass but could see no marks or scuffs. Then I flipped the catch and swung the tall pane open. It was well oiled and moved smoothly. Outside there was a stone parapet. I was looking for a place where the gunman might have rested his weapon. I didn't find any sign of that.

I turned back and saw Davie draping a blanket over the seemingly lifeless woman. He didn't bother covering up the tourist.

"They're on their way," he announced.

"Right. Let's see if we can find the Mist's spotter."

"Aye." Davie hit the buttons of his mobile again and got through to the command centre. As he waited for an answer to his question his expression became more serious. "Are you sure?" he barked. "All right. I'll check it myself." He signed off, shaking his head. "Bugger's not answering. It turns out they haven't heard from him since not long after the guardian went down. What with all the chaos, he was forgotten about. I'll have someone's barracks badge for this."

"Never mind that now," I said, heading out of the door. "We need to find the way to the roof. There must be access around here somewhere."

"How about there?" Davie was pointing to a green baize door marked "Fire Exit" further down the corridor. When we reached it, he tried the handle. It moved, but the door didn't. "Not much of a fire exit, is it?"

"Do your Open Sesame trick again," I said, standing aside.

He used the other shoulder this time. The effect on the door was no less shattering.

"Why would the guardsman have put a broom handle up against the door?" Davie said from the other side, rubbing his collarbone.

I looked around cautiously. Steps led downwards into the bowels of the building but I was more interested in the steel ladder at the other end of the narrow landing. "Got your auxiliary knife?" I asked, glancing round to see that Davie had already drawn the weapon. Although I've always had an aversion to firearms, at that moment I wouldn't have minded if Davie had one in his hand.

"I'll go first," he said, brushing past me.

I wasn't going to argue with him. I watched as his heavy frame moved slowly up the ladder.

"There's an angled trapdoor," he said, grunting as he applied pressure to it. "Christ, there's something bloody heavy on it." He drew himself back then drove upwards. "Shit!" he yelled with a great effusion of breath.

Natural light flooded into the stairwell. Davie disappeared rapidly out of the hole and the sun shone in even more brightly.

"What have you got?" I shouted as I started up the ladder.

"Fuck!" His voice was hoarse. "Fucking hell!"

I poked my head out into the open air and realised why he was cursing. The trap opened just below the top of the slated roof. At the northern end of the building there was a semicircular gable and Davie was leaning against it, his arms round the motionless figure of a middle-aged guardsman.

"Take his legs," Davie gasped.

I did and we fought to get the auxiliary down the ladder, finally laying him out on the landing.

"That was bloody close." Davie panted. "The guardsman's legs were over the trapdoor. When I forced it, he went flying. I managed to grab him before he dropped."

I was on my knees beside the spotter. His eyes were open and unfocused and his skin was cold. "Another one for the medics," I said, glancing up to the square of blue above us. "Let's hope the effort you put in to catch him was worth it."

We spent another hour in the Skin Zone then headed for the street. The three inert bodies had been removed to the infirmary and hooked up to whatever machines Sophia could muster. Apparently they were all alive and in a similar state to Dead Dod, their functions reduced to the level of complete catatonia. The toxicologists were no nearer identifying the compound that had brought that about, nor was the Medical Directorate clear about how it had been administered: no needle marks had been found on Faulds or the latest victims.

"What next?" Davie said when we were back in the Land-Rover. On the other side of the road tourists were hanging around outside the hotel, attracted by the stream of ambulances and guard vehicles. Perhaps some of them were waiting for their turn in the brothel. If so, they were going to be disappointed: the premises had been closed while the SOCS went over them with a nit comb.

"What next indeed?" I said, trying to gather my thoughts. "To tell you the truth, I'm surprised we haven't been pulled off the investigation by now, big man."

"Maybe the Mist hasn't got as much influence as she thinks."

"Maybe not." I looked at my notes. "We haven't got much to impress the Council with ourselves."

"I don't know," Davie said. "We've found the shooter's location."

I gave him a sceptical glance. "Have we? The shooter didn't leave anything behind: no shell casing, no scrapes on the parapets. I'll bet you there are no identifiable fingerprints either."

"Come on, Quint. We found three comatose people in there."

I was rubbing the stubble on my cheek. "But no staff members who saw anyone they couldn't account for, no clients your people haven't questioned; their statements have all been compared with the prostitutes they visited, haven't they?"

He nodded slowly. "What if the shooter was dressed up in a guard uniform?"

"Like may have been the case at Ramsay Garden?" I shrugged. "We spoke to the local commander. She was able to account for the movements of all her personnel. The only person on the upper floors was the spotter." I screwed up my eyes. "It's hard to see what happened up there, right enough. Let's say the sniper managed to get into the Skin Zone without being spotted."

"Aye, it's possible," Davie put in. "The place is a rabbit warren. There are doors on different levels round the back where it gives on to the steps leading down to Market Street."

"Doors that are supposedly alarmed," I said, looking at my notes.

Davie stared at me grimly. "It looks like this individual has the skills to handle most obstacles."

"Mmm." I gulped water from the guard flask in the glove compartment. "And the local knowledge. Anyway, let's say he – or she, I suppose – has made it to the top floor. Why does he knock out the Arab and the hooker?"

"He was looking for a secure place to make his shot."

"Yeah, he could have fired from that window, though there were no marks on the stone."

"Maybe he's such a good shot that he doesn't need to rest his weapon on anything."

"That's a comforting thought, guardsman."

He grinned weakly and started rooting around in the glove compartment. His face lit up when he found an oatmeal ration biscuit.

"But if the shot came from the room, why was the spotter on the roof taken out?"

Davie chewed hard and swallowed. "He must have seen him earlier and decided to deal with him."

I shook my head. "Not necessarily. The shooter might have a solid gold source of local information."

"What do you mean?" Davie demanded, his mouth full.

"I mean he might have known there was a spotter up top. I mean he might be monitoring guard communications."

Davie's mouth opened even more. "Bloody hell. Sounds a bit far-fetched, Quint."

"No, it doesn't. I reckon it was him – and this suggests that the shooter is male – who made the call to the command centre after Hamilton went down, not the spotter. I think he drugged the guardsman before he took the shot – whether from the window or the rooftop doesn't really matter. And he knew enough about guard reporting procedure to convince the command centre operative." I opened my hands. "Ergo he might well have been listening in."

Davie still looked dubious. "You'd need pretty sophisticated gear to do that. We don't have anything like that in the guard."

I looked at him seriously. "Edinburgh's not exactly at the cutting edge of scientific endeavour, guardsman. But I can think of one city that is."

The look of enlightenment that spread over his face suggested that Davie didn't need me to tell him that the name began with the letter "O".

A few moments later my mobile rang.

"Quint, it's Sophia. Something urgent."

"Oh aye?"

"I've sent the bullet I extracted from Lewis Hamilton to the ballistics man. He's ready to report and I'm going over there now."

"I'll join you at the range. Out."

Davie already had the engine running. "The range? Don't tell me. We're summoned to an audience with Trigger Finger."

I nodded, the grin immediately wiped from my face by the hundred-and-eighty-degree turn he put the Land-Rover into. Trigger Finger, a.k.a. Nasmyth 99, was one of the few remaining colourful personalities in the City Guard. I'd never had anything to do with him because of my aversion to firearms, but he was notorious for being as camp as the tented city on the Meadows where auxiliaries used to be trained.

"I hate that guy," Davie said, shaking his head. "He gets right up my—"

"Spare me, guardsman," I said, watching as the solid grey walls of the university's Old College flashed past on the right. The original Council regarded it as the Enlightenment's spiritual home since so many of the guardians had been professors; recently there's been more of an emphasis on animal cunning, Sophia excepted. "You can wait in the vehicle, if you prefer."

"No chance," he growled, giving an elderly citizen on a bicycle the benefit of his horn. "I want to be in on everything to do with this case."

I glanced at the burly figure at the wheel and realised how much Lewis Hamilton's death had affected him. Until the aftermath of the investigation in Glasgow in 2026 Davie had been the public order guardian's blue-eyed boy. It would be too much to say that Lewis had been grooming Davie to succeed him – the old martinet probably thought he was immortal – but the two of them definitely had an understanding. If I hadn't cultivated a taste for free-thinking and insubordination in him, Davie might well have been as bone-headed a guard commander as the rest of his colleagues.

"Fair enough," I said in a low voice. "We'll get the bastard who killed Lewis, don't worry."

He nodded, his expression determined.

I was bloody glad my feet weren't in the shooter's boots.

Edinburgh's only firing range had been set up during the drugs wars on a piece of land just inside the city line that forms the fortified inner ring of defences. The place had been a shopping centre called Cameron Toll before independence. In the months after the last election, mobs of desperate citizens ransacked the stores and burned the complex down. The large expanse of asphalt that had accommodated the cars that people used to own was now covered by a series of long, dun-coloured sheds, all of them flying the City Guard pennant. In the centre was a low stone-built edifice surrounded by a double line of razor wire and guarded by a squad of armed gorillas. That was the armoury, Trigger Finger's lair.

There were a couple of guardians' Land-Rovers by the fence. One of them I assumed was Sophia's. Who else was attending the ballistics report? It wasn't long before I found out. After our ID was checked, Davie and I were admitted to the yard outside the weapons store. The steel-panelled door opened as we approached.

"Hurry up, Dalrymple," the Mist said, her cheeks blotched with red. "We're waiting."

Davie and I exchanged glances and went inside.

"Hello, Quint," Sophia said, her voice clipped. She favoured Davie with a frosty nod. "Raeburn 124 has been trying to rush things." She looked at the Mist with no attempt to hide her contempt. "I told her that driving a guardian vehicle before the Council has approved elevation to the rank is contrary to regulations. Not to say disrespectful."

I nodded. "I agree." I went over to Sophia. "What did the post-mortem show?"

She held the Mist at bay with her eyes. "Lewis Hamilton died of heart failure. The impact of the bullet caused massive shock."

"What about the wound?"

Sophia's face was stern. "I've never seen a bullet like this one. It's large but the trauma is much less than I would have expected, even though the shell didn't exit the body. That's why I want to hear the expert's report."

A barred door at the rear of the entrance hall banged open.

"Are we all ready?" A short, thin auxiliary in a white lab coat that hugged the contours of his body walked in, swinging his hips. "At last?"

"Ready, Nasmyth 99," Sophia said with a faint smile that seemed to gratify him enormously.

"Oh good." The ballistics genius turned his hazel eyes on to me. His beard was fair and scant. "And who's your friend, guardian?"

"Dalrymple," I said. "Special investigator."

"The famous Quintilian," he said, offering me a surprisingly strong hand. "Delighted. I'll call you Quint, shall I? You can call me Trigger." He looked past me towards Davie. "I know this big laddie already." He turned to me. "He doesn't like me, you know."

The stage whisper didn't impress the Mist. "Stop mincing about, Nasmyth 99," she ordered. "Remember that your superior officer was shot earlier today," she said, demonstrating the senior auxiliary's ability for hypocrisy. "Proceed with your report."

Trigger ushered us to the door, his lips repeatedly mouthing a word that ended in "itch".

His inner sanctum was a gun-lover's wet dream. Every bit of wall space was hung with firearms, ranging from heavy, Border Guard-issue assault rifles to dull black machine-pistols to the single-shot pen guns occasionally given to undercover operatives. Glass cases at the far end were filled with stacks of numerous types of ammunition. There was even an antique anti-tank gun suspended from the ceiling, the draught from our entry making it swing to and fro like a bird of prey on the wing. The place had an acrid smell, a mixture of gunpowder, hot metal and lubricating oil. In the centre of the room was a high bench covered in tools and stands, a burner with a tall flame at the end.

"Well, boys and girls, gather round. This is what you've come to see," said Trigger, climbing on to a stool and pointing at a shell he'd mounted on a metal plate. "And I'm here to tell you that I've never seen a little beauty like this before."

I looked at the metal object through a glass that he'd set up over it. "Not exactly little, is it, guardsman?"

"Trigger," he said, his voice even higher. "No nasty ranks here, please. No, Quint, you're right. An inch and a half in length, three-quarters of an inch in diameter. And it weighs nearly an ounce."

"What?" Davie was incredulous. He knew more about firearms than I did. "No wonder it took the guardian out."

Sophia was bending forward too. "It's an odd colour too, isn't it?"

Trigger nodded. "Burnished gold, you might say. Very attractive. Very hot at the time of impact as well, I'd hazard."

"Any markings on it?" the Mist asked, her eyes fixed on the slug.

"Not a one," the expert replied. "The only feature I can see is a bevelled edge round the base."

"What kind of weapon would have fired this?" Davie asked.

"Good question," Trigger replied, giving the big man an approving look that didn't go down well. "The simple answer is I have no idea. Possibly a gas-powered rifle, possibly even a long-barrelled target pistol."

"We reckon the shooter was three hundred yards from the guardian," I said.

"My dear," said the auxiliary with an exaggerated gasp. "I am impressed."

Sophia stepped closer to him. "Nasmyth 99, I am extremely interested in finding out how this shell produced the wound it did. Can you give me any idea of that?"

"Low to medium velocity, given the shape and weight." He stroked his wispy beard. "Wide-ish entry wound, no exit wound," he muttered, then looked up. "I can't understand how there was no exit wound, though. This shell could go through a brick wall." He shook his head in frustration "No, guardian, I can't help you."

Sophia's shoulders dropped. "Then I'm wasting my time."

"You are, guardian." Then Trigger raised his hand, his face suddenly more animated. "Unless you give me authorisation to take the shell apart. I've already photographed it extensively."

"What are you waiting for?" Sophia said impatiently.

The Mist moved closer. "One moment. Perhaps we should obtain clearance from the Council." There was a sheen of sweat on her forehead.

Sophia looked at her icily. "Unlike you, Raeburn 124, I am a guardian. I have all the authority I need."

I managed to stop myself applauding.

"I go ahead?" Trigger asked, picking up a high-powered cutting tool.

"You go ahead," Sophia confirmed.

That turned out to be a decision she regretted for the rest of her life.

CHAPTER SEVEN

There was a sharp crack and a blindingly intense eruption of light from the lab table when Trigger applied his instrument. I felt myself jerk back and collide with Davie's solid frame. Hands grabbed my shoulders and stopped me hitting the floor. As the vision began to seep back into my eyes, I became aware of a high-pitched keening nearby.

"Be quiet, Nasmyth 99." The Mist's voice was firm. "Injury report – now!" She may not have come up through the ranks of the City Guard but she'd obviously learned the relevant emergency procedure. Now I thought of it, the same controlled tones had been audible after Hamilton went down.

"Hume 253," Davie said. "No injuries."

The screaming coming from the ballistic expert was hoarser now.

"My eyes," he wailed. "I can't see! My eyes!"

Blinking, I watched as the acting public order guardian stood over Trigger's prone form and drew her forearm slowly across his face. Her tunic sleeve was quickly soaked with blood.

"How many fingers?" Raeburn 124 asked, giving the auxiliary a reverse V-sign.

"Two," he gasped. "Two." His tremulous tone had

suddenly disappeared. He ran his hand across his face and smiled slackly. "I can see after all."

The Mist stepped away, shaking her head. "Citizen Dalrymple?" she said, opening her eyes wide at me.

"No damage," I replied, brushing a sheen of tiny glass fragments from my jacket. Then I heard a low moan to my right. Christ. Sophia. We'd forgotten about the most senior person in the room.

"Quint?" she said unsteadily, one hand extended. "Is that you?"

I pushed the bent metal frame of a stool out of the way and kneeled down beside her. She was in a terrible state, her tweed jacket in shreds and her features criss-crossed by dotted trails of blood. There was a thick coating of dust and debris on her short white-blonde hair and she was holding her right hand over part of her face.

"If anything happens, see . . . see that Maisie's looked after, Quint," Sophia said, catching her breath between the words. She took her lower lip between her teeth for a few moments, then she withdrew her hand. "What's in my cheek?" she asked calmly.

I looked at the ruptured skin and gave an involuntary grunt.

"Maisie . . ." she repeated, the final vowel tailing off as her eyes fluttered.

I dragged my eyes off the vicious-looking shard of metal that was protruding from her face about an inch beneath her right eye. "Get an ambulance," I croaked.

"It's on its way, Quint," Davie said, pocketing his mobile.

He pulled me gently away and we watched as Raeburn 124 did what she could to make the now unconscious Sophia comfortable. But all I could see was the little girl and her impish, smiling face.

* * *

"What the hell happened, Trigger?" I demanded. Sophia had been carried away by a team of medical auxiliaries. They'd decided against removing the object from her cheek on the spot. There was no way of telling how far it had penetrated towards the eye above. They'd stabilised her and left before I could ask for a prognosis; unsurprisingly, the guardian was being treated with a lot more solicitude than the average citizen gets.

"What happened?" The weapons man winced as a medic dabbed iodine on his ear. "The bastard shell went off in my hands, that's what happened, you fool." Apparently Trigger's lip had escaped serious injury.

The Mist approached, mobile in hand. "The wee girl's all right for the time being," she said with unlikely tenderness. "The crèche will keep her until we know how things are going to be with the medical guardian." She gave Trigger Finger a malevolent glare. "So you've finished whining, have you, guardsman? Not before time. Let's have your report."

Davie was eyeing the ballistics expert with evil intent as well.

"All right, all right." Trigger pushed the medic away and went towards the shattered remains of his worktop. "God almighty, my equipment!" he exclaimed like the female lead in one of the melodramas that the Culture Directorate forces citizens to sit through every month.

"You and what's left of your equipment will be down the nearest coal mine if you don't hurry up with that report," the Mist threatened.

Trigger was bobbing up and down, magnifying glass in hand. After a few moments he disappeared beneath the table. "Ah-ha," he said triumphantly. "We're in luck."

We gathered around him as he stood up, holding a

piece of darkened metal about a quarter of an inch across in a pair of tweezers.

"Aye, we're in luck, all right," I said, squinting at the piece of shrapnel. "Which is more than can be said for the medical guardian."

Trigger was given ten minutes to sniff around the lab for more traces of the bullet. It was the only tangible link we had with Hamilton's killer, even though it was now in small pieces, and I wasn't going to let it go.

The Mist spent the time clearing the staff out of the next-door lab room and arranging for the projection gear the weapons man wanted. It didn't take him long to get a detailed view of the fragment up on a wall screen.

"Apart from this piece there's nothing but minuscule fragments left of the projectile," Trigger said, shaking his head.

"Apart from the much larger piece in the medical guardian's face," the Mist put in. She didn't sound too distressed about what had happened to Sophia.

Davie, Trigger and I stared at her sullenly.

"Yes, well, I don't have that available for analysis," the ballistics expert said after a frosty silence.

"You set the bullet off, didn't you, guardsman?" the Mist said.

Trigger's lacerated cheeks reddened even more. "I did not set the bullet off, Raeburn 124," he said in aggrieved tones. "The only thing I can think of is that it was fitted with an anti-tamper device. I've heard that you can get those on the new generation of smart ammunition." He peered at his superior disconsolately. "Not that we ever see that kind of thing in the guard." He wasn't the only auxiliary who reckoned the best way to deal with gang violence was to use firearms. "Anyway, let's see what we've got," he said, turning towards the screen.

We stared up at the image he projected.

"What's that mark in the top left corner?" Davie and I glanced at each other after we came out with the question in unison.

Trigger fiddled with the projector and produced a close-up. "Mmm, interesting," he said. "Are those letters, do we think, people?"

I nodded. "I reckon. Three of them. Can you get in any closer?"

More fiddling, then a satisfied shout. "Gotcha!"

"Gotcha indeed," I said under my breath.

"N . . . O . . . X," Davie spelled out. "Nox." He turned to me. "Mean anything to you, Quint?"

I could feel the Mist's eyes boring into me, but I didn't meet them with my own. I kept those focused on the three letters.

"Well, citizen?" Hamilton's deputy asked impatiently.

"Nox?" I said, chewing my lip. "Nox means 'night' in Latin, doesn't it?" I glanced round at the Mist and registered the release of tension in the skin of her heavy face. I held my peace and let her imagine that I didn't have any other ideas about the significance of those three letters.

"It's a miracle."

I was standing in the corridor outside the operating theatre. "There's no serious damage?" I said in disbelief.

The surgeon shook his head. "The shard of metal entered about half an inch beneath the eye. There's some damage to the cornea from smaller fragments, but I don't expect any sight impairment. As I said, it's a miracle."

"I won't tell the Council you described the injury in that way." I smiled at the wizened medic. He was an auxiliary and auxiliaries have to swear an oath of atheism. Belief in miracles didn't exactly comply with that, though it was fair to say that Edinburgh needed a miracle to save it from the youth gangs – and from the current Council. "So she'll be up and about soon, will she?"

The surgeon nodded. "You know the guardian, citizen. She'll need a day or two to get over the immediate effects of the trauma, but I won't be trying to keep her on her back for long." He was too old and straight for innuendo, otherwise I'd have wondered if he had a fancy for his directorate chief.

"You'll arrange for her to see her daughter when she comes round," I said.

He nodded. "The nursing auxiliaries have that under control. Goodbye, Citizen Dalrymple." He turned to go then spun back to me. "Get whoever's behind this," he said, his breath on my face. "People can't be allowed to shoot at guardians." He stepped back, his head twitching. "What's the city coming to?"

I'd asked myself the question often enough in recent years, but I didn't have an answer to give him.

"Dalrymple?" The voice emanating from my mobile was a combination of sharp and oily.

"The same." I wasn't going to give the senior guardian the satisfaction of acknowledging his rank.

"You know who this is," he said, refusing to play the game. "Where are you?"

"On my way out of the infirmary. I've just been checking on the medical guardian." I paused for a moment. "Are you interested in your colleague's condition at all?"

"I know how the medical guardian is, Dalrymple. It's not your job to tell me. Why aren't you looking for Lewis Hamilton's killer?"

"What makes you think I'm not?" I walked into the courtyard and towards the Land-Rover containing Davie.

The senior guardian gave that a couple of seconds' thought. "I want you in my office at six o'clock. I've called an emergency Council meeting for seven and I want you to brief Administrator Raphael and her party before it. Out."

There wasn't much of the afternoon left. I didn't intend waiting till six to see the Oxford delegation.

"Where's the Mist?" I asked.

Davie pulled on to Lauriston Road and headed for the castle. "Gone off to see the senior guardian, she said." He turned and grinned at me. "Not planning on following her, are you?"

I shook my head. "Act your age, big man. Can you check out the command centre for any surveillance shots they might have overlooked – anything from yesterday evening to the opening ceremony?" I glanced at him. "Especially in the vicinity of the Skin Zone."

He nodded. "Okay, but I'll be surprised if they've missed anything. They're very careful with those new machines." He peered ahead as we approached the Museum of Edinburgh. "Christ, look at those idiots," he said, stopping at a pedestrian crossing.

A male-female couple dressed in silver suits passed in front of us: silver suits as in single-breasted lounge suits made of silver material, not spacemen outfits.

"Pilots," I said. "From that Oxford contraption. I wouldn't fancy going up in that, my friend."

Davie laughed. "Chicken. I'd love it. I've never been in an aircraft." He'd been a kid in the years leading up to independence, when the first drugs gangs started taking out civilian planes with black-market

Russian missiles and the travel industry took a major nosedive.

"Believe me, it's nothing to write home about," I said, recalling sweaty trips with my classicist parents to archaeological sites in Italy and Greece when I was a kid. "The pilots were pissed half the time. Then there were the poisonous food and drink that they had the nerve to make you pay for, the stewardesses with stiletto eyes and the overflowing bogs. Forget it."

"You mean they have toilets on board planes?" Davie said slowly.

"Of course they . . ." I caught the creasing of his eyes. "Screw you, pal. Where did you learn to be such a smartarse?"

"University of New Oxford correspondence course," he said, glancing at me as he swerved on to the Royal Mile. "If I'm checking the surveillance, what are you doing, Quint?"

"So suspicious," I mocked. Then I remembered what I was planning and got serious. "I'm going to pay Administrator Raphael a surprise visit."

"Oh aye?" Davie raised an eyebrow. "Take a look in her bath before you get stuck into high tea."

The look I gave him got lost in the gloom between the narrow buildings on Castlehill.

I asked the senior of the three guards on the door to the VIP accommodation in Ramsay Garden if the Oxford group were in situ.

"Aye, Citizen Dalrymple, they're all up there," he replied, his expression as impassive as a statue's.

To keep Slick and the Mist off my back, I had a simple choice. I could either act the tough guy and wave my authorisation at the guard squad leader: it guaranteed me co-operation without approval from guardians, but that didn't mean guardians weren't to be advised if I appeared at a secure location; or I could appeal to the auxiliary's sense of irony: though that had its own risks. I made up my mind and noted his barracks number.

"Could you help me out, do you think, Scott 247?" I moved closer. "Only, the Mist seems to have developed a worrying interest in my groin."

The squad leader's face remained set in stone for a long time, then he gave me a thin smile. "Bad luck, citizen. I've heard she's a real ballbreaker."

"What a surprise," I said in an undertone. "So can you let me know if she shows up?"

He nodded. It looked like Scott 247 was no more of a fan of the acting public order guardian than I was. I reckoned I'd bought myself at least half an hour.

Inside I felt my boots sink into the thick pile carpet and breathed in the inert atmosphere of opulence. The corridor leading to Administrator Raphael's apartment was dead quiet, as silent as a barracks hall during morning inspection. I disturbed the serenity with a series of raps on the thick door panel.

For what seemed like a long time nothing happened. Then the door was opened, not more than a couple of fingers' width.

"Yes?" came a fierce voice. "Who is it?"

I put my eye up to the gap and clocked Doctor Verzeni. "Relax," I said, taking in the sweat on his face. "It's me, Dalrymple."

"What do you want?" he demanded, his tone no less hostile.

"I want to speak to the administrator, please," I said evenly. "There have been developments in my investigation."

The academic stared at me. "Wait."

The door closed and I stood picking my nails, wondering if Raphael was calling the senior guardian for confirmation. Fortunately the chain rattled before she could have managed that.

"Citizen Dalrymple." This time the administrator herself was at the door, her eyes glinting under the artificial light and her tall form bending towards me. "What a pleasant surprise. Come in." The woman's aura – controlled but curiously seductive – began to work on me immediately. There was something odd about her, but I wasn't about to try putting my finger on it.

I followed her into the plush room. Verzeni, Yamaguchi and Raskolnikov were seated at the dining table, their heads bowed. At first I thought it was some kind of weird ritual; then I noticed they had their miniature computers on the surface, their fingers running over the tiny keys.

"Sit down, citizen," said Raphael, lowering her frame gracefully into an armchair.

"Call me Quint." I paused for a moment to show that I didn't jump to her every command then sat down on the Walter Scott sofa, sinking into *The Black Dwarf*.

The administrator ignored my attempt at informality. "My colleague mentioned developments," she said with what sounded to me like a fair amount of eagerness. "What are they?"

I raised my hand. "Wait a minute. First tell me what you've heard in the last hour or so." I wanted to find out how closely she was being kept in touch by the Edinburgh authorities – i.e. Slick. Setting up an exchange of information at least gave me a chance of getting under her guard.

She looked at me steadily then nodded. "I was told by the

senior guardian that his medical colleague was injured when the bullet taken from Lewis Hamilton exploded." Her eyes were still on me. "Exploded? Is that correct?"

I got the impression that the projectile was much more interesting to her than the state of Sophia's health. "The medical guardian was lucky. Her eyes escaped serious injury and she's not in danger."

Administrator Raphael's breath was expelled slowly, making an extended hissing noise. "Yes, I understand that, citizen. I asked about the bullet. Did it really explode?"

I felt my heartbeat speed up. Like a fisherman in a deep fjord, I'd got the faint tug that told me I'd hooked something big. "Oh yes, administrator, it exploded all right. I was about a yard away at the time."

"I see you escaped injury as well," she said lightly. "So the bullet was destroyed, was it?"

I leaned forward. "No. Not as destroyed as it might have been." I gave her a tight smile. "Back to the drawing board for whoever inserted the anti-tamper mechanism, I'd say."

Raphael's breathing remained steady but her eyes were locked on mine. "What have you found, Citizen Dalrymple? I can see you're bursting to tell me."

"You're right," I said, nodding. "I am. Administrator Raphael, can you tell me how a bullet made in New Oxford ended up being fired into an Edinburgh guardian?"

Now the apartment was as silent as a cemetery at midnight.

While the three academics were making their way towards us in response to the administrator's command, I feigned indifference and looked out of the leaded windows. To the north-west the city was shrouded in low cloud, the lights of the luxury hotel at the end of Princes Street glowing like a convention of will-o'-the-wisps.

"The citizen has made a very interesting discovery," Raphael said, eyeing her acolytes impassively. She gave them no encouragement to sit down. "He thinks the bullet taken from the public order guardian's body came from our home state."

Raskolnikov gave me a smouldering glare, while Professor Yamaguchi let out a string of high-pitched laughs – until he saw Raphael's expression. Verzeni was the only one who seemed capable of speech.

"What do you base this . . . this position on, Citizen Dalrymple?" the Italian asked in a low voice.

I smiled at him; he was hunched up like a cobra about to strike. "Can I have a look at your nostrum, doctor?" I asked.

He glanced at the administrator then handed over the small metallic device.

The screen was blank. "Turn it on, please," I said.

Verzeni spoke a few words in his native tongue. The grey panel lit up immediately and several rows of letters appeared. Most were blue, but it was the red ones at the top that I was after: I'd noticed them when I'd first seen Raphael's nostrum.

I spelled out the letters. "N . . . O . . . X." I looked round at the delegation. "Am I right in thinking that's an abbreviation of New Oxford?"

"No, citizen," the administrator replied, a thin smile flickering briefly on her lips. "But you're on the right lines. It's actually an abbreviation of Nova Oxonia."

"Pardon my Latin," I muttered. "What is it? A trademark?"

"Something like that," Raphael said. "Am I to infer that you found the mark on the bullet? You said it was destroyed."

I took in the three academics before I answered. Raskolnikov was still glowering at me, his brow furrowed. Yamaguchi, his head bowed over the sofa, seemed to have acquired a major interest in upholstery. Again, it was only Verzeni who was inclined to talk.

"Yes, citizen," he said quietly, "surely the bullet was destroyed when you tried to take it apart."

This was getting interesting. Raphael and her team seemed to have made the assumption that the bullet had disintegrated, which suggested that they knew exactly what its capabilities were. I suddenly wished that I'd brought Davie along as back-up. It looked like I'd have to proceed with extreme caution.

"The bullet blew up into a lot of very small pieces," I confirmed. That didn't make them look much more cheerful. "However, two larger fragments were found. One ended up—"

"In the medical guardian's face." Raphael completed my sentence with unusual impatience, her serene expression absent for a few seconds. "There was another?"

I nodded, watching as Yamaguchi looked up and gave the administrator a wide-eyed stare. "There was indeed. And on it were the letters—"

"N . . . O . . . X." This time it was the Japanese who supplied the conclusion.

"So what's going on?" I demanded, dispensing with caution. I'd had a sudden flash of the damage to Sophia's face and her desperation as she said her daughter's name. "Did you bring a gunman with you on that flashy helijet, Raphael?"

Raskolnikov stepped forward, his fists clenched. Although he was a lot older and skinnier than me, I still felt a tremor of concern.

"No one speaks to the administrator like that, Dalrymple," he said, his monk's beard hanging over me.

Raphael pronounced some words I didn't recognise and the Russian immediately stepped back. "This discussion is at an end, citizen," she said. "I shall inform the senior guardian that I no longer require the briefing he arranged for six o'clock. Good afternoon."

It was obvious that I wasn't going to get anything more out of the Oxford delegation, so I gave them a last, unwavering look and headed for the door.

My mobile rang before I made it to the command centre in the castle.

"What are you playing at, Dalrymple?" The senior guardian sounded very unhappy. "I expressly told you to brief Administrator Raphael in my presence."

"Your friend the administrator knows a lot more about Lewis Hamilton's death than she's letting on," I countered. "Why do I have the impression that your dealings with New Oxford matter more to you than the shooting of a fellow guardian?"

That shut Slick up for a few moments. "I'll pretend I didn't hear that," he said. "Provided you come to my office to explain yourself right now." His voice had increased in volume by the end of the sentence.

"Sorry," I said. "I can't spare the time." The only chance I had of keeping hold of my authorisation was to involve all the guardians. "I'll be at the Council meeting. Out."

This case had suddenly gone into overdrive. That's the way I like them.

The Council of City Guardians meets in the chamber that was used by the Scottish Parliament before the mob laid into the building and its occupants in 2003. One of the main reasons for the violence was the gigantic overspend on the premises that the people's representatives occupied; that and their general incompetence, venality and self-righteousness. You'd have thought the Council would have preferred to keep its distance from that tainted power structure, but the guardians hightailed it down to the foot of the Royal Mile as soon as the main building had been repaired. Maybe they felt the need to work in close proximity to the ruined Palace of Holyroodhouse, another symbol of governance gone to the bad.

Guards who had obviously been told to look out for me ushered me into the grandiose pile and pointed towards the heavy doors of the chamber. Not that I needed directions – I'd been up before the Council often enough in the past. There was a clang as the steel panels closed behind me.

I walked into the centre of the bear pit and sat down on the single chair that had been placed there. The guardians were at their seats on the elevated sides of the rounded debating chamber, their leader on a larger, more throne-like piece of furniture straight ahead of me. Glancing around, I counted fourteen: Sophia was the single missing body. Unfortunately the Mist had taken over Lewis Hamilton's seat, even though she wasn't yet wearing the tweed jacket that goes with the rank of guardian.

"Citizen Dalrymple," the senior guardian began, "you have a lot of explaining to do."

"I'm not the only one," I said. After years of manipulating guardians, I knew that the way to get ahead was to go for their collective jugular – and to hope that at least some of them remembered the Platonic ideals that underpinned the Enlightenment. "I've uncovered evidence pointing to the involvement of New Oxford in the murder of the public order guardian."

There was an outburst of gasping and exclaiming, which culminated in the senior guardian making repeated use of his gavel. As he did so, I caught the Mist's eye. That was not a pleasant experience.

"New Oxford is a great supporter of Edinburgh," the labour guardian said. He was a heavily built individual with a bald head and a notoriously short temper. "You don't know what you're talking about, man."

His words drew a flurry of approving calls.

So I hit them with the NOX factor. That took the wind from their sails, but not for long.

"You call that evidence?" the culture guardian said ironically. He was a dilettante who'd recently started wearing even more sumptuous Italian suits than he used to, thanks to Slick's version of a presidential campaign fund, I reckoned. "New Oxford is a major manufacturing and trading centre as well as a university-state. Even if the bullet is a genuine product of that city – and since you succeeded in destroying it, how will we ever be able to tell? – it could easily have been purchased by a third party."

As his colleagues vented their support, I wondered what deals his directorate had been setting up with the administrator.

"Is that really all you have to go on, citizen?" the senior guardian asked. I thought I caught a hint of relief in his voice but I may have been mistaken.

I shrugged. "That's enough for me." I looked around the stern faces above me. "That, and the fact that Administrator Raphael and her entourage refused to talk about the bullet."

"It's probably the result of top-secret research," the Mist put in. Then she gave me a bitter smile. "No doubt your notoriously direct way of asking questions was not to their taste either."

"Wake up, will you?" I shouted. "One of your colleagues was assassinated today. Don't any of you want to find out who was responsible?"

There was a stony silence.

I pressed on with my attack. "I think the administrator and her sidekicks knew from the start that the bullet that killed Lewis Hamilton was one of theirs." I looked up at Slick. "You've been keeping them fully informed. You gave them a description of the bullet, didn't you?"

The senior guardian nodded slowly. "Administrator Raphael asked me about it, yes."

I nodded. "You see? She could have warned us about it before we examined it, she could have told us about the anti-tamper device. Instead she kept her mouth shut and the bullet exploded, nearly killing another of your number. I reckon it was a misfire. It should have atomised completely. If it had, the medical guardian might not have been hit by the larger fragment." I stared at the Mist, wondering how much she knew about all this. "And there wouldn't have been a fragment with the NOX mark on it, leaving them completely in the clear."

There was another heavy silence, during which I reminded myself that Administrator Raphael had been pretty nervous before the shooting. How did that fit in with what had happened?

Then Slick got to his feet. The firmness of his jaw told me that I was for it. "Colleagues, this is intolerable. On the day our oldest and most experienced fellow guardian was done to death, we are forced to listen to a stream of uncorroborated accusations against Edinburgh's greatest benefactor state. I ask you, why would New Oxford want to assassinate a guardian?"

That was a good question. I hadn't got anywhere with identifying a motive.

He turned his gaze on me. "Citizen Dalrymple, do you have any other evidence to offer? Have you uncovered any witnesses of the shooting, any sightings of the gunman?"

I shook my head. Davie had told me that the command centre's surveillance system had drawn a blank.

Slick smiled tightly. "That is not good enough, citizen. It is clear that you are unfit to carry out the investigation." He glanced around his fellow guardians. "Colleagues, you will be aware that the special authorisation held by Citizen Dalrymple – an authorisation, I might add, that has always struck me as highly irregular – can only be revoked by a unanimous vote of the Council. I hereby propose that the said authorisation is revoked. Those in favour?"

There was a pause, but not much of one, while the guardians thought about it. Then all their right hands came up like targets on a shooting range – the Mist's included.

"Hang on," I objected. "Raeburn 124 isn't a member of this body."

"Oh yes she is," the senior guardian countered. "She was elected a few minutes before you arrived. Unanimously, of course."

I gave him a questioning look. "And how exactly did the medical guardian signal her approval? She's been sedated."

Slick stared at me. "Not that it's any of your concern, citizen, but the City Regulations allow for guardians to be elected by all colleagues who are conscious at the time of the given Council meeting." He gave me a taunting smile. "As will also apply in the vote applying to you." He looked around the chamber in perfunctory fashion. "Those not in favour?"

Before he could announce the absence of opposition to his proposal, the steel doors burst open. The sentry outside stepped away and a figure in a raincoat draped over a hospital gown moved slowly forwards.

"Sophia!" I went towards her quickly and took her arm. "What are you doing on your feet?"

"What does it look like?" she said in a low voice. "Coming to your rescue." There was a large raised dressing over her right cheek and eye.

I led her to the chair I'd been using, feeling her wilting against me.

"What is going on here?" Sophia asked, her voice unsteady but clear enough. "I came round and tuned in to the debate."

She took a small black box sprouting wires from her coat. Recently the Council had equipped itself with a digital link so that members unavoidably detained on directorate business could follow meetings. I didn't need to exercise my imagination too much to come up with the name of the city that had provided the gear.

"What do you think you're doing?" Sophia cast a sharp glance round the chamber. "Citizen Dalrymple is the only person in Edinburgh who can handle a case of this complexity and you know it." She placed a hand over the dressing protruding from her chest. "I want to find out who was responsible for the death of Lewis Hamilton and I want to find the bastard who almost left my daughter an orphan." She was staring at the senior guardian now.

He returned her stare and ran his tongue round his lips. "I presume you were not conscious when the vote for the new public order guardian was taken?"

Sophia gave the Mist a disparaging look. "Unfortunately not."

"So at least that decision is unaffected." The senior guardian sounded relieved. "I take it you're not in favour of rescinding Citizen Dalrymple's authorisation, guardian."

"Correct," Sophia said, her voice fading. "Meeting concluded." Her body sagged even more against mine. "Now get me back to the infirmary."

I led her out of the chamber and thanked her after the doors slammed behind us.

"I've bought you some time, Quint," she said, her face beaded with sweat. "That's all. Make sure you use it."

I nodded then took her down the steps carefully. I had a feeling I was going to need a lot more than time to solve this case.

CHAPTER EIGHT

I spent the rest of the evening with Davie in the cubby-hole we'd taken over in the castle. I'd given him the option of abandoning my rat-infested ship, but he declined. He reckoned he was soiled goods already as far as the new public order guardian was concerned. We pored over the guard reports and witness statements again, we checked the condition of the one-armed Leith Lancer – still comatose – and we ran through the lists of tourists leaving from the airport. I wasn't surprised when none of the city's departing visitors turned out to have a heavy-calibre firearm in his or her luggage. All in all, we drew a complete blank.

A little after midnight I left the big man to the snack he'd ordered from the mess. I could have walked back to my place, but the curfew had just kicked in and I didn't fancy flashing my authorisation at every guard patrol I met. So I jumped into the nearest Land-Rover on the esplanade and told the middle-aged driver where to go.

"Are you making any progress, citizen?" the guardsman asked, his voice sombre. "Have you found the lunatic who killed the guardian?"

"Making any progress?" I repeated, looking to my left as we passed the Oxford delegation's accommodation in Ramsay Garden. Raphael's nervous demeanour was still on my mind. "Well, we've made a start." It was only after

I'd spoken the words that I realised how lame they sounded.

"Get the fucker," the driver said. "The guardian was a great man."

I nodded. The guy was obviously a fully paid-up member of the old guard. I'd had too many run-ins with Lewis Hamilton and seen too many of his failings to go along with the characterisation of him as great.

But that didn't mean I was going to let the bastard who shot him slip out of my hands. No way.

I saw the faint line of light under the bedroom door as soon as I entered my flat. The electricity is shut off at midnight in citizen areas, making us rely on the poor-quality candles doled out by the Supply Directorate.

"Is that you, Katharine?" I called, concentrating on avoiding the sofa.

"Yes, it's me." Her voice was slightly less hostile than it had been the last time I saw her outside the infirmary. I'd considered ringing her earlier on but I'd chickened out.

I opened the flimsy bedroom door and looked at her apprehensively. "I wasn't expecting to see you tonight."

Katharine was sitting up in bed, the blankets pulled up to her neck to fend off the chill in the unheated room. "Yes, well," she said, her eyes off me, "I may have overreacted a bit." Then she turned her head towards me in a rapid movement. "But violence is no solution, Quint. You of all people must know that."

I sat down on the bed and started unlacing my boots. "Of course I bloody know that," I said. "But the head-banger tried to—"

"It's okay, I understand." Katharine stuck out a hand and rested it on my shoulder. "They don't know any better. The system's to blame, not the kids."

"You'll get no argument from me on that count," I said, standing up and preparing to jettison my clothes as quickly as I could to minimise my exposure to the chill in my bedroom.

"Aah!" Katharine gasped, pulling away. "You're freezing!"

"You'll soon warm me up," I said, pressing against her.

"Stop it." She turned her back on me. "Quint?" Her voice was serious. "I heard a story that Lewis Hamilton took a bullet. It isn't true, is it?"

"It's true all right," I replied. The Council had decided to make no announcement about the guardian's death yet; there was a feeling that the city's lowlife might take it as a licence to wreck the joint. But Edinburgh's only heavy industry is its rumour factory and clearly it had been working overtime. "He was hit during the prison inauguration and died on the spot."

"At the inauguration? That must have caused a stink."

"You could say that." I felt the warmth of her begin to spread slowly towards my feet.

"Are you in charge of the investigation?"

I nodded then stretched over and blew out the candle. "In charge for the time being at least – and having a lot of problems."

"No one's ever shot a guardian," Katharine said. "Not even Hamilton deserved that. Who do you think was behind it?"

Sleep was hovering over me like a shroud stretched out by a pair of undertakers.

"I'm working on that," I mumbled, sinking fast. Before I slipped under it struck me that, despite the fact that she'd suffered badly under Lewis Hamilton, Katharine sounded sorry that he'd gone. I didn't know what to make of that. "Funeral's tomorrow morning," I managed, then succumbed to exhaustion.

Warriston Crematorium is in the northern suburbs, about a mile west of the port at Leith. After independence it became the city's main gateway between life and death. The other crematoria had been torched during the drugs wars and the first Council banned burial in order to save space and to discourage religious ritual. So everyone, from long-serving guardian to humblest citizen, ends up in the furnace at Warriston. Not that the facility's major role in Edinburgh life has guaranteed it special status. It receives no more funding than any other service unit, so its walls are stained and pocked, its roof leaks and its gardens are maintained with much less diligence than the parks in the central tourist zone.

Davie picked us up in a guard vehicle at ten thirty, showing little enthusiasm for Katharine's presence. She'd insisted on attending the funeral without offering any explanation; Lewis Hamilton had been in charge of the Public Order Directorate when she'd been sent to the high-security prison on Cramond Island for three years for terrorist activities. Maybe her concern was just a blind and what she really wanted was a metaphorical dance on his grave.

"I thought this was supposed to be a restricted event," I said as we swung into the crematorium drive.

There were long lines of guard vehicles on both sides and the road was clogged with auxiliaries in full dress uniform, medal ribbons on their grey tunics and maroon peaked caps rather than the normal berets under their arms.

Davie grunted. "It is." He gave a warning blare of his horn and the guard personnel stepped aside when they saw him. "My colleagues are ignoring the Council directive. They want to give the chief a decent send-off."

Katharine, her head high, made no comment. She'd been back to her flat and changed into a white blouse and cream trousers that definitely weren't standard issue – she must have run them up herself. The sun was out so the thin material of her dark blue jacket was probably just about sufficient.

Davie let us off at the gate and we walked through the throng of auxiliaries to the main building.

"Citizen Dalrymple. It's been some time since we've seen you here." The thin citizen with yellow teeth attempted a welcoming smile but didn't make the grade.

"Hello, Haigh," I said. "Still enjoying life with the dead?" I'd had several unpleasant experiences with the crematorium supervisor; he took a distinctly ghoulish pleasure in his work.

He checked his clipboard. "Yes, you're on the list." He glanced up at Katharine and licked his lips. "Your barracks number or name, please?"

"She's with—" I broke off as I saw Katharine flash her "ask no questions". That put a stop to his tongue.

We stepped into the chilly building and breathed in an atmosphere that had always made me queasy. Even though the rapid throughput means that bodies don't stay in the place for long, it still smelled of the ultimate corruption. Then I caught sight of the senior guardian and the recently promoted head of the Public Order Directorate. They didn't look like they were enjoying inhaling either.

"Morning," I said, moving up on them unobserved. "You'll never get all of the City Guard in here."

The senior guardian stopped in mid-sentence and turned to me. "They will pay for this insubordination, citizen, never fear. My colleague will see to that."

The Mist gave me a humourless smile.

"What's wrong with people mourning their chief?" I asked. "You shouldn't have tried to hold the funeral in secret."

"What do you think the youth gangs are getting up to as we speak?" the new public order guardian asked sharply. "With a minimal guard presence on the streets, the suburbs will explode."

Katharine came closer. "They will not," she said. "The youth gangs are nothing like as dangerous as you think. The guard taunts them and antagonises them. I think you'll find that there's less criminal behaviour than usual this morning."

The Mist looked like she was about to throw Katharine out. Then Administrator Raphael and the Oxford delegation appeared, surrounded by a detail of tall guardsmen. Slick and his sidekick were off to greet them before I could count to one.

Katharine and I moved into what had once been called the chapel and was now known as the Meeting Hall; Haigh had wanted to call it the Last Meeting Hall but even the guardians had baulked at that. It was drab and cheerless, the only decoration a large maroon and white flag on the wall above the bier. Even in death the guardians were watching over you. In this case, even the occupant of the unadorned, recycled coffin was a guardian. Suddenly the reality of Lewis's passing struck me and I felt my stomach turn sour. I'd watched him die, but the trappings of death brought home how final and ineluctable the process was. At times like this, being an atheist wasn't the easy option.

The long room was almost full, the only vacant seats to the rear. A movement to the left caught my eye. Bloody hell, my father. I'd told him about Hamilton's death on the phone but he hadn't said anything about coming to the funeral. As a former guardian he was entitled to attend.

Hector didn't attempt to get up from the pew as we joined him. He was wrapped in a heavy, tattered raincoat, a scarf in the black and white Enlightenment tartan round his slack neck.

"Hello, old man," I said, taking his arm and feeling how thin the flesh was.

"Hello, failure." He looked beyond me. "Hello, Katharine." Ever since he'd once confused Katharine with Caro he'd been fastidious about addressing her correctly.

They started conversing, so I got down to checking out the gathering. All the guardians apart from Sophia were on parade, though none of them looked exactly heartbroken. Among them at the front I saw Andrew Duart. The Glasgow headman was dressed in a dark suit that must have come from his city's finest designer – and Glasgow had become a major fashion centre. Yet again I found myself wondering about his presence in Edinburgh. He seemed to be on good terms with plenty of guardians and senior auxiliaries. Then the crowd parted and I caught sight of a hunched figure in a wheelchair. Billy Geddes, Edinburgh's financial genius. He'd never had much time for Lewis Hamilton, but that hadn't stopped him inveigling the old guardian into one of his schemes a couple of years back.

Then a hush spread across the packed room like a squall sweeping over a cornfield. Haigh, wearing a black sash over his ancient suit, led a procession towards the coffin. The senior guardian was immediately behind him, while he was followed by Raphael and her three academics. The Mist brought up the rear, resplendent – at least in her own mind – in a guardian-issue tweed jacket that was at least one size too large. (Interesting symbolism, I thought.) Edinburgh's de facto president, then a delegation from a foreign state, then the newest guardian: what did that say about the balance of power?

The service turned out to be nothing but preparation and build-up, a funerary version of all mouth and no trousers. Haigh announced the name, rank and date of birth of the deceased, as he did for everyone in the city. Then the senior guardian got up, a look of mild distaste on his youthful features, and told us why we should celebrate the life of Lewis Hamilton. Except he missed out all the laudable parts – his commitment to the Enlightenment Party in the dark days before independence, his doggedness in eradicating the drugs gangs over a decade of extreme violence – and concentrated on his loyalty to the Council. In recent months that had probably been Lewis's most dubious claim to fame.

I could feel my old man fidgeting throughout the address. Eventually he couldn't hold himself back any longer.

"Sanctimonious bullshit," he said in a stage whisper which caused several scandalised senior auxiliaries to look round. "When's he going to say something about the man himself?"

I nudged him to shut him up. Not that I had a problem with his line of questioning. Lewis could be a boneheaded, stubborn old bugger when he was in the mood. Hector had fallen out with him so badly that he'd resigned from the Council years back, and I'd been on the rough side of Hamilton's tongue often enough myself. But at least, to the end, he'd possessed a grudging faith in humanity – which is more than can be said for a lot of guardians.

Slick ran out of words soon afterwards. After an awkward pause, a guard piper stepped forward and played a pibroch. The notes of his instrument were piercing in the enclosed space but no one had the nerve to head for the exit. I looked to the right and watched Administrator Raphael as she stood motionless, her face rigid and her eyes staring straight ahead. What was it about the woman? I wouldn't class myself as anything approaching an expert on her gender, but even I sensed that she was unusual in the extreme. Although she was stern and unemotional like your average Edinburgh guardian (Sophia excepted, occasionally) there was more to her than that: hidden depths, repressed feelings, some inner conflict that she was only just managing to contain. Then she leaned forward slightly, the upper half of her body at an angle to the lower for a few seconds and I had a flash of déjà vu.

Suddenly I was back in the exercise yard at the New Bridewell, the seagulls crying in the clear blue sky as the inauguration got under way. Little Maisie was dashing forwards, tripping; Hamilton and Raphael were lunging to reach her. Hamilton and Raphael. Her reactions had been quicker than his, she'd dived to the gravel ahead of him. Bloody hell. Lewis had been left behind, closer to perpendicular – exactly between the administrator and the shooting position on the top of the Skin Zone. Bloody hell. I saw it now. The shot had been meant for her. That went a long way towards explaining her unease about the bullet and its provenance, as well as her nervousness before the ceremony.

"Quint?" Katharine's elbow was in my ribs. "What is it?" she whispered. "You look like you've seen a ghost?"

I turned my eyes towards the coffin and watched as it disappeared from sight behind the black curtain in the front wall. Lewis was making the last journey, his journey to the fire. Soon he would be nothing but ashes, a scattering of dust over the fields of a city farm.

"A ghost?" I said hoarsely as the funeral party began to break up. I shook my head. "I don't believe in them." I looked into Katharine's bright green eyes. "What we've got to be frightened of is one hundred per cent human."

After the committal we stood around in groups outside, heads bowed and conversation muted as is the way at funerals. Everyone was keen to be away, but the crush of guard personnel heading back to their posts was blocking the gate.

"Davie will get you back to the home, old man," I said, holding Hector's arm.

"Aye, well," he said, nodding slowly, "it won't be long before I go the same way as poor Lewis."

I glanced at Katharine.

She stepped closer and took my father's other arm. "What are you saying, Hector?" she said with a smile. "You've got plenty more years with your books to come."

He looked at her with rheumy eyes then moved them over the crowd of guardians and senior auxiliaries. "To be honest with you, lass, I hope I haven't. These idiots have buggered the city up irreparably."

I'd never known the old man to be wrong about affairs of state.

"Interesting," Davie said, poring over the detailed central zone map we'd spread over the table in the small room near the command centre. Katharine had gone back to her work. "I think you might have something, Quint. Are you sure about the positioning of their bodies?"

I held up the sketches I'd drawn of Lewis Hamilton and Raphael. "That's the way they were," I said. "I've got a clear picture in my mind of how they moved."

Davie stood up and ran a hand through his heavy beard. "So what exactly are you saying?"

I took a gulp of cold and gritty mess-hall coffee. "I'm saying that the shooter was aiming at Administrator Raphael."

"All right," he said testily. "I gathered that. But why? You reckon the bullet comes from Oxford—"

"The bullet definitely comes from Oxford, my friend. All the members of the delegation were shifty as hell when I told them about the NOX mark."

Davie was nodding. "Fair enough. So we think the shooter's from New Oxford too, do we?"

"Hold on a minute," I said, raising a hand. "You're jumping to conclusions." I gave him a rueful smile. "Your former boss was a dab hand at that too."

"Let's leave Hamilton out of this," Davie growled. He wouldn't grieve openly for his former chief – senior auxiliaries don't make a show of emotion, even to their friends – but he was feeling the loss all right.

"Okay," I continued. "We haven't got much to go on as regards the identity of the shooter. Obviously he could be from Oxford, though what we know about that city's expertise with the theory and practice of punishment suggests that not many pot shots are taken at its leaders."

"Which could explain why the attempt on Raphael took place in Edinburgh."

I nodded. "It could do. But the assassin could just as easily come from outside Oxford." I caught his eye. "The shooter could even come from our own fair city."

Davie raised an eyebrow. "You're guessing, Quint."

"Well spotted, guardsman." I smiled ironically. "I was just demonstrating that we haven't much of a clue about the identity of the assassin. Or why the arm was taken from the Leith Lancer." I looked at him again. "Of course, the fact that the arm was put in the administrator's bath is another solid link with Oxford."

Davie was glaring at me in frustration. "So, apart from your nice theory that the shot was meant for Raphael, what have we got to go on?"

"The motivation," I said. "Why was the arm put in her bath? Why was a youth gang member chosen for mutilation? Why wasn't he killed to ensure his silence? And most significant of all, why is a university administrator being targeted for assassination?"

A grin spread across Davie's face. "No doubt you've got the answers to all those questions, Quint."

"You know I haven't, big man. But I'm working on them."

"That's all right then," he said, heading for the door. "I'm going to check the latest patrol reports. Let me know when you're ready to make an arrest."

A few minutes later I was running into the command centre after him, my mobile in my hand.

"Davie!" I shouted.

The heads of all the guard personnel at the screens and desks turned in my direction.

"What now?" he demanded, getting up from a surveillance monitor.

"Dead Dod," I gasped. "The Leith Lancer in the infirmary. He's come round."

He was with me in a couple of seconds. We headed for the door – and ran into the Mist, literally.

"What's going on, commander?" she asked, pushing me away and straightening her new jacket.

Davie glanced at me then told her what I'd just told him.

She thought for a bit, ignoring my urgent gestures, then nodded. "Proceed." Before Davie could do so, she poked a finger in his arm. "And commander? I'm relying on you to keep me fully informed of developments in the hunt for my predecessor's killer."

Davie looked like he'd swallowed the chalice as well as its poisoned contents.

The sun, weaker now, was still managing to poke through the cloud cover and I felt traces of warmth on my face as we ran down the cobbles to the esplanade. Davie turfed the female guard driver out of the first Land-Rover he came to and we careered round the parking lot towards the narrow beginning of the Royal Mile. This time there were no tourists blocking the road. Given the speed Davie had already attained, that was just as well.

As we passed the museum at the end of Chambers Street we were hit by the scream of high-powered jet engines. A panic-stricken pigeon – so decrepit that not even Edinburgh citizens desperate to increase their meat intake would bother trapping it – missed our windscreen by a few inches.

"There it goes," Davie said, angling his head upwards. "The afternoon helijet flight to Oxford." Suddenly he was a schoolboy plane spotter.

"Maybe our assassin's on board," I muttered. "Poxy machines. You'd think the smartarse engineers could have worked out how to silence them."

"Ah well, it's tricky with turbines, you see. They . . ." Davie's words trailed away as he noticed my glare.

"Spare us the lecture, guardsman," I said. "I'm trying

to preserve my hearing for the statement from Dead Dod. Maybe he'll be able to identify his assailant."

Except there wasn't anything. No statement identifying the arm wrestler, no description, no nothing. The mutilated Leith Lancer didn't even know his own name.

"A very bad case of amnesia."

Davie and I, standing at the glass partition of the intensive care unit, turned at the sound of the medical guardian's voice.

"Sophia," I said. "Shouldn't you be flat out?"

She handed the youth gang member's file to a nursing auxiliary and shook her head at me carefully. "I'm all right, Quint. Just a bit of damage to my face." She smiled unconvincingly. "What does that matter?"

Davie had stepped away and struck up a conversation with the attractive young nurse.

"Are you sure you're all right?" I asked in a low voice.

She nodded, touching the dressing over her upper face gingerly. "I'll survive. I told Maisie I'd walked into a door." She looked away, towards the figure with the bandage-covered upper torso in the ICU. "Your victim's still very vague, Quint. The psychiatrist has only had time to run initial tests."

"Could the amnesia fade? Could it be post-traumatic?"

Sophia gave me a thoughtful look. "It could, on both counts. On the other hand . . ." She put her hand in the pocket of her white lab coat and took out a folded sheet of paper. "The toxicologists are still unclear about the exact nature of the chemical compound in the patient's blood. But—" She broke off.

"But what?" I said impatiently.

"If you have a scientific background it goes against the

grain to pass on unverified test results, Quint," she said fastidiously.

I raised my eyes to the ceiling. "For Christ's sake, Sophia, you aren't giving the keynote speech at an international conference. Just tell me what they've found."

She nodded. "Very well. In layman's terms, the indications are that the drug given to the victim was a complex compound. It induced deep coma, but also prevented infection and blood-clotting. It probably also caused the memory loss we are now registering."

I stared at her and tried to make sense of what she'd said. "You mean the drug was both beneficial and harmful?"

Sophia was looking puzzled. "Yes, so it seems. It's almost as if the attacker didn't want his victim to suffer, either physically or mentally."

"So we're on the trail of someone who removes a limb – pretty clear evidence of abnormal behaviour, if you ask me – but doesn't want the kid to have a bad time. This has got to be a first." Something else struck me. "Am I right in thinking that this compound is highly unusual?"

Sophia nodded. "That's why toxicology's having such difficulty analysing it."

"So the likelihood is that it was produced in a very advanced laboratory?"

"Very," she confirmed. "I'd say it's the product of a major research project. I've never heard of a single substance causing all the effects we've logged."

"We've nothing like that in Edinburgh, have we?"

Sophia laughed. "Much though I respect the chief toxicologist—" She broke off. "No news on him, I suppose?"

I shook my head. "He hasn't exactly been top priority recently."

"Much though I respect Lister 25," she continued, "the Science and Energy Directorate has never had the funds to do much research."

That wasn't entirely true. The case that led me to Glasgow a couple of years back had involved a major and very secret research project, but I let Sophia's statement go. My mind had gone in a different direction altogether.

"I suppose a successful university-state would be capable of undertaking research like this?"

That made Sophia's mouth gape.

I spent the rest of the day wrestling with my suspicions. Part of me – the impulsive, suicidal side of my character – wanted to confront Raphael and the senior guardian with what I was thinking. The other more sensible side counselled caution, and eventually that prevailed, not least because I failed to come up with anything more conclusive before the Council meeting. It wasn't the first time that I'd spun the guardians a line and I was conscious that my authorisation was in the balance. Fortunately Sophia agreed to play down the toxicologists' initial findings, which gave me a bit more time.

I intended to spend some of that listening to the blues. I needed to unblock my thought processes and I had a hankering for an infusion of rhythm and melancholia. I'd already decided which cassette I was going to slot into my aged machine: the misanthropic Furry Lewis fitted the bill and my mood perfectly. Davie ran me down to Tollcross then headed off with a faint smile on his face. He'd arranged to meet the nursing auxiliary he'd been chatting up in the infirmary. He always was a quick worker.

As I approached number thirteen, I heard my name

being broadcast from the end of Gilmore Place. It was Katharine. I waited for her to catch me up.

"You took a chance on finding me here," I said.

"Nice to see you too." She came up to me and kissed me. "What's wrong with your mobile?"

"Sorry," I said, holding my face against hers. "I turned it off an hour ago. I'm lying low, trying to keep Slick and the Mist off my back."

She put her arm through mine. "Do you really think they won't be able to find you if they want to?"

"Course not," I said ruefully. "Surveillance is the name of the game these days." I glanced around the street, wondering if there was a camera in the vicinity. You can never be too paranoid.

"What's the matter?" Katharine asked solicitously as we went into the dank stairwell.

"Oh, the Hamilton case. The mutilated boy. That kind of stuff."

"How is George Faulds?"

I was lost for a moment. "Oh, you mean the man with one arm. I'll tell you later. After I've had a heavy slug of malt and a blast of the blues."

She laughed. "I'm so glad I decided to come over."

"I'll make it worth your while, darling."

Unfortunately I didn't get the chance.

We drank, we shivered in the chill of the gloaming – as it was April, the coal supplies had been reduced – we listened to the old bluesman and we picked at platefuls of hash that I'd made with a lump of bright pink sausage meat. I told Katharine my concerns about Oxford, then she described a normal session at the youth centre: verbal abuse, table tennis and the occasional smile from the city's alienated kids. We even talked about Lewis

Hamilton. Katharine didn't seem to harbour any antagonism towards him. Maybe death really does heal all wounds.

"What are you going to do then, Quint?" she said, stifling a yawn.

I moved closer to her on the sofa. "I was thinking about bed. It looks like you're in need of it too."

She gave me a sidelong glance. "In need of sleep, yes."

"Aw, come on," I said. "It's been a long, lonely time."

She laughed. "That'll be right."

I put my arm round her graceful neck and pulled her gently towards me. "What do you reckon then, pretty lady?"

Katharine looked at me disapprovingly. "Cut the sweet talk, pal. You're crap at it."

I sat back, deflated. "Well, thanks."

"All right," she said, smiling more encouragingly and getting to her feet. "Give me a minute to wash."

I touched her rear as she stepped over my legs and got another blast from her eyes for my trouble. These days everything was on Katharine's terms or on no terms. I wasn't over the moon about that, but the hard object in my groin told me to live with it.

There was the sound of running water from the sink in the alcove off my bedroom. Soon the Big Heat would be on us and the water restrictions would kick in. Even in spring, you had to wash your entire anatomy in the sink on the days you weren't on the bathhouse roster. I sincerely hoped Katharine wasn't undertaking that lengthy process. Then the water stopped and the screaming started.

I jumped up and threw myself through the doorway. "What is it?" I shouted.

Katharine was naked above the waist, the small

Supply Directorate towel clutched to her chest. She swallowed the last of her screams and nodded mutely towards the head of my bed.

I swung round and felt my stomach cartwheel.

Jesus.

Carefully positioned in the middle of my pillow, the bloody nail pointing at the wall, was a severed finger.

That wasn't all.

Words had been scrawled in red letters above the bedhead, dribbles of what looked very like blood having run down the faded wallpaper. They were words that did nothing to put a brake on my pounding heart.

What they said was "ALL ROADS LEAD TO OXFORD".

I'd have preferred a less graphic confirmation of my suspicions.

CHAPTER NINE

We spent the night at Katharine's place – what was left of the night after the scene-of-crime squad had set up camp in mine. The digit was sent to the pathology lab in the infirmary. From a cursory examination I could see that the surface of the wound had a similar appearance – uneven rather than cauterised – to the stump on the hand of the Leith Lancer's severed arm. The Mist made an appearance, her nose held high in the air as she inspected what she was no doubt classing as the squalor I lived in. Eventually Katharine and I left them to it. The SOCS wouldn't report until the morning and I had the feeling this was going to be my last chance of sleep for some time.

I woke up early and tried to get out of the narrow bed without waking Katharine.

"Where are you going?" she said, her eyes suddenly wide open and focused on me as I buttoned my faded black trousers – the Supply Directorate has never been well endowed with functioning zippers.

"Infirmary," I mumbled. I've never been good first thing. "Want to confirm the finger came from Dead Dod."

She sat up and swung her long legs out from the covers. "I'm coming with you."

My face was obscured by the sweatshirt I was pulling

on. By the time I'd got my mouth clear she was taking clothes from the rack that ran along the wall.

"Don't argue," she said, before I could. "George – that's his name, by the way, not Dead Dod – is one of my kids. I'm sick of him being treated like an animal. I want to know what the hell happened to him."

"You're not the only one." I sat down to lace my boots. I'd been in situations like this with Katharine often enough. Resistance was useless when she set her mind on something. "What are you going to do then? Leave the drop-in centre to look after itself?"

She shrugged as she ran a brush through her short auburn hair. "The Welfare Directorate will send another operative down." She turned to me, her jaw jutting. "Don't forget, I've got an 'ask no questions'. I can go anywhere I want."

I wondered how long the new public order guardian would let her keep the undercover authorisation, but I didn't voice that thought. I needed all the help I could get.

We never made it to the infirmary. On Lauriston Road I was called to the castle by the Mist. Her tone was already more dictatorial than it had been a few hours earlier.

Hamilton's replacement hadn't been wasting any time. Little more than a day had passed since her promotion, but she'd already changed Lewis's office in the castle beyond recognition. The heavy, dark-stained furniture had been replaced by tables and chairs of stripped pine with gleaming tubular frames. Instead of a desk she'd purloined a surveillance unit from the command centre, complete with screens, headphones, keyboards – the lot. It wasn't hard to see where public order in Edinburgh was heading. Big Sister is watching you.

Next to her stood the Council's version of Big Brother.

Fresh-faced, youthful and vicious as a starving stoat, the senior guardian looked at Davie and me with a mixture of impatience and contempt. Fortunately I'd managed to convince Katharine to wait in the cubby-hole by the command centre. There was no point in irritating the city's great powers any more than was strictly necessary.

"Citizen Dalrymple," Slick began, "we called you and your—" He broke off and I could tell from the look that spread over his face that he was about to make what he reckoned was a witticism. "You and your Doctor Watson here to give you one last chance."

If Davie was unimpressed by the characterisation he made a good job of dissembling. He stood motionless, his hands behind his back and his chest in the grey guard tunic thrust forward. Then again, maybe he took it as a compliment. Conan Doyle was one of the few crime writers approved by the original Council. The guardians thought Sherlock Holmes, that stalwart defender of establishment values, was a suitable role model for auxiliaries. Shame about the cocaine addiction.

"One last chance?" I said, trying to concentrate on what the senior guardian had said. "What does that mean?"

Slick stepped out from behind the console and brushed a piece of fluff from the arm of his perfectly pressed suit. "It means that we're on to you, citizen."

The new public order guardian managed to tear herself away from the surveillance camera images she'd been following. She stood up and joined her superior in the middle of the spacious room. "We're prepared to accept that you had nothing to do with the appearance of the finger on your pillow," she announced.

"Thanks for the vote of confidence," I said.

The Mist's face reddened. "But we know that you were responsible for the words written above it." Her voice was painfully loud. "Your antagonism towards our friends from New Oxford has been obvious ever since you started this investigation. The scene-of-crime squad reports that the blood used to mark the wall came from a rat. Admit that you wrote the words and I'll consider a reduced sentence in the dungeons."

So that was her game. I was still thinking about how to return serve when there was a knock on the door.

"Not now!" the senior guardian yelled.

That didn't stop the door opening.

"I beg your pardon?" Sophia asked, her expression showing what she thought of Slick's tone.

"Ah, medical guardian," he said uncertainly, glancing at me. "Was there something you wanted?"

Sophia closed the door behind her and came towards us. The dressing over her eye and cheek was smaller and she looked less pale than yesterday.

"I have a report to pass on. Several reports actually, senior guardian." She followed his lead in addressing him by his title. When they're not in front of auxiliaries like Davie, guardians have been known to use their first names. I had the feeling Sophia never called the head honcho Lachlan. She turned to us. "Good morning, citizen. Hume 253."

"Guardian." Davie's tone was reserved, his body tense.

Sophia looked thoughtful.

"Well, guardian?" the Mist said.

Sophia looked at her new colleague like she'd just risen from a grave. "Well, guardian," she countered. "First, the finger Citizen Dalrymple found." She slapped a maroon and white folder on the top of the console. "It's definitely from the severed arm of George Faulds. I estimate that it was removed from the hand at approximately the same time. There are no traces of blood from any other person."

"What about the trauma?" I asked.

"I was coming to that." Sophia was back in full empress mode. "The surface of this wound is different to those on the arm and torso." She glanced around. "They are completely beyond our ken: some kind of high-temperature device that effectively sealed and cauterised the wound. But the finger was removed by a well-honed, non-serrated, single-blade knife." Sophia raised her shoulders. "There are probably thousands of such blades in the city."

"Very helpful," the senior guardian said dismissively. "What else?"

Sophia slapped another folder down. "Progress report on the victim George Faulds. He's still exhibiting the signs of total amnesia. He appears unable to recognise even the nursing staff who are in and out of the ICU all the time."

The Mist let out an impatient sigh. "And the last file?" she said, extending a hand.

Sophia ignored it, this time laying the folder down carefully. "Ballistics report on the fragment of the bullet removed from my face."

Shit, I'd forgotten all about that.

"Nothing significant," she said, shaking her head. "No letters or markings at all. It's the same alloy as the other piece, of course."

"Thank you very much, guardian," Slick said, attempting to usher Sophia to the door. He overplayed his hand.

"Just a moment," she said. "I have a personal interest in this investigation." She raised a hand to her face. "What's this I hear about some kind of message on the wall in Citizen Dalrymple's bedroom?" When we'd been together, Sophia had passed quite a few nights in that particular room – not that she was giving any sign of recalling those times now. "'All roads lead to Oxford', was it?"

The Mist stepped closer. "Message?" she scoffed. "That was your friend Quint's idea of a joke. We all know how much he dislikes the Oxford incarceration initiative."

Sophia's eyes were on me. "This isn't true, is it?" Her expression showed how little credence she was giving her colleague's words.

"Of course not. You don't imagine I'd have gone for such a cliché of Golden Age detective fiction?" They all stared at me blankly. "Anyway, Katharine Kirkwood was the one who found the finger. Ask her if I did the writing."

Slick laughed humourlessly. "We can trust her testimony as much as we can trust your Doctor Watson's."

Sophia looked at him blankly. "What's going on here, senior guardian?"

"What's going on is that Citizen Dalrymple is about to take up residence in the dungeons for the foreseeable, and indeed the unforeseeable, future," he said. "We cannot tolerate the fabrication of evidence."

There was a hubbub of voices, mine to the fore. Then the Mist's mobile went off. She'd programmed it to emit the most high-pitched tone on the menu.

"Public order—" Her head jerked back as the caller interrupted her. "Yes indeed," she said after a few moments. "You'd better speak to my superior." She handed the phone to Slick.

"Hello? Yes, administrator. How are—?" He broke off and listened. "I see," he said, his brow furrowing. "Very well, I'll bring all of them." The connection was cut before he could sign off.

"We have been summoned by the Oxford delegation,"

he said in a low voice. "That includes you, medical guardian." He kept his eyes off me. "And you, Dalrymple. You'd better bring your dogsbody too." With that he strode towards the door.

From Watson to dogsbody in the course of a meeting – Davie must have been suffering a hell of an identity crisis.

On the way to Ramsay Garden I called Katharine. I was under all-out attack by Slick and his heavy, and she was a good person to have around when the shit started flying. Her presence didn't raise any objections. Then again, she'd already managed to get herself involved in the case.

The esplanade was bathed in sunshine as we walked across it, the buds showing on the trees against the northern wall. Spring was definitely on its way. If I didn't come up with a survival plan pronto, I'd be spending it and the subsequent seasons in the bowels of the castle.

"What the fuck's going on, Quint?" Davie said in an undertone. "Is the Mist serious about nailing you?"

I shrugged as Katharine looked on uncomprehendingly. "If it's a bluff, it's a pretty good one. She's got the senior guardian on her side."

"What's going to happen now, do you think?" Davie asked, acknowledging a guardsman who was standing to attention beside a Land-Rover.

"They're going to jump to Administrator Raphael's every word."

"Is that where we're going?" Katharine asked.

There wasn't time to brief her. I nodded. "Your role is to be as disrespectful as possible."

Katharine laughed. "I think I can manage that."

Davie gave a grunt. "I know you can manage that." His relationship with Katharine was as rocky as ever. It was comforting that at least one thing hadn't been changed by the incursion of New Oxford into Edinburgh.

The atmosphere in the administrator's apartment was distinctly strained. I took that to be a good sign. The sun was streaming in through the leaded windows, but Raphael and her trio of academics looked like their breakfast kippers had been boiled in lubricating oil. They were standing at the dining table, their nostrums – nostra? – round their necks and their faces solemn. Then I got a surprise. Andrew Duart, the Glasgow first secretary, appeared from behind Raskolnikov. What was he doing here? A moment later Billy Geddes rolled out of the shadows in his wheelchair. His presence wasn't exactly a surprise; more of a confirmation that some deal involving large amounts of money was going down.

Raphael nodded at the guardians, then at me and my team. Her eyes rested on Katharine. "Who is this?" she asked.

"This is—" My introduction was interrupted – I should have known better.

"I'm Katharine Kirkwood," came the firm voice from my right. "I work with Quint on major cases."

Duart moved to the administrator's shoulder and whispered a few words. He knew who Katharine was from the investigation in Glasgow back in '26.

"You're in the right place," Raphael said, smiling briefly at Katharine. "It would be fair to say that this is rapidly turning into one of Citizen Dalrymple's major cases."

The way she said it made that sound almost encouraging. I turned to Slick and the Mist and was pleased to see that their expressions had soured. Sophia's was non-committal, the patch of bandage looking like a growth that she was trying to ignore.

"I gather one of the earlier Councils used to conduct its meetings in peripatetic fashion," the administrator said.

The senior guardian nodded without enthusiasm. "That did occur in the early years of the decade." He gave a supercilious smile. "We've moved on, so to speak."

"If it was good enough for Plato's academy . . ." Raphael let her words trail away in an obvious rebuke to Slick. "In order to ensure our minds remain on the subject in hand, I suggest we do the same."

"Excuse me if I rest my arms," Billy said with a slack grin.

The rest of us started pacing slowly up and down the long room like a gang of philosophers chewing the fat about the major questions of existence. But it soon became clear that the administrator's problem wasn't an abstract one at all: it came down to a simple proposition, one directed at me.

"Citizen Dalrymple, you feel that my colleagues and I have been concealing the truth from you." Her tone was polite enough but I sensed disquiet beneath the surface.

"I . . . yes, I do," I said, deciding that I might as well be straight with her.

Raphael caught me in her gaze and I felt the power in her eyes. "Good answer," she said, beckoning me to approach her. We were at the far end of the room, near the Walter Scott settee. She spoke some words I didn't recognise and then held up her nostrum, the screen towards me.

"Shit," I muttered as I made out miniature versions of myself and Davie hunched over the table in the room near the command centre. I could hear myself arguing the case for Raphael being the sniper's target. "You bugged the place."

The administrator gave an almost imperceptible shrug. "It was actually my colleague Professor Yamaguchi who placed the device. During a tour of the castle facilities with the former Raeburn 124."

The Japanese fended off the Mist's accusing glare with a twitch of his thin lips. "We had our reasons," he said.

"I don't suppose you put one in my bedroom, did you?" I asked. "You'd have got some interesting shots of whoever left the finger last night."

Yamaguchi shook his head. "Regrettably, I did not," he said.

The senior guardian moved quickly to catch up as Raphael set off up the room again. "I don't understand," he said. "What does this mean?"

The administrator stopped suddenly and turned towards the rest of us. "It means that my colleagues and I have come to a decision."

"You have some information you'd like to share with us," I said ironically.

"Indeed, citizen." Raphael's voice was level, giving nothing away. "Why do you think we placed a transmitter in your work room?"

"Search me," I replied. "You've been getting up-to-the-minute reports from your pals here." I inclined my head in the direction of Slick and the Mist.

"Don't pretend that you've been keeping your superiors fully informed, citizen."

I accepted the administrator's gibe with a laugh. "Why did you bug the cubby-hole? To satisfy yourselves that I knew what I was doing with the case."

She opened her eyes wide. "Very good, citizen."

Raskolnikov came closer, his long beard caught beneath the flap of his suit jacket. "You'll be glad to hear that you passed the test, Dalrymple."

A burst of slow clapping from the table made everyone look in that direction.

"Well done, Quint," Billy called. "You've pulled the wool over some more clients' eyes."

Raphael's stony gaze put paid to my former friend's bravado. "Let's have your thoughts on the finger and the words that were written on your wall, citizen," she said, turning back to me. "I've already heard the scene-of-crime report from the public order guardian."

"I'll bet you have," I said, glaring at the Mist. "She hasn't shared it with me yet." I straightened my back and rubbed my hands together. "The finger. Sophia – the medical guardian – has confirmed it's from the victim whose arm was found in your bath."

The administrator glanced at Sophia and nodded. "Continue."

I glanced at a piece of paper Davie had just handed me. "As for the writing on the wall, I gather that the author used rat's blood. It would be easy enough to find a donor in this city." That didn't go down well with Slick. "Presumably he didn't want to use his own blood. The message was very interesting," I said. "'ALL ROADS LEAD TO OXFORD.' Written in capitals to make the handwriting less easy to identify."

"A reasonable conclusion," the administrator interjected.

"The words themselves are a paraphrase of the proverb about all roads leading to what used to be the capital of Italy," I continued.

"And is regrettably now a theme park called Pasta, Pizza and Circuses," Doctor Verzeni put in.

Raphael stared at her colleague to shut him up. "But

what do the words mean?" she asked me. "What do they mean in this context, do you think?"

"Assuming you don't go along with the theory that I wrote them," I said, giving the Mist a disparaging look, "I'd say the perpetrator is trying to point me in the direction of your fair city."

"That much is obvious," Raskolnikov said bluntly. "Have you nothing more profound to suggest?" I got the impression that he was less keen on my investigative talents than his boss.

I looked straight at Raphael. "More profound?" I asked. "Well, how about this. The same individual is responsible for the removal of the youth gang member's arm and the attempt on your life, which mistakenly resulted in Lewis Hamilton's death. That individual has significant connections with New Oxford, as proven by the NOX bullet fragment and by the sophisticated drug used on Faulds." I turned towards the senior guardian. "That individual also has a substantial knowledge of City Guard working practices – remember the ease with which the security in this building was compromised – and of Edinburgh geography. He – and I'm assuming the perpetrator's a male until I get evidence to the contrary as the footprints found in Leith were size eleven – managed to discover where I live as well." I flicked my eyes back to the administrator. "Final conclusion: you've got a lot to come clean about."

Raphael gave me a neutral look, then smiled with a surprising amount of warmth. "Very well, I will come clean, as you put it." Then she turned away. "On this afternoon's helijet to New Oxford."

The Joseph Bell Rooms were suddenly as silent as a pharaoh's dusty tomb.

* * *

Somehow I managed to get what I wanted. Slick wasn't keen, but his resistance crumbled in the face of the approval Administrator Raphael gave to my request: Davie and Katharine were allocated seats on the plane as well. We went back to the cubby-hole to make sure we had all the files we might need.

"Bloody hell," Davie said, shaking his head in disbelief like a kid who's finally found the key to his old man's booze cabinet after years of searching. "I'm going up in the air."

Katharine was standing with her arms crossed, her lips pursed. "Is that the only thing you can think about, guardsman?" She turned to me. "What's going on, Quint? Are you sure this is a good idea?"

I looked up from my notebook. I'd been so caught up in the practicalities of the unexpected development that I hadn't considered the big question: was I jumping out of the frying pan?

"Em, possibly," I said. "I don't know, Katharine. Christ knows what we'll find down there. But I haven't exactly got many options left in Edinburgh. Slick and the Mist were about to lock me up and melt down the key."

She looked at me dubiously. "But why does this administrator woman want you to go to Oxford? Shouldn't you be staying here to track down Hamilton's killer?"

"What makes you think Hamilton's killer is in Edinburgh any more?" I asked. "Let's face it, there are enough indications that he's linked with the university-state."

Davie grinned at her. "You don't have to come if you don't want to, Citizen Kirkwood."

Katharine raised a finger at him. At the same moment the door opened and Sophia walked in.

"Glad to see your team's operating in perfect harmony

as usual, Quint," she said, an icy smile on her lips. The medical guardian and Katharine had always been an even more lethal combination than Davie and Katharine. She came up to me and handed over a thick maroon folder. "Here's all the data on the amputee and on Lewis Hamilton. The drug specs – such as they are – examination and p-m reports, everything. They might be useful." She gave me a penetrating stare. "Are you sure that leaving the city is a good idea?"

I raised my eyes to the vaulted ceiling. "Not you as well. Look, what choice have I got? Raphael's got Slick's balls in a vice. If she wants us in New Oxford, we're going, period. Anyway, Slick and the Mist were about to consign me to the nearest dungeon."

Sophia nodded. "You're probably right." The smile returned. "Though it's the first time I've seen you do what a woman asked without playing for time."

"She didn't ask, Sophia," I said. "She ordered."

"Now I see where I went wrong."

Katharine moved closer. "Have you finished, guardian?" she demanded.

Sophia kept her eyes on me. "Good luck, Quint. Come back in one piece."

I felt my stomach flip. "Thanks a lot. You'll keep the senior guardian and his sidekicks on the right side of the City Regulations?"

She nodded, raising her hand to her face. "I'll try," she said. She walked slowly to the door. "As long as the painkillers have an effect."

I wondered how long she'd be able to hold the line in the Council chamber.

"We've only got three-quarters of an hour till take-off, Quint." Davie sounded uncharacteristically nervous. He swung the Land-Rover round a citizen on a bicycle in Inverleith Row, eliciting a yell of alarm.

"Calm down, big man," I said. "You won't miss your inaugural flight. I have a feeling they'll hold the helijet for us."

He glanced at me. "They're that keen on the great Quintilian Dalrymple's abilities, are they?"

I shrugged, gazing out at the soot-stained barracks block to my right. "I don't know. Raphael certainly seems to think I can solve her problem."

Davie sniffed. "Pity we don't know what that problem is."

"The external manifestation of it is that someone's trying to kill her, guardsman."

He shook his head. "It doesn't feel right to me, Quint. We should be tearing Edinburgh apart to find the bastard who shot the chief."

I knew what he meant; but I was also finding the prospect of a trip beyond the borders of Edinburgh pretty exhilarating. Maybe the old man would be able to put a damper on my enthusiasm.

Wrong. As soon as I told him what was happening, Hector's wrinkled face cracked into a wide smile.

"Oxford?" he wheezed. "You'll have a great time, laddie."

I pulled the blanket up his chest and tucked it in under his arms. As usual he was in his armchair, a heavy volume of Latin text on his lap.

"I'm not going there for a symposium," I said in irritation, glancing at Davie. "I don't really know why I'm going there."

"Ah, Oxford in the spring," the old man said wistfully. "The cherry blossom, the river, the gardens . . ."

"Spare us the lyricism," I said.

"Don't you remember the time you came with me when I gave the Innes Lecture, Quintilian?"

"I was sixteen, old man," I said. "I had other things on my mind."

Davie moved into the centre of the room in the retirement home. "You didn't tell me you'd been to Oxford, Quint."

"I've had other things on my mind," I said pointedly. "It was a long time ago. I'm sure the new city isn't anything like it was back then."

"I seem to recall that you were particularly keen on the female undergraduates on bicycles," Hector said, licking his lips.

"I wasn't the only one," I countered.

"What do you mean?" the old man demanded. "I was completely engrossed in Seneca's position on imperial corruption."

"Aye, that'll be right." I gave him a serious look. "Anyway, I don't know how long I'll be gone. Will you be all right?"

Hector gave an impatient snort. "Don't worry about me, lad. I've lived my life." He lowered his gaze, shaking his head. "Not always wisely, but to the best of my ability. I tried to change the way other people lived." Then he raised his head again. "Whatever good I did has been pissed away by the idiots in later Councils. You go where you have to go, Quintilian. Don't bother about me."

I stared at him. "Well, thanks for the maudlin farewell speech. That's really going to make me leave Edinburgh with a spring in my step."

An arthritis-twisted, liver-spotted hand shot out from the blanket. "I'm serious, laddie," he said, gazing at me steadily. "I don't want you taking me into account when you're making decisions."

"I'll bear that in mind," I said, suddenly finding it hard to speak.

Hector nodded. "Look in the fourth shelf of the bookcase on your way out. You'll find an Oxford guidebook."

I squeezed his forearm then turned away. The book was blue and well worn, the unfamiliar name on the flyleaf suggesting that the old man had bought it second-hand. He was always a fearful hoarder of books. This was the first time he'd ever offered me one of his own free will.

I clung to that bittersweet thought as I followed Davie to the guard vehicle.

We screeched to a halt at the corner of Chambers Street and jumped out, leaving the Land-Rover's doors open. A guardsman waved us towards the museum entrance, keeping a group of aggrieved tourists waiting behind a barrier.

"Lift number three takes you to the roof, commander," he said, ignoring me.

Davie looked at his watch as the doors closed in front of us. "Four minutes to go, Quint. I told you we didn't have time."

I put the book Hector had given me into my holdall. "And I told you we would have time. Just watch."

The doors opened and we stepped out on to a clear space underneath the great transparent, curved blast shields. The helijet, all slim lines and massive engine nacelles, loomed above us like a dark-feathered bird of prey perched on its eyrie.

A guy in a silver suit nodded to us punctiliously and handed over plastic cards. "These are your seat controls." He pointed to a small panel at the top. "Touch these pads" – he played over the surface with his fingers – "and you can change position, order drinks, access webnet, increase ventilation . . ."

We watched as the appropriate words appeared on the panel. It seemed the high-tech world of New Oxford started on the Museum of Edinburgh roof.

"The other passengers are over there," the steward said, indicating a group standing by a heavy steel door. "I'll take your bags."

We declined that offer and kept our luggage to ourselves, provoking a disappointed twitch of Silver Suit's lips.

Katharine stepped forward as we approached. "Where have you been? I almost ended up on the plane without you."

"I don't think so." I pulled out my mobile and called Sophia. I wanted to ask her to watch over the old man, but the call was diverted so I left the message with her secretary. I hoped Sophia was resting. Knowing her, I reckoned she was more likely to be hard at work in her lab.

"So you have finally decided to grace us with your company, Citizen Dalrymple." Professor Raskolnikov's voice was deep and disapproving. "I hope you are more punctual when you are a guest in New Oxford."

He turned away and rejoined Raphael and the rest of her entourage. Beyond them was a large group of well-dressed men and women. I recognised none of them and wondered who they were. Probably more consultants for the prison initiative.

Then I heard a voice I recognised behind us.

"I don't care if there is no reservation for me. I am the public order guardian of this city and I order you to let me on the helijet."

Davie and I exchanged glances.

"Don't tell me the Mist's going to be on our backs," he groaned.

We watched as Raphael strode over to meet the guardian, who'd barged past Silver Suit.

"Administrator," the Mist began, "I really must insist—"

"You really must leave this area, guardian," Raphael interrupted, making no attempt to conceal their conversation from the rest of us. "I've already told you, we do not require any other Edinburgh personnel." She looked over towards me. "Citizen Dalrymple and his team will be quite sufficient."

"But we are investigating the death of a Council member," the Mist spluttered. "One of the most important people in—"

"Enough!" The administrator's voice was sharper than the blade of an auxiliary knife. "Go back to the senior guardian and tell him I will be in touch. Goodbye."

Lewis Hamilton's successor stood limply on the concrete, strands of her lustreless hair protruding from the normally tight elastic she fastened round it. Then she fired a poisonous glare at me and turned on her heel. I couldn't understand why the newly appointed guardian was so keen to leave Edinburgh, or why she was suddenly so outraged by Lewis's death. And I was surprised at the way Raphael had publicly humiliated her. It was almost as if New Oxford's dealings with Enlightenment Edinburgh had moved to a different level – one of master and servant rather than equal partners.

The man in silver moved towards us with a smile on his face, then sobered up rapidly when he saw Raphael's expression.

"Ladies and gentlemen, we are ready to board. Please follow me." He ran his fingertips over a small device he was holding in the palm of his hand and watched as the door leading to the apron opened.

We walked up a short flight of steps that led directly into the rear of the helijet. I breathed in a mixture of aviation fuel and leather – the spacious dark blue seats were of that material – and blinked. The interior of the aircraft was sleek and well lit, the fittings all in silver. I had a flash of the science-fiction movies I used to watch when I was a kid: vast metallic spacecraft with powerful weapons, astronauts in bulky suits and highly intelligent computers. They suddenly seemed very close. Then I remembered the alien beings that often haunted the dripping cargo spaces and scurried through the ventilation ducts to ambush all available humans – and felt a crushing wave of apprehension.

Davie obviously didn't. He was taking his seat avidly, a broad smile on his face.

I sat across the aisle from Katharine and fiddled with the card I'd been given. A cup with a lid was ejected slowly from a panel in the rear of the seat in front of me.

"Did you mean to do that?" Katharine asked.

"Of course," I lied.

Then the lights were dimmed and the engines on each side of the wide fuselage began to whine, though the noise was much less than it was at street level beneath the blast shields.

"Here we go," Davie said from behind.

I nodded. "Here we go. Goodbye, Edinburgh."

For a few seconds I found myself wondering when – or if – I'd see my home city's buildings again. Then the engine nacelles swivelled round and the noise level increased.

We had lift-off.

CHAPTER TEN

Despite the automatic belt that had moved over my lower midriff with a hum and a click, I was clutching the sides of my seat, expecting a sudden surge of power. Although I hadn't been on a plane since the early years of the century, I still remembered the way your stomach suddenly seemed to empty as the brakes were released and the gunned-up engines sent the aircraft down the runway like a giant artillery shell.

I was to be disappointed, or rather, pleasantly surprised; I was never the world's best passenger. The helijet was making a fair amount of noise but it lifted itself off the museum roof smoothly, no blast or jolt to shake its occupants up.

"Bloody hell," Davie gasped, staring out of his egg-shaped window. "Isn't this something?"

"It's an aircraft," Katharine said sarcastically. She closed her eyes and relaxed, unmoved by the hyper-advanced machinery.

I was with Davie on this one. What we were seeing really was something. From the window on my side I watched as the centre of Edinburgh sank away beneath us, the castle's imposing bulk getting more like a kid's toy by the second. Even Arthur's Seat was reduced to the status of a minor mound, the aerial perspective flattening the green hill and the dark scars of the crags. Initially I could distinguish the inhabited areas inside the city line, but soon the devastated buildings and potholed roads of the outer suburbs where the drugs gangs once held sway looked no different from the rest of the city. It was as if twenty-five years of Council rule, of penning the city's remaining populace inside the carefully guarded border, had achieved nothing. The guardians should all have been given a trip on the helijet. It might have taught them humility.

"Look," Davie said. "The mines."

Directly beneath us the patchwork of fields – green pastureland, cereals and root crops interspersed with brown ploughed areas – was pockmarked by blackened earth and rundown buildings. For ordinary citizens it was difficult to decide which punishment rota was worse: a month underground hacking out the coal essential for electricity generation, or a month being drenched or parched, depending on the season, on the city farms. I couldn't recommend either.

Then we began to ascend more steeply, cutting through layers of cloud that soon became thick enough to obscure the view. Edinburgh was gone, lost in the mass of white. I wasn't sure whether to laugh or cry. I let myself sink into the luxurious seat and had a more detailed look at the control card I'd been given. After a few minutes of fumbling I managed to work out how to access the different options that appeared on the small screen when I touched the numbered keys. That way I made the back of the seat move backwards and forwards like a tree in a strong wind, got myself a packet of what looked like desiccated rabbit droppings, though the label called it Nox Vitamin Snack, and obtained my very own strong wind from a panel above.

"Have you finished playing, citizen?"

I jerked forward. The voice came out of a speaker next to my ear that I hadn't noticed.

"If so, come to the front of the cabin. I want to talk to you." Administrator Raphael was in her autocratic mode. When she said "want" she meant "require", not "desire". I gave her a minute to wonder whether I was going to respond.

Before I did, I entrusted my bag to Davie. Then I walked up the gently sloping floor, feeling my boots sink into the thick dark blue carpet.

It was about time Raphael came clean.

I passed Professor Raskolnikov on the way. He gave me a scowl that made me wonder if I'd unwittingly deleted all his crime and punishment files when I was fiddling with the control card. Then I saw the empty seat across the aisle from the administrator and realised that he'd been expelled to make room for me.

"Sit down, Citizen Dalrymple," she said, inclining her head to the right.

I decided to take my life in my hands. "You can call me Quint, you know," I said as I obeyed her command. "What's your first name?"

For a moment she looked nonplussed, then she turned her piercing eyes on me. "Administrators in New Oxford are not addressed by forename."

"But you do have a first name? Family and friends use it, don't they?" I took in the unrelenting expression. "You do have family and friends?"

Raphael seemed uncertain for a moment, the skin on her face less taut than usual. Then she went back to type. "Administrators are expected to give all their attention to their work," she said, raising her nostrum from her chest and glancing at the display. All I could see was a matrix of numbers and letters. "We avoid all distractions."

"Now I understand why you've been getting on so well with Edinburgh guardians," I said. Although Sophia had recently had a child, she was the only one of her rank to have taken advantage of the loosening in the Council's celibacy regulations and to have rejoined the human race.

Raphael gave me a sharp look. "Be serious for a while, citizen. If you can."

"I am being serious, administrator," I replied with a grin.

"And grow up."

That was a trickier one. I let it pass.

"Very well." Raphael pushed her thin frame back in the leather seat and formed her hands into a pyramid underneath her chin. "I said I would impart certain information to you during the flight and that's what I intend to do." She glanced at her nostrum again. "We only have half an hour at most."

I looked out of the window and saw that the cloud layer below was passing at what seemed like a very high speed.

"First of all, some points of detail you should know. The footprints you found on the floor of the derelict flat in Leith."

"Oh aye?" I said, remembering the heavily ribbed mark from a shoe or boot.

"An identical print was found on the staircase outside your own flat."

"What? I never heard that."

The administrator gave me a tight smile. "I'm sure the public order guardian didn't intentionally keep the updated scene-of-crime report from you."

I was as sure about that as I was that the drinking

water ration would be increased in the summer, but I kept my thoughts about the Mist to myself; although Raphael bawled her out before we left Edinburgh, the pair of them had seemed to be pretty close before that.

"Anyway," the administrator continued, "that isn't the most important point about the print."

That sounded interesting. "It isn't? What is then?"

She looked down at her knees. They were pressed tightly together, the black material of her trousers creased out of line. "That particular marking is to be found on a make of boot produced by Nox Footwear Industries." She looked at me sternly. "I understand that its design number is NF138B and that it is sold exclusively to students of the university."

I started to scribble in my notebook.

"I will supply you with a full digital record of our conversation, citizen," the administrator said.

"I prefer to write my own record." I turned to watch her. "Sold exclusively to students, you said. Does that mean only students wear that kind of boot?"

She nodded. "And – to pre-empt your next question – none of the Oxford personnel who have been in Edinburgh is a student."

I raised an eyebrow. "Students wear different shoes from university staff?"

"You'll find we're very organised about that kind of thing, citizen."

"Is that right? So how do you explain the prints in Leith and outside my place, administrator?"

She met my eyes with her own. "That's one of the things I'm expecting you to do."

Before I could take her up on that the man in the silver suit appeared and leaned over Raphael. I couldn't hear much of their whispered conversation but I did hear a reference to "the large man with the beard". Oh shit. What was Davie up to?

The administrator looked at me round Silver Suit's legs. "Apparently your colleague Hume 253 has asked to visit the cockpit. Can you vouch for him?"

I nodded. "He's never flown before."

She dispatched the steward and shortly afterwards Davie came past, looking like he was in seven times seventh heaven.

"Let's move on," Raphael said briskly. "The next—"

"Hang on, we haven't finished with the footprint yet."

"I told you, citizen, you'll get a full record." Her eyes were steely. "Kindly refrain from interrupting."

I got the feeling that there was a lot more discipline in the university than there had been in the past, as the New Oxford incarceration initiative back home suggested.

"The next matter is the bullet." She knew that would get my attention and she met my eyes impassively. "As you correctly deduced, it too was made in Oxford. By Nox Ballistics and Weapons Technology. That is one of the university's most successful commercial operations." She took another look at her nostrum. "It's an experimental model known as the Eagle One."

I was scratching my head, taken aback by her sudden openness. "Why didn't you admit that when I told you about the NOX marking on the bullet?"

Raphael raised her hand. "I knew nothing about the Eagle One at that stage. It's a highly sophisticated, top-secret development. I needed to be sure."

I bit my lip and watched as Davie came back from the cockpit, a beatific smile on his face. "I need to be sure too," I said in a low voice. "You're telling me that a hot design product from your home city was fired at you by someone who isn't a student but was wearing a student's boots. Jesus Christ, Raphael, someone tried to kill you. Why?"

The administrator didn't react to my use of her surname. "Again, citizen," she replied in a cool voice, "that's what you're here to find out." She rubbed her hands together. I caught sight of the implant in her wrist and wondered again about its function. She ran her tongue along her lips. "There's something else."

"Oh great," I said with a groan, still trying to work out why she wanted me to catch an assassin from her own city.

"With hindsight I realise I should have told you sooner." Raphael was taking care to avoid my eyes now.

"This is getting better and better. Let's have it then."

The administrator pressed her forefinger against her lips. "Very well." She turned towards me, eyes still lowered. "A week before we left for Edinburgh, the mutilated body of a young man was found in central Oxford."

I felt my heart start to beat faster. "Mutilated," I repeated.

She nodded. "But on that occasion both arms had been removed."

Administrator Raphael certainly had been keeping a lot to herself.

Shortly afterwards Raskolnikov came back to his seat and signalled to me to get out of it. "We'll be arriving soon, citizen," he said, giving me the usual stony stare. "Then you'll have to show how good an investigator you really are."

I returned his stare and threw in a smile for good measure. "Just watch me," I said, brushing past him. As I went I heard the administrator say something to him in a muted voice. After she'd told me about the Oxford murder, she shut up shop and started to commune with her nostrum. Perhaps she urgently felt the need of some time with a machine after spending half an hour with a human being who answered back.

I passed Davie and repossessed my seat. The Russian had left a curious smell behind, something sweet and sickly like incense cut with sweat. It seemed that Nox Underarm Protection Industries wasn't a world leader in its field. Across the aisle Katharine was asleep, her head in profile against the soft leather. In repose she had none of the fierceness she'd cultivated over years of hardship in prison and working the land. Her long eyelashes and high cheekbones still gave her an exotic air, but the slackness of the skin around her mouth made her look like a child at rest – a child who was innocent of the horrors of the world.

"Look what I managed to get," Davie said, turning to me and holding up two handfuls of Nox snacks.

I tossed over the one I'd declined to open. "Don't eat them all at once, big man," I said.

"Eat them?" he said. "No chance. I'm keeping them to throw at the locals. Here, what did the woman in charge have to say?" he asked, his expression suddenly intent.

"I'll tell you later," I replied. "When Katharine comes round."

He glanced at her then shook his head. "She doesn't know what she's missing. Do you know what our cruising speed is?" He wasn't going to let me answer, not that I had a clue. "Nine hundred and fifty kilometres an hour." He looked at me. "How many miles is that?" The original Council went back to imperial measurements in an attempt to erase the supposedly malign effects of the crumbling European Union in the early years of the millennium.

"About six hundred," I estimated.

"Aye. And the pilot told me we're flying at over twelve thousand metres."

"About forty thousand feet," I translated. "Why so high?"

"Because there are some headbangers around what used to be Leeds who have ex-Russian army ground-to-air missiles that can reach ten thousand metres. It seems they don't like anything from New Oxford." Davie grinned. "Any idea why?"

I laughed. "Nice, easy-going people like Raphael and Raskolnikov? An overriding interest in discipline and imprisonment? Beats me."

Suddenly there was a reduction in the engine noise and I felt my stomach jump. Then, almost imperceptibly, the front of the aircraft tilted groundwards.

"We're on our way down," Davie said, sounding disappointed.

"Aye," I replied, shaking Katharine's knee gently. "The fun's about to start."

"Mmm?" she asked, her voice languid. "What fun?"

Good question.

For a short time everything was obscured by clouds. Then we were through them and descending at an angle that wasn't too threatening. Looking down, I made out a curiously regular band of grey earth that must have been at least ten miles wide. As I sat back, Silver Suit came down the aisle.

"What happened down there?" I asked, pointing out of the window. "Looks like a desert of ash."

The operative glanced nervously towards the area

where Raphael and her team were sitting, then nodded. "You're not far off. They're the Poison Fields. They surround the university-state on all sides. There was massive pollution caused by the fertilisers they used at the turn of the century. There's only one safe way through them and that's to the south of the city." He looked round again and continued on his way.

The Poison Fields. That sounded pretty ominous. I took them in again, seeing no sign of habitation or infrastructure. Then I remembered the bloody message on my wall. In this area there were apparently no roads leading to Oxford at all.

Davie's nose had been glued to the window. "Have you seen the way it looks down there, Quint?" he asked, turning to face me. "It's like a bloody great dartboard."

I looked again, this time to the front beyond the helijet's swept wings. He was right. We were in the airspace over a huge roundel, the ashen fields forming an outer ring. Then there was a wider band of what seemed to be intensely cultivated land – the green fields much larger than the ones around Edinburgh – and, further ahead, a distant centre circle of buildings. The angle of descent became more acute. It looked like we were in the process of scoring a bull's eye. Or an ox's eye.

The sun was lower in the west now and the nerve centre of the university was caught in its light. As we approached, I became aware of the shape of the city: a long, narrow strip running from north to south, separated from other built-up areas to the east and the west by the thin, meandering blue of rivers and the green of fields and woods. The streets in the suburbs were much shorter and closer together than those among the central buildings.

"Shit!" Katharine snapped her head back from the

window and ran her hand over her eyes. "Watch out. You need sunglasses."

I peered out again gingerly and blinked as the sunlight was reflected off what seemed to be a large expanse of glass near the centre of the city. Shielding my eyes with one hand, I made out several more patches of shiny roofing in the area. Either the university's scientists had come up with a new building material or a double-glazing salesman had made a major killing. Looking to the left, I realised that the suburbs were not endowed with reflective roofs.

The belt tightened itself over my belly and a few minutes later we were hovering over the golden heart of New Oxford. The crenellated towers and battlements of the colleges came into focus as the final descent began. Directly below us was a large area of parkland, in the centre of which was a landing zone surrounded by transparent blast walls. There was a large black identification mark on the white concrete.

"X" marked the spot.

"Citizen?"

The speaker by my ear made me jump again.

"What?" I replied, deliberately omitting Raphael's title.

"I have arranged for the proctor to meet you and your people."

"Really? And what's a proctor?"

I heard a faint sigh. "The proctor is responsible for order and discipline in New Oxford."

"Ah," I said. "Your equivalent of the Mi— The public order guardian."

"Along the same lines, yes," she replied. "He combines university duties with those previously undertaken by the late and unlamented Thames Valley Police Force."

"So the proctor was in charge of the armless murder case."

"Correct. He will give you a full briefing. And you will give me your preliminary thoughts at dinner this evening. Farewell." There was a muted click from the speaker.

The belt round my midriff had undone and rewound itself. I stood up and watched as the administrator and her entourage disappeared through the front door.

Silver Suit was standing just in front of us, pointing to the rear. He smiled unconvincingly and nodded. "Farewell."

That seemed to be the standard term around here. I began to wonder if the helijet was a time machine. Or maybe today's Oxford people just got a kick out of speaking like characters from the stories of H.G. Wells.

We walked down the ramp into the late afternoon sun. It was being refracted as it came through the blast wall and my eyes registered rainbow flashes. I squeezed them shut then opened wide and experienced another time shift.

"Quintilian Dalrymple?" asked a heavy, red-faced man in a full-length red and blue academic gown. He even had a tasselled mortar board under his arm. "I am Doctor Connington, proctor and fellow of Corp." He didn't extend a hand.

"Corp?" I said. "As in corpse?"

He gave me a restrained smile. "After a fashion. As in Corpus Christi. For ease of diction, the colleges no longer use their full names."

"Is that right?" I said, wondering if that was also New Oxford's way of breaking with the past. I introduced myself and the others. "For ease of diction you can call us Quint, Katharine and Davie." I looked beyond him and worked hard to suppress an explosion of laughter. "Who are your friends?"

Connington glanced at the pair of tall, muscle-bound guys in dark suits and bowler hats. "Ah, these gentlemen are bulldogs. Security operatives." He looked at me dubiously. "I imagine what you would call policemen."

"No, we wouldn't," Davie put in. "We'd call them—"

"Thank you, guardsman," I interrupted, giving the doctor an encouraging smile. "I gather you're going to brief us on a murder."

The proctor nodded gravely. "Indeed. I'll take you to headquarters and tell you all you need to know." He stepped aside and ushered us towards a door in the transparent wall. "I hear you are an expert investigator, citizen," he said from behind me.

"I told you, call me Quint. What should I call you?"

"You choose," he replied. "Doctor or proctor."

I resisted the temptation to compose a limerick on the spot. Obviously he fancied first-name terms as little as the administrator did. "Investigator?" I said. "Oh aye. Expert? That depends on how much information you give me, doc."

He stiffened, as did the two bulldogs. "I've been instructed to answer your questions and to give you all the help you need," he said in a lofty tone.

"Make sure you do." I've learned from long experience of dealing with guardians that it pays to show your teeth to senior personnel as soon as you can.

We walked out on to a path that ran through a wide expanse of uncultivated parkland. Beyond it a tall bell-tower rose from a cluster of college buildings of different vintages. I seemed to remember it was Magdalen. Presumably they called it Maud these days, as in "come into the garden". There was a group of people in front of the nearest stone accommodation block who'd done just that. As we got nearer I saw that most of them were young – some of them worryingly young – though there were a few figures in black robes among them. What struck me was that the young ones – students, presumably – were all wearing similar clothes: the males were in pale-coloured cavalry twill trousers and sports jackets, while the females were in white blouses and knee-length tweed skirts.

"Looks like a convention of trainee guardians," Katharine said with a hollow laugh.

Davie was right behind me. "They're having a tea party," he said. "I wonder if they'd give me some cake?"

"Haven't you got your pockets full of those snacks from the plane?" I asked.

"I want real food," he complained.

"Later, big man."

Katharine pointed away to the left. "What's that over there?" She sounded seriously surprised.

"Haven't you ever seen deer before?" I enquired.

"Not the deer, you moron," she replied. "Behind them. It's just going round the corner."

"That waddling bird?" said Davie.

"Yes," Katharine said excitedly. "It can't be."

I hadn't managed to see what they had. "It can't be what?"

She stared at me, shaking her head slowly. "It looked like one of those fat things in kids' books. The ones that are extinct."

"Dodos?" I suggested with a laugh.

"Exactly. It looked like a dodo. What do you think, Davie?"

He shrugged. "I didn't see it clearly. I don't know . . ."

"Oh, for Christ's sake," Katharine said. "Take it from me, it was a bloody dodo."

The proctor was walking sedately down the path, paying no attention to our conversation.

I was beginning to get the feeling that we had landed in an extremely weird place.

That feeling stayed with me as we came on to the High Street. Apart from a lot of silver boxes sprouting aerials and tubes by the porter's lodge the college looked much as I remembered it from when I was a teenager. After the old man had given his lecture, he took me for sherry with a shrivelled old classicist in Magdalen. I drank too much and had to make use of a bush afterwards, much to Hector's amusement. But when we got outside the college now I realised there had been some pretty major changes.

"What are they for?" I asked, pointing up at the see-through panels that extended horizontally from the walls about thirty feet above the ground.

"Protection from the elements," the proctor said, leading us towards a wheeled contraption at the roadside. "There was a major problem with acid rain when New Oxford was in its formative stages. Most of the industry that produced it was destroyed during the drugs wars, but there's still a residual danger. The panels also act as screens from the summer sun – they have a computer-controlled tint facility."

"What the hell's that?" Davie demanded, pointing at what looked like a cross between a pick-up truck and a rickshaw. It was shrouded in clear glass, through which eight comfortable seats were apparent. The wheels were large and thin, like those of late nineteenth-century cars.

Connington stopped by the vehicle. "That is the Nox

Transportation Systems gas-powered people transporter. Its popular name is the Chariot."

Davie was staring in the windscreen. "How do you steer it?" he asked. "There aren't any controls."

The doctor shook his head and smiled tolerantly. "You are incorrect. The Chariot has a full set of operational controls." He opened the glass door and pointed at a small mesh-covered button on the roof. "The driver has only to speak simple commands and the chariot's on-board computer does the rest."

"Really?" Davie looked impressed. "Can I have a go?"

The smile faded from Connington's lips. "I don't think so. You must first learn the commands I referred to."

Davie wasn't giving up. "You're a teacher, aren't you?"

"Not of students at your level," the proctor said sharply. "Take us to the Camera, Trout."

One of the bulldogs nodded and got into the front of the Chariot, his colleague joining him. The doctor gathered his garish robe about him and clambered in behind them, while we brought up the rear.

Trout wasn't playing fair. He spoke in a low voice that was difficult to hear; he obviously didn't want us to learn the control commands. There was a hiss, then the Chariot moved forward at surprising speed, overtaking a couple of students on pedal bikes before they even noticed us.

We followed the gentle upward curve of the High Street, past imposing academic façades and colleges that were better fortified than your average castle. The streets beneath the rain shields were busy despite the hour, students in the garb we'd seen earlier walking purposefully, gowns flapping around their hips. When I was last in Oxford, students only moved like that when the pubs were about to open, but I reckoned from their serious expressions that this lot were on their way to lectures or tutorials.

Then a shopfront caught my attention.

"Stop!"

I was glad to see that the Chariot understood my instruction. I told the door to let me out before Connington and his canine escort could respond.

The door to the shop slid to the side automatically as I approached.

"Good afternoon, sir." A middle-aged man with thin hair plastered over his scalp, and restless hands, came out of the shadows. The words on the shop sign – NOX University Outfitters – were written in old-fashioned script and the interior was a replica of what seemed to be an early twentieth-century gentlemen's apparel supplier. The lights were low and the place smelled of leather and heavy-duty fabric. The attendant was dressed in a dusky suit and high collar, and he was giving my tatty Supply Directorate gear the once-over. "How may I be of service?" The way he was licking his lips suggested that he reckoned he was about to double his day's takings.

"Footwear," I said. "Specifically, model NF138B."

"Size, sir?" he enquired, his eyes wide.

"Eleven," I replied.

The salesman looked at my feet – I take an eight. "For yourself, sir?" he asked dubiously.

I ignored the question. "Do you have them in stock?"

"Let me see, sir," he said, going over to a small screen. After a moment he looked back at me. "It's not a standard model," he said. "Could I recommend NF73s for everyday wear?"

I could tell he was stalling. "Do you have them in stock?" I repeated.

I felt a rush of air as the door opened again.

"What are you doing, citizen?" Connington asked. "Taking steps to improve your wardrobe?"

"You don't, do you?" I said to the salesman, ignoring the proctor. "Who do you normally supply them to?"

He rubbed his hands together nervously, keeping his eyes off Connington. "I think . . . I think there have been production problems . . ." His voice tailed away and the only sound in the shop was his rapid breathing. "Who do we supply them to? I can't . . . I really can't say . . ."

"What's this all about?" the academic demanded.

I turned to the door. Even though I moved fast, it was way ahead of me and opened before I got there.

"Citizen?" Connington's voice was raised. "What were you doing?"

"I'll tell you later," I replied. "After you've given me that full briefing."

Further up the High Street, Trout turned the Chariot right into a cut that had been made in the pavement and took us into Radcliffe Square. I felt Connington's eyes on me all the way. My detour to the outfitters was puzzling him, but I was pretty confused by it too. Why was the salesman so reticent about the NF138Bs? Raphael herself was the source of that information. It was hard to believe she'd made a mistake with it.

I let the thought go and looked out of the canopy. This was the part of Oxford I could remember most clearly, the part that all tourists thought of as the iconic heart of the city. To the south, on the side we'd just passed, stood the university church – St Mary the Virgin, as far as I could remember. It looked exactly as it had done twenty-eight years ago, its great spire adorned with pinnacles and statues giving off a deep golden glow. Then I turned my gaze to the front and got a shock. Here was the Camera that we were being taken to, the Radcliffe Camera; it was then that I remembered Raphael's use of the term when she was speaking into her nostrum in Edinburgh. But what the hell had happened to the great rotunda?

The Chariot stopped and we spilled out on to the elliptical lawn surrounding the structure. Apart from some patches of lighter-coloured stone around the arches of the ground floor and the double columns of the central section, the lower parts of the mausoleum-like building were intact. It was what had happened to the upper area above the transparent shields that took my breath away.

"What's that up there?" Katharine asked, shading her eyes as she bent her head back.

"Search me," I muttered, trying to make sense of the huge uneven ball made of hundreds of opaque glass panels that surmounted the Camera. "There used to be a domed roof."

Connington stepped forwards. "Impressive, don't you think? This is New Oxford's security centre." He looked upwards proudly. "We keep an eye on everything that happens in the city from here."

"What's inside that glass thing?" Davie asked.

The proctor was unimpressed. "That glass thing, as you put it, contains our main surveillance equipment. I'm quite sure that your imposing frame is filling a screen as we speak."

Security centre? Surveillance equipment? Those words didn't exactly make me feel on top of the world. Still, installing it in a building called the Radcliffe Camera suggested that at least some people in Oxford had a sense of humour. Then it struck me that perhaps the city's rulers had chosen the place as a heavy-handed statement of intent to the native population rather than a smartarsed pun. That made me even more suspicious about the set-up.

As did the realisation that, despite this state-of-the-art security facility, there had recently been a particularly brutal killing in the city; one whose perpetrator, according to Raphael, had completely escaped the attention of the watchers in the sky.

CHAPTER ELEVEN

Connington led us up to a door of dark glass. In front of it was a chest-high metal post with a line of green light running down it. The proctor parted the flaps of his robe and spoke into his nostrum.

"I take it you all still have the cards you were given on the helijet," he said when he'd finished. "Good. I have now programmed them to allow you entrance to the Camera."

That explained the absence of sentries. Everything seemed to run like clockwork in New Oxford – as long as you had the right bits of plastic.

The opaque door opened silently and we followed the man in the robe into the building.

"Bloody hell," Davie muttered, looking up at the great arches that supported the upper floors. "The new command centre back home's a doll's house compared with this."

He had a point. Although the outside of the Camera – apart from the glinting ball on top – retained its classical lines, the interior was like something out of the twenty-fifth century. The walls were sheathed in polished steel, the windows shielded and light provided by long strips that were suspended in the air by almost invisible wires. The circular floor was filled with screens and small computer terminals manned by operatives dressed in dark suits like the ones worn by Trout and Perch. In the centre there was a wide and transparent column of glass which, as we got closer, I realised was a lift shaft.

Doctor Connington stopped next to it and glanced upwards. "The elevator gives access to the surveillance equipment in the dome," he said, stepping in as a panel opened with a sibilant breath. "But we are going down." He leaned forward and spoke inaudibly at a half-inch fine-meshed dot on the glass wall.

The lift moved so quickly that it was impossible to make out anything of the subterranean levels we passed, apart from the fact that there were a lot of them. Then the brakes were applied and we stopped with more of a jolt than I'd expected.

"That was pleasant," Katharine said with an ironic smile.

We stepped out into a corridor that ran further than the eye could see in both directions.

"Are you sure you wouldn't like the bulldogs to look after your bags?" Connington asked. He'd already tried to get us to leave them in the Chariot after we arrived at the Camera.

"Quite sure," I said. I didn't want his heavies rummaging around in the files I'd brought, let alone laughing at my small stock of tattered clothes.

"Very well." The doctor sounded uninterested. "I'll take you to the Viewing Room."

"What are we going to view?" Davie said in an undertone. "Dark blue movies?"

"What floor are we on?" I asked Connington.

"Minus eight," he replied. "We're approximately forty-five metres underground."

I glanced round at the walls. They were of the same silvery steel material as those upstairs. "It must have cost a fortune to dig this place out. Did you run out of space at street level?"

The doctor looked over his shoulder at me. "Not exactly. The city went through a sustained period of conflict during the first decade of the century. Some buildings were completely destroyed. This one survived, though not unscathed; you saw the damage to the exterior. The underground security centre was designed in response to the threat posed by the drugs gangs."

"But they were driven off years ago, weren't they?" I said, catching up with him and looking at his florid face. "Why do you need so much security now?"

Connington declined to answer that question. He brought us to a halt outside a steel door. It was unmarked apart from a small panel in the centre bearing the letters HOMVR.

"Let me guess," I said. "VR is viewing room, obviously."

"And HOM must be homicide," Katharine put in, staring at the proctor. "Just how many killings does the university-state have on an annual basis, doctor?"

Another good question; and another the man in red and blue didn't favour with an answer.

The door hissed shut behind us and we breathed in the sterile smell of air-conditioning. The Viewing Room was about fifty by fifty feet. Its main features were the complete lack of furniture and the profusion of large and small screens built into every wall. I gave up counting after twenty. The only other occupant was a young blonde woman in the standard dark suit, set off by a dark blue tie with the emblem of a closed book beneath the knot.

"Haskins," Connington said with a nod. "Have you prepared the disks?"

"Yes, proctor," she said in a clear voice. "Everything's ready."

"Run all!" Connington commanded.

The voice sensor activated the four largest screens, one on each wall, and we suddenly found ourselves in the middle of a very real crime scene.

"Quadrihypervision," the proctor said proudly. "Developed by our technicians. Takes you straight to the location of the recording."

"Oh aye?" I was turning in circles, trying to get a grip on what I was seeing. "It would help if I had eyes on every side of my head."

Connington gave me an encouraging look. "You'll get used to it."

I spent half an hour trying and ended up with a headache for my trouble. However, I managed to get some idea of what had happened to the murder victim. His name was Ted Pym and he was a thirty-year-old cleaner who'd worked in the Department of Metallurgy in the northern city centre. On 27 March he'd finished his shift at five a.m. – university regulations apparently permitted cleaning operations only at night to give maximum access to researchers – and was on his way home to the suburb of Cowley on his bicycle. What happened next was unclear. His body was found in the middle of a pathway called Dead Man's Walk to the south of the High Street, the severed arms laid one across the other in the shape of a cross a couple of feet above his head. His bike turned up three days later in the River Cherwell a quarter of a mile away.

"Jesus!" Katharine was shaking her head. "You were right about this Quadrihypervision putting us on the spot."

All around us were great gouts of blood, the result of extended spurting from the ruptured artery in each shoulder. The poor guy's face was set in agony, the teeth bared and the eyes bulging. This was as messy a scene as the one in Raphael's bath in Edinburgh was bloodless. That wasn't the only difference.

"What was the cause of death?" I asked.

Connington nodded to the blonde bulldog and the pictures changed. Now the screen in front was showing the victim's naked body on the mortuary slab, while those to the right and left had the pathologist's and the investigating officer's illustrated reports. I took in as much as I could.

"He bled to death?" I said, walking up to the front screen. "And the damage to the sternum is taken to be from a heavy boot?"

The proctor was nodding. "Correct. We posit that the killer knocked the victim to the ground – notice the large contusion around the left eye – and then held him down with his foot while he severed the arms."

I swallowed hard. "The murderer then kept his boot on the victim till enough blood had gushed out for him to succumb."

Davie cursed out loud, bringing a glare from Connington.

"Whoever did that must have been covered with blood," Katharine said.

"Yeah," I agreed. "Though he – or she, if it was a very strong woman – could have been wearing protective clothing which was subsequently discarded." I turned to the proctor. "You didn't find anything?"

He shook his head. "We only found the bicycle by chance. It was caught up in the branches of a weeping willow."

"Any footprints?" I asked, thinking of the mysterious NF138Bs.

The proctor pursed his lips. "It had been dry for days. What marks there were had been carefully obscured with a rough fabric."

Shit. "What about the weapon used to sever the arms?" I asked.

The image on the front screen changed again.

"Computer reconstruction of the likely instrument," Connington said. "Single-edged, non-serrated knife. Like the kind favoured by the drugs gangs of old."

"And by the City Guard back home," I said thoughtfully, running my hand over the stubble on my chin.

Davie glanced at me. "It's a common enough kind of knife," he said. "And this is only an extrapolation from the trauma data."

"Our extrapolations are usually very accurate," the proctor said firmly.

"Uh-huh." I gave him a slack smile. "Which is more than can be said for whoever was in charge of the surveillance camera in Dead Man's Walk that night."

The academic was looking sheepish.

"Don't tell me," I said. "You've got enough cutting-edge gear to set up a colony on Mars, but there was no operational camera down there."

Connington's face had turned as red as his gown. "Something went wrong with the power unit."

Dalrymple's Nineteenth Law of Criminology: do not put your faith in cameras. No matter how good your system is, any criminal who's worth chasing will find a blind spot.

We spent more time in the Viewing Room going over the data before Connington called a halt. We were expected for what he called "pre-prandial drinks" with the administrators at seven thirty. That gave us less than an hour to clean up and change.

Trout and Perch escorted us out of the Camera and headed towards the nearest college. The heavy wooden gate was open and they left us in the porter's lodge without saying a word. It looked like bulldogs were better at biting than barking.

A gruff old guy in pinstriped trousers and a black jacket took our control cards from us and keyed in room numbers. "Your rooms are all in Old Quadrangle." He pointed through the arched entrance. "That's it there." He turned back to us. "The lady is in staircase five, the gentlemen in staircases two and seven." He gave us an intimidating glare. "No gentlemen in ladies' rooms or vice versa. No movement about the college after midnight without special permission. And no fraternising with the students."

I made sure I didn't give any indication that we were going to go along with his instructions. "Isn't this Brasenose?" I asked, trying to resurrect my local knowledge.

"Brase," he corrected, looking less than happy. He'd probably been around when the original names were in use. "And make sure you keep your noise down. I don't like noise."

I went through the gateway, wishing I'd brought my Screamin' Jay Hawkins cassettes.

"Shouldn't we have told the administrator that we wanted a double room?" Katharine asked with a tight smile.

I shook my head. "It's better that they've split us up. Sniff around and see what you can find out from your neighbours."

We separated and headed for our staircases. The quad, its central carpet of lawn cut immaculately, was deserted apart from us. Never mind no fraternising with the students – there didn't seem to be any. I went up the worn stone stairs and found my room easily enough. I could hardly miss it as my surname, prefaced by the title "Mr" was lit up on a black panel on the door. I moved to slide my card into the slot under the handle but the dark blue wood swung open as I approached. Perhaps it smelled me coming – I needed a wash.

On first appearance the rooms – a spacious sitting room and a much smaller bedroom – were a blast from the time of Evelyn Waugh and his drunken pals, though there wasn't anything approaching a handful of dust in the place. The furniture was brown going on black, the wallpaper was in your face and the sofa could have done with a new set of covers. The main room was a strange brew of medieval and futuristic. I couldn't fail to notice a large screen set into the wall above the roll-top desk and discovered that the humming cabinet beneath it contained a fridge – empty, unfortunately. I was about to give the accommodation the thumbs up when I saw the bathroom, or rather the shower hole. There was no cabinet or curtain, just a pipe with a battered head and a single, cold tap. High-tech New Oxford seemed to have an ancient Spartan heart.

Then I saw the dinner suit laid out on the bed. Holding it against myself, I realised it was the right size. Someone must have been measuring me up covertly. There was also a dress shirt, a pale green bow tie and matching cummerbund, and a pair of gleaming black shoes. I picked up my mobile to see if Davie had been given a change of clothing too, then remembered how far from Edinburgh I was. I fingered his number anyway and was amazed to hear a ringing tone.

"Here, have you been kitted out with a penguin suit?" I asked after we'd got over the shock that our clapped-out Supply Directorate phones worked in Oxford; maybe the technicians in the Camera had programmed the control cards to do something magic to our handsets.

"Aye," he replied. "I'm not planning on wearing it though. It makes me look like a right—"

"You are wearing it, pal," I interrupted. "Just go along with everything they want. That way we stand more of a chance of picking up the stuff they're keeping hidden from us."

He started grumbling so I cut the connection. It occurred to me that if they'd facilitated our phones, they might be listening to our calls.

At twenty past seven the screen in my sitting room let out a high-pitched bleep and a mechanical voice instructed me to proceed immediately to the front gate. Fortunately the bow tie was on an elastic so I'd almost finished my preparations. No shave though. I didn't want to look too clean-cut. Earlier I'd knocked on all the other doors on the staircase in search of a friendly local. Nobody was at home – or at least nobody who wanted to risk opening up to me.

Davie was already waiting under the archway, his bulky frame fitted up surprisingly well in a suit identical to mine. Next to him was a woman I initially didn't recognise. It was only when she turned round, the knee-length ochre evening dress carving out an elegant flourish, that I realised it was Katharine. She was wearing what looked like a silk shawl round her otherwise bare shoulders and her shapely legs were given even greater effect by high-heeled leather pumps. I was glad to see that she'd managed to maintain some integrity: her short brown hair had been brushed straight up and gelled in a striking clash with her formal get-up.

"This way." Trout had appeared outside the gate. I was relieved to see he was still in his bulldog suit. Even though he'd demonstrated that he could speak after all, I didn't fancy sitting next to him at dinner.

"Where are we going?" Davie asked as we stepped out into the square around the Camera.

"You'll see," replied Trout, keeping his eyes to the front.

"Sorry I spoke," Davie muttered.

I turned to Katharine. "You look . . . well, spectacular."

"I'm not sure if I feel that way," she said, looking down at her legs. "I haven't worn a dress for a hell of a long time."

"You want to complain. I haven't *ever* worn a dinner jacket."

She smiled. "I'd never have guessed. Actually . . ." She ran her eyes over me. "You don't look too bad either. I'm not sure if green's your colour though."

"I *am* sure that green isn't my colour." I glanced at Trout and moved closer to her. "Anything or one interesting on your staircase?"

She shook her head. "No one around. The door screens only said that the occupants were out; there wasn't any more information about them."

I gazed around as the bulldog led us through a narrow passageway, the ubiquitous sensor post on the outside.

"This is the Bodleian Library, isn't it?" I asked.

"Was the Bodleian Library," he replied after a pause.

We came out into a quadrangle which instantly took me back about five centuries – and also to the days of my youth. The flagstoned square and the buildings with their battlements and tall windows were exactly as I remembered them; Hector had talked one of his professor friends into getting us temporary passes back in 2000. It didn't look like the drugs gangs and their heavy artillery had done much damage here.

I came back to what Trout had said. "What do you mean? What's this place now?"

"The university doesn't use books very much these days," the bulldog said, suddenly loquacious. "Everything the students need is in digital form." He opened his arms wide and spun round in a surprisingly light-footed movement. "This is the university administration centre – Noxad for short."

I stared at him and then took in the glorious towers and façades again. They'd turned one of the most famous libraries in the world into an office block.

What did that say about the people who ran the university-state of New Oxford?

"Hurry up, citizen." Professor Raskolnikov was standing at the entrance to the Gothic western side of the quad. As ever his beard and long gown gave him the look of a medieval monk, his tone suggesting that he'd been fasting far too long. "We can't keep the administrators waiting."

"Just watch me," said Davie, stopping to inspect the bronze statue of an armoured nobleman that stood before the door.

"Come on, jackass," I hissed. "This is serious." I had a lot to lay on Raphael and her friends, and I was expecting plenty in return.

"Is it true that the university doesn't use books any more?" I asked as the Russian led us up a winding staircase.

He gave me a pained look. "This is the twenty-first

century." He lifted the nostrum from his chest. "What do you think technology is for?"

"You mean you do your research with a two-inch piece of metal?"

"Don't be an idiot. I mean we use the technological advances in data processing to cut out the drudgery. You have a wall screen in your accommodation, do you not?"

I nodded. "So you, the students, whoever, can access whatever documents or publications are required without going anywhere near a library?"

"Precisely." Raskolnikov stopped at the top of the stairs and gave the three of us the once-over. "I'm glad to see you've got rid of those Edinburgh rags. We try to maintain some standards in New Oxford."

Davie raised his middle finger at the professor's back as we were taken past a pair of regal busts and into a long room filled with stalls. They weren't for animals, though. The shelves above the sloped desks were lined with old tomes and incunabula, some of them attached to the stanchions by chains. It looked like even the classics were subject to incarceration in the university-state. Above us, the panels of the ceiling were covered with coats of arms and the hall reeked of learning and devotion to reading; at least there was one place in the city where those pursuits weren't served up digitally.

Raphael appeared out of one of the stalls at the head of a small group. From the other side of the central passage Doctor Verzeni led out a gaggle of academics, among them Yamaguchi. Gowns of various colours were draped over their dinner jackets, but the administrator and several other individuals were more soberly dressed, in high-necked black suits of the kind she had worn in Edinburgh, their nostrums glinting in the subdued lighting.

"Duke Humfrey's Library," she said, opening her arms expansively. "Built in 1444, restored by Sir Thomas Bodley at the beginning of the seventeenth century. What do you think of it, Citizen Dalrymple?" She accepted a minuscule glass of what I took to be sherry from a white-coated waiter and sent him in our direction.

"Very impressive," I replied, taking a larger glass than hers from the tray. "Do you consult the volumes here regularly?"

She gave me a tight smile. "Few of them are relevant to the modern world." She looked at the group of dons as they took possession of the remaining glasses. "Besides, I am only an administrator, not a scholar."

"Only an administrator indeed!" said a pallid guy whose neck was too long even for the raised collar he was wearing. He gave Raphael an admiring look then turned to me. "You realise you are talking to the chief administrator, the university's de facto chief executive."

Raphael nodded at him. "This is Administrator Dawkley," she said. "He oversees the university's science departments." She introduced five more administrators, two of them women and all of them attentive but extremely reserved.

I tried to keep up with their names, but I was more interested by the fact that Raphael was the university's number one and that administrators rather than academics apparently called the shots. From what I could see, the university ran everything in the state of New Oxford. I wondered why she hadn't come clean about her position earlier. It certainly gave some insight into the shooter's motivation. Putting a bullet in the head of state was a lot more significant than killing a faceless bureaucrat. Then again, what was so important about the incarceration initiative in Edinburgh that New Oxford's supreme commander felt she had to drop everything and make a personal appearance?

Verzeni and Yamaguchi, along with Connington, had taken charge of Katharine and Davie and were introducing them to other academics. I hoped they'd both be on the lookout for any potentially interesting information, but predictably the big man was more keen on the tray of canapés that was circulating.

Raphael gave me a penetrating look and beckoned me to another stall. I leaned back against an angled medieval desk top and waited for her next move.

"They made them like this to stop scholars falling asleep," the administrator said, resting her haunches on a desk across the aisle from me.

"No danger of me falling asleep here," I assured her. "What exactly is the deal then?" I drained my glass and looked for somewhere to put it down.

"Here," Raphael said, extending a hand. "I'll take that." She raised an eyebrow at me. "The deal, citizen?" she asked.

"The deal, the play, the rules of engagement." I returned her stare. "You wanted us down here so we came. What do you want us to do?"

"I've already told you that, citizen," she said brusquely. "You're to find Hamilton's killer – the one who in all probability was aiming at me and who may well have been involved in the murder here."

So my thinking had been right. I kept my eyes on her. "Yes, but you've got a massive security and public order system in place in Oxford. Why do you need me?"

Raphael laughed. "Because you are an unorthodox, inquisitive, awkward investigator. Doctor Connington and his people are competent but they could hardly be described as imaginative."

I wasn't sure if I bought that, but I let it go. The waiter appeared and offered us more sherry; it was dry enough to provoke a tear from the most heartless of topers, but I never leave a drink unfinished on principle. I also grabbed a couple of biscuits covered in a pale brown substance.

"Foie gras," the administrator said. "From the Department of Agricultural Zoology's farm."

My mouth was filled with a magnificent and overpowering taste. Not even the richest tourists in Enlightenment Edinburgh got a sniff of this class of product. I was silenced for a couple of minutes.

Raphael stood straight when I'd finished chewing and brushed invisible dust motes from her suit. "Very well, citizen. The deal, as you put it. Tell me your requirements."

"Right. If you really want me to get to the bottom of this, I need a guarantee of free access to all parts of New Oxford." I gave her a questioning look. "And to all databases. And to all people: students, academics, workers, the lot."

"I am listening, citizen," she said, her expression neutral. "Assume I approve your terms unless I tell you otherwise."

I nodded, surprised that I'd got as far as I had without opposition. "I also want a guarantee of no surveillance. I need a completely free hand. No worries that my every word and movement are being recorded. And no moronic computer voices telling me what to do all the time."

No reaction.

"I also want transport – one of those Chariots will do – and I want us to be able to move around without bulldogs escorting us. Or on our tails."

Still no response. There had to be a catch somewhere.

"And I want a nostrum for each of us, fully programmed, each one accessible to all our voices."

Raphael glanced to her right and nodded at the waiter. "Is that all, citizen? Dinner is about to be served."

I shrugged. "That's all for the time being."

"Very well," she said, stepping away. "I'll expect your plan of action after we've eaten."

I followed her out, kicking myself for not having demanded a Chariot-load of gold bars as well.

Any remaining doubts I'd had about who ran the place were blown away when I saw the seating arrangement. Raphael was placed at the centre of the long table, a fellow administrator on each side and the dons towards the ends; the latter definitely below the salt, which was contained in ornate, solid-silver shakers. We'd been led downstairs and into what was once the Divinity School, a six-hundred-year-old Gothic hall with a glorious vaulted, arched and bossed ceiling. While we were taking our seats, Verzeni remarked that divinity had ceased to be a subject studied at the university after the drugs wars; apparently no one was interested in theological matters any more. That would explain why no one said grace, not that I was complaining.

"I don't suppose you've been to Oxford before, have you, Citizen Dalrymple?" Professor Yamaguchi said. He was sitting to my left, with Katharine on my right, while Administrator Dawkley was following what was said from the other side of the table.

I considered keeping quiet about my visit with the old man, then decided to see if I could provoke an unguarded response. "I have, actually," I replied, watching the Japanese's face. It remained unreadable. "Back in 2000. My father was a professor at Edinburgh University before the last election. He delivered a memorial lecture on ancient rhetoric at Christ Church."

It only lasted a second or two but Yamaguchi suddenly looked less sure of himself. I glanced across at Dawkley and registered a similar uncertainty on his bloodless features. Then the moment passed and the administrator handed me a basket of rolls.

"Try one of these, citizen. We've been working on a new modification of wheat. The taste is remarkable."

I took a bite and nodded in agreement. "Modification?" I said, remembering the civil disorder caused by that word in the early years of the century, especially when it was collocated with another. "That wouldn't be genetic modification, would it?"

Dawkley laughed, a strident noise that might have meant more to a horse. "We're well past that stage, I can assure you," he said disdainfully. He turned to his colleague and paid me no more attention.

The food was superb, courses of the best soup, freshwater fish, lamb, cheese and fruit that I'd had since I'd been in Glasgow a couple of years back; it certainly bore no resemblance to the primary-school slop I'd been served with on my last visit to Oxford. There was also a succession of excellent wines. I didn't ask, but I had the feeling that New Oxford probably ran to a Department of Oenology and Viticulture; the torrid summers of recent years would have made the production of top-quality wines feasible as long as there was enough water. From what I'd seen from the helijet, the university-state had no shortage of rivers and lakes.

"Do I get the feeling we're being fattened up?" Katharine asked as the port decanter appeared in front of Raphael, not that the chief administrator poured herself any.

"There's a quid pro quo," I replied. "Any minute now I'm going to have to tell them how I'm going to solve the case."

She smiled and sat back in her chair. "Sounds like a fair exchange to me."

Then Raphael tapped a spoon against her glass of water and called on me to address the company.

I swallowed the last of my claret and got to my feet, concentrating on not pushing my chair over the edge of the platform. Looking round at the glorious high windows and the fine old stonework, I found it hard to believe I was in the middle of a city that had put its faith in ultra-smart computers and the surveillance dome on the top of the Camera. That was as good a place as any to start.

"Administrators, doctors," I said, looking to soften them up by using their titles – I've never known that tactic to fail. "Ted Pym was found in Dead Man's Walk. That is, in the immediate vicinity of colleges and close to the High Street." I shot a glance at Connington. "And yet the camera covering the pathway was out of action." I looked around the table. "What conclusions can we draw from that?"

Raskolnikov snorted. "That we need to repair it immediately."

That provoked a chorus of mild laughter.

"Not quite what I was thinking," I said. "Any other ideas?"

"The killer knew there was surveillance there." Raphael's voice was low and unwavering. "He took steps to deal with it."

I nodded, looking at the notes I'd made in the Viewing Room. "Exactly. The victim was cycling down the High Street towards Cowley, as recorded by the camera on the corner of Longwall Street. So he must have been intercepted immediately afterwards, before he reached the lane that leads to Dead Man's Walk. Unfortunately the camera there also suffered a fault that night and transmitted no pictures. Could the killer have tampered with it too?"

Dawkley shook his head. "I don't think so. Unlike the low-level box on the path, that equipment is located six metres above ground level and is fully protected. Anyway, there was no sign of any tampering on either unit."

"Is that right?" I said. "Surely, in New Oxford, of all places, the technology exists to disable cameras electronically." I ran my eyes round the administrators' expressionless faces. Their silence made my point for me. "Getting back to Dead Man's Walk. Was the killer also making some kind of point by leaving the body there?"

Verzeni sat up straight. "Of course," he said, clapping his hands together. "Why didn't I think of that before?"

I'd only been referring to the obvious symbolism of the walk's name, but the Italian was a lot more excited than that seemed to merit.

"Dead Man's Walk," he said, nodding repeatedly. "Of course. It is believed that the Jews of medieval Oxford took their dead along that path outside the city walls to their burial ground."

I looked at him quizzically. "Where does that get us, doctor?"

He pursed his lips. "Think of the arms. They were placed in the shape of a cross above his head."

"Are there Christians and Jews in New Oxford?" I asked, remembering what I'd heard about the lack of religious interest.

Raphael leaned forward on her elbows. "Not in the university. Religious affiliation is banned; we expect our students to be far beyond that atavistic stage of human development before they commence their courses. There may be some vestigial sects in the suburbs." She looked up at me. "Are you suggesting the killing was religiously inspired? How would that square with the events that occurred in the Council's atheist Edinburgh?"

I shrugged. "No idea." The angle didn't excite me.

"What about the modus operandi?" Raskolnikov was glaring up at me from the far end of the table.

"I was coming to that," I said, putting him even further below the salt cellar. "I'd say the killer was highly trained. He left no incriminating traces." I glanced at Raphael. "On the other hand, Ted Pym was slaughtered with extreme savagery, which doesn't sit easily with the idea of a skilled assassin. He was also killed with a knife, a weapon very different to whatever was used to sever and cauterise the arm of George Faulds, though similar to that used to remove his finger – and note that no fingers were removed here." I suddenly remembered the unidentified drug that had given the Leith Lancer amnesia, among other things. Raphael hadn't mentioned it on the helijet and there was no reference in the post-mortem report to any unusual substances in Pym's system. I decided to sit on that for the time being.

"So do you now think there may be no connection between the two cases?" Raphael asked, her eyes fixed on mine.

I held her gaze then looked down at my notes. "It's too early to say, administrator. I need to work on the murderer's motivation here. Was Ted Pym simply in the wrong place at the wrong time, or was he chosen deliberately? More to the point, if the two assaults are connected, why are there so many differences? Not only in the mutilations and the weapons, but in the traces at the scenes." I looked back up at Raphael. "Why were the footprints obscured here but left untouched in the gang house in Leith? There was no attempt there at – so to speak – a cover-up."

Raphael declined to comment on my deliberately provocative terminology. She nodded and pushed her chair back, making it clear that my time was up.

"One more thing," I said, smiling at the diners. "This city's wired up better than an electric chair." I took out my control card and brandished it at them. "You can't go anywhere without the right codes being input." I grabbed Yamaguchi's wrist and held it up so the implant sparkled in the light of the nearest candle. "Which is why all you people have these pieces of jewellery buried in your flesh, isn't it?"

"They perform the same functions as the cards you've been given," the chief administrator said. "What's your point, citizen?"

"This is my point. Whoever cut Ted Pym's arms off, held him down till he died, then disappeared into the night in the centre of New Oxford also has one of those implants." I took in their uneasy expressions. "The killer isn't just a legitimate citizen of your city. The chances are the killer can get into plenty of places you imagine are totally secure."

It looked like they found that observation a lot more indigestible than their dinner.

CHAPTER TWELVE

We were heading out of the Bodleian – or, rather, Noxad – when Doctor Connington came up behind us, his gown billowing and his face crimson.

"You're not following us, are you, proctor?" I said, giving him a hostile look.

"No, no," he stammered. "Of course not. I . . . well, the chief administrator wanted me to make certain things clear to you."

Katharine, Davie and I formed a half circle round him in the brightly lit quadrangle. That didn't put him at ease.

Connington glanced at Katharine. "Em, earlier today you asked about killings in New Oxford. Well, the fact of the matter is that there hasn't been a murder in the centre of the city for over five years. Until the wretched Pym, that is."

The way he stressed the word "centre" caught my attention. "And how many people have been killed outside the centre?" I asked.

"Ah." The proctor was suddenly pensive. "That is a different story. The subs in certain areas are hard to control."

"The subs?" Davie and I said in unison.

Connington nodded. "That is how non-university citizens of New Oxford have been designated."

"What's that short for?" Katharine demanded. "Sub-human?"

The proctor looked affronted. "Certainly not. Subs simply refers to inhabitants of the suburbs beyond the university boundary."

"Couldn't you have found a less demeaning name for them?" Katharine said, her eyes flashing. She was always quick to defend those she perceived as underdogs.

Connington tried to give the impression that he didn't know what she was talking about, but the nervous movement of his lips gave him away.

"You're saying that some of the suburbs are out of control?" I asked before Katharine could savage him more.

The proctor shook his head. "Absolutely not. We maintain order, but with a degree of difficulty. What I wish to draw to your attention is that murders are not unknown in the suburbs, especially those to the south-east of the city centre such as Cowley and Blackbird Leys."

"Ted Pym came from Cowley, didn't he?" I said. "You think he might have been in some kind of trouble there? There was nothing in his personnel file to suggest that. And even if that was the case, why would he have been killed in the university area?"

Connington raised his shoulders. "I don't know, Citizen Dalrymple." He turned away. "Administrator Raphael gave you a free hand," he said over his shoulder. "Use it."

I just managed to restrain myself from using it on him.

Although it was a few minutes after midnight, the door that was inset into the great wooden gate of Brase opened automatically as we approached. The porter we'd met earlier was still on duty and he cast a wary eye over us as we passed his lodge. I guessed his screen was telling him to give us carte blanche, but he didn't look too happy about it.

We walked into the front quad. On the north wall there was an antique sundial under the gabled windows of the top storey. I checked my watch. A mobile spotlight had been rigged up on a cable to replicate the movement of the sun at night. I wasn't sure what to read into that: the light of learning is never extinguished in New Oxford?

Davie waved a hand and went towards his staircase.

Katharine stopped outside hers. "Well, isn't this exciting?" she said with a mocking smile. "A romantic tryst in an ancient seat of contemplation." She came closer. "How about breaking the rules and spending the night in my rooms?" She gave a throaty laugh. "You could see how far that free hand of yours gets."

I glanced around the deserted, preternaturally quiet college. "I told Raphael that there was to be no surveillance on us, but how can we be sure? No one else around here seems to be taking any chances."

Katharine draped her arm round my shoulders and pressed herself against me. "Screw the surveillance. How can you resist a woman in a dress like this?"

I couldn't.

It was just before six when I woke. Katharine's rooms were almost identical to mine and the major drawback to illicit nocturnal activities was the single bed. I'd retired to the floor and spent a night that didn't do my back much good. I got dressed and flitted across the quadrangle, feeling like a fool in the dinner suit trousers with the silk strip down the leg. Fortunately, yet again, there was no one around.

Back in my own rooms, I checked the state of my bag and the files inside. As far as I could tell, nothing had been interfered with. So I had a very quick cold shower and kitted myself out in my own clothes: the black strides and sweatshirt were well-worn and definitely not the height of fashion, but at least they weren't what everyone else was wearing in the university city.

Despite the fact that I'd dined like a dissolute monarch the night before, I felt pangs of hunger. Outside, there were at last signs of movement, a few students scurrying around in their jackets and gowns. The smell of bacon was hanging over the quad in the still morning air. I decided to follow my nose to the hall. Opening my door, I saw a small cardboard box on the floor. It must have been left there while I was changing. For a few seconds I wondered if I'd been presented with a case-breaking clue – an ear, maybe, or another severed finger – but inside all I found was the nostrum I'd asked for, along with a booklet aimed at first-year undergraduates with the title *The Nostrum for Virgins*. Just what I needed.

I followed a group of fresh-faced students into the dining hall. The males' college ties were knotted neatly and their hair was short, back and sides, while the females were all in sober skirts and – believe it or not – blue stockings. The kids seemed to be normal enough, if distinctly well behaved. Their conversations were pretty serious for first thing in the morning: one lot was on about the benefits of free trade, while others were arguing about the laws of thermodynamics. I stuck to filling my tray. The food here was a lot more basic than on the administrators' table, but it was still a hell of a sight better than the Supply Directorate's efforts back home. The bread was wholemeal and healthy, the bacon lean and the tea aromatic – the university probably maintained a plantation on the slopes of Boar's Hill.

I headed for an empty table and sat down. At the far

end of the hall, above what was presumably the high table, an ancient metal door knocker in the shape of a lion's head had been hung on the wall.

"The original brazen nose," said a man who'd arrived silently behind me.

I looked round and took in an elderly specimen with greasy off-white hair. He was wearing a jacket that had almost as much leather patching as tweed on it and his dark blue university tie was spattered with enough stains to keep a forensics operative busy for weeks.

"Ah," I said, swallowing bacon. "I see."

"It dates from the twelfth or thirteenth century," he said, putting his tray down unsteadily. "May I join you?"

"Go ahead." I watched as he strained to swing his leg over the long bench.

"The name's Burton," he said, smiling crookedly and revealing uneven yellow teeth. "Elias Burton." He raised his shoulders apologetically. "I'm afraid you'll have to call me doctor. According to Hebdomadal Council Regulations, all academic staff apart from readers and professors are to be addressed thus." He laughed drily. "Even those, like me, who never bothered to undertake a doctorate."

"I imagine it wasn't a requirement to do so when you started your career," I said, vaguely remembering Hector telling me during our visit that plenty of dons at Oxford weren't doctors. This old man looked like he'd been around since I was in nappies.

"No, it wasn't," he said, looking at me curiously. "And who are you, young man?"

"Quintilian Dalrymple," I said, gratified that at least there was one person in the world who classed forty-four as youthful. "Call me Quint."

Doctor Burton's heavily lined face broke into a smile

that couldn't be said to be attractive. "Well I never," he said, shaking his head. "Who in this benighted land would name their son after the old Roman orator?"

I might have known that my full moniker would be familiar to some of the university's denizens. I went for another point of contact. "My father chose the name," I said. "He was a classicist."

The old don's pale blue eyes opened wide. "Not Hector Dalrymple?" he gasped. "Not the world authority on ancient rhetoric?"

I nodded. "Did you know him?"

Elias Burton twitched his head. "Not personally. But I am familiar with several of his papers. You see, I too am a classicist, though my interests were originally more centred on the Horatian ode." He looked despondently at the pot of marmalade on his tray. "I am one of the few remaining scholars of antiquity in Oxford."

I noticed that he didn't give the university-state its qualifying adjective. "I seem to remember there being hundreds of classicists here."

Burton nodded, then thrust his knife into the marmalade with surprising speed. "Indeed there were. The university was one of the world's major centres for the study of classical languages and literature, as well as history and philosophy." He screwed his face up. "Then the drugs wars came and the old university was torn apart. The—" He broke off and glanced around. Apart from the solemn figures in gowns on the paintings, there was no one in earshot. "The damned modernisers – the so-called administrators who took over the Hebdomadal Council which used to consist of academics – they changed everything when they took control and re-established the university. Now the only courses offered are those judged to serve a vocational purpose. That was a condition of the companies, the multinationals, transnationals, whatever the money-grabbing shysters call themselves, who invested in the place."

I pushed my plate away and concentrated. This old guy was giving me insights into New Oxford that I hadn't got from Raphael and her crew. "So everything's business and science, is it?" I asked, recalling the conversations I'd heard on my way in.

Doctor Burton nodded as he loaded up a piece of toast with dark brown marmalade. "The applied sciences primarily. Biotechnology, software development, engineering, agriculture, that sort of thing. Oh, and I mustn't forget criminology. That's the largest faculty, along with business and economics."

"Criminology?" I said, thinking of the prison in Edinburgh, and Connington's surveillance operations. "What about law?" I seemed to remember plenty of bent politicians who'd read that subject at Oxford in the years leading up to the dissolution of the United Kingdom.

He gave a hollow laugh. "Law? That's nothing more than a minor component of the criminology foundation course that every first-year student must complete. The administrators don't care a fig about law. They rule by decree."

Given Raphael's autocratic demeanour, I wasn't too surprised by that revelation. "Where do all the students come from?" I asked, peering round at the subdued young people with their respectful eyes and old-fashioned clothes. "There aren't many schools left in these islands, are there?"

"Where do you come from yourself?" Burton asked, his watery eyes on me.

I told him.

"Good God," he scoffed. "I heard that Edinburgh was nothing more than a fortified village run by lunatics."

There was something in what he said. I gave him a slightly more objective take on the Council's efforts, though I decided against mentioning that Hector had been a guardian.

"I see," he said when I was done. He finally had enough of the marmalade, screwing the lid on and slipping the jar into his pocket. "Well, your understanding of the state of what used to be Great Britain is somewhat out of date, Quintilian. Although the major cities and towns were severely damaged – most of central London is still under water after the Thames barrier was blown up – several of them have got back on their feet now and instituted local regimes of varying hues. So students do come from the English free cities, but many more originate abroad. The companies sponsor them, you see. The university's nothing but a production line of willing labour nowadays." His voice was bitter.

I saw Davie appear at the hall entrance in his guard uniform and waved to him. "Em, excuse me asking," I said, turning back to Doctor Burton, "but if the courses are all vocational, how come you've still got a job?"

He laughed sharply. "No use for the poetry of Horace in the modern world, you mean? Quite so. That is the administrators' position too. I give a series of lectures on Latin terminology in the sciences." He shook his head. "Pathetic. I have also been compelled to study the economics of early imperial Rome. There are many similarities between Roman trading practices and international business in the 2020s."

"Really? I thought the Romans took what they wanted and wiped out anyone who objected."

The old don looked at me approvingly. "Exactly." He banged his fist on the table. "Of course, I struggle to accomplish my research because so many of Oxford's finest libraries have been closed."

"So I heard. Everything's supposed to be accessible with this." I pointed to the nostrum that I'd hung round my neck.

"Rubbish!" Burton's voice was shrill. "All you can get from the database and the webnet are the basic course materials. In their wisdom the administrators have sold off thousands of the most valuable manuscripts and incunabula to the few foreign universities that still care about original texts."

Well, well. Maybe Raphael wasn't quite as incorruptible as her manner suggested. "What's the webnet?" I asked, remembering that I'd heard the term in Edinburgh.

Davie showed up on the other side of the table, his tray piled high. The students had refrained from staring at his unusual clothing, but Elias Burton's eyes were wide open. I introduced them then gestured to the doctor to go on.

"Where were we? Ah yes, the webnet. It's the university's version of the Internet – remember that virtual monstrosity?"

I nodded. In the years before independence in Edinburgh the role of the global network in promoting civil disorder and drugs trafficking had become a major issue. Then the violence erupted and personal computers disappeared from the "perfect" city, leaving the Internet a virtual void.

"Obviously a restrictive utopia like this one can't allow its population access to the real Net," Burton said ironically. "So they've set up their own. Highly controlled, highly censored – there's no pornography, for example – and highly tedious. I never bother with it myself." He was gazing at Davie. "What's that uniform?" he asked. He turned to me. "What exactly are you people doing here?"

I stood up and beckoned Davie to follow suit. He glared at me and started stuffing toast into his pockets. "I don't think you want to know that," I said, smiling at the don. "Thanks for the background information."

"Think nothing of it," Burton replied. "I've enjoyed letting off steam. Perhaps we'll meet again, Quintilian Dalrymple."

I moved away, then stopped. "I don't suppose you attended the Innes Lecture back in 2000? It was at Christ Church."

Elias Burton gave what looked to me like an involuntary start then, after a long pause, shook his head. "No, I don't think so," he said. "Your father? I would have remembered, I'm sure. I must have been . . . must have been on sabbatical." He turned to the front again. "Farewell."

"Goodbye, doctor," I said, steering clear of the archaic term that seemed to be standard in New Oxford.

As I headed for the door, I thought about his reaction to the college my old man had lectured at. That was the second time a reference to Christ Church had provoked a startled response. Maybe, even these days, it was full of upper-class loudmouths with beagles and hunting horns who drove everyone else in the city to distraction.

We met Katharine in the quadrangle.

"I wondered if I'd find you in the dining hall," she said, watching as Davie retrieved a piece of toast from his pocket.

"I wasn't allowed to stay for long," he complained.

"Sorry, big man," I said. "I reckoned I'd dallied with that old academic long enough."

Katharine was playing with her gleaming new nostrum. "Did you not find the breakfast facility in your rooms?" she said.

That explained why the hall hadn't been very busy.

"No." Davie sounded even more aggrieved.

"If you'd bothered to familiarise yourself with your nostrum, you'd have found all sorts of useful things." She moved her fingers dextrously over the miniature keys. "I don't fancy talking into machines so I've been using the touch facility." She looked up. "For instance, you can activate the hot water in your shower."

I let out a groan. "That would have been good." Apparently New Oxford wasn't as Spartan as I'd thought.

"As well as get a delivery of coffee and rolls from the flap next to your desk that you probably didn't even notice." Katharine eyed Davie. "Though no doubt you'd still have made a visit to the hall, guardsman."

Davie concentrated on swallowing.

"All right, children," I said, looking at the sundial on the wall across the quad. The shadow it cast was accurate even though the sun hadn't got above the college walls yet. "Time for a plan."

"Aye," Davie said, brushing crumbs from his uniform. "Where are we going? The murder scene?"

I shook my head. "Maybe later. After all, we've already seen it in Quadrihypervision. The first priority is the bullet that took out Lewis Hamilton."

Katharine looked up. "Aren't we trying to find a connection between the murder here and what happened to Lewis Hamilton? The guy in Dead Man's Walk wasn't shot."

"No," I said, setting off round the lawn towards the gate. "But he was a cleaner in the Department of Metallurgy. I want to check out his place of work."

"Because the bullet was made of metal?" Davie said doubtfully.

"We've got to start somewhere," I said, glancing round.

Neither of them looked particularly enthusiastic about that line of enquiry.

Trout and Perch were standing on the kerb that ran round the Radcliffe Camera. Next to them was a medium-sized Chariot, its transparent shell shining brightly even in the early morning light.

"Two faithful bulldogs ready for a walk," Katharine said under her breath.

"We're not taking them anywhere," I said as I headed over. "Is this ours?" I asked.

Trout nodded once. "The activation code is 37 Morris."

"Right," I said. "I don't expect to see you two again today," I added.

"You won't," Perch said, a vertical vein in his forehead pulsing. Maybe his bowler hat was too tight.

We climbed into the Chariot, Davie taking the front seat. Katharine and I got in behind.

"You do realise that you can be a back-seat driver in this contraption," I said, taking my old man's battered Oxford guidebook from my pocket.

"Forget it, Quint," Katharine said. "If you drive, I'm going on foot."

"I don't know what you've got against my driving," I said, finding the city plan in the book.

Davie spoke the activation code and prompted a quiet hum from the Chariot's power system. He turned round. "Do you want a fully itemised list of complaints?" he asked.

"All right, all right," I said. "I'll stick to navigating."

"Good," he said. "Where to?"

I held the map out to him. "Let's take a tour to acclimatise ourselves."

Davie nodded and read out the name of the street I was pointing at. The Chariot moved away, gliding sinuously round the bicycles and pedestrians.

Looking up at the great panelled ball on the top of the Camera, I wondered if the proctor and his outfit were watching where we went. Despite Administrator Raphael's agreement to my terms, I was pretty sure that no surveillance wasn't an option in New Oxford.

"God, this is spectacular," Katharine gasped as we moved along Broad Street.

I couldn't fault her judgement. The golden-hued stones of the old buildings were cleaner than I remembered them. There was little sign of drugs war damage to the Clarendon Building's massive four-columned Doric portico designed by Hawksmoor. A couple of the lead muses on the roof that my guidebook referred to seemed to have disappeared though.

"That's the Hebdomadal Council Block," Katharine said, looking up from her nostrum.

I could see a grid on her screen, with red lettering around it. "Is that a street plan you've accessed?" I asked.

She nodded. "Central University Area High Definition Map is the file." She glanced at my book. "They seem to have changed that building's name and function."

I nodded. Raphael and her fellow administrators had certainly left their mark: the Bodleian renamed Noxad, this pile bearing the name of the city's ruling body.

"What does your map call this?" I asked, pointing at the D-shaped structure behind the railings and their oversize stone heads. When I was last in Oxford most of them had been festooned with college scarves or traffic bollards, but the contemporary student body was leaving them well alone. Were the students just well behaved by nature or did they live in fear?

"The Mendoza Memorial Theatre," Katharine replied.

"Amazing," I said. "They've changed its name."

Katharine's fingers moved rapidly over the nostrum keys. "The description says that the former Sheldonian Theatre was one of Sir Christopher Wren's least successful buildings, an ineffectual and unimaginative copy of a Roman theatre."

Trust the new regime to have the last word. I looked to the right and took in the cottages that stood in front of Trinity College's open garden space. At least that was how my guide put it. In reality there was a fifty-foot-high, windowless concrete block stretching up behind the humble buildings on the Broad.

"What the hell's that?" I asked.

Katharine's fingers played again. "Don't know," she answered after a pause. "There's nothing about it in the Trin College description." She looked at the concrete monstrosity again. "I'm not surprised. It's unsuccessful, ineffectual and unimaginative."

"Aye," Davie said. "But this heap's even worse." He told the Chariot to stop and we gazed out at the nightmare building on our right.

"Hang on . . ." Katharine fiddled with her nostrum then shook her head. "It doesn't say anything about this place at all, doesn't even show the outline of the walls on the map."

I didn't have to look at the guidebook to remind myself what used to stand here. Balliol College was one of the few that had stuck in my sixteen-year-old mind: first because Hector had gone on about its Scottish connections and its intellectual traditions; and second because

I'd watched a group of underdressed female students playing volleyball on the lawn outside the dining hall while he was talking to some classics don. What had then been drab Victorian Gothic walls had now disappeared, replaced by a great metal-sheathed block that must have been a hundred yards long and at least twenty high. Like the concrete lump in Trinity, this construction had no windows, its smooth silver walls as out of place in the street where Cranmer and his friends were burned in the sixteenth century as a carbuncle on a child's face. The administrators had certainly had a ball with what used to be Balliol.

We took a right turn on to Magdalen Street then headed north towards the science zone. Although I could recognise the main buildings and monuments in the guide, there was more evidence of reconstruction and repair. What was the Taylorian Institute, now apparently the headquarters of the Criminology Faculty, still retained its neo-classical columns and entablatures, but the windows were shuttered in heavy steel. So too the façade of St John's College – no doubt known as the john if there were any piss-artists remaining in Oxford – was patterned with replacement blocks that were much lighter in colour than the original blackened stone. Presumably a drugs gang had used the place where Charles I and Archbishop Laud once held sway to try out every one of their weapons.

"Seen enough sights?" Davie asked as we moved out of the city centre, past lines of trees with bright pink and white blossom.

"For the time being," I replied, nodding thoughtfully. Everything I'd seen so far was telling me that a lot of major changes had been made to Oxford. That impression wasn't reversed by the sight of the polychromatic brick walls and chimneys of Keble College, which Katharine informed me was now called Keeb – it still looked like a High Victorian public lavatory. The Hebdomadal Council had obviously attracted plenty of funding for the university; but why had Raphael's coterie spent so much of it on buildings that looked more like concrete bridge caissons than colleges?

"Where to now?" Davie asked as we drew up at a corner with a view across the university parks. According to the old man's guide, they accommodated numerous rugby pitches in the winter, as well as the pavilion used by the university cricket team in summer. Now there was a vast tented encampment beyond high barbed-wire fences. Katharine's nostrum wasn't forthcoming about what went on there either. I almost headed for the heavy metal gate to see if the free access I'd been promised applied in the parks, but the muscle-bound bulldogs inside put me off.

"Let's hit the Department of Metallurgy," I said.

Davie repeated the direction and the Chariot turned obediently to the right. It was time to find out what the top-secret research project that had produced the bullet was all about.

The university science area started opposite Keeb, nondescript twentieth-century buildings interspersed with tall modern towers of glass and steel. There were even more sensor posts around here and numerous pairs of bulldogs were on patrol, their hands behind their backs. It struck me that New Oxford's police officers didn't carry any obvious weaponry. I wondered how they managed to handle the suburbs where, according to Connington, murders were perpetrated. Maybe their bowler hats were more sophisticated than they looked.

The access codes that had been fed into our control cards seemed to work all right. We were allowed to proceed to a squat block of dark glass.

"Nice place," Katharine said ironically. "Looks a bit like that insurance company building by the big swimming pool back home."

"I hope it doesn't end up the way that place did," Davie said. "At least not when we're inside." After the last election in 2003 a mob of citizens whose savings had gone walkabout vented their wrath, among other things, on the building. It experienced meltdown, literally.

There was a screen with the department's name above a panel that didn't look like a door, but which slid open at our approach. Inside, the atmosphere was antiseptic, hardly any noise audible. I thought I'd walked into a vacuum and was relieved to find that my lungs managed to find something to work on.

"State your business."

We glanced around but failed to locate the speaker.

"State your business." The voice was metallic and neutral, though this time it seemed to be slightly louder.

"Quint Dalrymple," I said. "Here on the authority of the Hebdomadal Council."

There was a pause while the voice's owner – human? mechanical? – gave my words some thought. Then there was a low hiss and a section of the floor in front of us started to open, revealing a short staircase leading downwards.

"Enter," said the unseen receptionist. "Doctor Verzeni will be with you shortly."

Well, well. Look, or rather hear, who was here. We followed the instructions and found ourselves in a long, narrow corridor.

"See if your card lets you in anywhere, Davie," I said,

pointing down the passage. There were no obvious doorways, but those hadn't been a feature of the department so far.

Davie presented himself to the dark glass walls at regular intervals. They remained solid. He moved to the other side. "Here, Quint," he called. "There's some kind of sign here."

Katharine and I went down the corridor. At eye level on the wall there was a small dark blue metal plaque embossed with four letters in white.

"N-B-W-T," Katharine read. "What do you think—?"

"Bingo," I said.

They stared at me.

"All right, smartarse," Davie said when I held my peace. "Tell us what it stands for."

"When Raphael was telling me about the bullet on the helijet, she mentioned the name of the company that developed it." I nodded at them. "This is it. Nox Ballistics and Weapons Technology."

"As you say, citizen, this is it."

I turned to find that Doctor Verzeni had crept up on us. He was wearing a pristine white lab coat and there was a tight smile on his olive-coloured face.

"Come into my lair," he said with an extravagant flourish of his arms. Either that or the word he spoke in an undertone made the floor suddenly jolt beneath our feet.

"Shit!" Davie grunted as Katharine and I each grabbed one of his arms.

Verzeni was standing with his feet set apart on the square lift platform that had dropped downwards. "I wasn't expecting you, citizen," he said mildly. "You should have let me know you were coming."

"Like you didn't know," I muttered, certain that the

Chariot had been observed heading in his direction. "I wasn't expecting to find you here. You never mentioned that you were a metallurgist." Then I remembered his interest when I questioned Raphael and his colleagues about the bullet after it self-destructed.

"Didn't I?" he replied, blinking. "You never asked."

"Did you design the bullet that put the public order guardian down?" I demanded.

"Patience, citizen," Verzeni said as the lift came down in the middle of a large, well-lit laboratory. "That's exactly what I'm going to explain."

And he did – after a fashion. In the next hour he took us through the design specifications of the Eagle One and showed us the projectile in both integrated and disassembled forms. Even though I'd seen it before, it still raised the hairs on the back of my neck. The shell was as long and as thick as an all-in wrestler's thumb, and the burnished alloy casing tapered to a vicious point at the contact end. But the contents took my breath away even more. There were circuit boards, armatures, wiring systems, Christ knows what else; all so tiny that high magnification was necessary for us to make them out.

"What are the capabilities of this bullet?" I asked when the doctor paused. "You admit that it has an anti-tamper device?" I tried to keep a grip on myself as I remembered what that had done to Sophia's face.

Verzeni nodded. "It wasn't clear to us initially that an Eagle One had been used on Lewis Hamilton, but . . ." His voice trailed away.

"What else can it do?" I said, keeping the pressure on him. "What was the rationale behind its development?"

The Italian stood up straight, his lower lip between his teeth. "The Eagle One has a unique command facility which enables the shooter to control what level of damage is done to the target. It can produce an explosion that will destroy a small building. It can disintegrate into enough fine shrapnel to disable dozens of people." Verzeni looked at the object on the surface in front of him. "It can also be programmed to penetrate up to three metres of concrete or steel."

"Jesus," Davie said. "Sounds like the chief got off lightly."

"Exactly," I agreed, staring at the doctor. "What happened in Edinburgh? Why wasn't Hamilton blown to pieces?" I shivered as I remembered what had happened in Trigger Finger's lab. "Why weren't we killed when it did finally detonate?"

Verzeni was chewing his lip again. "Ah. Yes, well, incorporated into the Eagle One is another top-secret device." He ran his forefinger over the projectile's surface and returned my gaze. "Its programmed activity can be altered after firing."

"What?" I leaned back against the workbench and tried to make sense of what he was saying. "You mean that whoever shot Lewis Hamilton rendered the charge inert?"

The Italian nodded. "Precisely. The Eagle One was subject to massive deceleration immediately before impact, meaning that it caused no potentially fatal exit wound."

That explained the curious sound I'd heard seconds before Lewis hit the ground.

"If the guardian's heart had withstood the shock of the impact," Verzeni continued, "he would probably have survived."

"But surely there isn't enough time for the shooter to do anything after the trigger's been pulled?" Katharine said.

Verzeni opened his eyes wide. "Yes, there is. That is exactly what we have managed to achieve. The software is so sophisticated that, in effect, it overrides the normal constrictions of time."

"What?" I was struggling to grasp what the academic was saying.

Davie's face was grim. "So the shooter attempted to minimise the trauma suffered by the public order guardian. Why?"

Neither Verzeni nor any of the rest of us came up with an answer to that.

CHAPTER THIRTEEN

Davie was studying the projectile from a few inches' range. "What kind of weapon fires a monster like this?" he asked, straightening his back.

Doctor Verzeni regarded him thoughtfully. I reckoned he was struggling to reconcile the free access Raphael had given us with an inbuilt tendency to extreme secrecy. Finally he led us over to an empty glass cabinet and put his hand into a slot; presumably it was some kind of fingerprint sensor. There rose up before us a collection of what initially looked like junk, an array of black plastic tubes and rectangular boxes. It suddenly began to move when Verzeni gave an almost inaudible command.

"What's going on?" Katharine asked, her eyes wide.

"It's a system we've been developing in conjunction with the Department of Cybernetics," the doctor said. "The Advanced Self Assembling Rifle, or ASAR, is designed for undercover operations."

I watched as the weapon took shape in front of me. When the movements ceased, it still didn't resemble any rifle I'd ever seen. The barrel was short and thick, while the main assembly consisted of several irregular compartments. I could see no sign of a sight or a trigger. The whole device wasn't much more than a foot in length.

Verzeni spoke in an undertone again and the ASAR came to life, a series of underlit screens appearing on the rear surfaces of the rectangular components. "Sighting, control and firing units engaged," the Italian said. "All the materials are completely secure. They cannot be detected by any surveillance or search systems."

"Undercover operations?" Davie asked. "You run a lot of those in New Oxford, do you?"

Verzeni gave him a superior look. "We have no need of such activities in this city. The ASAR and the Eagle One are purely for export." He gave a patronising smile. "They have been extremely successful in several locations around the world."

"Not least in Edinburgh," I said. "Who has access to the weapon and ammunition, you murdering bastard?"

The metallurgist's head snapped back. "No one," he answered. "No one apart from me and the administrators."

I stared at him to register my disbelief then changed tack. "Ted Pym. The murdered cleaner. Did he work in this part of the department?"

Verzeni was watching the ASAR as it obeyed his instruction to disassemble. "I believe the proctor has provided you with the sub's file," he replied in an offhand manner.

That got me going again. "The sub, as you call him, was cut to pieces," I yelled, aware that the heads of all the researchers in the vicinity had turned towards us. "I've read the file but I want to hear about him from you as well, doctor."

The scientist gave me a look of measured contempt. "Do you imagine I concern myself with the cleaners, citizen?"

"Did he work in this area?" I demanded, keeping the volume up. "Yes or no?"

Verzeni drew himself back like a cobra about to strike. "I believe so," he answered in a low voice. "According to the records, he was in this lab on the night he died."

"No surveillance cameras in here?" Davie said.

The Italian shook his head. "All the equipment is fully protected and alarmed. There is no need for visual observation."

I wondered about that but let it go. It was about time we checked out the suburb where the dead man came from.

I only realised it was drizzling when I stepped on to the road beside the Chariot. The rain shields around the Department of Metallurgy had protected us until then; only in the city centre did the shields extend all the way across the streets.

"It must be weird when those shields get a dark tint in the summer," Katharine said as she climbed in.

"Weird is par for the course in this place," I said.

Davie activated the Chariot.

"Rain dispersal system in operation," stated a robotic voice.

We watched the windscreen as the vehicle pulled away. Who knows how it worked, but there wasn't a single drop of water anywhere on the transparent canopy, despite the absence of wipers.

"I'm surprised they haven't got a mechanism that sends the clouds to Cambridge," Katharine said.

"Ha." I glanced at her. "That's a point. Do you think a university still exists over there?"

She shrugged. "Who knows? Who cares?"

I'd never heard her views on élitist education, but I could believe she wasn't a fan. I hadn't been one myself when I grew up in pre-independence Edinburgh. Until now it had been a dead issue since the Council was committed to lifelong education for all its citizens. Seeing New Oxford with its incongruous blend of dinner-jacketed, gown-clad tradition and progressive high-tech had brought the debate back to mind. The old don Elias Burton had told me that students came from the former United Kingdom as well as from abroad. I wondered how many of them came from places like Cowley.

The Chariot was taking us down what my father's guidebook described as "dreary modernistic buildings" on South Parks Road. There were some fairly dreary-looking students in corduroys and gowns in evidence too. Then we were round a couple of corners and heading down Longwall Street to the High. The grandiose buildings of Magd where the helijet had landed were on our left.

"Do you think this will get us anywhere, Quint?" Davie asked, looking over his shoulder.

"You told the Chariot to take us to Cowley, didn't you, big man?"

"Very funny," he growled. "I mean, how are we going to find out why Ted Pym was killed by asking around in the suburb? Surely the answer's in the university area."

I nodded. "You're probably right." I looked out as we crossed Magdalen Bridge and approached a roundabout. "But maybe the so-called subs will be a bit more forthcoming than the academic tight arses like Verzeni."

"Aye, maybe," he conceded. "On the other hand, they might just tell us to make enemas out of our questions like they do in the Edinburgh suburbs."

He had a point.

There were some buildings around the junction that bore a resemblance to the worst barracks blocks that had been erected back home. There was also a construction faced with red tiles and standing on stilts that combined grandstand and giant's pissoir very imaginatively, if you like that kind of thing.

Signs on the roundabout exits proclaimed the start of separate suburban zones, each with its own checkpoint. Vehicles like ours which were programmed with the appropriate authorisation weren't bothered, but individuals pedalling bicycles had to stop to flash passes at bowler-hatted bulldogs. Those individuals were wearing clothes that definitely didn't come from the university outfitters: loose-fitting denim trousers, jackets in bright check material and heavy workboots. Most of the men had hair down to their shoulders and were unshaven.

"No more rain shields," Katharine said, pointing upwards.

She was right. The subs had been left out in the rain and they weren't enjoying it. The drizzle had turned to a much heavier downpour and pedestrians were bending their heads as they struggled down the Cowley Road. Some of them gave the Chariot hostile looks. It moved rapidly past unkempt shops and under-maintained two-up two-down housing; the gas line that fuelled it apparently continued down here. It wasn't long before I discovered why the infrastructure was organised that way. The university had more interest in the suburbs than I'd thought.

"Bloody hell," Davie gasped. "What's this?"

"The university's engine room," I replied, clocking the large screen in front of the complex of tall, white, corrugated-metal buildings. It read "NOX Industry Park No. 1". Underneath the luminous red letters was a long list of company names, most of them prefaced by the New Oxford abbreviation and many of them containing the words "digital", "hyper-conductor", "software" and "technology".

Katharine sniffed and grimaced. "It's noxious enough around here, all right."

"You kill me, Katharine," Davie said, looking past her at me. "What do you mean, the university's engine room, Quint?"

"This is how it makes economic sense," I replied, recalling what the old don had told me about the transnational companies and their sponsorship of research and development. The names of major concerns that I could remember from the early years of the century were on the display too. "It's a business, not an educational foundation. The administrators have set things up so that every faculty makes a pot of money."

Katharine grabbed her seat. "Where are we going now?"

The Chariot had made a sudden turn on to a wide carriageway and was hurtling northwards, overtaking slow-moving trucks that looked similar to the vehicle we were in but were ten times larger. Stacks of boxes and containers were visible through their canopies. I wondered where they were going. If it was true that New Oxford was surrounded by the so-called Poison Fields, perhaps there was a commercial helijet base somewhere outside the university boundary.

"Ah, I've got it," Katharine said, her nostrum in operation. "Ted Pym lived in Appleby Terrace. It's the next left."

Sure enough, the Chariot slipped smoothly off the main road and entered a housing estate that had seen better days; better days about fifty years ago, judging by the overgrown gardens, the plastic sheeting that was replacing many of the windows and the spatter of missing tiles.

Despite the rain, ragged children were playing in a desultory way between the potholes in the street. The Chariot wove competently round both kids and cavities, having informed us that it was switching to its onboard fuel tank. No gas lines in this neighbourhood.

"Number thirty-two," Katharine said. "This is it."

The vehicle hissed to a halt on Davie's command. He told his door panel to open, then hurriedly changed his mind. "Close!" he yelled.

The three of us leaned towards the onside and I felt the Chariot cant over before its computerised suspension got a grip. A large black dog with foam-specked jaws was snarling at us from the pavement. Then it made the mistake of jumping up against the transparent plastic. There was a sharp crack and it arced back through the air in a spray of urine, landing on its back.

"Shit." Katharine was out before I could stop her. She kneeled down beside the beast and stroked its head. Then she looked round at us. "Get out, you cowards," she said angrily. "Our bastard Chariot has dealt with the poor thing."

Davie and I squatted down beside the motionless dog.

"Is it dead?" he asked.

Katharine shook her head. "No, I can feel a pulse." She glanced back at the vehicle. "The bloody plastic cuddy must have turned on an anti-tamper device as soon as we entered the suburb."

I watched as she eased the dog on to its side, then saw two pairs of small feet appear on the uneven paving slabs nearby.

"What you done to Shelley?" asked a small girl with a muddy face.

"They topped her, Fran," said a boy with long blond hair and a fine collection of dried snot.

"No, we didn't," Katharine said gently. "She went too close to the Chariot." She smiled at them. "You make sure you stay away, okay?"

They nodded uncertainly then looked round at the sound of quick footsteps.

"Fran, Rex, what you doing?" The woman's voice was on the edge. "What happened to Shell?"

I stood up and opened my arms. "Sorry . . . she jumped up on the vehicle . . ."

"Who the fuck are you?" The voice was harsh now. "What the fuck you done to my dog?"

"We . . . we're—" I broke off, wondering how to explain myself. "You're Mrs Pym?"

She looked at me uncomprehendingly. "That's old language," she said, her eyes screwed up. "I'm Maddy Pitt." She stared at the comatose dog and then at Katharine, whose smile seemed to encourage her. "I lived with Ted, if that's what you mean."

I nodded. "We're trying to find your husband's . . ." I was suddenly aware of the children's blank faces. "We're investigating—"

"You're not bulldogs," she interrupted, her eyes now fixed on Davie's guard uniform. "Who are you?"

There was a murmur of voices and I realised that a crowd of people was gathering in the street.

"Trouble, Maddy?" called a large, long-haired man in a dirty vest which displayed his massive biceps.

She glanced at me again. "I don't think so, Pete. I'll let you know." She smiled briefly and her face was transformed. Although she was young, her drooping shoulders and aggressive demeanour had made me think she was the kind of citizen that pushed around a wheelbarrow full of grudges. Now I could see that she was a fighter. "You better come inside, whoever you are," she said. "Shelley'll be all right. It's not the first time she's got herself pulsed."

"Pulsed?" I said, following her up the uneven path.

"You're not from Oxford, are you?" she said, looking back at me. "Didn't you see the warning signs all round the industry park: 'Danger – Unauthorised Personnel Will Be Pulsed'?" She held the flimsy front door open. "Just one way to keep us in our place."

I walked into a surprisingly well-kept living room. The furniture was basic and old, but the place was clean – no sign of any dog hairs – and the small collection of ornaments on the ancient television was neatly arranged and dusted. The volume was low, but it was still easy enough to see how much of a moron the man wearing a floral suit was. He was running some sort of quiz show and he was egging the contestants on like their lives depended on getting the answer right. Maybe they did.

"You kids, go and play upstairs," Maddy Pitt said, her voice soft now. "It's too wet outside."

"What about Shelley?" said the little girl.

"Don't worry," Katharine said, stroking her hair and smiling. "I'll keep an eye on her."

Maddy shooed her children out then eyed us dubiously. "What you want then? You must be working for the bulldogs even if you're not wearing stupid hats. Otherwise you wouldn't have a Chariot."

"We're not working for the bulldogs," I said. "The administrators have asked us to investigate your man's death."

"Why?" she demanded.

"Because it might be linked to one in our city," Katharine said.

"Where's that then?" Maddy said.

"Edinburgh," Davie replied, pointing to the maroon heart on his tunic.

"Never heard of it." The Oxford woman turned away and took a silver packet from the dresser. "Smoke?"

We shook our heads.

"They're safe," she said. "No cancer." She stared at the packet. "'Least that's what they tell us. Course, people still end up in the hospital."

I glanced round and realised there was a complete absence of books, magazines, any kind of reading material in the room. "Edinburgh," I repeated. "It's in Scotland."

"Never heard of it," she repeated.

"Didn't you do geography at school?" Davie asked. "Or history? Or modern studies?"

Maddy Pitt looked at him and laughed. "School? There aren't any schools out here."

Christ. The significance of the term "sub" was beginning to become apparent.

After ten minutes of jousting, Maddy seemed to decide that we were at least worth opening up to. I got the impression that the bulldogs investigating Ted Pym's death hadn't shown much interest. She produced a tray with tea and some hairy-chested oatmeal biscuits that Davie approved of.

"So have you got any idea—?" I broke off and stared at the TV. "Can't you turn that thing off?"

She shook her head. "You can't turn it off," she said. "Or cover it up. Or put the boot into it – unless you want the bulldogs round. Only thing is to turn the volume down and I've already done that." She looked at me curiously. "Anyway, there's nothing wrong with *Want to Make a Mint?*. It's the only way you can get a better house or give your kids a chance of going to boarding school in the centre – though they're prisons like everywhere else in this fucking place and I'm not sending Fran and Rex there, no matter what the dogs say, I'm not and . . ." She ran out of words and let out a desperate sigh.

I looked at the television again and saw that it formed an integral unit with its frame, the legs of which were welded to the floor.

Maddy caught the direction of my gaze. "It's on all day from six in the morning to eleven at night. All you can do is drown it out with the O-blues." She smiled crookedly. "But if we do that, you won't have any chance of hearing what I say."

"The O-blues?" I said. "What are they?"

Katharine's eyes flipped upwards. She'd never shared my passion for the devil's music.

"The sound of the suburbs," Maddy said. "A mixture of old rhythms and guitar crash. The Cowley version's definitely the best."

It obviously had nothing much to do with any other kind of Oxford blues.

"Get on with it, Quint," Katharine said.

"Right." I looked at the woman who'd lived with the dead man and wondered if she had anything useful to impart. "Your man Ted," I began.

"He wasn't dirty," Maddy Pitt said, her words coming out in a rush again. "The dogs never caught him for nothing." Her eyes were wild and she'd taken a step towards me, fists balled. "He wasn't like some of them out here."

I nodded, trying to placate her. "I know. There was nothing in his personnel file."

She stared at me, her expression gradually slackening. "I mean . . . he . . ." She turned to the tray and busied herself with the teapot.

"What do you mean, Maddy?" Katharine asked, warning Davie and me off with a stern look. "You said he wasn't like some of them."

The woman raised her head slowly then shook it. "Leave me alone," she said in a low voice. "I don't know you." She let out a sob. "You can't bring Ted back." She started to weep quietly.

"What the fuck are you doing to her?" The heavily built guy she'd called Pete had appeared at the door. He barged in, heading straight towards me.

Davie had him in a neck lock before he even got close.

After a few minutes things calmed down. A crowd of locals had blocked the light from the front window, their faces fierce. They stayed where they were when they saw how Davie was holding Pete. Katharine spoke to Maddy Pitt while I tried to convince the man in the vest that we had nothing to do with the bulldogs. Eventually he nodded his agreement to my suggestion that he send his friends away. Davie wasn't convinced we were in the clear, but he loosened his grip and the stand-off turned into a sit-down.

"This is Pete Pym," Maddy said, handing the big man a mug of tea. "Ted's brother."

Pete glanced at Davie, who was between him and the door. "Fair enough," he said. "You can't be undercover dogs wearing rags like those." He grinned. "I'll get you, Black Beard. Where did you learn that lock?"

Davie looked down as Maddy's dog wandered unsteadily into the room, and patted her head. "Never you mind, pal. I've got plenty more to show you if you're interested."

"All right, boys," I interjected. "Shall we get on?"

Pete Pym peered at me suspiciously. "Get on with what?"

"We're trying to find your brother's killer," I said. "Can you help us?"

He shrugged. "Too late to do anything for Ted now," he said, shaking his head.

"But not too late for other people," I said. I told him what had happened to George Faulds back home, leaving out the differences between the cases. "Have you any idea why Ted might have been chosen as a victim?" I looked at Maddy Pitt. "What did you mean when you said your man wasn't like some out here?"

She glanced at Pete nervously. "I . . . I just meant he had a clean record."

I looked at the victim's brother. "Come on, give us a hand, Pete. We're not going to put the bulldogs on to you."

"Wouldn't care if you did," he said with a grunt. "I've been inside most of their fucking prisons."

I stared at him. "Most of their prisons? How many are there? And what did you mean about undercover bull-dogs? I was told that they didn't run that kind of operation in New Oxford."

Pete and Maddy both burst out laughing.

"Come on, mate," the victim's brother scoffed. "What did you say your name was again?"

"Call me Quint."

"Well, Quint, it seems to me you need an education." He grunted again. "And not the kind they give those poncey fucking students up town." He looked at Maddy. "I hope I'm not cocking up here, opening up to these foreign goons."

She took in Katharine's encouraging smile, thought for a bit then shook her head.

"All right," Pete said, pulling back his arms and watching the muscles ripple. "Here's how it is."

What he said turned out to be more than a little enlightening.

"Where are you taking him?" the bulldog at the checkpoint on the slip road off the bypass demanded. This time the Chariot had stopped automatically because Pete Pym didn't have the necessary access code.

"Murder investigation," I replied. "We have full Hebdomadal Council authority."

The bulldog looked up from his nostrum. "I can see that. I still need to know where you're taking him."

Davie leaned across. "Look, he's not co-operating. I'm going to find a secluded spot and beat the shit out of him."

Pym let out a high-pitched moan.

The bulldog cast his eyes round the inside of the Chariot then smiled at Davie. "Very good. Let us know if you need any help."

That brought another petrified whine from Pym.

The vehicle moved off smoothly and in a few minutes we were passing through thick woodland. There was no sign of anybody and Pete Pym gave us the nod.

Davie told the Chariot to stop. "Right, you sack of pus," he said, turning to Pym. "Out."

We all stepped down, our feet sinking into the mulchy forest floor. Katharine and I followed as Davie dragged the prisoner deep into the dank undergrowth.

Pete ran his eye over us as we gathered round him. "Okay," he said, completing the check. "No Nox gear, no nostrums?" We all shook our heads, having left the devices in the vehicle on his whispered instruction. "We're out of range of the Chariot's surveillance system now."

"I got agreement from the chief administrator that we wouldn't be subject to surveillance of any kind," I said.

Pym laughed. "Did you, Quint? Bloody good for you. And you believed the cow?"

I raised my shoulders.

"We rigged up an anti-snooping field in Appleby Street last month," he said, "so what was said in Maddy's place shouldn't have got back to the bastards. But your visit will have made them suspicious. That's why we're playing this game."

I examined the burly figure leaning against a gnarled oak trunk. He looked more like a fairground heavy than someone capable of standing up to Raphael's system.

"Why didn't we stay there if it's secure?" Davie asked.

Pete Pym's face was split by a broad grin that displayed gaps between dirty teeth. "I told you – they'll have sent a squad to Maddy's by now. Besides, I want to show you something, Black Beard." He turned towards the tree. "But first I need to make it look like you roughed me up." He drew back his head and smashed it three or four times into the damp green bark. A blackbird burst out of the bushes, its cries of alarm echoing through the trees.

I swallowed hard. Headbanging was never one of my favourite pursuits.

"See that?" Pete pointed to the east.

We were on the summit of a wooded hill, fields and distant buildings stretching away in front of us. The rain had stopped and the sun had begun to burn off the few remaining clouds.

Davie was looking through a pair of City Guard-issue pocket binoculars that he'd taken from his breast pocket. "Some kind of blockhouse," he said. "There are a lot of people on the land near it."

Pym nodded. He must have been having difficulty seeing anything. The skin above his eyes was broken and there was blood around his eyes, not that he seemed to care.

"Chain gang," he said, shaking his long hair back from his face. "Planting spuds."

"So much for high-tech agriculture," I muttered.

Pete Pym turned to me. "Oh, they've got modern machines, all right. They use them in other areas. The eastern parts are punishment zones." He laughed humourlessly. "The eastern parts and the centre of New Oxford itself." He pointed to the left of the chain gang. "Over there – see those low buildings? – they're a children's prison." He swung his arm round. "Down there, that village is what they call a family detention unit. I was in that with my woman and our six nippers."

"What did you do?" Katharine asked.

"Me? Nothing." Pym's eyes narrowed. "Our Kevin, he got picked up with his mates. They nicked a Chariot, messed about with the command system and went hot rodding in it. All the families got banged up for six months of something called intensive social skills."

I raised a hand. "Hang on, Pete. You're moving too fast."

He glanced around. "I'm also taking a big fucking risk standing out here in the open with you. Get back in the woods."

We followed him into the cover, Katharine giving me a puzzled look.

"Start from the beginning, Pete," I said, squatting down beside him. "You're making New Oxford sound like a prison-state."

The big man clapped his heavy hands together slowly. "Well done, son. That's exactly what it is."

I looked at him in disbelief. "Come on, there's more to

it than that. Nox is all about the university and the money it can make."

"I'm not disagreeing with you," he said. "As far as you've gone. All right, history lesson." He grinned. "You're in luck. I actually went to school and learned to read and write. They don't give many of our kids that chance these days. Anyway, the city got fucked up big-time during the drugs wars."

"Like most places," Davie put in. "Including Edinburgh."

"Okay, Scottish git," Pym said with a laugh. "I'm not saying we got it any worse than the rest of you." His face darkened. "Not in the beginning, at least. Except the farmland all over central England got polluted to buggery by those arsehole big companies with their arsehole chemical fertilisers and their arsehole genetically modified crops. Not to mention the thousands of cattle with BSE that were buried all over the place when the disease came back strong in 2005."

"The Poison Fields," I said.

He looked impressed. "You know about them? That's a start. Anyway, they were a disaster for everyone else, but a godsend for the scumbags who wanted to set up the university again." He stood up and moved an arm round in a great sweep. "The Poison Fields were an excuse for them to cut the city off from prying eyes."

I nodded, remembering how the first Council had done the same thing with Edinburgh, blowing the bridges and railway lines, blocking the roads and putting up high fences on the borders.

"You had the same kind of thing, did you?" Pete asked. "Yeah, well, the administrators managed to attract money from the big companies – the same fuckers who'd destroyed the UK, of course – and they got the university going again." He raised a thick forefinger. "But on a lot of conditions." He slapped the finger against the flesh of his palm. "One: they were only to teach courses the companies wanted." Another slap. "Two: they were to set up factories producing high-quality gear to pay back the companies' investment." He looked round at the three of us and brought his finger down again. "And three: they were to turn the whole state into a living laboratory."

We were all staring at him.

"A living laboratory?" Katharine asked. "What do you mean?"

Pete Pym ran the back of his hand across his mouth. "We subs – you know they call us that? – we subs are their guinea pigs."

"Jesus," I said, thinking of the incarceration initiative back home and the windowless blocks in the colleges on Broad Street. "This city's a criminologist's dream."

"Yeah," Pete said grimly. "And a citizen's worst nightmare."

After a while Pete Pym looked at his badly scratched watch. "We'd better get back. The dogs will be beginning to wonder what we're up to." He moved off through the woods.

"Did your brother say anything about his place of work?" I asked, catching him up. "Did he say anything that might explain why he was killed?"

He shook his head. "Nah. He used to talk all the time about how strange the people in the lab were. Apparently the ones who work nights are the ones even the administrators don't want to see. But he never told me anything that'll do you any good." He stopped and leaned against a fallen trunk. "You've got to understand, Quint. They treat us like morons. Slaves, actually. All we're allowed to do is menial work – fetching and carrying, cleaning like Ted, working the fields. The students and researchers do all the brain work. We haven't got much of a clue what goes on in the labs." He caught my eye. "But I'll tell you something. His killing, the arms hacked off, blood all over the shop – it wasn't the first like that."

"I heard it was the first inside the university area," I said. "They did tell me that there are murders in the suburbs from time to time."

"I'm not talking about those," Pete said, shaking his head. "They're usually provoked by Nox undercover people for research reasons and they're just knifings or bludgeonings – minor gang warfare stuff. No, I'm talking about full-scale mutilation." His face darkened. "Like happened to my poor bloody brother." He glanced at Davie. "They send the biggest and nastiest bulldogs out to the farms nearest the Poison Fields to patrol. There've been stories about infiltrators and escapers being torn to pieces out there."

"Christ," I said under my breath. "You think Ted was killed by a bulldog?"

Pete Pym shrugged. "My money's on that. Probably another fucking research project. But you'll need a hell of a lot of proof to force the administrators to change their ways." He started walking again.

"Pete?" Katharine said, moving alongside him. "Maddy said something about boarding schools for the most gifted children. Why don't they educate all the kids?"

He laughed bitterly. "It's obvious, isn't it? They only want the kids they can place in the transnationals afterwards. Those ones become students. You've probably seen how scared they are." He shook his head. "They're not getting any of mine, even if it means they end up working on the farms or cleaning up after the shitheads in the colleges."

He strode away and I heard him singing part of a song I thought I recognised.

"Here, Pete," I called.

He stopped and looked round.

"Big Maceo and Tampa Red," I said, smiling. " 'County Jail Blues.' "

He stared at me. "No, Quint. That's an O-blues standard. I haven't got a clue who wrote it." He started to sing again. " 'The Oxford jails, they ain't no place to go . . .' "

As we followed him towards the Chariot, I heard a cuckoo for the first time since I was a kid.

CHAPTER FOURTEEN

"Now what?" Davie asked as the Chariot went through the bulldog post at the western boundary of Cowley and moved towards Magdalen Bridge.

All the way back from the woods I'd been pondering what Pete Pym had told us about the regime in New Oxford. None of us had said much since, so I assumed Katharine and Davie had it on their minds too. Everything the dead man's brother had described made sense: Administrator Raphael and her team's involvement in the prison back home, the sophisticated surveillance dome on the Radcliffe Camera, the subjugation of the university's activities to profit. Now it was impossible to look at the city's buildings without wondering what kind of prison or research facility might be housed in each of them. I took in the eccentric grandstand-like structure on stilts on the other side of the roundabout. Maybe it was a detention centre for dissidents; I could remember that football grounds had been used for that purpose in Holland before mainland Europe went back to the Dark Ages in 2004.

We crossed the bridge, the great bell-tower on our right. I hadn't noticed when we passed it earlier that a screen had been placed over the recessed openings beneath the pinnacles. Large red numbers informed us that it was 15:03, as well as advertising the name of the donors. Presumably NOXON was some kind of power company.

"Let's take a look at the murder scene," I said, bending towards the transparent door as the Chariot responded to Davie's direction with a rapid left turn.

We got out when the vehicle stopped at the end of the lane.

"Are they playing what I think they're playing?" Davie asked, squinting at a group of young men in whites.

"And you think they're playing?" Katharine asked impatiently.

"Cricket," Davie said. "They showed us a film about it in the auxiliary training programme, remember?"

Katharine looked blank and watched as there was a loud shout, then a round of applause from the players.

"Aye," Davie continued, "there was some reference to it being a good example of English society's inherent degeneracy. The national team's players were allegedly all on the take."

I nodded. "I had to play the game at school when I was a kid. In shorts, of course. And not on the take."

"I'm sure you looked very fetching," Katharine said.

"Very. Scraped knees, frostbite in the toes. In the old days Edinburgh wasn't the place for summer sports."

Davie grunted. "It's too sweaty for them now, thanks to the Big Heat."

Katharine had walked on ahead. "Here it is," she called, pointing to an area on the gravel path that was marked by a cluster of short metal posts, one of them bearing the faulty camera unit. As soon as we approached, a metallic voice started announcing that this was a crime scene. The warning was repeated at one-second intervals, the volume rising when we stayed put.

I waved my control card around. That shut the alarm system up.

"Not much to see," Davie said after we'd inspected the place.

As I'd expected – apart from the posts and the slightly different colour and texture of the gravel, there was little sign that Ted Pym had been held down while the blood drained from his severed axillary arteries.

I kneeled on the grass beside the path and took out my notebook. I'd written down the salient points while we'd been in the Viewing Room with Connington. Now I was trying to reconcile what we'd been shown in Quadrihypervision with the reality of the locus. It wasn't long before something struck me.

"The only prints came from Ted Pym's shoes," I said, flicking pages. "Obtained from Cowley Footwear Factory Outlet, model number twelve."

Katharine was playing with her nostrum. "That's right. Brown work shoe, Plastex upper, Plastex sole, size ten."

Davie stepped closer. "What have you got there?"

"The full murder file," she said. "We've got access to everything, remember?"

Davie took the device he'd been issued with from his pocket and looked at it dubiously. "If you can trust this thing."

"Shut up, Davie," I said, glancing up at Katharine. "No other shoe or boot prints recorded."

Katharine nodded as her fingers played across the keys. "The bulldog in charge of their version of the SOCS said she thought the murderer had deliberately obscured all prints."

"Mmm." I gave that some thought. "Why did he take that precaution here and not in Leith? That's still puzzling me."

Davie was scratching his beard. "This murder happened a week before the attack on Faulds. It might not have been the same perpetrator. Or the killer might have got more confident."

"Or the lunatic might have started laying a trail," I said.

There was a loud crack from my left and a dark red ball shot across the grass towards us. The fielder chasing it gave us a curious look as he cut it off ten yards away.

"Laying a trail?" Katharine's eyes had come up from the nostrum.

"'All roads lead to Oxford'," I quoted.

She and Davie nodded slowly.

"The Eagle One that did for Lewis Hamilton is one of those roads, isn't it? I'm bloody sure the arm amputation is another, for all the discrepancies."

I moved further down Dead Man's Walk, the walls and gables of Merton College – now known as Mert, no doubt – immediately to my right. Ahead, the path pointed directly towards the massive buildings of Christ Church. What did they call that now? I wondered. Christ? If so, what tone of voice was appropriate. Then the look of surprise on the old don Elias Burton's face when I mentioned the college came back to me, as well as Yamaguchi's similar expression at dinner. I quickened my pace, eyes locked on the ecclesiastical architecture ahead. It was only when Katharine called out that I realised we had company.

"What the . . .?" I stopped and stared at the outlandish creature that had been keeping pace with me about five yards away on the grass. It had ground to a halt too, its beady eyes fixed on me.

Katharine came up, her movements slow and cautious. "I told you I saw a dodo yesterday."

We stared at the heavy bird, taking in its dowdy grey feathers and the feeble wings that were folded against its body. The overall impression it made was of a sweet but dotty aged aunt – apart from the vicious curved beak.

"They're extinct," Davie said, his voice low. "We learned that at school."

"Apparently not," I replied.

The dodo kept its black eyes on us, its steady gaze disturbing. Then it seemed to lose interest. It moved away slowly, its webbed feet flopping over the grass inelegantly but with surprising speed.

"Lewis Carroll was a don at Christ Church," I said, my eyes again on the buildings towards which the bird was heading. There were two narrow dark-coloured metal columns extending high above the wall: they looked like chimneys, the tops crowned with mesh filters.

Davie and Katharine stared at me.

I didn't go into the dodo's role in *Alice in Wonderland* as there was something I needed to check. I took out my old man's guidebook and found the appropriate page. My memory hadn't been deceiving me.

"What are you looking at?" Davie asked.

I pointed at the photograph in Hector's book. "The Tom Tower," I said. "Designed by Sir Christopher Wren, containing the six and a quarter-ton bell known as Great Tom. One of Oxford's most striking monuments." I glanced at them. "Where is it?"

There was no sign of the Gothic tower with its sublime dome.

Katharine's fingers were at work on the nostrum again. "It's probably gone the same way as Christ Church," she said. "According to the street plan, there's no such college."

"What's on the site now, then?" I asked.

She looked up at me and gave a bitter smile. "Guess."

I nodded. "There's nothing marked."

"Nothing at all." She turned her eyes towards the imposing cluster of buildings. "I wonder what kind of research facility they've got in there?"

So did I. I was also concerned about the dodo. It seemed to have disappeared behind the forbidding walls.

The Chariot glided to a halt outside the Nox University Outfitters shop on the High Street.

I was through the automatic door before the salesman – it was the same subservient guy – could do anything but take a step back in alarm. Maybe he still hadn't got used to my Edinburgh clothes.

"Yes, sir, good afternoon, sir," he gabbled. "How may I be of—?"

"Never mind that," I interrupted. "You dumped a load of dodo shit on me the last time I was in here, pal."

His eyes jerked from side to side. No one came to help him. Maybe tea breaks were still permitted by the Hebdomadal Council.

"You told me that there were production problems with model NF138B boots."

The salesman's eyes focused on me but he didn't speak.

"Which was all bollocks, wasn't it?" I yelled. "Just so you know where you stand, we're handling a murder investigation on behalf of the Hebdomadal Council."

He licked his lips and lowered his gaze.

"I'm going to give you one more chance." I turned and beckoned Katharine forward. "My colleague has accessed the webnet. She can't find any reference to model NF138B boots in the Nox Footwear Industries' records. Isn't that right?"

Katharine gave the salesman a chilly smile. "None at all. Are you by any chance covering something up?"

He twitched his head. "No . . . no, not at all." He glanced at the door, where Davie's large form was blocking out most of the light. "I . . . I made a mistake. I thought you were referring to model NF128B, you see." Suddenly he was very eager to speak. "It was a simple confusion on my part."

Katharine's hands had flown across the nostrum keys. "I don't think so," she said, fixing him with her eyes. "NF128B are standard don-issue slippers. And there's been no problem with production of those."

The shop assistant went quiet again.

"Davie," I called. "Have you got your knuckle-dusters?"

He stepped forward, one hand rummaging in his pocket. "Oh yes," he replied with a hollow laugh.

The salesman let out a gasp and clutched the nearest display case. "I . . . NF138B, you say . . ." he stammered. "Yes, of course, silly of me . . . I should have . . ." He looked at me imploringly. "I'll talk, sir, I promise. Just call off your . . ."

I raised a hand. "NF138B boots are issued to . . .?" I asked, making it easy for him.

He gulped, swallowed hard, then raised his eyes to mine. "They're issued to Grendels," he said. "Those boots are manufactured exclusively for the Grendels."

That stopped my own boots in their tracks.

"I wish I did have a set of knuckle-dusters," Davie said wistfully when we were back in the Chariot.

"I'll bet you do, big man," I said, glancing at my watch. A thought had struck me.

Katharine was playing with her nostrum again. "This is interest— Ow!"

I loosened the pressure my fingers had applied to her upper thigh and looked at her meaningfully, my lips making a sibilant "shhh". I directed that at Davie too. After a few seconds of bewilderment, he got my drift too.

"Head for the helijet pad," I said to him.

He gave the Chariot its driving orders. We swung across the High Street in front of a posse of students on bicycles and headed back towards Magdalen, or rather Magd. The vehicle soon stopped outside the side entrance on Longwall Street.

I put my nostrum on the seat and gestured to the others to do the same. Then I got out and led them past the sensor posts towards the high, transparent blast shields. I glanced at my watch again. This time yesterday the helijet was making its final approach with us on board. I gathered the others into a huddle, facing inwards.

"What's going on, Quint?" Katharine asked, her eyes screwed up.

The familiar high-pitched whine of the jet turbines was becoming audible in the distance. I waited a few seconds longer then put my arms round their shoulders and drew them even closer.

"I don't know what game Raphael and her people are playing yet," I said. "So we have to assume they're watching us all the time and listening to everything we say." I still couldn't understand why the chief administrator had put me on to what seemed to be a secret model of boot.

"Just like the guard would do back home if they had the equipment," Katharine said.

"Just like the Mist *is* doing back home," I reminded her. Already we were having to raise our voices against the engine noise. The dark blue aircraft had appeared above the trees to the north. "Anyway, keep things to yourselves till we can find a secure spot like this."

"Maybe we should communicate by Morse code," Davie suggested. "You know, tap messages out on each other's hands."

"Save Our Souls?" I said, watching as the helijet drew near. "That'll be right. We haven't much time. What did you find on your nostrum, Katharine?"

"Grendels," she shouted, the blast almost deafening now. "I wanted to know what the guy in the shop was on about."

The salesman had refused to say anything else, even when Davie stepped in close. Sweat was running down his face and he was twitching like a rabbit in a snare, but all the guy would do was refer us to Doctor Connington.

"Wasn't there some kind of monster called Grendel?" I yelled. "In an Old English poem?"

Katharine nodded. "That's what I found on the web-net. Grendel was the embodiment of evil – supposedly descended from Cain – in the poem *Beowulf*. He killed and ate a large number of warriors until the hero of the poem caught up with him."

A dim memory of the poem came back to me. I went through a phase of being fascinated by heroic poetry: *The Epic of Gilgamesh*, Homer, *The Song of Roland* – any kind of violent, glorious tale. I was in my mid-teens at the time and I soon realised that the kind of mayhem going on around me as the UK fell apart was very far from being heroic.

"What are you saying, Katharine?" Davie shouted. "I haven't seen many monsters around New Oxford. You remember that the salesman referred to them in the plural?"

I nodded and watched as the helijet neared the ground, its flimsy-looking undercarriage lowered. "Monsters provided with rib-soled boots? That is interesting. Let's see what we can find out about them later on. The thing to do now is increase our options."

Katharine's lips were close to my ear, but she still had to raise her voice. "Meaning what, exactly?"

"Meaning we split up." I looked at Davie. "You go back to the Department of Metallurgy, guardsman. Question the researchers and any other staff you can find and see if what they say about the dead cleaner squares with the statements on file." The noise from the turbines was suddenly cut. "Also," I said more quietly, "see if you can find out if anyone could have got access to an ASAR weapon and Eagle One ammunition illicitly."

"Right," he said.

"What about me?" Katharine asked.

"How do you fancy making a nuisance of yourself?"

Davie grinned. "Aye, you're good at that."

"Screw you, guardsman," she said.

"Calm down," I said. "Go and get in Doctor Connington's way. Don't mention the NF138Bs and the Grendels till we know more about them. Tell him you want to review all the data on the Pym murder again. That might distract him from what I'm doing."

"Which is?" Katharine asked.

I drew back from the huddle and looked across at the now silent helijet. People were coming out of the exits, most of them in the dark suits worn by Raphael's administrative staff. I wondered if they'd come from Edinburgh.

"Which is?" she repeated.

I smiled. "I'll tell you later. How about a glass of sherry in my rooms at seven o'clock?"

Davie laughed. "Only if it's a pint glass."

I didn't even know he liked sherry.

Katharine went off to the Radcliffe Camera on foot, while Davie took me up to the science area in the Chariot. Conversation was muted at first; there's nothing like the thought that you're being monitored to shut you up. But, to keep up appearances, we managed a debate about whether the students of New Oxford could get away with doing as little work as some of my contemporaries at university in Edinburgh had. The young people's sober faces and purposeful gait showed how spurious the discussion was.

"Right," I said, as the Chariot drew up outside the dark glass of the Metallurgy building. "I'll see you later. You keep the wheels."

Davie nodded, watching me thoughtfully as I walked away. There was no point in telling him where I was going, even by tapping the words out on the back of his hand – I didn't know Morse. Anyway, I'd had to find out from my nostrum where the place I wanted was located, so my interest might well have been noted already. The fifty-foot-high smoked glass and white concrete block I was headed for was located right in the middle of the science complex, though the panel above the main entrance wasn't displaying a science faculty name. These laboratories belonged to the Faculty of Criminology, one of the university's largest if the old don Elias Burton was to be believed – and this was the Department of Forensic Chemistry.

I went through the same procedure as we'd experienced at the Department of Metallurgy. My control card got me past the sensors. In the vacant reception area I was greeted, or rather accosted, by another imperious mechanical voice. I kept quiet and waved my card around. A door ahead of me slid open. I got about five paces beyond it when I was met by a familiar face.

"Citizen Dalrymple." The blonde young woman gave me a restrained smile. She was wearing a white lab coat over the black bulldog suit she'd had on the last time I saw her.

"It's Haskins, isn't it?" I said. "You were running the Viewing Room in the Radcliffe Camera yesterday."

She nodded once.

"Taking chemistry lessons in your spare time?"

She eyed me dubiously; humour definitely wasn't the bulldogs' strong suit. "This facility and the Camera both come under the aegis of the Faculty of Criminology," she said.

"You mean Doctor Connington's in charge of all law and order concerns?"

Haskins looked at me like I was a four year old. "The junior— The proctor's role is largely ceremonial." That would explain why we'd been fobbed off with him. "The faculty is run directly by the Hebdomadal Council."

"So much for academic independence," I said ironically.

That went over her head.

"Is there something I can help you with, citizen?" she asked. Her tone was efficient as well as officious.

"Call me Quint." I looked at her. "What's your first name?"

Haskins stiffened. Spots of colour appeared on her cheeks. "Bulldogs are not permitted to disclose their first names."

That made me think of the way auxiliaries in Edinburgh had to stick to their barracks numbers – one of the many similarities I'd begun to notice between the apparently dissimilar states. "Come on," I wheedled, "you can tell me. I'm an outsider. I won't let on."

She hesitated. "Oh, very well. My name is Harriet."

Just what you'd expect a dark bluestocking to be called. "Right. So, Harriet, are you a chemist?"

She shook her head. "No. But we're moved around all the departments during our training. I've done some time in the forensics labs."

"You know your way around here?" I asked, peering down the brightly lit corridor. The walls on both sides were solid, the only sign of doors coming from the small touch screens at chest height.

Harriet Haskins nodded. "What is it that you need, citi— I mean, Quint?" She stumbled over my name to demonstrate that she wasn't comfortable using it.

I held up my notebook. It was open at the page on which I'd copied down the details of the drug found in George Fauld's veins: the combined anaesthetic, anti-infection, amnesia-inducing compound. That was why I was in the labs. Administrator Raphael hadn't made any reference to it, either in Edinburgh or on the way to New Oxford, so the impression given was that, unlike the bullet, it didn't originate in this city. I wanted to see if I could establish if that was the case. And not only that: if the compound didn't come from Oxford, these high-tech labs with their transnational backers should at least be able to identify its provenance.

The blonde bulldog ran her nostrum over the page. "I presume you want a check run on this?" She turned her shapely form away from me and spoke into the device round her neck.

I nodded. "Who produces it? Is it available in New Oxford? That sort of thing." I felt my stomach flip as the floor suddenly started moving. "Thanks for the warning, Harriet," I complained.

"My pleasure," she said, smiling briefly. "Quint."

Sometimes first-name terms are more trouble than they're worth.

I spent the next hour giving myself an unguided tour of the Forensic Chemistry facility. Harriet Haskins offered to show me around; in fact, she tried to insist that I play Follow My Leader with her in the starring role. That was when I got tough and reminded her that my Hebdomadal Council authority gave me free, unaccompanied access everywhere. She gave a little pout that made her look even more fetching, then retired to a corner office to sulk and call her superiors, probably in reverse order.

I wandered around the banks of computer terminals and gleaming equipment, smiling encouragingly at the researchers like a visiting head of state from the time when heads of state could temporarily leave home; when the drugs wars kicked in across Europe presidents and monarchs had to barricade themselves inside their palaces, but the mobs still got most of them. The chemists and technicians knew that I must have had clearance. I remembered what happened to Maddy Pitt's dog when it jumped up against the Chariot. I was pretty sure that anyone trying to enter university premises would get pulsed terminally. But the white-coated ones were still keeping their eyes off me, trying to pretend I wasn't there. I hadn't realised my dress sense was so offensive.

"Where do the toxicologists work?" I asked a skinny guy with pimples who was wearing what I assumed was a college tie. He was busy directing a flow of green liquid around an array of glass tubes.

He glanced round and I saw that Harriet had appeared

at the work surface further along from us. She gave an almost imperceptible nod.

"Fourth floor," the researcher said, his voice reedy and heavily accented. Italian, I reckoned.

"*Grazie*," I said, giving him a broad grin. That seemed to terrify him. Maybe he thought I was after his body.

I turned and walked quickly over to Haskins. "You're beginning to piss me off, Harriet," I said in her ear. "Go back to your screens and follow what I do on them, all right? Otherwise it's the end of a beautiful friendship."

She tossed her head and strode away. I smiled to myself. She could watch where I went and listen to what I said if she wanted, but she couldn't see inside my head; you develop a talent for living inside yourself in Enlightenment Edinburgh.

I went up to the fourth floor and was taken down an identical moving corridor. It stopped by a touch screen and, before I could attempt to activate it, a door appeared in the wall. Even the building knew where I was going. I'd have to do something about that.

I found myself in another large laboratory, the atmosphere tinged by something unpleasant like a blue cheese that had begun to liquefy. None of the men and women at work paid any attention to me. That was fine. It was I who wanted to pay attention to them. Because the other reason I'd come to the department was Lister 25, Edinburgh's missing chief toxicologist. I had no evidence linking him to New Oxford, but there seemed to be more connections between the two cities than I'd realised. I was also thinking of the message written in blood above my bed. Was this another road that led to Oxford? It was worth checking.

Except, of course, it was a waste of time. I understood that as I walked up and down between the rows of work stations, looking for an elderly specimen with heavy jowls humming Robert Johnson songs. There was no sign of him, though they'd had plenty of time to get him out the back way if they'd wanted to. There were no unoccupied desks and no untidy experiments that betrayed the signs of a hasty departure.

My nostrum chirped and Harriet Haskins appeared on the small screen.

"Citizen Quint," she said, frowning and trying to focus her eyes. There must have been a miniature camera on the device that relayed a picture of the respondent.

"Bulldog Haskins," I replied in kind.

"We do not use our rank as a title," she said, her voice sounding robotic through the nostrum's speaker.

"Mea culpa," I said. "And you want?"

"I want?" she asked, hesitating. "Oh, I see. I've got the results of the check we've run on your mystery compound."

"Surprise me," I said, holding the metallic device in front of my face. "It was developed and produced by Nox Pharmaceuticals for the lucrative Chinese sex industry."

Now she was staring at me. "Do you want this information or not?"

"Proceed, Harriet," I said, wondering if my flippancy had put her off her stride. I had a feeling I was about to be fed a heap of ox excrement.

"The compound in question does not feature in any of the university's databanks," she said, looking straight at me from the display. "It is completely unknown, I'm afraid." She cocked an eyebrow. "Are you sure you wrote down the specification correctly?"

"Oh yes," I said, slipping the nostrum cord over my head. "Thanks for your input, Harriet. See you soon." I put the device into the back pocket of my trousers, hoping she approved of the new camera angle.

It was time to turn the heat up.

As the lift took me down to the ground floor, I pondered the ethics of what I was about to do. It wasn't long before I gave myself the green light. This was the only way I could make sure Lister 25 wasn't on the premises.

When the lift door hissed open, I stuck my head out and ascertained that no one was around. It seemed that everyone who worked in the department stayed at their desks until their shift was complete; presumably they each had a personal chamber pot under their feet. Then I kneeled down in the corner of the lift, tore out some blank pages from my notebook and took the box of matches I'd imported from Edinburgh out of my jacket pocket. Fire one. I pressed plus six on the panel, wondering how quickly the smoke detectors would smell a rat. Not immediately. The door closed behind me and there was a sigh as the lift moved upwards again.

I exited the building and took up position behind a low hedge. From there I could see the exit from the emergency staircase on the right of the building as well as the main door. As soon as I squatted down, there was a shrill blast from what sounded like a full horn section of sirens, both inside and outside the Forensic Chemistry block. The blaring was interspersed by a shrill mechanical voice proclaiming, "Evacuate! Evacuate!"

Which is what the occupants did, at high speed. I had difficulty keeping track of them and had to bob up and down and from left to right to ensure that Lister 25 didn't escape me. After a couple of minutes there must have been several hundred flustered people in white coats assembling obediently in designated areas away from the block. My small fire must have ignited the plastic surface of the lift's floor. But there wasn't any sign of the old toxicologist.

Then things really did start to hot up. There was a blast of mobile sirens and three large silver vehicles shot up the access road, the late afternoon sun glinting from their pipework and windscreens. Numerous hefty individuals in metallic blue suits and masked helmets leaped down and started hauling hoses. I turned back from them towards the building and saw Harriet Haskins stepping towards me, an expression that was definitely not friendly on her face. And at the same moment I saw something that made me jerk back as if my eyes had been stung by the deadly killer bees that decimated Paris in 2003.

I blinked involuntarily at what I'd seen. Or rather, at the people I'd seen. There were four of them, on their way out of the fire exit. Two were bulldogs, one without his bowler hat on, but I wasn't interested in them. The man and woman they were protecting were the ones who had made me flinch. It was only about thirty hours since I'd seen the male with the goatee beard in Raphael's suite in Edinburgh. On reflection, it wasn't that much of a surprise that Glasgow's first secretary was here. He'd made no secret of his city's connections with Oxford.

It was his female companion who really rocked me back on my heels. Dressed in dark blue overalls, she was thinner than she had been when I last saw her in October 2026. Her face with the button nose was gaunt and lined. But her hair was exactly as it had been, the thick brown curls cut short. Jesus. Hel Hyslop, former chief inspector in the All-Glasgow Major Crime Squad. She was supposed to be locked up permanently in the secure unit at Barlinnie. What was the woman who'd been involved in some of the most gruesome murders I'd ever investigated doing on the loose with Andrew Duart?

Even more perplexing, what was she doing on the loose with him in Chief Administrator Raphael's New Oxford?

CHAPTER FIFTEEN

I glanced at the old sundial in Brase front quadrangle as I hurried towards my staircase. Ten past seven. I tried without much success to keep my excitement in check. Davie and Katharine would be as amazed as I'd been by Hel Hyslop's presence in Oxford. I kept telling myself it could be a coincidence but the temptation to look for a link between her, Duart, and what had happened in Edinburgh was irresistible. I paused as I reached the doorway. The evening was warm and still. Somewhere nearby a choir was giving what sounded to me like a faultless rendition of a medieval religious piece. It definitely wasn't the O-blues.

I ran up to my rooms and put my control card in the slot by the door. It swung open and voices cascaded out.

"Ah, Quint, there you are," Davie said, grinning at me and holding up a glass. It wasn't a beer mug, but it must have held close to a half a pint of pale brown liquid. "We decided not to wait."

"How did you get in?" I asked, looking at my card.

"We had some help." Katharine was standing at the armchair by the open window.

A figure in tweeds stood up shakily. "How are you, Quintilian?" The old don Elias Burton nodded at me, his bright blue eyes glinting beneath his lank yellow hair. "You don't mind if I call you by your full name, I hope?"

"Nah," Davie said. "He loves it."

I raised an eyebrow at him and turned back to Katharine. She was sipping from a smaller glass. "You had help?" I asked.

Burton took an unsteady step towards me. "Forgive me. I found your friends on the stair. My rooms are on the floor above." He pointed to the nostrum that was dangling from his wrinkled neck. "I managed to access your entry code."

"Brilliant," I muttered, wondering how many other people had been through my door during the day.

"And I managed to work out how to access the college cellar," Davie said, looking pleased with himself.

"With a lot of guidance from me," Katharine said, smiling at him acidly.

I shook my head at them, glad to see that they were still observing their traditional hostilities but frustrated by Elias Burton's presence; it was getting in the way of my news.

Katharine took the old academic's elbow and steered him back to the armchair. "Doctor Burton's been telling us more about the set-up in New Oxford," she said, giving me a meaningful look. "Apparently there are over thirty incarceration facilities in and around the city."

The classicist nodded. "That's right, I'm afraid. The Faculty of Criminology is a law unto itself."

I took the heavy glass that Davie handed me. "Is it right that the faculty is controlled directly by the Hebdomadal Council?" I asked, remembering what Harriet Haskins had said.

Elias Burton took a sip of sherry and nodded again. "That's because of the huge amount of funds generated by Crim Fac." He looked up at me, his head twitching. "You see, a different research project is run in each prison. The transnational companies and the independent foreign states are desperate to find the most cost-effective ways of handling the huge prison populations that have resulted from the breakdown in law and order all over the world."

That squared with what Pete Pym had told us. I remembered the windowless blocks we'd seen in the colleges on Broad Street.

"What research goes on in Balliol and Trinity?" I asked. "I mean Ball and Trin."

Elias Burton pursed his dry lips. "Terrible things in the former, Quintilian. The facility in the former Balliol College was constructed for political prisoners. They are sent here from numerous countries." He shook his head. "Keep this to yourselves," he said, lowering his voice, "but I've heard they even torture the inmates."

I glanced around the room, hoping for the old don's sake that we weren't under aural surveillance. Maybe he was past caring.

"And Trin?" I asked.

"Ah," Burton said, looking less despondent. "Trin isn't so bad. The prisoners there live communally. They're encouraged to do their own cooking and laundry."

"But they're still locked up in a concrete pile without any fresh air," Davie said, shaking his head.

"What about the people who live in the suburbs?" Katharine asked. "They're treated as little better than slaves, aren't they?"

The old man nodded, his head bowed. "That's true. Why do you think they're called subs?" He put his glass down carefully on the window ledge. "The university authorities don't really need their labour. They simply use them as laboratory rats." He looked up at us. "You've been out there. You've seen how they live."

I glanced at Katharine and Davie. They'd obviously let slip something about what we'd been doing.

"But the children aren't given any schooling," Katharine said, impervious to my concern. "Apart from the ones who are chosen to be indoctrinated in the boarding schools."

Burton laughed bitterly. " 'Twas ever thus, dear lady. This university has operated a strict selection policy ever since the thirteenth century. The school you went to usually counted much more than any natural ability."

I remembered the guy in the outfitters and decided to throw the word he'd used at the old don. "Tell me, doctor, what exactly are Grendels?"

He took the question without any giveaway twitches. The only thing that suggested he might have been surprised was his brief silence. Then he looked straight at me. "From your use of the plural form, I infer that you are not asking about the creature who caused the early Danes no end of bother in the old poem?"

I nodded, keeping my eyes on him. The choir was still singing the Lord's, or more likely the administrators', praises in the background.

Burton ran his tongue over his lips. "Grendels? You have been busy, Quintilian. Even I have heard very little about those individuals." He smiled. "And I, as you may have gathered, am quite a collector of information."

"Gossipmonger is the word," said Davie in a low voice as he refilled our glasses.

Burton raised an unsteady hand to decline more sherry. "The Grendels," he said, lowering his voice again, "are the Faculty of Criminology's pride and joy. A highly trained, highly" – he glanced at Katharine – "to use your term, highly indoctrinated group of paramilitary operatives. They patrol the outer reaches of the state, especially the so-called Poison Fields, and deal with both interlopers and escapees."

"Highly trained?" I said.

"Lethal, I should say. Capable of killing people with their bare hands. They're also heavily armed." The old don looked out of the window at the shadows that had now fallen across the lawn. "They are violence personified. So much so that they are restricted from entering the central university area. The bulldogs are lightweights compared with Grendels."

I glanced at Davie and Katharine. It looked like they too were thinking about the mutilated bodies we'd seen in Edinburgh and in the Viewing Room here.

There was a trill from my nostrum. I raised it from my chest and saw Administrator Raphael's face appear on the screen.

"Citizen Dalrymple," she said, looking straight at me, "I want a full report from you. Kindly present yourself at the Hebdomadal Council Block immediately. And citizen?"

I returned her stare but didn't speak.

"Come alone." There was a dull click and her face disappeared.

"Do you know where you're going, Quintilian?" Burton asked.

I nodded. "What used to be the Clarendon Building, on the far side of what used to be the Bodleian." I drew Davie and Katharine towards me as I headed for the door. "Did you find out anything interesting?" I asked in a low voice.

They both shook their heads.

"No one in the Department of Metallurgy would give me much more than the time of day," Davie complained. "Verzeni sat on my back all the time. I got nothing more than what the murder file shows."

"Surprise, surprise," I said, turning to Katharine.

"Same here," she said. "Though I think Doctor Connington needed a drink by the time I'd finished with him. You?"

"Oh yes," I said. "I struck twenty-four-carat gold." I shrugged. "I'll have to tell you about it later, though."

"Quint!" they exclaimed.

I pushed them aside and went back. "One more thing, Doctor Burton," I said, thinking of the high walls and chimney-like towers we'd seen from Dead Man's Walk, and flying a kite. "What kind of prison facility is located in Christ Church?"

The old academic was leaning forward in the armchair. "Christ Church?" he repeated in a voice that was suddenly even shakier. "Christ Church? They . . . they call that—" He broke off and gave me a pained look, as if the words he was about to speak were already burning his mouth. "They call that the House of Dust." He didn't say anything more.

That kept my mind occupied as I went to meet Raphael. Until I remembered my act of arson at the Department of Forensic Chemistry. Maybe the flames were about to be lit under me.

I cut through Noxad, the high walls of the former library glowing pale gold in the failing light, and walked across the path to the administrator's lair. A pair of bulky specimens in black suits and bowler hats were standing outside the central arch of the two-storey Hawksmoor building. Trout and Perch.

I nodded to them as I approached. "Evening, gentlemen. Or should that be—?"

"Don't," Trout said, his heavy face set hard.

"Fair enough," I said, deciding on discretion. "The chief administrator's expecting me."

"You think we don't know that?" Perch asked, his lips curled.

I tried to look unconcerned as they made a point by blocking my way for a few seconds. The Grendels that Burton had told us about must have been seriously worrying if they were worse than these apes.

After they'd stepped aside, I followed the line of red lights that had suddenly appeared on the floor in front of me into the old building. Well, the outside was old – early eighteenth century, I guessed – but the interior was stunningly high-tech; like the flight deck of a spaceship in one of those high-budget, low-intelligence Hollywood movies that used to be served up, before California fell to the religious right in the first decade of the century. Everything was shiny metal and tinted glass, with wall panels dotted and traced with multicoloured lights thrown in for contrast, the panels being scanned by personnel in high-necked dark suits.

The red line on the floor stopped in front of a highlighted section. I suspected that I'd just stepped on to an elevator pad. The only question was whether the sherry I'd drunk was going to be shaken up or down. There was a sigh of compressed air as a curved glass safety panel came up to my waist. Then, like an Old Testament saint, I was translated upwards. Not, I was relieved to see, to the pastures of heaven but to the first floor. I found myself in a long, airy room with deeply recessed windows looking out over Broad Street. I could see Administrator Raphael at the far end, near her a small group of individuals in the clothing worn by that rank, as well as a few others in academic robes.

The safety panel dropped down and I moved towards the occupants of the expansive room. The walls were hung with portraits of university worthies from days gone by, the sober paintings at odds with the gleaming metal and the glass screens. I wasn't paying too much attention to the artwork though. I had plenty I wanted to nail Raphael about, as well as certain things I wanted to keep to myself. I was keen to see how she and her colleagues reacted to the outrage I was about to express; it had been building up since we'd been in the suburbs and had got even more intense since Burton confirmed what Pete Pym had told us about the prisons and the slave culture. I also wanted to see how she explained the Grendels. I was beginning to have major suspicions about them, though if it was true that they were kept out of the city centre one of their number would have had trouble murdering Ted Pym. And, last but not least, I wanted to know what Hel Hyslop and Duart had been doing in the Department of Forensic Chemistry.

As it turned out, I didn't get the chance to broach any of those issues. I reached the gaggle of officials and realised immediately that something critical had happened. Their faces betrayed extreme anxiety and their voices were strained. Doctor Connington, resplendent as usual in his blue and red gown, looked like he was about to keel over. Even Dawkley, the science administrator, was jerking around like a puppet on a string, talking in a hoarse whisper to Professor Yamaguchi and Doctor Verzeni.

Raphael had moved a couple of paces to the rear and had turned her back to the others. She was speaking in a clear voice to nobody in particular and I realised that she was using the voice facility on her nostrum. Through the high window behind her I made out the Bridge of Sighs that was originally built to connect parts of Hertford College, now presumably called Hart. I wondered if the enclosed structure with its elegant arch was used by condemned prisoners like the Venetian original had been.

"Why is his nostrum not responding?" I heard the chief administrator say, her voice more animated than I'd ever heard it. "At the very least, why is the tracking signal not being received?" She listened and obviously didn't get the answer she wanted. "Find him," she shouted. "Or I'll send your whole section to the fields. Off."

I watched as she swung round, her nostrum deactivated. The fields? Did she mean the Poison Fields? And what was that about a tracking signal?

"Citizen," she said, breathing what sounded very like a sigh of relief. "Just the man I need."

Her tone, steely but also curiously vulnerable, put me off making a risqué response.

"Someone gone absent without signed and countersigned leave?" I asked.

She nodded, biting her lip.

I ran my eye over the group behind me. None of them was talking now. "Let me guess. Professor Raskolnikov."

Raphael inclined her head forwards again. "He should have been here half an hour ago. No one is ever late for a Hebdomadal Council meeting. No one. And there is no sign of him on any of the Radcliffe Camera's surveillance systems." She looked at me with eyes wide open. "He's disappeared without trace." It was clear from her demeanour that no senior academics ever did that either.

I wondered about the gloomy, bearded Russian. Had he tempted fate by taking the name of Dostoevsky's axe-murderer?

There were a few moments of feverish silence. I let them stretch out. It's always good to put the squeeze on your employers – especially if they haven't bothered to propose a fee.

"So you want me to find the professor?" I asked, looking at Raphael with what I hoped was a convincing degree of nonchalance.

"That's what you're good at, isn't it, citizen?" she said, regaining the control she usually exercised over her voice.

"But he's only been missing for half an hour. Maybe he's fallen asleep over the latest burglary statistics from the suburbs, maybe he's got gut rot, maybe—" I broke off when I saw the stony stares my suggestions were inspiring. "All right," I conceded. "So Raskolnikov would normally be here at this time of day?"

Dawkley stepped forward, his pale face above the spindly neck even more bloodless than before. "Yes, Dalrymple, he'd be here. There is a Hebdomadal Council meeting every evening. He and his colleagues" – he glanced at Yamaguchi and Verzeni – "are special advisers. They attend all our meetings."

I glanced at Raphael; her face was tense. "And it's already been made clear to me that arriving late for one of those is a capital offence."

"So is being facetious, citizen," the proctor barked. "Professor Raskolnikov is a Fellow of Souls. We've already checked. He is not in his rooms there."

I presumed that Souls was what they now called All Souls. I vaguely remembered that the place was a dons-only establishment, notorious before the break-up of the UK for giving a comfortable home to intellectuals who were too far removed from reality to fit in anywhere else. "How about his place of work? I presume he has an office in the Faculty of Criminology."

Raphael nodded. "In the Taylorian. He left there at four minutes past seven."

"The surveillance camera on top of the Martyrs' Memorial tracked him to the shed on the corner of Broad Street immediately afterwards," Connington said. "He then took a public-use bicycle and—" The proctor broke off, looking embarrassed.

Raphael was glaring at him. "And . . .?" she prompted, not letting him off the hook.

"And then," the doctor concluded in a low voice, "all contact was lost."

There was an uneasy lull.

"It happens from time to time," the proctor said, trying desperately to look like he knew what he was talking about. "There were a lot of students on bicycles on the Broad. My people are reviewing the tapes. We'll trace him soon enough."

"Sounds like you don't need me," I said.

Connington's nostrum made a noise. He glanced at it and breathed a gasp of relief. "We have him." He spoke into the device and moved towards the nearest room-high transparent plastic panel. "There he is."

The panel darkened and a detailed image appeared. I recognised the streets of central Oxford. A red square appeared around a specific area and the image was magnified. A digital timer on the screen showed that the footage had been taken at twelve minutes past seven.

"The High," Connington said. "You observe Queen on the left." He was referring to Queen's College. "Increase resolution." The last words were spoken as a command.

There was the professor, instantly recognisable by his long monk's beard, which was being blown back in the slipstream along with his gown. He was perched on a bicycle with a silvery frame, his legs perfectly still.

"Gas-powered," Raphael said, noticing my stare. "Provided free of charge to university members."

Raskolnikov moved out to the centre of the road as he went past what used to be the Examination Schools. I'd noticed when we'd driven past the building earlier that it now housed the Department of Comparative Penology.

"He's going to turn," I said, watching the figure on the screen and feeling a shiver of anticipation run up my spine. He was approaching Rose Lane, the street leading to Dead Man's Walk. Was that where he was heading?

But he went past the junction, still in the middle of the road. On his left were the buildings and walls of what used to be called Magdalen. Then the image disappeared in a flurry of black and white dots and the screen turned back into a blank plastic sheet.

"What has happened now?" Dawkley demanded, glaring at the senior proctor.

Connington was peering at his nostrum. "Em . . . it seems there was a fault on the camera unit outside Magd."

"A fault on another unit?" Raphael asked.

Doctor Connington was floundering, his mouth open but no words being produced.

I stepped in to bail him out. "Did the cameras further down the road record Raskolnikov?"

He muttered into his nostrum and a shot of the bridge came up on the screen. He zoomed in on it. There was no sign of the professor.

"Go back a bit," I said. I pointed at the area that had come up. "What's that place?"

"The Botanic Garden," Dawkley said.

"Known as Bot?"

No one answered. They were all too busy staring at the

screen. If I'd listened hard enough, I'd have picked up the sound of numerous pennies dropping. The gardens were no more than a couple of minutes' walk from where Ted Pym's body had been found on Dead Man's Walk.

"See you down there," I called as I headed for the exit, taking my mobile out of my pocket.

I wanted Davie and Katharine to help me with this. What had been so urgent that Professor Raskolnikov had skipped a meeting with the administrators? And more worrying, why weren't his heavy features coming up on the nostrums of the colleagues who'd been calling him non-stop for nearly an hour?

It was time to do some digging.

I was taken to the Botanic Garden in Raphael's top-of-the-range Chariot, the canopy an opaque dark blue from the outside. Although there was no siren, everyone else on the roads got out of the way at speed. I thought back to the traffic jams, the lung-burning fumes that had ruined Oxford when I was a kid. At least the new regime had solved that problem – but at what cost? Behind us, a couple of slightly less flashy vehicles brought the rest of the administrators and their advisers. They had their headlights on even though the evening sun was still surprisingly bright. It was glinting through the rain shields and suffusing the old walls in shades that almost seemed to bring them to life.

"What's going on, administrator?" I asked as we moved rapidly past the Radcliffe Camera.

She looked at me. "That's what you're here to find out, citizen."

"Cut the oxshit, chief administrator," I said, raising my voice. I was beginning to suspect she was operating several different agendas. "If you really wanted me to catch the killer or killers, you'd tell me a fuck sight more about the set-up here."

She didn't show any reaction to my deliberately pumped-up language – apart from a tight smile. "You're perfectly capable of obtaining all the information you need on your own, Quint."

I wondered if she'd been monitoring all my conversations. If I asked her, she wouldn't admit it. I considered telling her that I'd seen Duart and Hel Hyslop, but decided against it. I didn't want to show her too much of my hand yet.

We soon pulled up outside the Botanic Garden. There were several Chariots with opaque canopies already on the pavement. Bulldogs were standing around them with their chests inflated, waiting for a command from their handlers. As I got out, I saw Davie and Katharine standing by a grandiose neoclassical gate. I went to join them.

"What's the story, Quint?" Davie asked. He wasn't showing any effect from the sherry. No doubt he'd managed to find something to soak it up since I'd seen him.

"Professor Raskolnikov," I said. "He's gone missing. He was last seen on the High Street near here."

"On a bike?" Katharine asked, pointing past the fussy stonework of the archway to a silver two-wheeler with the words "Public Use" stencilled on the seat.

"On a bike," I confirmed. I waved Raphael and her group over. "Look what we've found."

"Most impressive, citizen," Dawkley said drily. "There are over seven thousand public-use bicycles in central New Oxford. How do you know this is the one the professor was using?"

I tapped the side of my nose. "Call it intuition, administrator."

"Or a highly developed sense of smell," Davie said under his breath. He looked at the science administrator with distaste.

I put my hand on his arm. "Doctor Connington," I called. "We'll take the centre. Get the bulldogs to spread out and start searching. See if they can find anyone who saw the professor." I looked through the gateway and into the gardens. There didn't seem to be a soul around.

"You'll be lucky, Dalrymple," Dawkley said with a shake of his head. "The garden is out of bounds after seven o'clock. Students and university staff are expected to be at their desks in the evenings."

I gave him a dubious look. "That doesn't apply to university professors then?"

He turned away abruptly.

"Let's check this place out," I said to the others.

So we did. There was no sign of the Russian in the garden itself. He wasn't lurking behind a tree or hiding in any of the greenhouses, he wasn't in the rockery, he wasn't up to his knees in the cultivated bog. I led the line out into the meadow to the south. Twilight was well advanced now, but I could still see the walls and twin shafts of the former Christ Church beyond Dead Man's Walk. It was then I remembered that Elias Burton had called the college founded by Henry VIII "the House of Dust". What was that about?

We followed the path down towards the river, Davie and Katharine a few yards on either side of me and the bulldogs spread out across the playing fields. A branch of the Cherwell – now the Char? – swung round close to us and I heard the soft purr of a motor.

"Punting for lazy folk," Katharine said, pointing to the low craft on the water. A pair of aquatic bulldogs were manning the punt, their bowler hats replaced by bright orange helmets.

I saw what Katharine meant. Although the men had poles, they were using them to probe the depths of the water. The craft was powered by a small engine and presumably steered by some kind of programmed rudder as there was no helmsman.

Then I looked to the front. At the same moment a bulldog on the shore let out a loud cry. Before I knew what I was doing, I was sprinting forwards. Not that there was any point in hurrying. The figure strung up among the verdant branches of a weeping willow on the riverbank wasn't going anywhere.

"What has happened to him?" Administrator Raphael's voice was faint but the words were enunciated clearly enough.

"Hard to tell," I said, stepping back from the missing professor. I'd noticed a jumbled pattern of footprints and had been marking the area off so that they could be identified. "I can't feel any pulse." I looked round at her. "I'd say he was dead, but I made that mistake in Edinburgh with George Faulds."

She looked at me then nodded. "Are there any obvious injuries?"

I shook my head. "His face is bruised. Apart from that and the dribble of blood from his mouth, nothing that I can see."

Raskolnikov's academic gown was in a heap on the path. He was still wearing his dark suit and the dark blue tie with the closed book emblem worn by university staff. His shoes were still on his feet. If it hadn't been for the position his body was in, you'd have thought he was taking a nap. But people taking a nap don't tie themselves to branches with pieces of plastic cord under their armpits and round their ankles. The Russian's head was leaning back, the willow's new leaves like a crown or a cushion, while his arms were dangling by his sides. His legs were about a yard apart, the feet lashed to the tree's lower branches. He looked like a rag doll that had been thrown aside by a bored child.

"Here is the medical examiner," Dawkley said, ushering forward a tall, balding man in a white protective suit with a mask round his neck.

I moved aside to let the expert look Raskolnikov over, but I stayed close. I wanted to hear everything he said to his superior. As it turned out, he didn't have a lot to say. He fiddled around with some sophisticated instruments, spoke some medical jargon into his nostrum and then stepped back, a puzzled expression on his face.

"All organs are inactive," he said. "This man is indubitably dead. But I am at a loss to explain how."

"Hang on," I said, drawing up to Raskolnikov again. "What's this?"

I moved forward on to the damp path and examined the cuffs of the Russian's suit jacket under the bright lights that had been set up.

"What have you found, citizen?" Raphael said, moving closer.

"Bloody hell," I said, feeling my stomach flip. "His sleeves have been sewn up."

"What?" Katharine's voice was sharp. "Why?"

I stood up slowly. "Why?" I repeated, turning to face them. "Remember what happened to the others?"

"Arm amputation," Raphael said slowly. She turned to the nearest bulldog. "Cut him down." Her eyes blazed. "Carefully."

In a couple of minutes the body was stretched out on

plastic sheeting beside the path. The crime-scene cameramen who'd already taken footage of the willow and its strange fruit were recording everything.

"Remove the jacket," Raphael said, standing over the motionless form.

The medic kneeled down and ran a small blade down the arms of Raskolnikov's suit and parted the material, as well as the unstained white shirt beneath.

Davie was the only one who spoke. "Shit," he said, shaking his head.

The killer had repeated what had been done to Ted Pym. Both of Professor Raskolnikov's arms had been amputated in the region of the upper humerus, but this time the limbs had been sewn up inside his shirt. The condition of the body was different to that of Ted Pym too. The wound surfaces were clean and free of blood like those of George Faulds. However, the youth gang member back home had been left alive, even if he was comatose.

What had been the cause of the Russian's death?

We found out the answer to that question soon enough. The balding medic had been prowling around the body, his fingers running across the keyboard of a metallic instrument with a tube coming out of its side. He kept pointing the end of that tube, presumably some kind of scanner, at Raskolnikov's neck.

Finally, he straightened up and nodded. "I thought so. There's something between the back of the tongue and the epiglottis. It's partially obscured behind the bone, cartilage and muscle structure." He called forward an assistant in protective whites. "Tilt the head back," he ordered.

The medical examiner leaned forward, a pair of

forceps in his hand. He moved them around for a few moments then pulled them out carefully.

"Is that what I think it is?" Davie asked.

"An Eagle One," Katharine said, peering at the bullet.

I turned to the medic. "Presumably he was asphyxiated."

"That's a good possibility," he agreed, eyeing the heavy projectile uncomfortably.

Raphael was standing with Dawkley and Yamaguchi. Verzeni was also there, his gaze fixed on the bullet. There were beads of sweat on his forehead.

It didn't seem like the right time to ask them if they had any idea why a specimen of New Oxford's most sophisticated ammunition should end up in their colleague's throat, so I left that for later. At least we had a connection with Hamilton's shooting and the murders, not that it was getting us any nearer identifying the killer.

Davie was on his knees by Raskolnikov's discarded gown. "Here's something else, Quint," he said, holding up the shattered remains of a nostrum by its cord.

"Good God," Dawkley gasped. "That's impossible."

I looked at him. "What do you mean?"

He glanced at Raphael. "The nostrums issued to senior personnel are made of the highest quality tungsten steel."

"Of course they are," said Katharine.

Dawkley ignored her irony. "They're guaranteed indestructible by Nox Nostrum Industries. How could this be?"

"Guaranteed indestructible?" I repeated, gazing at the crushed device and wondering how the damage to it had been carried out. "The factory needs to improve its quality control." I turned to Raphael. "And you need to improve the security of your senior staff. Without delay."

The chief administrator nodded, her face wan.

Things were evidently getting a little too close to home.

CHAPTER SIXTEEN

The rest of the evening was a drag. It transpired that high-tech, utopian New Oxford's take on handling murders wasn't much different to Enlightenment Edinburgh's: a slog through the tedious procedural part, plenty of frantic running around and, at the end, nothing much to show for it. By two in the morning, we called it a night.

Katharine, Davie and I retired to Brase with Raphael, Connington and Dawkley to see where we stood. The chief administrator seemed to know her way around the college. She led us straight to the Senior Common Room, having instructed the suddenly obsequious porter to send over food and drink – no messing about with self-service touch pads and delivery units for her.

"Kindly take us through your preliminary conclusions, Citizen Dalrymple," Raphael said after a pair of white-jacketed scouts had laid trays of sandwiches, wine and coffee on the oak table that took up one end of the long room. Academics who looked like they'd spent too long filleting ancient texts stared down at us from the walls, the extravagant gilt frames of their portraits in tune with the opulent antique furniture.

I wolfed down a sandwich filled with blue cheese that almost took the roof of my mouth off and sank a glass of vintage claret, then pulled out my notebook. Raphael and her colleagues had been playing with their nostrums all evening, but I preferred my handwritten notes: the fact that even an experienced graphologist would struggle to make sense of my scribbles was curiously comforting.

"Right," I said, running the stump of my right forefinger down the page. "The crime scene. We've found no witnesses to the murder. Not even anyone who spotted Professor Raskolnikov or a potential assailant on the way into the garden." I glanced at Dawkley, who was taking small bites from a banana and sipping water with a virtuous air. "You were right. The entire population of central New Oxford was doing its homework."

"Spare us the satire," the chief administrator said sharply.

I shrugged. "As for traces at the scene, neither we nor your operatives found any obvious material – fabric, hairs, whatever – that might point to the murderer's identity."

"Subject to further analysis," Doctor Connington put in.

"Of course," I said, nodding and then looking at each of the New Oxford officials. "The footprints were more interesting, though. There was no shortage of them and they didn't all come from Raskolnikov's size nine senior academic-issue Oxfords."

The three of them stared back at me impassively.

"There were the marks of a size eleven, as in the tenement in Leith. The ridging on the sole is identical." I gave them a tight smile. "It's our old friend Model NF138B."

No response.

"Model NF138B," I repeated. "As issued exclusively to Grendels." I looked at the chief administrator. "Not students."

Connington's eyes flicked open in surprise, but the two administrators were giving nothing away.

"What exactly are Grendels?" I asked Raphael. "Or is that another detail you want me to find out for myself?"

Raphael glanced at Dawkley then looked back at me. "Grendels are top secret for reasons that I cannot go into now. I suggest you follow whatever angles you see fit, citizen. I do not wish to prejudice your enquiry in any way."

"Aren't you prejudicing it by withholding vital information?" Katharine demanded. She was standing behind me, her hands on the top of my chair. I could hear her fingernails scrape on the polished wood.

Dawkley raised his eyes to Katharine and gave her a withering look. "How do *you* know such information is vital to the case?" he asked, his tone harsh. "That is for Citizen Dalrymple to decide."

I swivelled my head and shook it in her direction. If that was how they wanted to play it, I'd find a way to get round them. Maybe the whole issue of the boots was a sideline; maybe anyone could obtain a pair of the supposedly exclusive boots on the black market. I was pretty sure there would be one of those operating in the suburbs.

"As for the modus operandi," Davie said, having dealt with a large plate of sandwiches and emptied the claret jug. "The arm amputation was performed with what looks very like the same weapon that was used on the youth gang member in Edinburgh; the surfaces of the wounds were cauterised." He glanced around. "The precise nature of that instrument is still undetermined."

I turned to Dawkley. "Have your people been working on anything that could have removed the arms?"

He nodded slowly. "We have advanced expertise in

many fields." He frowned. "Are you suggesting that a New Oxford scientist killed the professor?"

"As you said, administrator," I replied, "that's for me to decide." I gave him a slack smile.

"But why both arms?" Raphael said. "What is the point of that . . . that horror?" She was looking uncharacteristically shaken.

"You tell me," I said. "The perpetrator, assuming the same individual was responsible in all three mutilation cases, has obviously got a thing about arms. At this stage, I haven't got a clue why." It's always best to declare ignorance, especially when you think you're on to something. I was positive the modus was significant, but I didn't want to make my interest too obvious yet.

"What about the post-mortem?" Katharine asked, turning to Davie. He'd attended it.

He raised his shoulders. "Too early to say. They've taken all the relevant samples for testing. Cause of death is definitely asphyxiation due to the bullet Raskolnikov was forced to swallow. Time of death – well, there's no argument about that. We already know it was between seven fifteen and eight p.m."

"You'll have the test results first thing in the morning, Dalrymple," Dawkley said. "The equipment we have at our disposal is the best there is and the laboratories are working as we speak."

Raphael stood up, her hand to her forehead. "Anything more?"

I nodded. "Raskolnikov's nostrum. Is it possible to reconstruct its memory cells? I'm pretty sure he must have received an urgent message that sent him hightailing down to the Botanic Garden."

Connington, also on his feet, nodded. "My technical people are working on that."

"Good." I smiled at him. "Maybe they'll also be able to ascertain how it was destroyed." The proctor's face fell but I still hadn't finished with him. "And maybe they'll also be able to find out how the surveillance cameras near the locus were tampered with. I presume you accept that they didn't go down by accident?"

Dawkley glanced at the proctor. "I'll provide a team of expert fibre-optic engineers, Connington."

I nodded. "Okay. Then it's time for you to hit the sack."

Raphael twitched her head at me and led the others towards the door.

"Oh, one more thing," I called, focusing on the chief administrator when they turned round. "The Eagle One bullet that Raskolnikov choked on."

"What about it, citizen?" she asked tersely.

"You might want to think about why it was used," I replied. "After all, that model of ammunition isn't exactly common and access to it is supposedly strictly controlled." I gave her a tight smile. "Don't forget: the assumption is that the one we removed from Lewis Hamilton's body was aimed at you."

She swallowed audibly then moved off again. "Report to the Hebdomadal Council at eight tomorrow evening, citizen," she said. "Goodnight."

I wished her sweet dreams – inaudibly.

Katharine, Davie and I moved to the leather armchairs at the far end of the long room.

Davie yawned massively. "I want to hit the sack too."

"What's keeping you?" Katharine asked.

"Calm down, children," I said. "We're all going to bed in a minute. I want to work out what we're doing tomorrow first."

"You mean today," Davie said, looking at his watch and shaking his head.

"Aye. You keep on the pathologist's back, big man. And check that Connington keeps his eye on the ball too."

He nodded.

"Katharine, can you take a look at Raskolnikov's rooms in his college? While you're there, see if you can find out anything about his private life."

"Do they have private lives in this place?" she asked. "New Oxford's even more obsessed with control than the Council back home."

"Who can control his fate?" came a wheezing voice from behind us.

The three of us jumped like performing monkeys.

"Jesus!" I said. "You shouldn't sneak up on people, doctor."

Elias Burton looked over his shoulder. "My apologies. Perhaps you hadn't noticed the alternative door."

"Perhaps not," I said. "Who can control his fate? Is that a quotation?"

"Very good," Burton said, clapping his hands and gazing at the table beyond us. "It's from *Othello*. Is that wine I see there?"

"Help yourself," I said, glancing at the others. I wondered how long the old academic had been lurking in the shadows.

Burton returned with a glass of Nox Chardonnay and sat down. "You and your friends appear to be working overtime, Quintilian," he said.

"Don't worry," I said with a laugh. "It'll be reflected in the bill."

He smiled. "I wish you luck. Extracting payment from the Hebdomadal Council requires a heroic temperament."

"Oh, we're all endowed with one of those," I said.

"That'll be right," Katharine said, getting to her feet. "I'm away to my bed. Coming, Quint?"

I shook my head. I was dog-tired and I didn't fancy another night on her floor. Besides, there were things I wanted to ask the old guy.

"Sleep well, then," Katharine said, tossing her head. "Goodnight, doctor."

"Night, Quint. Doctor." Davie followed her out.

Elias Burton was looking at me thoughtfully. "You and the lady are a couple, are you not, Quintilian?" he ventured, dabbing wine from his lips with a discoloured handkerchief.

I nodded. "After a fashion."

"Romantic attachments are discouraged in New Oxford. Be careful they don't put the two of you in a cage to observe your every move." His voice was bitter, his head moving from side to side. "They experiment on everyone in this city," he said.

"I know. We saw what happens in the suburbs."

"I'm not just talking about the suburbs," Burton countered. "It's even worse within the university, you know. Surveillance everywhere, conversations logged . . ."

I looked at him. "Hadn't you better be more careful then?"

He laughed hoarsely. "They don't care about me. I'm dead wood. I'll soon be on my way to the House of Dust."

I pricked up my ears. There it was again. That was one of the things I wanted to ask him about. "It's the second time you've used that expression, doctor," I said. "What does it mean exactly?"

The old don was gazing at me. "Ah, the House of Dust, Quintilian. Man's long home, as it's called in *Eccle-*

siastes." He smiled sadly. "The university has spurned the teaching of ancient literature and culture. Even the Bible is ignored, except when it comes to the teaching of effective business practice in the few remaining Catholic countries."

I felt a yawn coming on and swallowed it with difficulty. "Yes, but what is the House of Dust?"

Elias Burton registered my impatience. "Never fear, Quintilian," he said, getting his lips round my full name with evident pleasure. "You will visit the House of Dust when your time comes. We all will." He smiled again. "In the old Mesopotamian epic poem the hero Gilgamesh laments his friend Enkidu, who dies and descends to the House of Dust." His eyes were on mine. "The House of Dust is the underworld, Quintilian. The realms ruled by Ereshkigal, Queen of the Dead. We are all bound there." He sat back, the wine glass held loosely in his hand.

I stared at him. "But what's that got to do with the buildings that used to be Christ Church?" I demanded. "You referred to them as the House of Dust."

Burton was sprawled in his chair, his limbs loose. After a few moments he shook his head feebly. "Enough, Quintilian. I've said enough." He waved me away, his appetite for talk suddenly sated. "Goodnight to you." He bowed his head, already lost in a reverie.

I got up and left him to his thoughts. I had the feeling that, even though I was ready to drop, sleep would not come easily.

I was wrong. The combination of a long day and a late intake of food and booze knocked me out as efficiently as a cosh to the cranium. Never mind the House of Dust – I spent what seemed like aeons trying to walk through a viscous, sucking sludge that threatened at any moment to drag me downwards and clog my lungs terminally. I was distantly aware that I'd been writhing around, the thin, temperature-regulated quilt wrapping itself round my limbs like a winding sheet.

Then everything suddenly became much clearer. I heard a clock chiming in the distance. The dim lights in the quadrangle were lining the outside edges of the curtains, but otherwise the room was pitch dark. I tried to move, but my legs still seemed to be caught up in a glutinous morass and my arms refused to rise from my sides.

That was when I saw the figure. It was surrounded in what seemed like a hazy aura and it was large, both tall and bulky. I felt my heart begin to pound, but, apart from my eyes, that was the only movement in my body. My brain was sending frantic messages to nerves and sinews that were resolutely off duty.

So I lay where I was and watched the figure as it approached, then leaned over me. My heart was thudding like a bass drum that was providing the backing to a particularly explosive solo by some old blues maestro. I still couldn't move a muscle. The face was lowered to within a foot of mine and I could hear the susurrus of steady breathing. I tried as best I could to make out the features but they were amorphous and unstable, as if an electric field were distorting them. And then, for a moment, the image solidified and I saw a heavy male face with unnaturally smooth skin. But it was the eyes that made me stop breathing. The irises were jet black, immobile and completely devoid of life. I heard myself gasp as my lungs filled with air, but by then the face had been withdrawn, the features losing their shape again. There was a brief hissing noise and I felt myself falling, losing touch, entering the void.

The last thing I remembered was a sensation of joy. Somehow I'd managed to evade the night visitor with the terrible staring eyes.

I came round slowly, my eyes gummed together and a jumble of unconnected thoughts cascading through my mind like a mountain stream in spate. Then I remembered what I'd seen and sat up so quickly that I almost put my back out. I rubbed my eyes and ran through the vision, gradually coming back to the real world – or at least the New Oxford version of it. Outside I could hear the restrained voices of students on their way to the hall or to early lectures. I moved my arms and legs gingerly and found that they were in working order again. Then I got up and crumpled to the thin carpet like a house of cards beside an open window.

"Shit," I said, trying to remember how many glasses of claret I'd got through. I didn't think it had been enough to floor me.

I pulled myself up and staggered to the wash basin, then bent down and sluiced my head with cold water. I still hadn't worked out how to programme hot on my nostrum. Clarity gradually returned to my consciousness. I stood up and rubbed my head and face with a towel. And opened my eyes to get another shock.

Two lines of letters and numbers had been written on the mirror glass in marker pen:

Crim Fac Access Code
RED3694T00699

I stepped back a couple of paces and tried to make sense of what was going on. Here, at least, was proof that the apparition had been real. Given how terrifying the guy was, I could have lived without confirmation of that, but at least I hadn't been seeing things.

Then I looked down. On the carpet beneath the basin pedestal was a prime piece of evidence. It was a heavily indented muddy footprint. I estimated that it was a size eleven sole – and it was ribbed in exactly the same pattern as the ones we'd found at the crime scene in Leith. An NF138B. Jesus. I sat back down on the bed and tried to get a grip.

The idea that I might have been in close proximity to one of the mysterious Grendels took me some time to digest.

I eventually managed to get some coffee – acrid and murky – out of the delivery unit. My stomach seemed to be experiencing a delayed reaction to what had happened during the night, so I decided against eating. I copied the writing into my notebook and took a tracing of the footprint. After carefully cleaning the writing off the mirror, I left my rooms. To my relief I didn't see Katharine or Davie as I headed for the college gate. I wanted some time to think about what was going on, as well as to check out the code reference that had been left for me. I had the feeling that prefix "RED" meant that it was top secret in spades. The question was, how could I guarantee myself a reasonable shot at accessing whatever it was that the mystery visitor wanted me to see?

I decided to let that stew for a while and walked across Radcliffe Square towards Noxad. As I went, I looked up at the gleaming panels of the surveillance dome on the Camera and wondered if my steps were being tracked. If I'd had any money in my pocket I wouldn't have bet against it, but New Oxford apparently worked on a digital credit system. Then a thought struck me. Had the cameras and sensors picked up the night visitor? If they hadn't – and that seemed likely, considering no one had come to investigate – then perhaps the Grendels had some kind of anti-surveillance device. On the other hand, Grendels were denied access to the city. What the hell was going on?

I cut through the former library and on to Broad Street. The clouds above were darkening: it looked like the rain shields were about to come in useful. The usual bustle of sober students was all around me, some of them piling into the Faculty of English Language across the road. I vaguely remembered that the building used to be a world-famous bookshop. There were very few books in New Oxford, of course. If what Elias Burton told me about the vocational nature of the university's courses was right, those would probably be foreign students learning English rather than native speakers reading *Beowulf* and the like.

That thought made me perform an emergency stop, causing a tall, black female student to collide with my back. She was the one who apologised, though I hardly noticed. Christ, *Beowulf*. It came back to me out of the mists of my youth. In the old poem the eponymous hero lays into the marauding monster Grendel and rips his arm off at the shoulder. Christ. Could that similarity to the killer's modus operandi only be a coincidence?

I was still pondering that when I passed the thin finger of the Martyrs' Memorial and reached the Faculty of Criminology at the bottom of St Giles. Was my adolescent passion for epic poetry reimposing itself unduly? I didn't think so, especially after what I'd seen in the night. It seemed clear enough that one or more of New Oxford's most lethal servants were connected with the murders, but I needed hard evidence if I was to stand any chance of convincing Raphael. She knew more than she was saying about the Grendels, but she had given me the footwear reference that initially put me on to them. I still didn't have a clue about her agenda. Maybe I'd find one in the headquarters of the university's most repressive faculty.

The high neoclassical façade rose up before me, four great Ionic columns stretching skywards like the bars of a huge jailhouse window. I looked at my father's guidebook and discovered that each column had originally been surmounted by a figure representing the languages of France, Italy, Spain and Germany. Like the UK, those four countries had been torn apart by drugs gangs a couple of decades back. Presumably that explained why all that was left of the statues was the odd shattered leg.

Inside the tall doorway was a panel showing the location of the various sub-faculties and institutes. I was amazed to see that there was a Department of Crime Writing – maybe fiction was as significant to the criminologists as fact. Surprise, surprise, it was in the Dorothy L. Sayers Wing. I recalled that she had an unhealthy interest in heroic poetry too.

"Can I help, Citizen Dalrymple?"

I turned at the sound of the female voice. "If it isn't Harriet Haskins," I said. "We must stop meeting like this." I gave the blonde bulldog a cold smile. "I mean it."

She looked at me with what I was pretty sure was feigned surprise. "I don't know what you mean. I happened to be on my way to—"

"Where are Trout and Perch?" I asked. "I haven't seen them today."

"Really, citizen," she protested. "I don't know what—"

"Forget it," I interrupted. "Since you're here – for

whatever reason – you can direct me to Professor Raskolnikov's office."

"I can do better than that," Haskins said eagerly. "I can take you there."

"All right," I said. "And then you can leave me on my own."

"Very well." She led me to a transparent lift shaft, her lips pursed.

I've always found it effective to take enthusiastic officials down a peg. Or six.

Up or down? I flipped a mental coin before the floor moved and got it wrong. We shot upwards and hissed to a halt on the third floor.

Haskins led me to a heavy oak-panelled door. "The professor liked the old style," she said, nothing akin to grief in her voice. Members of her rank were strangers to emotion. She admitted me to a huge split-level room that, unusually for this computer-driven city, was lined with fully occupied bookshelves.

"I see what you mean," I said, running my eye round the place. "Was this once a library, by any chance?"

"I believe so," the bulldog replied. "The professor's desk is behind that bookcase." She pointed to a wide antique piece made of dark wood and stacked with bound volumes.

"Right," I said, turning to her. "Close the door behind you."

She gave me a perfunctory nod and complied with my instruction. No doubt she'd be telling Doctor Connington exactly where I was. I wondered if senior academics' offices were subject to surveillance. It didn't take me long to come up with an answer. Of course they were. I grabbed the nearest chair and leaned it against the door, the backrest under the handle. That would give me a few seconds' grace if anyone came to stop what I was about to do.

I scouted around the cavernous office. A glass cupola was casting light over the central area, the clouds that were visible through it even blacker than they had been. From what I could see of his personal possessions – icons, a samovar, bottles of vodka – the Russian had been very receptive to his own country's culture. I couldn't fathom how that tied in with his role in the Faculty of Criminology. Then I remembered the Siberian gulags and the industrialisation of crime that had started with Stalin and ended up with the so-called Mafia governments of the early twenty-first century. Plenty of crime and bugger-all punishment.

The professor's desk would have won a Nobel Prize for untidiness in the times before Stockholm and Oslo were turned into communes by Vietnamese and other Asian immigrants. For someone who used to fiddle with his nostrum as much as any of his colleagues, Raskolnikov had been very keen on bits of paper. There were hundreds of them scattered over a large mahogany worktop, the few I glanced at in a Cyrillic scrawl that did absolutely nothing for me. So I could find nothing obvious linking him to the murders, and nothing to explain how he obtained a starring role in the latest one. Time for plan B.

On the left of the desk there was a flat screen with the letters "NOX" in red at the top. It was similar in style to the one in my rooms at Brase, but it looked a lot more sophisticated. I tried unsuccessfully to find a keyboard. Shit. The professor must have used voice recognition. I didn't think my limited impersonation skills would be able to replicate his guttural accent. I sat back in the leather swivel chair and spun myself round. After a while that shook my ideas up. Of course. I didn't need Raskolnikov's terminal. I had my very own nostrum. I wished Katharine was here to give me a quick tutorial. Then again, I suspected that what I was about to key in would bring the house down on me. I swallowed hard, tried to dredge up a remnant of the heroic temperament and typed access code RED3694T00699 on the tiny keys.

For a few seconds the nostrum was silent. Then it emitted some high-pitched bleeps and suddenly the miniature screen was filled with closely compacted writing. I did what I'd seen Connington do in the Camera and pointed the nostrum at the screen on the desk. That did it. The backlight came on, then the file was transferred to a more legible format. I leaned forward and scanned the contents as quickly as I could.

There was plenty of technical guff that I scrolled past quickly, the language an unpalatable blend of scientific, bureaucratic and academic. From what I could gather, the Faculty of Criminology, represented by the Department of Forensic Chemistry, and the Faculty of Biological and Physical Sciences' Department of Applied Bioengineering – whatever that was – were involved in a joint research project. I looked in vain for the word "Grendel" but got no joy. This project seemed to be all about toxic pollutants and the human nervous system. Then a light went on in my head when I saw a reference to the Poison Fields. I remembered what Pete Pym had said about the savage bulldogs who patrolled the contaminated outer regions of the state. Now I was getting somewhere. The departments' joint venture had produced a method of rendering humans immune to high levels of toxicity. Experiments had been extensive and the personnel who'd been treated had shown no signs of tissue or organ damage. And the original test subjects were referred to by names from works of English literature: there was a Volpone, a Miranda, a Tamburlaine, a Pardoner and a Plowman. No Grendel, but it was a pattern of sorts.

Then two things happened in quick succession. The first I'd been expecting. There was a thunderous pounding on the door. I looked over the bookcase and saw the chair I'd lodged under the handle judder. The second I definitely hadn't anticipated. Underlined in blue on the screen, the print sticking out like an operation scar, was a combination of letters and numbers that made my eyes burn. Next to them was a location that was very close to where I was.

The chair finally gave way and the door burst open. Trout careered through, his pal Perch not far behind. Then came Haskins, followed by Professor Yamaguchi. None of them looked at all pleased with me as I closed the file and shut down my nostrum.

But I didn't care. I'd just managed to track down Edinburgh's missing chief toxicologist.

What Lister 25 was doing in New Oxford was another question altogether.

"Citizen Dalrymple." Yamaguchi came towards me. "What exactly are you doing?"

"You know exactly what I'm doing," I replied. "The file I accessed had enough alarm bells attached to it to wake up the dead of Jericho."

The professor gave a brief smile. "Yes, I'm afraid code red files are restricted to administrators and senior academics. If it's vital to your investigation, you can ask the Hebdomadal Council to allow you to see the contents."

"So much for free access," I said under my breath.

Trout and Perch stepped forward, their faces set in stone.

Yamaguchi raised a limp hand. "Could I ask how you obtained the file code, citizen?" His tone was light but I registered the interest beneath it.

"You could," I said, nodding. "In fact, you just did."

When I said no more, the professor looked pointedly at the male bulldogs. Then he shook his head in annoyance. "Be careful, Citizen Dalrymple," he said quietly. "There are things in this city that you do not want to meddle with."

"Uh-huh." I stepped to the side of him and headed for the door. "Let's talk to Raphael about those this evening." I could feel my heart pounding in my chest as I walked out, but the academic and his canine friends stayed put. Probably trying to find out if there was anything else I shouldn't have seen on the dead man's desk.

I got out of the Taylorian in one piece but I knew that the chains were tightening around me. I needed to make a breakthrough in the case or I'd be taking up residence in one of New Oxford's many incarceration facilities.

A visit to the chemist seemed like a good idea.

Davie came on the mobile as I was walking down Beaumont Street. I'd turned it off when I was in the faculty to avoid being disturbed. Heavy rain was pounding on the protection shields above.

"Where the hell are you, Quint?" he demanded. "You didn't show at breakfast."

"Couldn't stomach the idea of you taking advantage of the porridge, big man."

"Very funny. The test results are beginning to come in."

"Oh aye?" I said.

"The pathology team's been through all the samples from Raskolnikov." His voice was even. "Nothing out of the ordinary."

I stepped aside to allow a procession of gown-clad students to pass. "You mean, no chemical compounds?"

"Correct."

"Jesus. So his arms were removed without an anaesthetic." I was thinking what a horrific experience that would have been if the Russian had still been conscious. Why hadn't the assailant used the compound that had put Dead Dod into a coma? And why was there no blood from the wounds?

"Correct again. They're not sure if the victim had choked on the Eagle One by the time the knife or whatever it was cut into him."

"I hope so for his sake. What else?"

"Connington's people have reviewed all the surveillance records. No sign of anyone suspicious. And something definitely happened to the cameras at the bottom of the High Street and in the Botanic Garden. The team Dawkley sent hasn't worked out how it was done yet."

"All right. Where are you, Davie?"

"On my way to Souls," he replied. "To see if Katharine needs a hand."

"Don't wind her up, will you?"

"Me?" he said, laughing. "What are you doing?"

"Tell you later. Out."

I stopped at the junction to let a Chariot glide by and gazed up at the imposing, three-storey recessed block in front of me, wings extending on either side of it. It looked about as welcoming as a Victorian workhouse, which may well have been what it had been turned into by Raphael and her mates. I crossed the road and walked past the ranks of bicycles that were piled up against the railings. Signs of student life. Maybe the establishment was still a place of learning. According to my guidebook, it used to be called Worcester College. The black display panel proclaimed in pink letters that it was now known as "Worc"; I presumed that wasn't pronounced "worse". I passed the sensor posts without any problem and walked through the gateway into a quadrangle that wasn't a quadrangle. Stepping beyond the loggia, I looked round at the asymmetrical buildings. On my right there was a long, graceful façade, while the end straight ahead had been left open. Over to my left was an uneven but picturesque terrace of medieval cottages. Neat architectural contrasts, but they weren't why I was here.

I looked at the staircase and room numbers I'd scribbled in my notebook when the file had been on the screen: 18/25. I wandered around the main quad and soon realised I'd have to look elsewhere. I went through a low passage and found myself in a wide expanse of garden, a lake to my right and a well-tended lawn dotted with trees all around. There were several late twentieth-century stone and brick buildings at the far edges of the grass. I ran over – no rain shields here – and located staircase eighteen in one that a screen identified as the Masterman Building.

And then, not for the first time that day, I felt a frisson of shock. The curtains to the first room that I reached on the ground floor were half open. Being an investigator – and also a nosy bastard – I couldn't resist a peek. Jesus. Wiping the rain from my eyes, I concentrated on the two partially clad individuals, one male and one female, who were closely entwined. I recognised the man with the goatee beard instantly: Andrew Duart, Glasgow's first secretary. He was getting around a lot in New Oxford. I had to wait till the woman turned, her head leaning back as Duart nuzzled her heavy breasts. This time I wasn't quite as surprised as I had been yesterday. It was Hel Hyslop, former Glasgow detective and, apparently, former convict.

What was this pair of migrant lovebirds doing three floors beneath Edinburgh's missing chief toxicologist?

CHAPTER SEVENTEEN

I slipped past the sensor posts at the entrance to the accommodation block – my control card really had been programmed to allow me access everywhere, it seemed. The building was functional, late twentieth-century drab, a major let-down after the spectacular old buildings in the main quad. The brickwork was discoloured and pocked with unfilled bullet holes. It wasn't the kind of place Andrew Duart would usually frequent.

I felt my way down an unlit passage, estimating where the door to the room would be. I thought about knocking, but decided against it after a couple of seconds' thought; surprise is always a useful weapon, especially with people who normally dispense orders. I waved my card at the metal wall panel. There was a dull click and the door swung open. I was in.

So was Glasgow's first secretary. There was a partition wall separating most of the small study cum sitting room from the sleeping area. Through the gap next to the window I could see a tangle of bare legs and two fused sets of loins. The couple had collapsed on to the bed, the floor around it littered with items of clothing. Hel Hyslop's hands, fingers apart and bent for purchase, were exerting what looked to me like excruciating pressure on Duart's buttocks. Relief was at hand.

"Ding ding," I said, sitting down on the wide ledge beneath the window. "End of round one."

Andrew Duart's rapid pumping stopped. He glanced round, his cheeks beaded with sweat. Hel Hyslop's head appeared over his shoulder. She looked much more in control of herself, her grey eyes fixed on me and her lips set in a tight line.

"Dalrymple!" the first secretary gasped, pulling away and lunging for his trousers.

I averted my eyes but couldn't miss a flash of the thickly curled hair in Hyslop's groin. She made no attempt to cover herself.

"What the fucking hell are you doing here?" Duart yelled.

I stared at him until he realised what he'd said.

"Well?" he demanded, his anger fading. "Do you normally walk in on people when they're . . . when they're . . ." He seemed to have lost the verbal proficiency that political operators like him are born with.

"When they're overcome by passion?" Hyslop's voice had an edge to it. She got off the crumpled bed slowly and pulled on a dressing-gown. Her breasts, fuller than I'd imagined, swung provocatively as she moved.

"Hello, Hel," I said, giving her a cautious smile. I'd been on the wrong end of her temper more than once in the past. "What happened? Did your friend here get you out on parole?"

"That's nothing to do with you, Quint," she said, turning to the washbasin and starting to dash water over her lower torso.

I glanced at Duart. "What's going on, Andrew?" I glanced around the room. The walls were painted in an unappealing shade of beige. The only decoration was a large overhead photo of central Oxford with the words

"NOX Secure Imaging Inc. – Vision is Power" in red over the Radcliffe Camera: one of Crim Fac's money-spinning sidelines, I guessed. "Surely your friends in the Hebdomadal Council could have found you somewhere better than this."

"I'm not staying here," he said with a sneer. "This is the inspector's . . . em, Hyslop's room." He was fully dressed now. Donning his expensive dark suit and glistening black loafers had enabled him to regain most of his authority. Most, but not all: his cheeks were still glowing and his hair was ruffled. "Guests from New Oxford's trading partners are accommodated at the Rand."

I'd noticed the Victorian Gothic hotel opposite the Taylorian earlier. "Convenient for the Faculty of Criminology," I observed.

Andrew Duart stared at me aggressively. "What's that supposed to mean?" he asked, tightening his florid silk tie.

"I saw the pair of you yesterday," I said, aware that Hel Hyslop had stepped closer. She was rolling forward on the balls of her bare feet like a large feline that had just spotted its evening meal. "Coming out of the Department of Forensic Chemistry. Which, as you no doubt know, is a branch of the Criminology Faculty." I stood up to face them. "Any chance you might tell me what you were doing there?"

Hyslop took a pace nearer. "I suppose that fire was your doing, Quint. It didn't occur to you that people could have been injured?" I wasn't keen on the way she was flexing her hands. I was pretty sure that she'd learned plenty about unarmed combat in the All-Glasgow Major Crime Squad.

Duart raised a hand to restrain her. "Our movements

in this city are no concern of yours, Dalrymple," he said in an icy voice.

"Dalrymple?" I said. "What happened to Quint? We used to be so close." I glanced at Hel. "Until I discovered that you'd let a major criminal out after a few months. Been getting around, have you, Hel?" I was wondering if she could have had some involvement in the murders and mutilations.

They both stared at me.

"What's the point of that question?" Duart asked.

"How long have you been in Oxford, Hel?" I demanded. "Have you been in Edinburgh recently? And where were you between seven and eight o'clock yesterday evening?"

They were looking seriously puzzled now.

"To answer your questions in order, Quint," Hyslop said. "Two days. No. At a seminar in this building. Satisfied?"

I shrugged. It wasn't very likely that she'd committed the murders; for a start, she didn't have size eleven feet, though the wearing of oversize footwear by miscreants isn't unheard of. What she did have was a history of complicity in numerous killings – except I'd never established if she carried out any of them herself.

"I don't suppose you'll be giving us an explanation as to why you burst in here," Hyslop said.

"Not unless you tell me what you're doing in Oxford." I glanced at Duart. "Both of you."

The first secretary was straightening the creases of his trousers. "I'm here on business, not that it's any business of yours."

"Ha," I said, not laughing. "Signing Glasgow up for more Nox systems? You'd better be careful, Andy. They might take you over." I might have been imagining it, but for a second I thought he looked unsettled.

Then Hel Hyslop moved towards me menacingly and I decided that I'd said enough.

Now it really was time to visit the chemist.

I went up the stairs, having ascertained from the display screen on the ground floor that 18/25 was on the third. There was no one around and the place smelled of polish and detergent rather than of human bodies. Maybe the list of names on the panel referred to old members who'd donated funds to the college rather than to living residents. But where would that leave Hyslop? Why was she being put up here?

This time I knocked. Not that it got me anywhere. I put my ear to the door and heard nothing. It looked like I was going to have to rely on the control card after all. Then there was a click and the door opened. On the other side of it was a face I recognised. But the condition of the body had changed a lot.

"Ramsay?" I said, using the chief toxicologist's first name. "Is that you?"

Lister 25 was propping himself up on one of those frames that old people use to get around. It was a long time since I'd seen something like that – the Council's welfare budget doesn't run to what the guardians see as fripperies.

"Dalrymple?" he said with a gasp. He screwed his eyes up. "Quint Dalrymple? Is that you?" Tears filled his eyes and began to run down over his jowls. They were looser and even more pachydermic than they had been.

I stepped inside and let the door swing to. "Aye, it's me," I said, going up to him and smiling. "Don't worry, I'll get you out of here."

The toxicologist manoeuvred himself awkwardly towards a high armchair and let his shrunken body drop into it. Then he dabbed his eyes with a dirty handkerchief and glanced around the room. "Get me out of Death Row?" He gave a bitter laugh. "You'll have to carry me. Think you can manage that?"

I followed the direction of his eyes, trying to understand what he meant by Death Row. The room was much larger than Hel Hyslop's, the living area broad and high, with a sofa as well as an armchair. A slatted wooden staircase led up to a platform on which there was a bed. It was a lot more comfortable than your average condemned man's cell.

Lister 25 laughed again, his head twitching uncontrollably. "This is their idea of retribution, Quint. When I couldn't work any more they put me in a room where I couldn't reach the bed except by crawling." He gave one of his trademark pouts. "Fuck 'em. I've been sleeping on the settee."

I squatted down in front of him. "What's happened, Ramsay?" I asked in a low voice. "You've been working in the Poison Fields, haven't you?"

He opened his eyes wide. "How did you find me, Quint? What do you know about the PFs?" He started coughing.

I stood up and looked for a glass. I found one by the sink in the far corner of the room. By the time I got back to him, he was in a full paroxysm. I managed to take his hands away from his mouth and get some liquid down. Eventually the tearing sound subsided.

"My lungs," the toxicologist said, shaking his head. "They're done for. I'll not make it back to Edinburgh." He looked at me sadly. "Or hear another Robert Johnson song." The old bugger was still addicted to the blues – I found that reassuring. He made a throaty noise and I thought he was going to start choking again. Then I realised he was laughing. "'Hellhound On My Trail' would seem appropriate." He swallowed and stared at me. "How did you find me?"

I told him about the reference to him in Raskolnikov's file, editing out the part about the nocturnal visitor and the message on my mirror. I also mentioned the murders in Oxford. He hadn't heard about either of them.

"So the criminals in charge of this festering utopia brought you here to do their dirty work," Lister 25 said, shaking his head in disgust. "I'm surprised you agreed, Quint. Or did they hold a gun to your head?"

"Uh-uh. The killings here are linked to things that happened in Edinburgh. A Leith Lancer had his arm amputated." I looked at him. "And Lewis Hamilton was shot, probably by mistake. I reckon the bullet was meant for Administrator Raphael."

The old chemist was peering at me, his eyes watery but focused. "The public order guardian was shot? Is he dead?"

I nodded. "Heart failure."

"Bloody hell." Lister 25 shook his head slowly. "Poor bastard. I didn't like him much, but . . ." His words trailed away. Then his body stiffened and he gripped the arms of his chair. "It's a pity Raphael didn't get it. That woman's deranged."

"Have you met her?" I asked, glancing up at the Nox Imaging Systems photo of Oxford that was on the wall above the armchair, the Radcliffe Camera's high-tech dome its centrepiece. I wondered if everything we were saying was being overheard and relayed to the chief administrator.

The toxicologist nodded, clearing his throat with

difficulty. "After her people hustled me on to the helijet in the middle of the night a couple of weeks back, she made a personal appearance on the nostrum they gave me." He nodded at me. "Smart devices, those. Have you got one?"

I took mine out of my pocket, then let it slip back.

"Aye, well," Lister 25 continued, "she made it very clear to me that the work I was instructed by the senior guardian to do on certain soil samples had suddenly become even more crucial: absolutely essential to the security of New Oxford, as she put it." He gave a dry laugh. "Have you noticed how the top brass here sound exactly like the guardians?"

"Oh yeah," I replied, noting Slick's involvement for future reference. "Something to do with people who wield power unchecked."

"Aye," the old chemist grunted. "They begin to speak like machines. Anyway, she was there waiting for me when the helijet arrived. She was as welcoming as a cold fish can be. Not that she apologised for spiriting me away from Edinburgh. She even took me down to the research station herself. There was another top-ranker with us, a character by the name of Dawkins . . . no . . . what was it?"

"Dawkley?"

"Aye, that's it. Fancied himself as a scientist. Sounded more like a bureaucrat to me."

I had my notebook out. "Where was this research station, Ramsay?" I asked.

Lister 25 drew the back of his hand across his brow. "Research station? It was more like an army camp. Checkpoints everywhere, electronic surveillance, heavies much worse than any guardsman back home." He let out a cracked laugh. "Or guardswoman. The place is known as Sutt. It's a village about ten miles south of the city. I found out from one of the lab assistants that it used to be called Sutton Courtenay. Apparently some Prime Minister lived there back at the beginning of the last century." He broke off and drank from the glass I'd given him, then laughed again – it was more like a croak. "I'll tell you something funny, Quint. I went for a walk one day – before the contaminated samples got to me – and wandered round what was left of the church. The drugs gangs had blown the buildings to pieces but the cemetery was still in pretty good shape. Guess whose gravestone I found."

I looked across at him and shrugged. "John Mayall's?"

"Ha!" The noise that erupted must have traumatised what was left of his lungs. He gulped water. "John Mayall. Very good, lad. He could play the blues. Not that it was the real thing. No, this grave was much more appropriate to this twisted state."

I raised my shoulders again.

He leered at me. "Eric Blair."

For a moment I got caught up on the surname: nasty memories of image-obsessed, terminal governments from the years before the break-up of the UK. Then the juxtaposition of names hit me. Jesus. Eric Blair, that was the real name of one George Orwell. I should have spotted it the second I heard it – I was born in 1984, after all.

"You're kidding?" I said. "Was it really him?"

Lister 25 nodded solemnly. "Apparently. I eventually found someone in the place who confirmed it. The rest of the morons didn't even know who Orwell was."

"So symbolism is alive and well." I shook my head to bring me back to the real world. "What was the research you were doing out there, Ramsay?"

The toxicologist's face fell. "Don't ask, Quint," he said in a low, unsteady voice. He coughed agonisingly. "Look what it did to me."

"I'll get you home," I said, leaning towards him.

He shook his head. "I've seen what happens. Two or three days is all it takes." He clutched my forearm with surprising strength. "The pollution in the Poison Fields is more severe than anything I've ever studied. Apparently it's been getting even worse in recent months. If it goes on like this, the city will soon be uninhabitable. That's why they've sent every scientist they can find out to the station in Sutt. Unless they can control the toxic gases and counter the effects they have on the immune system, they're lost."

Things were coming together. The RED code file I accessed referred to the human immune system, as well as to the Poison Fields. Was this what the case was about? But how did that tie up with the murders and mutilations?

"Ramsay," I said, my voice no more than a whisper. "Have you ever heard of the Grendels?"

His bloodshot eyes opened so wide that I thought they were going to slip out of their sockets. "The Grendels?" he said hoarsely. "You know about them?"

I shook my head in frustration. "Not enough. What are they like?"

Slowly he closed his eyes, his head twitching. "The Grendels?" he repeated in a weak voice. "Remember what I said about a hellhound on my trail?"

"Aye. And?"

But before the chief toxicologist could say anything more, there was a loud knocking. The door behind me opened.

I let out a groan and turned to face the music.

* * *

Except it turned out to be a different genre to the one I'd been expecting – along the lines of a female vocalist singing *a cappella* rather than a group of howling bulldogs.

"I hope you haven't been tiring my charge out," said a thin, middle-aged woman in a green and white striped jacket as she stepped past me. The strong smell of antiseptic came in with her.

I glanced down the corridor. She seemed to be on her own. "Not as much as you just did by flagellating the door."

She looked round at me from the armchair containing Lister 25. "Flagellating?" she repeated, her voice expressing bewilderment. "What do you mean?" She stood up straight, suddenly more interested in me than in the sick man. "Who are you?"

"You know exactly who I am," I said, moving towards her. "You were sent up here to interrupt us, weren't you?" I was pretty sure that someone – Connington? Dawkley? Raphael herself? – had been listening to our conversation and had decided to pull the plug before the old chemist said any more. Information in New Oxford seemed to be controlled by drip-feed. But why were they letting me find out anything at all if they were so touchy about the Grendels and the research projects at Sutt?

There was a strangulated sound from Lister 25. The nurse or whatever she was bent over him and loosened his clothes. Then she started speaking urgently, presumably into her nostrum.

"Code nine, Worc Masterman 18/25, top priority," I heard. She turned to me. "You'll have to go," she said, her voice taut. "The paramedics will be here in a few minutes."

I peered over her shoulder as she put a stethoscope to

the chief toxicologist's chest. He was only semi-conscious, the breath dragging audibly in and out of his ravaged lungs.

"Go!" the woman shouted.

There was nothing more I could do for Lister 25, so I complied.

But I didn't intend to forget the old toxicologist. Whoever was responsible for what had happened to him was in an abyss of trouble.

Back on ground level I stopped outside the door and watched as a pair of hefty medics pulled up in the ambulance version of a Chariot, red lights flashing. They rushed past without giving me a second glance.

I gave a second glance to Hel Hyslop's window. This time there was no opportunity to play the voyeur. The blinds and curtains were open but the room's human contents were no longer in situ. I set off back towards the main college buildings. Although the rain had let up, the grass underfoot was still very soggy. Then a loud scream almost made me lose my footing. It had come from my left. I looked through the trees and across an ornamental lake with Canada geese and other waterfowl standing guard on the bank. I could make out a group of people in dark blue overalls on a large grass-covered area. They seemed to be gathered around someone or something on the ground.

Call it professionalism, call it rabid curiosity, I threw caution to the still air and headed quickly for the trees that ran alongside the path. The new leaves were well advanced and they gave me some cover, but not as much as I'd have liked. Fortunately there was no one else around. I picked my way through the undergrowth, aware that there was a high fence on my left. It presumably marked the boundary of the college's extensive grounds.

Ahead there was a squat wooden pavilion. It was so run-down that I didn't bother trying to guess its age. The medieval buildings in the main quad looked more modern. Years of catering for swaggering rugby players and half-cut cricketers had taken their toll. At least the unkempt construction would give me cover.

When I was about twenty yards from it I heard a loud rustling in the bushes to my right. I froze, glancing around for a piece of timber to defend myself with. Shit – there was nothing but twigs. Then I heard a flip-flopping noise that seemed familiar. The leaves parted and out stepped a dodo.

"Christ, you again," I said under my breath. "Or does every college have its own?"

The formerly extinct bird held its shiny black eyes on me and stood motionless for a few seconds. Its curved beak was levelled at me like a loaded banana. Then the dodo flicked its head at me disdainfully and waddled off through the mud, its tail feathers twitching. I watched it move round the lake. The water birds took one look at it and scattered, the air filling with outraged honks and shrieks. It looked like dodos had pariah status – probably because the other avians knew they were zombies.

I made it to the pavilion and crouched down by the corner. I couldn't see any sign of surveillance units up above. That proved nothing. Nox cameras weren't always obvious. Moving my head cautiously round the splintered planking on the corner, I took in the throng on the open ground. Some of them were gazing across the lake, alerted by the birds' cries.

Then I saw her. Hel Hyslop was grappling with a guy who was at least a foot taller and wider than she was.

What was she doing here? I didn't have her down as an ornithologist, let alone an all-in wrestler.

I was so busy watching Hel that I was taken by surprise. There was a heavy thud a few yards to my left. I pulled my head back and waited, my heart pounding.

"Leave him there," said a harsh voice. "He's soft as shit. Fuck knows how he ever made standard bulldog grade."

Feet squelched across the grass and after a while I risked another look. I wished I hadn't. The young man who was lying comatose on the steps of the pavilion had pulp instead of a face. His right ear was dangling, attached only by a small piece of flesh. Around his groin the overalls were soaked. Jesus. The auxiliary training programme back home was bad, but at least you got to keep your facial features.

There was a sharp whistle blast from out on the field.

"Form up in lines of five!" shouted the guy with the barbed-wire voice.

I watched as the figures in dark blue overalls raced to obey. They seemed to be evenly split between males and females, though there was no segregation. Women had been fighting men before, as Hel had demonstrated. I wondered if she'd been the one who had laid out the poor sod on the steps.

"Now then," the commander continued, "it's fun time." He ran his eyes over the ranks in front of him – I'd counted ten lines. "So you want to be Grendels, do you?"

I pricked my ears up, clutching the edge of the pavilion. Was that what was going on here? An audition for potential hyper-bulldogs? I was in luck. Then I remembered the access code I'd been left by the intruder wearing Grendel-issue boots. Maybe I was meant to find my way here.

"I can't hear you!" the speaker was yelling.

There was a mixture of loud and more muffled cries in the affirmative. It sounded like some of the recruits might have already lost their appetite.

"Well, this is where we find out if you make the grade, people." The headbanger swung his head round to take in the whole group. Even though I was about forty yards away I could see the deep scarring on his cheeks and head. There wasn't much more than a thin fuzz of hair on the latter. "Noke here will issue you all with probes."

I strained to see what the subordinate was handing out. Each of the candidates got a thin rod that was about two feet long. I couldn't be sure, but it looked like the front half was a thin metal blade. They were glinting, even in the weak sunlight.

"Right, people," the hard man continued. "Same rules as earlier when you were grappling. I want contact only to be made with your opponent's upper arm. The winner of each bout will be the first to pierce both arms between shoulder and elbow."

Oh aye? What was so significant about the upper arm? I was thinking of the amputation in Edinburgh and those down here. Another Grendel connection?

"Excuse me, leader," came an unsteady male voice. "You said pierce. You mean—"

"What do you fucking think I mean?" shouted the leader, squaring up to the tall trainee. "I mean stick your fucking probe as far as you can into your opponent's flesh. Do you get that?" He grabbed the unfortunate guy's weapon and, before I could blink, ran it through his bicep. I saw the blade protrude by at least six inches.

To my amazement the victim stood his ground. His face was screwed up in agony, but he kept quiet, his back straight. I reckoned he'd shown he was Grendel material, but what did I know?

"So, numbers one and three," the leader roared, "get to it."

A heavily built young woman and a male of medium height came forward and took guard. Then their blades flashed and they went at each other. They separated after a few seconds, the guy dropping to one knee, a hand to his face.

"I said upper arm, number one!" the trainer screamed. "You've taken his fucking eye out."

I rocked back on my heels. This was way beyond a joke. I was trying to think of a way of getting Hel Hyslop out before she lost a vital organ. Then I leaned forward again and saw the avid look on her face as she followed the next bout, her lips parted. Hell's teeth.

Then I blew it. Without realising, I'd been inching my head further round the pavilion corner. Suddenly one of the dark blue overalls saw me and let out a shout of alarm. After a few seconds of focusing, they all looked towards me. I wondered if Hel had recognised me, but I wasn't waiting to find out. To the sound of a ragged hue and cry I jerked my head back and got to my feet. The fence was about twenty yards away. It was high and forbidding, sensor posts in regular gaps at the base. At least there wasn't any barbed wire.

I threw myself towards the barrier, conscious of the yells and pounding feet close behind and even more conscious of what the leader and the fighter had done with their probes. Then I remembered what had happened to Maddy Pitt's dog.

I just hoped there wasn't an electric current running through the wire.

* * *

It turned out not to be electrified. Or maybe it was and my control card switched the juice off. Anyway, I was over like a mountain goat and sprinting to my left down what must have been a towpath – the stagnant strip of water looked like a disused canal. I fully expected Hyslop and her new friends to come after me, but I was able to reduce my pace when I neared a low bridge because there was no sound behind me. Glancing round, I saw I was in the clear. Sticking each other in the upper arm, or eye, was obviously more important than chasing unauthorised observers. Then it struck me that the training leader might have called up a pack of ordinary bulldogs to track me down. I followed the towpath under the arch of the bridge and squatted down in the dark.

All I could hear was the faint sound of water running from a rusty pipe, interspersed with the squeaking of what I took to be rats. No sirens, no high-speed hissing from gas-powered bulldog Chariots. Just when I'd concluded that I was being left on my own, heavy footsteps began to approach. I drew further under cover beneath the dank stonework, my heart racing. The regular sound grew louder, still louder, then passed me by. I swung my head round and realised that the walker had passed under the bridge on the other side of the water. I looked again and blinked. I recognised him. The large shoulders and long hair were easy to place. It was Pete Pym, the dead cleaner's brother. He was a long way from Cowley. I wondered where he'd been when Raskolnikov lost his arms and his life.

It was time to activate my own surveillance skills.

It isn't difficult to follow someone when they're on the other side of a stretch of water, even one as silent as the stinking canal. You just keep your distance and make use of the natural cover, which in this case was plentiful: overgrown verges, the trunks of long-dead trees, the odd abandoned shopping trolley from the time when the centre of the city was served by supermarkets rather than Nox outlets. This was definitely not one of New Oxford's well-maintained thoroughfares. I had the impression that I was the first person to go down the towpath on this side for a long time.

The problem I had was that Pete Pym was taking pains to make sure he wasn't spotted. He kept stopping and looking round, as well as regularly retreating into the bushes on his side. That made my life a lot more difficult. I wondered what he was up to. It was hardly the place for an afternoon stroll. Besides, I was pretty sure that the so-called subs weren't allowed to wander about the university area without permission. Judging by the way he was behaving, I reckoned Pym didn't have anything akin to permission.

I let him get further ahead of me and checked my guidebook to see where I was. According to the late twentieth-century map the waterway ran close to what had once been the prison. Well, well. I scrambled up the steep bank on my left and got an eyeful of high, solid walls. Behind them was a tall, square tower that looked like a castle keep. I became aware of high, keening voices. I got the distinct impression that the buildings were still being used to lock people up. What else would you expect in Raphael's Oxford?

Pete Pym had almost disappeared so I hurried after him – then dived behind a crumbling concrete litter bin when I saw him stop abruptly. By the time I looked round the rough surface, the bugger had gone.

Shit. I took a chance and ran down the towpath. The stream continued ahead of me but to the left there was an obscured entrance. Looking down, I saw wet footprints on the ground. Large footprints. There were ripples on the previously undisturbed surface of the water. Pete Pym had waded or swum across the foul canal. Why?

I followed the footprints. They went in through a low, arched gateway with no barrier across it and no obvious sensor post. There was a vile, putrescent smell emanating from there. The place was giving me a seriously bad feeling. I thought about giving the tail up, but I was too involved now.

Beyond the gate a long, dim tunnel with a paved floor stretched into the gloom. I held my hand over my eyes to acclimatise them. Then I realised that there was a faint, luminous strip in the middle of the roof. This place wasn't as unfrequented as I'd imagined. Apart from the dull pounding of Pete Pym's feet and the occasional drip of water from the brickwork of the roof, there was no sound. I moved forward as carefully as I could, but after a few minutes I understood that I was wasting my time. Pym was getting further away from me and he'd given up checking behind him. So I quickened my pace. I had no idea where I was. The tunnel had started out straight, but there had been a couple of bends since then.

I was taking frequent and shallow breaths, trying not to inhale too much of the mephitic atmosphere. Maybe that was why I didn't notice more quickly what had happened to the steps. I suddenly became aware that things had changed. For a start the regular footfall in front of me was louder, meaning that Pym was nearer. But that wasn't all. The footsteps had doubled. Christ. I wasn't tailing one man any more. There were two of them.

The tunnel curved to the left and I slowed down as I reached a corner. The double footfall continued, then stopped without warning. I stuck my head round and got a shock. So did Pete Pym. Standing about ten yards behind him was a large figure in dark clothes, arms dangling by its sides in a frighteningly simian way. I couldn't make out the face or any other features, though I thought there was some kind of covering on the head. But Pym could. He let out a gasp, his heavy features with the bruises he himself had inflicted suddenly transformed into those of a terrified child.

Then the bulky shape behind him leaped forward with surprising speed. Pym tried to run but he was nailed before he got more than five yards. The assailant crawled over his victim's prone form and clamped a hand on his throat.

I stood in the shadows trying to make up my mind. Did I owe Pete Pym enough to get what I feared was a Grendel off him? Foolishly, insanely, I reckoned I did.

So I sprinted round the bend, past the shadowy recess in the wall where the attacker must have hidden himself, and went for the pair on the ground. Halfway there I remembered that I still had the cosh I'd used on the Edinburgh youth gang member in my jacket pocket.

Looking at the solid form that was now rearing up on its knees over Pym, I didn't think it would do him or me much good at all.

CHAPTER EIGHTEEN

I was wrong. The cosh did do some good. I drew up behind the figure who was throttling Pete Pym and swung it down behind the ear, exactly as I'd been taught years ago on the auxiliary training programme. The blow made the attacker stiffen and take his hand off Pym's neck, his upper body still upright. Then he turned towards me. I wasn't waiting for an introduction. I belted him again, this time above the eye on the other side of his head. Still the bastard didn't go down; he didn't even flinch.

Pete Pym let out a long gasp. That was a relief – at least he was still alive. The sound seemed to affect the assailant. He was male all right, his muscular frame and bull neck more imposing even than those of the most fearsome prop forward in the inter-barracks rugby championship back home. He was staring at me, as motionless as a statue. It was difficult to make out his features under the nondescript peaked cap, but I caught glimpses of the empty black eyes I'd seen briefly in my bedroom and shivered. They regarded me with something akin to surprise. Then the big guy wiped his hands with improbable delicacy against the front of his overalls, pulled his headgear lower and turned away with what looked like a dismissive shake of his head. I watched as he disappeared round the next bend in the tunnel, his pounding steps eventually fading away, and for a moment I wondered where the underground passage led. Then I looked at my cosh and tried to work out how he'd sustained two heavy blows to the skull without visible effect.

Pete Pym groaned. I kneeled down beside him and put my arm under his head. I couldn't see any sign of injury apart from the livid marks on his throat. He was desperately trying to get air into his lungs.

"What . . .?" he said hoarsely. His eyes were darting around and his expression was still that of a quivering infant. "Where . . . where is he?"

"He's gone, Pete," I said, manhandling his upper body into a vertical position. "I chased him off," I added with a grin.

He gave a weak laugh in between the deep breaths he was taking. "No one chases off a Grendel," he said. "Grendels are trained to kill. I've never heard of one slipping up."

The words wrenched my gut and I remembered those blank, staring eyes again. It wasn't just that I'd seen them in Brase. There was something else about them, something else about the preternaturally regular features: they were familiar but in a way that was impossible to pin down.

"We'd better get out of here," Pym said, levering himself up from the damp tunnel floor.

"Where does this lead?" I asked, peering down the dank passage. "What were you doing down here?"

"You don't want to know," he said, moving off unsteadily in the direction we came from.

I caught up with him. "Yes, I do," I said. "You owe me something for getting that thing off you, Pete."

He glanced at me as he wiped muck from his long hair. "Yeah, I suppose I do." He looked over his shoulder and shuddered. "Where does the tunnel lead?" He was looking straight into my eyes now. "It leads to the House of Dust."

I'd been trying hard to stop myself jumping to that conclusion.

Pumping Pete Pym was hard work. He'd suddenly gone as coy as a male teacher giving a sex lesson in a girls' school.

"What's your problem, Pete?" I asked as we moved towards the patch of daylight at the end of the tunnel. "Yesterday you were keen enough to tell us about the prisons and the Poison Fields."

He kept his eyes off me. "Every kid in Cowley knows what I told you. Who the fuck are you, Quint?" he demanded. "What were you doing following me down here? Why should I trust you?"

"I picked you up on the canal by accident."

He stared at me in obvious disbelief. "That tow-path you were on is restricted. How did you get on to it?"

"I've got free access from the Hebdomadal Council." I saw I had to give him something, so I told him about the Grendel recruitment session I'd observed in Worc.

"Bugger me." He sounded impressed. "We never managed to get over the fence there."

"We?" I stopped him, my hand on his arm. "Come on, Pete, tell me what's going on. I'm trying to find out who killed your brother, remember?"

He screwed his eyes up as if he were trying to see inside my head. Finally he nodded. "All right. I must be out of my mind dealing with one of Raphael's—"

"I'm not one of hers," I interrupted. "If I was, I'd have let the Grendel throttle you, wouldn't I?"

He snorted. "That woman's poison, Quint. There's no telling what she's scheming."

"Take my word, I'm on your side," I said. "So who's we, Pete? Who are you working with?"

He squatted down and leaned his back against the damp brick wall. "You'd better not rat on us, Quint," he said in a low voice. "One way or another, we'll get to you."

"For Christ's sake, I don't give a shit about the Hebdomadal Council. I'm trying to find the shooter who killed a friend of mine in Edinburgh." If there was life after the crematorium, Lewis Hamilton would have been amazed to hear himself described in that way. Then I had a flash of Lister 25's ashen face. "And I've just found another friend of mine down here who's been fucked up by Raphael and her crew."

Pym was still looking at me intently. "Yeah, well, we've all had that experience." He thought for a few moments then nodded. "Okay, here's how it is. For two years some of us in the suburbs have been building up an underground movement." He smiled bitterly. "The stupid bastards give us nothing to do except clean up their mess and watch brain-numbing television programmes. Working out ways to shaft them is all that keeps us going."

I nodded. The guardians back home were learning the same lesson from the youth gangs.

"After a while we managed to turn some of the students," Pym continued. "Not many, mind. They're mostly as committed to the university and the companies that sponsor them as pigs are to the trough, but a few of them can't handle the way the subs are treated." He pulled a small matt black device from his pocket. "See this? We call it a sub-machine."

"Gun?" I asked.

He laughed. "I wish. It's basically a communication unit, but it also contains an anti-surveillance device."

"They don't know you're in here?"

He shook his head then his face darkened. "I'll bet they know you are, though. Will they be looking for you?"

I raised my shoulders. "Maybe." I had something else on my mind. "I thought Grendels were only allowed to operate outside the city. What was that specimen doing in here?"

Pete Pym let out a grunt. "The Council *says* that Grendels are only used in territory beyond the Poison Fields." He gave a hollow laugh. "Never believe anything those fuckers tell you, Quint."

I nodded. "I've been finding that out for myself." I smiled. "Not that I was ever very good at believing people in power." I caught his eye again. "So, are you going to tell me what you were doing down here? What is the House of Dust? You're not the first person I've heard mention that place."

He was returning my gaze. "Really?" he asked. "Who else told you about it?"

"Elias Burton," I replied. "A shrivelled-up old don at Brase. Do you know him?" It had suddenly occurred to me that the academic might be part of Pym's movement; he wasn't exactly New Oxford's number one fan.

But Pete shook his head again. "Never heard of him." He glanced down the tunnel in the direction the Grendel had headed and shivered. "The House of Dust? We've been aware of it these last few months, but it's only recently that we've managed to locate it." He looked at me blankly. "People disappear into the House of Dust and they don't come out again."

"Is it a prison facility?"

He bit his lower lip. "Don't know. It doesn't feature on any of the Crim Fac documents we've managed to access."

"Do you think it might be—?"

The loud blast of a siren drowned out my words. It came from the canal end of the tunnel.

"Shit!" Pym said with a gasp. "You've led them to me."

I opened my arms helplessly. "Not deliberately, Pete." I looked at the thin strip of yellow light in the roof that snaked away into the darkness. "I'll go out and take the heat. But you'd better go further down the passage."

He swallowed hard, a sheen of sweat on his forehead. "Yeah, I suppose I will. After all, I was on my way to see if I could find a way into the House of Dust." He gulped again. The expression on his face suggested that his encounter with the Grendel had put him off that idea. "I must be out of my mind. Let's hope that monster's long gone."

Lights flashed on the brickwork at the entrance to the tunnel. The blare of the siren was echoing down the curved walls like the cry of a hungry carnivore.

"Go, Pete," I said, pushing him gently.

He got up and headed off, giving me a rueful glance. I watched him vanish round a corner.

Then stood up to face the siren song.

"Citizen Dalrymple." Trout was standing on a motorised punt like the one that had been at the Raskolnikov murder scene. He was wearing an orange life jacket over his dark suit and his bowler hat was incongruous. "Kindly step out of the tunnel entrance." He had to shout above the racket the siren was making.

I waited for a few moments to show him that he wasn't boss, then walked into daylight. Perch was sitting at the stern of the punt. He held his eyes on me and deliberately refrained from killing the noise. Perhaps he was deaf as well as dumb. Eventually he pressed a button on the panel in front of him and calm was restored.

"What were you doing down there?" Trout asked. "Were you alone?"

I took my control card from my pocket. "I can go where I like," I said, waving it at him. "Without surveillance."

The bulldogs exchanged glances.

"Oh, we weren't watching you, citizen," Trout said. "We just happened to be patrolling the canal and noticed the footprints at the tunnel entrance. It's a restricted area."

"Is that right?" I turned and started walking up the towpath.

Perch executed a neat volte face with the punt. It drew alongside and kept up with me.

"Can we give you a lift?" Trout asked.

I gave him a look that I hoped he would understand.

"I see," he said. "Can we be of service in any other way?"

"Yeah," I replied. "Why don't you go and service your punt?"

After a couple of seconds the craft sped up and disappeared under the bridge. It seemed the bulldogs liked that idea a lot.

I got off the towpath and climbed on to Park End Street. The walls of the castle and prison reared up before me again. I could still hear crazed shouts. They made me wonder if the Department of Psychiatry was in charge of those premises. I struggled to imagine how New Oxford treated its mentally infirm citizens. Given the university's commitment to the profit motive, they probably supplied the screams for the blockbuster horror movies that I'd heard were very popular in capitalist Vietnam.

I pulled out my mobile and pressed buttons. "Davie?"

"Quint? Where have you been?" He sounded tense. "I've been calling you for an hour."

"I've been down in the sewer. Probably no signal. What's up?"

"Raphael's up. Connington's up. Dawkley's up. Will that do?"

"For a start." I moved to the side of the pavement as a pair of male students in rugby kit ran past. "What do they want?"

"You, pal. What have you been doing? They're all desperate to see you."

I reckoned Raphael knew where I was even before Trout and Perch called in my latest position. She'd been playing an elaborate game of double bluff ever since we arrived in New Oxford. "It's my innate charm, my cultivated conversation and, last but not least, my innovative sexual skills," I said.

"Oh aye?" he said, stifling a laugh. "Have fun with the administrators then."

"Have you turned up anything, Davie?"

"Uh-uh. Same old nothing of significance."

"What about Katharine? And don't say 'What *about* Katharine?', guardsman."

"All right, I won't. She's gone off to a house on – hang on while I check my notebook – Banbury Road. Apparently Raskolnikov used to visit it every other evening. No one seems to know why."

"Okay. Fancy looking over a desirable property before I hit the administrators?"

"Hold me back. Where?"

I told him and signed off. As I headed towards the city

centre, I called Katharine. Either she was otherwise engaged or there was something wrong with the signal again, so I left it for later.

At that moment I was keener on a building than on Katharine – not that I'd been intending to tell her that.

"Carfax?" Davie said, looking up at the old tower that rose above the crossroads. I'd met him there and told him we were going to the House of Dust. "Why's it called that? There aren't any cars around here, let alone any fax machines."

"Oh very good," I said. I had my father's guidebook open. "You'll find it comes from the Latin *quadrifurcus*, meaning four forks or ways." I glanced at him. "What's a fax machine?"

"You remember, those things they had in pre-independence times that sent bits of virtual paper down the tele—" He broke off when he saw the derisive look on my face. "Up yours."

"Come on then," I said, leading him across the road. "Leave the Chariot here. Let's do this on foot." I was struck again by how little traffic there was apart from students on public-use bicycles. This was how to ease congestion on the roads: make everyone walk or ride a bike. Pity no government before the break-up of the UK had had the balls to legislate for that. It would probably have stopped the mob laying into Westminster. Then again, people were deeply in love with their cars – until the oil companies upped their prices once too often and the refineries were torched by committed but short-sighted activists.

"What do you think you're going to see from the outside?" Davie asked, stepping out of the way of an elderly female academic with half-moon glasses and hair like a crow's nest.

"Don't know, pal." I looked across St Aldate's at an ornate building with arched mullioned windows and a grandiose entrance.

"What's that place?" Davie asked.

I glanced at Hector's book. "The town hall, as was. Jacobean gables, turrets, ogee roofs, balustrade of—"

"Change of function," he said, pointing.

I focused on the words on the dark blue display screen by the door. " 'Faculty of Criminology'," I read. "What a surprise." I looked again. "Department of Prison Privatisation."

"Oh aye," Davie said.

"Oh aye exactly. That'll be where the consultants they sent to Edinburgh came from. They no doubt make a pile of money from states that are desperate to get shot of the responsibility for their prisons."

"That's not what's happening back home," Davie argued. "The Mist's got Public Order Directorate personnel running the New Bridewell."

"For how long?" I asked. I was still puzzled about the relationship between the Council of City Guardians and Raphael's regime. What was in it for New Oxford?

We walked down the road.

"That's it, isn't it?" Davie said, pointing ahead. "The House of—"

I put my hand on his arm to silence him. There weren't many people about, but I knew that, unlike bicycles, the name Elias Burton and Pete Pym had spoken wasn't for public use.

From the north the amber walls of what used to be Christ Church were still impressive, even though the tall, narrow windows had been covered by steel shutters and there were large patches of shell damage. The pair of vast metallic columns shot up into the sky like the amputated legs of a giant. I could make out wisps of steam or smoke around the cowling at their tops. The two small towers on either side of the main gate were in reasonably good condition, their stone a darker shade. But my eye was irresistibly drawn to the vast stump of the Tom Tower above. Christ knows what had happened to it. Some drugs gang must have had a serious aversion to the college: maybe the leader was a former student who'd come from a state school. A massive amount of explosives must have been detonated around the Gothic tower's base. There was no sign of any debris. The raised edge of the stump's outer rim indicated that the tower had fallen inwards. I felt what remained of my right forefinger begin to tingle in sympathy.

"What the hell goes on here?" Davie demanded, tugging at his beard.

"Not much, by the looks of it," I said. "There's nobody at the gate." We were now standing directly opposite the heavy steel barrier. "It doesn't look like that entrance is used much."

"Are we going to cross over?" Davie stepped towards the road but I stopped him again.

"No. I don't want to look too interested." I screwed up my eyes. "Can you see a panel or sign saying what the buildings purport to be?"

After a few moments Davie shook his head. "Not a thing," he said in a confused tone. "Why not?"

I felt a shiver run down my spine. "Information in New Oxford is pretty much on a need-to-know basis, wouldn't you say? The people who know what goes on here don't need a sign."

Davie nodded, his face grim. "And the rest of the population pretends that the House of . . . I mean this facility doesn't exist."

I reckoned he'd hit the nail's head well into the surface of the wood.

Back at Carfax I came to a decision. I activated my nostrum, ignored the list of Missed Calls and highlighted "Chief Administrator" in the Contacts Menu. Almost immediately Raphael's face appeared on the small screen.

"Citizen Dalrymple," she said with a mixture of relief and irritation. "Where have you been?"

"Don't tell me you don't know, administrator."

She let that pass without comment. "Kindly don't deactivate your nostrum again. I need to see you urgently."

"Ditto," I said. "But I don't want anyone else present." I noticed her eyes open a touch wider than usual. "How about inviting me round to your private quarters?"

Raphael thought about it. "If you insist. I want you there as soon as possible."

"You want me where?" I said, looking at the mini-camera's eye on my nostrum.

"Queen, staircase one."

The picture flickered and died.

I laughed.

"What?" Davie asked. "Where is that?"

"Where do you think?" I replied. "What used to be called the Queen's College."

The way that people in power lose all sense of irony never fails to amuse me.

Davie had me down the High Street in well under a minute – he'd managed to work out the high-speed commands. I hadn't been able to tell where Raphael was on the nostrum screen, but I assumed she was in the Council building and wouldn't be down here for a while. I tried Katharine again while I waited. She still wasn't answering. I tried to call her up on the nostrum. The words "Transmission Failure" came up in red on the screen.

"Do you know the address of the place Katharine went, Davie?" I asked.

He pulled out his notebook. "Aye," he said, "465 Banbury Road."

"Get up there while I'm in with her majesty, will you? I don't know why Katharine isn't answering."

He looked at his watch. "It's not that long since she set off. Maybe she stopped for a walk in the park."

"The park's some kind of concentration camp, remember?"

"Oh aye," he said, his face grim. "I'll look after it."

I got out. "And Davie? Call me on the mobile in exactly one hour, okay? I don't want to lose touch with both of you."

"Don't worry," he said, grinning. "You don't get shot of me that easily."

I waved him away and walked slowly towards the college entrance. I had a bad feeling about Katharine, but I forced myself to ignore it.

My imminent meeting with the chief administrator was more than enough to worry about.

I walked past the sensor post and through an elegant gateway surmounted by what looked like a miniature ancient temple. At least the female statue in it wasn't of Raphael. Apart from a couple of shy students, the spacious front quad was deserted. I was about to ask my way from the porter when there was a loud buzz. A line of red dashes appeared on the flagstones in front of me and a mechanical voice said, "Citizen Dalrymple, follow the line." I glanced around and nodded at whoever was manning the surveillance system. For a change they were being open about watching me.

The arrows led round to the left. In front of me was a long colonnaded block with pediments and statues on the upper part. Looking round, I realised the front façade of the college was nothing more than a retaining wall, the accommodation forming only three sides of the quad. It was all too regular for my liking, too ordered. That was probably why Raphael had chosen to live here.

I was directed upstairs to the first floor. A door on the uncarpeted landing swung open.

"Come in, citizen," said an impatient voice when I didn't. "You aren't here to be diverted by the view."

I entered the chief administrator's pad and took it in. "Nice place," I said. "You don't think a carpet might improve the ambience? Maybe some curtains? Even the odd bookcase or escritoire?" Apart from a pair of distinctly aged armchairs and a low coffee table, the austere room contained no furniture. There was a bank of screens on the wall above a carved marble fireplace, none of them currently active.

Raphael was standing in the centre of the bare floor, nostrum in hand. "Sit down and refrain from making extraneous comments," she said, letting the device fall between her breasts. "It's time we talked."

"Okay," I said, giving her a bland smile. "But before we do that, answer me this: were you here when we spoke on the nostrum?"

She stared at me then shook her head. "If you must know, I was in the north Noxad building – what used to be the New Bodleian Library."

"So how did you get here so quickly? I didn't see you come in the main entrance."

"Really, citizen, what are you trying to prove?" she said testily. "The college has more than one entrance."

I took the guidebook from my pocket and looked at the street atlas. The New Bodleian was an ugly rubble-walled heap on the north side of Broad Street. How the hell had she got here so quickly? Supersonic public-use bike?

"May we proceed now?" Raphael asked.

"Be my guest."

The chief administrator sat down and waited for me to follow suit. "Very well, Citizen Dalrymple—"

"Call me Quint," I put in. "Even if you won't tell me your first name."

She glared at me. "Kindly do not interrupt," she said. "Citizen."

I turned up my palms. If that was the way she wanted it, fair enough. I was still going to run the conversation my way. "I had an interesting encounter today," I said, pausing to get her full attention. "With a Grendel."

"What?" Raphael's voice was suddenly animated. "Where?"

"Don't you want to know about when, why and how as well?" I asked.

Her eyes locked on to mine. "Remember that you and your friends are guests in this city." Her tone was caustic. "And remember that there are numerous incarceration facilities here."

I breathed in hard, wondering where Katharine had got to. I could have asked Raphael to put her people on to it. Or maybe she already knew exactly where Katharine was. This game was getting very complicated.

"All right," I said. "Here's the story." I told her about the tunnel and the Grendel, omitting Pete Pym's involvement.

"What on earth were you doing down there in the first place, citizen?" she demanded when I'd finished.

I shrugged. I wasn't going to tell her about the House of Dust angle yet. "Just following my nose." I fixed her in my gaze. "Are you going to come clean about the Grendels now or do I have to spell it out? It was one of them who fired the shot in Edinburgh, wasn't it?"

She looked away and I suddenly got the impression that we had company.

"You don't mind, do you?" I asked, standing up and moving quickly to the door behind her. I didn't wait for an answer, flinging it open and looking the place over. It was her bedroom and it was as drab as the main room: a steel-framed single bed with dark blue covers, a narrow wardrobe and a basin, that was all. The mirror above the basin was round and small. The chief administrator wasn't a great one for make-up. I closed the door and went over to the one on the other side of the fireplace. An identical bedroom, this one without a toothbrush between the taps.

"Guest room?" I asked.

She looked at me coolly. "These rooms were originally for two students." She pursed her lips. "I never have anyone to stay."

I sat down again. At least the likes of Connington and Dawkley weren't listening at the keyhole, even if they were watching us on a screen somewhere.

"Satisfied, citizen?" she asked.

I shook my head. "Several country miles from that condition. It's time you opened up to me." I used the double entendre deliberately to shake her up. "Why have you got a Grendel on your tail?"

Raphael leaned forward and smoothed her hands over the dark fabric on her thighs. I couldn't be sure if that was her way of showing that she'd registered my lewd implication. "You seem to have found out quite a lot without my help, citizen," she said in a dry voice. "Which, of course, is what I wanted you to do. It had become apparent that a fresh approach was necessary."

I wasn't convinced that she was being straight with me, but what she said squared with the way I'd been allowed to check all my leads – whether I was being watched or not.

"The Grendels," she continued, looking past me through the tall window at the block across the quad. "They belong to ExFor – the External Force. It is an élite cadre of paramilitary police. It was formed in 2012 and its primary functions were, and are, to patrol and to maintain the state's land borders. Drugs gangs and other criminal elements have been trying to infiltrate for years."

"Despite the existence of the so-called Poison Fields?" I said.

She looked at me and shrugged. "Yes. More fool them. Unfortunately it gradually became apparent that the contamination levels were increasing drastically. Many ExFor personnel succumbed to viruses that had never been identified before. So . . ." She paused and took a deep breath. "So the Hebdomadal Council was forced to take a major decision."

The atmosphere in the room was suddenly oppressive. I could feel sweat breaking out all over my body. Was Raphael finally about to tell me what I needed to crack the case?

"And what was it that you decided?" I asked in a low voice.

The chief administrator dropped her gaze. "We decided to implement research that several of the science departments had proposed." She licked her lips and looked straight into my eyes. "We decided to create an enhanced human being."

Outside the birds were twittering in the spring warmth, but all I felt was icy steel running up my spine like an executioner's blade.

It took me some time to find my voice. "A what?"

"You heard me, citizen."

"An enhanced human being?" I repeated, my heart pounding. "What the hell does that mean?"

Raphael was back in control of herself now. "It means a human being with an advanced immune system, one so sophisticated that none of the toxins and viruses in the Poison Fields can affect it." She glanced past me again. "We also applied certain other characteristics to improve the performance of ExFor personnel."

"Oh aye?" I said. What she'd said tied up with the code red file that I'd seen in the morning. I was also thinking of the Grendel recruitment session I'd witnessed. "What characteristics?"

"Massively increased physical strength, for a start." A shadow of what might have been doubt passed over her face. "We used psychological and chemical means to produce the ideal patrol operative."

"You mean you brainwashed them?"

Raphael gave me a disapproving look. "That term has no scientific validity, citizen."

I shrugged. "Neither does Grendel." Then I remembered the other code names I'd seen: Miranda, Plowman, Volpone and so on. The pattern suddenly fell into place. "Oh, now I get it. Reverse chronology. *Beowulf* is the earliest work, so the Grendels must be the most sophisticated ExFor personnel yet." I caught her eye. "What happened? Did one of them take exception to the process?"

Her face was pale and she didn't favour that question with a spoken answer, which told me that I was right.

I rubbed my forehead. "Surely you have some kind of monitoring system on these monsters. Why don't you just pick the miscreant up? Or is there more than one of them on the loose?"

Now she was shaking her head, her face sombre. "It's not that easy, I'm afraid. There are two classes of Grendels. Mark Ones, those who operate in the outer Poison Fields, are programmed to remain in designated ExFor areas; that is, no closer than fifteen kilometres from the city. All of those are accounted for."

I felt a sinking feeling. "Don't tell me," I said. "Mark Twos are like me. They have free access."

The chief administrator pursed her lips. "In principle, no. Mark Two Grendels were designed to be completely self-sufficient so that they can operate outside the borders of New Oxford. But the scientists discovered that the only way to achieve flexibility and independence of thought and action was to remove the monitoring facilities."

"You mean you haven't got a clue where any of these highly trained operatives is. How many are there?"

"Seven," she replied. "All male. The last was released from the borders in February. One of the few control mechanisms that we have over them is that their initial programming prevents them from re-entering the state of New Oxford."

"And you think one or more of them has managed to override that?"

She nodded. "The problem is . . . the Mark Twos are fully trained in anti-surveillance tactics, including the assumption of false identities and disguising their appearance. They are also issued with certain equipment which enables them to counteract cameras and other tracking units."

"That could explain what happened to the cameras on the High Street before the killings of Ted Pym and Raskolnikov."

"It could, yes."

Now I was having flashes of the crime scenes in Edinburgh: the stinking tenement where we found Dead Dod and the former burial ground where Lewis Hamilton had fallen. I leaned forward. "What is the Mark Two Grendels' function outside New Oxford?"

"They—" Raphael broke off, her reluctance to answer very obvious. "They carry out certain sensitive duties."

I remembered the ASAR rifle and its sophisticated ammunition. "Jesus Christ. They're assassins, aren't they? You use them to take out people you don't like."

"Um . . . that isn't really germane to this investigation," she said.

"Like fuck it isn't," I yelled, getting up and bending over her. "One of your fucking Mark Two Grendels put an Eagle One in the Edinburgh public order guardian."

The chief administrator raised her hand. "You're too close, citizen."

I leaned closer. "You're bloody right I am, Raphael. And getting closer to your septic secrets by the minute."

"No," she said, her straightened fingers jabbing hard into my chest. "I mean you're too close to me. I don't like physical intimacy."

I stepped back, aware that by doing so I was giving her back the initiative.

"There's something else you should know," Raphael continued.

"Don't tell me. You like to pull the wings off flies."

She twitched her head. "Not about me. About the Eagle One that hit Lewis Hamilton."

I moved towards her again. "What about it?"

She raised a hand to fend me off. "You've seen the specifications. You know what it can do. In this case, the shooter deactivated the detonation unit."

"That's right," I said, recalling what Verzeni had said about the software when he demonstrated the ASAR to us. "He stopped the bullet blowing Lewis to pieces."

Raphael nodded. "Not only that. Remember the low buzz that the projectile made before impact?"

I nodded, my mind flashing back to the scene in the prison yard and the sound I'd picked up.

"The shooter attempted to minimise the bullet's impact by initiating the velocity reduction facility."

"Maybe that was because he realised that it wasn't going to hit you."

"Maybe," she said. "The sighting system does allow for rapid response, despite the fact that the projectile's vector cannot be altered; during the trials there were cases of imperfect Grendels trying to fire round corners for their own amusement. However, there is another possibility."

I couldn't see where she was heading. "What?" I demanded.

Raphael opened her eyes wide at me. "Why would the shooter make such efforts to neutralise the Eagle One's effect?"

I ran my hand across my chin. "Why would he indeed? Grendels are trained to kill, aren't they?"

"Precisely. Their programming takes no account of misfires or wrongly identified targets." The administrator went on looking at me intently. "Perhaps this particular shooter had some reason of his own for trying to save Lewis Hamilton from serious injury."

I tried to imagine who in New Oxford would give a shit about an Edinburgh guardian. I didn't have long to get anywhere with that. My mobile went off, making me jump.

"Quint?" said a familiar voice. "It's Katharine. Davie told me you were worried about me. How sweet."

"Not now," I said.

"You're not worried now?"

"No. Yes. Oh, for Christ's sake. Meet me outside Queen. Out."

The chief administrator was sitting motionless. "News?"

I shook my head, keeping the relief I was feeling over Katharine to myself. "Right, about the errant Mark Two Grendel." I gave Raphael the eye. "What you say is very interesting, but it isn't much more than speculation. There's a more immediate question. Why would a Grendel want to kill you? Surely the first command that's drummed into your highly efficient killing machines is that administrators are untouchable."

She left my question unanswered for a time. "Yes, well, I presume that aspect of the programming has also been overridden." She stood up in a rapid movement. "You're the investigator, citizen. I leave the question of the killer's motivation to you. My colleagues and I do have an idea how to catch him though."

"Do you?" I wasn't sure if I wanted the administrators' help – I reckoned at least some of them were up to their elbows in the mire – but I was beginning to flail around. "And it is?"

"Tomorrow we are holding one of the bimonthly Encaenia."

"Translation?"

"Encaenia? Ceremony commemorating the university's

benefactors," she said. "It used to be an annual event, but these days our sponsors like a more frequent recognition of their generosity. There is a public procession of administrators and senior academics."

"And you think the Grendel will take another pot shot at you there?"

She nodded slowly. "I do."

Take out the university-state's leading light in front of the people who fund the place? I couldn't fault her thinking.

CHAPTER NINETEEN

Preparing for the procession took up the rest of the day and most of the evening. We spent several hours in the Hebdomadal Council building. The proctor wasn't impressed by Raphael's insistence that she would lead the parade as usual, but he was given no choice. On the other hand, Dawkley had trouble concealing his excitement; he seemed to be positive both that the assassin created by his scientists would make an appearance and that he would be caught, without suggesting how. The fact that he and Raphael were so sure of their strategy, as well as the carefully ordered dispositions of bulldogs and other security staff, prompted me to wonder why I was being made privy to the planning. Eventually I found out.

"You're joking," I said, my jaw slack. "I'm not dressing up in one of those patchwork gowns."

Raphael gave me a tight smile. "Don't worry, citizen. We'll find you a black one."

I glanced at Davie and Katharine. "Why do you need me in the procession at all?" I asked.

The chief administrator shook her head at me despairingly. "You're the only person who's seen the Grendel close up. If anyone can see through the disguise he'll surely be wearing, it's you." She gave Davie and Katharine the quickest of looks. "What your colleagues do is of no interest to me."

"Screw you too," Katharine said under her breath.

I put myself between her and Raphael. "All right," I said. "I'll do it. But there isn't much chance of me recognising the bastard. I hardly got a glimpse of his face and his muscle-bound body isn't exactly a one-off in this city." I directed my gaze at Trout and Perch who were standing at the far end of the room.

Raphael and Dawkley exchanged a look that I couldn't read.

"Here is a folder containing photographs of all the Grendel Mark Twos, citizen," the science administrator said, stepping forward. "Coming from technology-deficient Edinburgh, you may find it easier to work with hard copies than the digital versions. I suggest you study them carefully."

The meeting broke up before I could tell Dawkley where to stick his hard copies.

We walked back to Brase through the quadrangle of the former Bodleian. The great walls were floodlit and the Latin names above each of the Gothic-arched doorways were picked out in a different coloured light. You could almost believe that you were back in the old Oxford, the one that was confident about its academic standing and untouched by the real world's problems. Conversely, that anachronism had managed to preserve the ideal of intellectual freedom. As I left the passage to be confronted by the Radcliffe Camera and its high-tech surveillance dome, I found myself feeling strangely nostalgic for what the place had been when I'd visited it as a teenager. I blinked to banish the feeling. That world was irrevocably gone and it was probably just as well.

The night was warm, giving a hint of the burning summer that lay ahead.

"I wonder what they call the Big Heat down here?" I said, breathing in the scent of blossom from the trees in the college gardens.

"Summer?" Katharine suggested. The acidity in her voice told me that she was still seething about the way Raphael had dismissed her earlier.

"Roast Ox?" Davie proposed.

I looked up into the darkness. "Spare me."

"You'd better hope the shooter spares you too, Quint," Katharine said as we approached Brase. "You know what I think?"

The door in the heavy wooden gate hissed open automatically.

"Enlighten me," I said apprehensively.

Katharine led us out into the front quad. It was perfectly still: no snores from scholars who'd passed out over their nostrums, no insects rustling the leaves of the wisteria, no drunken students carousing. It could have been an ancient citadel deserted by all but the dead.

"I think," she said, turning to me, "that your friend Raphael is using you as bait, Quint. I suppose it makes a change. You've done that to other people often enough."

"I suppose I have," I agreed. I reckoned Katharine was right about the chief administrator too. The problem was, I didn't have any idea why the assassin was hunting her; or why he'd have any interest in me.

We managed to get something to eat and drink in the Senior Common Room. There was no one else there – no doubt even the dons were required to be in bed by now – but I didn't feel secure under the disapproving gaze of the college's old masters. I took the others back to my rooms.

"Let's have a look at these monsters then," Katharine

said, tugging the blue Noxad folder from under my arm. She pulled the photos out and spread them on the floor around us.

We moved our heads around in dismay.

"Bloody hell," Davie said.

"Shut up, guardsman," Katharine interrupted. "Can't you ever come up with anything original?"

He returned her gaze, a grin spreading across his bearded face. "All right." He looked down again. "Bloody useless. These photos tell us bugger all. The guys are like seven more or less identical brothers, and they're the seven most undistinguishable specimens you could imagine."

"Apart from their build," I said, running my eye over the Physical Specifications sheets that had also been in the file. "They're all exactly the same height and weight." I did a quick calculation. "Slightly over six feet tall and around fifteen stone. Solid citizens."

"Aye," Davie said, "but look at their faces."

I did, feeling a twinge in my gut. There was definitely a hint of the guy I'd seen in them all, something in the cold, unnaturally black eyes. The effect of the photos was weirder than it would have been if the seven of them had been exactly the same. They were *almost* the same – short, crew-cut hair, close-shaven and smooth skin, lips in a perfectly straight line, faces fleshy but firm – but somehow each one still projected his own identity.

"Him," Katharine said, pointing at the photo on the carpet in front of her. "He looks like the worst of them."

Davie and I studied the burly face that was staring up at us. He'd been designated Number Three – apparently Grendels didn't qualify for names, like auxiliaries back home.

"Aye," Davie nodded. "He does." He nudged me. "Was this the one you saw, Quint?"

I bent down to take in every detail of the photo. There was something marginally more familiar about that particular Grendel, but the feeling was vague, inchoate – like the flashes you get in dreams of people you haven't seen for years, flashes that are gone before you can identify them.

"Could have been," I said lamely.

Dave was running his fingers through his beard. "Course, what Raphael told you about *one* of these guys losing the plot could be bollocks." He opened his eyes wide at me. "All seven of them might be on the loose in New Oxford."

I stepped out of the ring of Grendels. "Thanks very much for that thought, pal." I headed for the dispenser. "Who wants a drink?"

The big man's face lit up. "Now you're talking."

I managed to get a bottle of pretty decent malt out of the system. After I'd handed glasses round, I looked at Katharine. "What was the story about the house Professor Raskolnikov used to visit: 456 Banbury Road, was it?"

"Four hundred and sixty-five," she corrected. "Well, it was a dead-end."

Davie guffawed. "You got that right."

I watched as they caught each other's eye. For once they seemed to be sharing a joke.

Katharine swallowed whisky. "Our Russian friend liked to have his backside thrashed with birch twigs. The place is a homosexual brothel catering for senior academics. Run with the Hebdomadal Council's full approval, of course."

"It was nothing compared with what the wealthy

tourists get back home, but it was busy enough," Davie said. "Raskolnikov had a special friend up there. A Cypriot called Yorgo."

"So he was into punishment," I said. "Where's the crime in that?"

"Very funny," Katharine groaned. "Could the professor's peccadillo have had anything to do with his murder?"

I shrugged. "Maybe. We still don't know what it was that got him moving down the High Street with such alacrity instead of going to the Council meeting. Did you check this Yorgo out?"

Davie nodded. "The bulldogs had already given him the fourth degree. He was terrified – said he hadn't seen the professor since the night before last. I don't think he was bullshitting."

I turned pages in my notebook. "What about the damage the professor's nostrum sustained?"

The others were both gazing at the Grendel photos again.

"Look at the state of those headbangers," Katharine said. "They could probably crush a nostrum with their bare hands."

That made me think of Pete Pym. He was bloody lucky to have got away with his throat intact. I hoped he'd made it back to Cowley in one piece.

Davie was stifling a yawn.

"Yeah, it's time to crash," I said. "But first I've got more to share with you." I sat down in the armchair and told them about the sights I'd seen in Worc: about Andrew Duart and Hel Hyslop, about Hel's involvement in the Grendel session, and about Lister 25's condition.

The last description sent them off to their beds without a spring in their steps.

* * *

I was about to hit mine when someone hit the door – not very hard, just a few gentle taps. I'd declined Katharine's offer to keep me company overnight because I didn't want her there if the nocturnal visitor reappeared. Now I was gripped by the panic-inducing thought that the guy with the killer's eyes was at my door.

I grabbed my mobile and pressed Davie's number, then touched the Open button on the door frame. There seemed little point in winding up the Grendel, given that he could probably pulverise the door if he felt like it.

"Oh, it's you, Burton," I said, taking in the shrivelled figure in a moth-eaten silk dressing-gown. "False alarm, Davie. Out," I said into the phone. That wouldn't have impressed him much. "What can I do for you?"

"I heard voices," the old academic said. "I was wondering if you had any . . . any booze." His leathery face cracked into an uneven smile. "The college governing body doesn't let me have any in my rooms, you see."

I glanced at my watch. "All right, doctor," I said, intending to get rid of him as soon as I could.

"Aren't you going to join me?" he asked after he latched his gnarled fingers round the tumbler I'd given him.

"If you insist," I said, pouring myself a slug and pointing him to the sofa.

"Tell me, Quintilian," Elias Burton said after he'd taken a sip. "How's your trip to New Oxford progressing? Is your investigation reaching a satisfactory conclusion?"

If it hadn't been so blatant, I'd have thought the old bugger was pumping me for information. As it was, he was probably bored stiff from gutting too many musty Latin tomes. That didn't mean I was going to tell him anything. I gave him a few vague details about Raskolnikov's death. The Hebdomadal Council had kept it quiet, but it seemed the university grapevine was in good nick because Burton had already heard about it. Then I remembered the references he'd made to the place I stood outside earlier in the day, the place that Pete Pym had been trying to penetrate.

"Doctor," I said, leaning forward and giving him a smile of encouragement, "you've spoken more than once about what used to be Christ Church, what you called the House of Dust. What exactly—?"

Burton's manic hand movements made me break off. He put his glass down carefully and got up, pointing towards my bedroom. Inside there, he went over to the shower and turned the water full on. Then he beckoned me towards him. He was standing about two inches from the flow. He must have read plenty of spy novels in his time.

"Quintilian," he said in a hoarse whisper, "be very careful. It's one thing for a crazy old fool like me to rattle on about that place, but anyone else who discusses it will be at the mercy of the bulldogs."

I had my ear close to his lips. I screwed my head round to look at him. "I've tied the House of Dust into my investigation," I said. "What the hell goes on there?"

Elias Burton was examining me, his eyes damp. "Hell is the right word, my boy," he replied. "If hell is what we do to others when we absolve ourselves of responsibility for our actions." He shook his head. "Let alone guilt."

I took a deep breath. "Yes, but what *is* the House of Dust?"

The old man nodded slowly. "I imagine you'll be finding out about it soon enough." He looked at the jets of water and spoke in a voice that caught even more in his throat. "The House of Dust is the worst of New

Oxford's many incarceration facilities, Quintilian. It is an underground composite of the Bastille and Belsen, Barlinnie and San Quentin, Newgate and Alcatraz." His eyes met mine again. "It is worse than any poet's depiction of the infernal regions, believe me."

I did.

After that, sleep was a suffocating blanket that I struggled with all night. At least I had no undesired company. I woke to the sound of church bells – presumably atheist New Oxford retained them to keep the students on time – and the smell of fresh bread. My watch told me it was eight thirty. I'd slept late. I closed my eyes again and reasoned with myself. I'd allowed myself to get distracted by what was nothing more than hearsay about the House of Dust; after all, Elias Burton hadn't been able to tell me anything specific about the place after he'd run through every prison name and underworld metaphor he could think of. I let myself sink back into the pillows. Then I remembered what was planned for the day and apprehension stabbed me in the gut.

I got up and went through to the main room. I noticed a line of text flashing on the screen above the desk. It informed me that a delivery of clothing had been made. On the other side of the door there was a heap of packages wrapped in transparent plastic. It was pantomime time.

Davie came on the mobile as I was finishing dressing. "Alive, alive oh, Quint?"

"So far. Have you had breakfast?"

"Oh aye. I made sure I got it in early. We'd better get over to the Camera." We'd arranged with Doctor Connington to go over the final pieces of the security operation for the Encaenia.

"Right. I'll see you at the porter's lodge. Any sign of Katharine?"

"Uh-uh. Out."

I called her and got no reply. Edinburgh phones weren't reliable in New Oxford, as I'd discovered yesterday when I tried to raise her. I couldn't get through on the nostrum either, which made me worry more. Then again, maybe she was in the shower. I picked up my gear, glanced in the mirror long enough to make me shake my head at my reflection and headed out. Rather than going straight to the gate, I crossed over to staircase five. The outer door to Katharine's rooms was closed but there was a message in green letters on the screen by the jamb.

Quint – checking a long shot.
See you at the Camera.
K

I went downstairs and across the quad.

"Did Katharine say anything to you about a long shot?" I asked Davie as I came up behind him. He was examining the college rugby team sheet.

"What?" he said, turning. "Oh, what?" he repeated, his voice rising. "Jesus, Quint. What the hell do you look like?" His mouth formed into a ribald smile.

"Yeah, all right," I said, glancing down at the dark blue pinstripe suit and the black gown that I'd been provided with. Fortunately the white bow tie was out of view. "The hood's not too bad," I said, pulling the blue and white silk garment round.

He swallowed laughter. "Aye, you're less of a target than a full-blown Doctor of Philosophy, I'll give you that."

"That long shot of Katharine's?" I repeated, giving him the eye.

He raised his shoulders. "Don't know, Quint. She didn't say anything to me last night. Where is she?"

"Search me. She's going to appear at the Camera."

Davie looked at me. "She's probably scouring the outfitters for the latest Nox frock." The smile died on his lips when he saw my expression.

He knew better than to joke about females and fashion.

Doctor Connington looked up at the ornate antique clock that was suspended from the high ceiling of the Camera. It was as incongruous as a Colt .45 in a collection of Roman swords.

"It's ten thirty, Dalrymple. We'd better get over to the muster area." He was wearing an even shinier version of his red and blue quartered gown. "Are you clear about everything?"

I nodded. I reckoned we were as ready as we'd ever be.

"Quint?" Davie said in a low voice. "Katharine."

I looked up expectantly, then realised he wasn't announcing her arrival. She should have been here by now. I hit the buttons on my mobile and my nostrum simultaneously.

"Dalrymple?" Connington asked. "What is it?"

I waited. There was still no response on either. "Our colleague Katharine Kirkwood," I said. "I can't get through to her and I don't know where she is."

The proctor frowned. "We don't have time for this," he said, turning away. "The chief administrator and her guests are waiting."

I glanced at Davie. He raised his shoulders in a gesture of helplessness. "Doctor," I called, "do me a favour. Get one of your operatives to check the recordings. She must have left Brase before nine a.m."

"My operatives are all fully occupied with the Encaenia," Connington said, his face darkening. "Do you seriously—?"

"Do it or I'm not coming," I interrupted.

He thought about it, but not for long. A bulldog was detailed to run the check and report as soon as possible.

Davie and I followed the proctor out of the Camera, Trout and Perch on our tails. As we cut through the former Bodleian, I tried to contact Katharine on the nostrum again. The same transmission failure message came up. I breathed in hard and tried to convince myself that she was all right; she'd been out of touch yesterday without coming to any harm and, anyway, she could look after herself. Then I remembered the empty eyes and lethal skills of the Grendel Mark Twos, and felt my stomach churn. Maybe Davie was right about them all being on the loose in New Oxford; maybe one of them had taken Katharine and the other six were lining their ASARs up on the procession.

"Don't worry about Katharine," Davie said. "I wouldn't take her on willingly."

I nodded but I was still nagged by doubt. Even if Katharine had gone off on her own, what was the long shot? Could it have something to do with Grendel Number Three? She was the one who'd picked his photograph out.

Then we came out of the northern passage into the courtyard beyond and my mind switched back to the Encaenia. The spaces between the walkways had been fenced off. They were already packed with crowds of people, many of them noticeably foreign: black women in brightly coloured full-length dresses, groups of Chinese in sober suits, Arab men – their heads covered – wearing white robes.

"Who are these people?" I asked Connington.

He was striding towards the Hebdomadal Council building, still anxious about being late. "They are representatives of the sponsor companies," he said in a clipped voice. "Their senior executives are about to have honorary degrees conferred on them. Hurry up, will you?"

The proctor led us through the arch and out on to Broad Street. It had been closed to Chariots and bicycles, and thousands of students in their best subfusc were crammed against steel barriers. All were wearing mortar boards. I noticed that their gowns, most of which only reached down to their groins, bore large coloured logos on the right breast. Even coming from a backwater like Enlightenment Edinburgh I could recognise some of the company names: they were major transnationals such as MacroNet, Conch, Chinair and Mango.

I caught up with Doctor Connington. "Are all the students funded by big corporations?"

He glanced at me. "Not all," he said. "There are several hundred who pay their own way. Mostly the children of wealthy families."

"Glad to see the university hasn't lost all its traditions," I said, shaking my head.

Glancing up at the screens and banners emblazoned with company names on all the surrounding walls, I came to the conclusion that there was even less room for free thought in New Oxford than I'd imagined. The presence of numerous bulldogs in bullet-proof vests and helmets at the windows beneath the rain shields reinforced that thought. As did the sudden recollection of what Elias Burton had told me about the House of

Dust. How many free-thinkers were in the underground caverns beneath Wolsey's and Henry VIII's Christ Church?

"Come on," Connington said, walking quickly up Parks Road.

On our left was the ugly façade of the New Bodleian. I remembered that Raphael said she'd been there when I contacted her on my nostrum. I still couldn't work out how she'd got to her rooms in Queen so quickly.

"In here," the proctor said, crossing the road.

There was a three-storeyed college building set back from the pavement, its impressive fan-vaulted gateway filled with bulldogs carrying vicious-looking prods. The red flashes on the hafts suggested that they packed a blood-boiling electric pulse.

I felt in my suit pockets for my old man's guidebook and realised that I hadn't brought it with me. "What is this establishment?" I asked Trout, Connington having dashed into the place ahead of us.

"Wad," he answered reluctantly. "It's used exclusively for sponsors, donors and their guests."

"Good name," Davie grunted.

"Aye," I said. "I remember now. It used to be called Wadham."

The bulldogs let us pass and we went through the gate into a symmetrical quadrangle with a tower on four levels directly in front of us. The lawn was filled with people in academic robes, scouts in white jackets circulating with trays of coffee. I glanced up and made out the armoured heads of several spotters behind the castellations on the roofs. No chances were being taken with the safety of New Oxford's cash bulls and cows. On the other hand, the chief administrator was willing to put herself up as a target, even though the Hebdomadal

Council hung on her every word. That had been puzzling me a lot.

Then the throng of people parted and I caught a glimpse of Raphael. She was wearing an intricately detailed dark blue robe with a heavy gold chain on her shoulders, not to mention a mortar board with a long gold tassel. None of that made as much of an impression on me as the pair of individuals she was talking to.

Billy Geddes, my former friend and financial genius, was in his wheelchair and behind him, hands in his pockets, was Edinburgh's senior guardian. Both of them were in dark suits and full-length academic gowns. Surely no one had been crazy enough to offer either of them an honorary doctorate.

"Well, well, look who's here." Billy's tone was characteristically mordant. "The great Quintilian Dalrymple. I hear you still haven't caught Hamilton's killer." He laughed raucously. "Stick to the donkey jacket, Quint. The gown doesn't suit you."

"And yours suits you?" I said, giving him the eye. "What the hell are you two doing here?" I turned my gaze on Slick.

The senior guardian was tightening his bow tie. His gown was an unpleasant shade of yellow that made his face look even more sallow. "Edinburgh has many links with New Oxford, citizen," he said, giving me a superior look. "Why should high-ranking representatives of the city not attend an Encaenia?"

I glanced back at Billy. "Since when did Edinburgh use demoted auxiliaries as representatives?" I demanded.

My former friend let out a manic cackle. "Since you were sent down here, pal."

"Where's the public order guardian?" I asked, looking around to see if the Mist's ambition to board a helijet had been fulfilled.

"Looking after things in Edinburgh," Slick said with a smile that didn't put me at ease.

Raphael had been talking to Dawkley, who was looking bilious in a green and white striped gown, and the proctor. She now turned her attention to me. "All is clear," she said, drawing me to one side. "The Camera has detected no trace of the target."

"He's got an anti-surveillance device, chief administrator," I reminded her. I looked back at the pair of Edinburgh natives. "You didn't tell me they were invited."

"Is that relevant to the case?" Raphael asked, raising an eyebrow.

I shrugged. "Probably not." I told her about Katharine.

"Really, citizen," she said dismissively, "I cannot concern myself with your—" She broke off and stared at me. "Do you think the target might have taken her?"

"I don't know. It's a possibility." I beckoned Connington over. "Any sign of Katharine?"

He shook his head. "I just spoke to the Camera. She still hasn't showed up on any of the monitors."

"Shit." I shook my head. "All right, let's get this over with." I caught Raphael's eye. "But I'm telling you, if the main man doesn't put in an appearance at this parade, I'm dropping everything to find Katharine."

Raphael looked at me and finally nodded. "Very well." She turned to Connington. "Proceed."

In a few seconds, with military precision, we did.

Raphael insisted that I walk just behind and to the right of her, at the very head of the procession. That brought home to me even more forcefully what Katharine had said. It was as if I were bait, or even an alternative target – but why? If a Mark Two Grendel was after her, why would he lock on to me instead? Number Three's face flashed before me, the eyes blank and the jaw set hard. I clenched my fists in frustration, still unable to fathom what was going on.

We walked at a slow pace out of the college and turned left on to Parks Road. I glanced round and saw the column snaking out of the gateway like a garish train exiting a tunnel. Davie was walking to the side, his hand on the grip of his auxiliary knife. God knows what good he thought that would do us against a Grendel. Then another familiar face caught my eye. Andrew Duart, the Glasgow first secretary. I wasn't surprised to see him. He'd been turning up everywhere I went in the investigation recently, not that I could think of a way to tie him to the killings. He was resplendent in a crimson gown and deep in conversation with Professor Yamaguchi and Doctor Verzeni. I couldn't see Hel Hyslop though. Perhaps she'd passed the Grendel recruitment test. That thought made me even more tense.

The crowd on the corner was clapping and cheering. Raphael took the acclaim with what she thought was an appropriate degree of froideur, her chin held high and her eyes fixed on the columns of the Council block ahead. I moved my eyes from side to side, scanning the crowd for the Grendel's neutral features. I saw nothing except the smiles and waves of the students. They really did seem to be enjoying themselves. I got the impression they weren't given many days off.

"Nearly there," Raphael said as we came out of the passage and into the courtyard. To our right the Mendoza Memorial Theatre rose up, as proclaimed by a large digital panel. Who was Mendoza? I wondered. I had the feeling there used to be a large Colombian drugs operation run by a family of that name. The former Sheldonian's curved wall and the blind arcade beneath the narrow domed tower gave the building a Renaissance feel, despite the multitude of screens bearing company logos.

I glanced at the chief administrator. She didn't look nervous but her voice had wavered slightly. Up in the old Bodleian, bulldogs stared down like statues, the muzzles of their snub-barrelled rifles just visible. I felt my heart begin to pound. Although there were hundreds of people in the enclosed areas, we made perfect targets on the wide walkway. This was as good a place to take us out as the shooter would find.

"We made it," Raphael said, dabbing her forehead under the mortar board with a blue handkerchief. She gave me a thin smile. "Thank you for escorting me, citizen."

I watched as she walked to the internal door that led to the auditorium. Immediately she started greeting the gowned benefactors and sponsors. It struck me again that they were from all over the world. A swarthy Mediterranean male was followed by a Japanese woman in a tight dress. Each of the guests acknowledged Raphael with overstated respect.

Davie appeared at my side. "What next?"

"You know the plan," I said. "There's a seat for you inside that door. I've got to go and hold Raphael's hand again."

"Mind she doesn't crush yours," he said as he moved away.

I watched as Billy Geddes manoeuvred himself up a ramp, refusing the help offered by a female bulldog with words that made her head flick back in shock. I'd found out the hard way that he had a major aversion to being treated as an invalid.

I walked into the hall. There must have been well over a thousand people in there, the seats close together and on several galleries. Above us the magnificent ceiling was covered in a great painted sky replete with classical figures and clouds. Raphael and her fellow administrators were seated on a multi-layered platform straight ahead, the professors beneath them and the honoured guests, including Duart and Slick, in a segregated area to the left.

Conscious of my ridiculous garb and of the fact that – apart from the bulldogs all round the walls – I was now the only person standing, I moved up the central aisle to my seat behind Raphael. From that raised position I had an excellent view of the audience, which was why I'd placed myself there during the planning. I started running my eyes over the ranks of people, searching for the figure I'd seen in the tunnel yesterday.

Then there was a blast from the organ and everyone followed the chief administrator's lead and got to their feet. Dawkley was immediately below me. It was as I raised my head above his that I saw the rapid flashes of flame on ground level straight ahead of me.

The shooter had been way ahead of me from the start.

CHAPTER TWENTY

For a couple of seconds nothing happened. There was no sound of gunfire audible above the racket from the organ, and by the time I reacted two of the figures in the rows below me had crumpled over. Then the man in charge of the music must have realised something had happened. The swell of notes collapsed into a discordant blare and was replaced by a steadily increasing wave of screaming along with the rush of feet as people stampeded for the doors. I tried to keep my eyes on the spot where the flashes had come from, but it was hopeless, so I looked down and took in the huddle of gowns that was forming around the two motionless bodies.

Stepping over the legs of one of the three bulldogs who had forced Raphael to the floor and positioned themselves over her, I made it to the multicoloured silk cocoon and pushed my way through.

Dawkley was on his knees by one of the bodies, his hands covered in blood and his head bowed. "Oh no," he was moaning. "Oh no."

I examined the victim. Judging by the suit trousers it was a male, but it was difficult to identify him. The entire upper torso was a lake of blood and the chest looked like it had exploded. The face was covered in blood and other body matter. "Who is it?" I asked the science administrator, trying to remember which of the senior academics had been wearing a grey hood over his gown.

"Yamaguchi," the science administrator said in a leaden voice. "It's Professor Yamaguchi."

The hubbub in the hall was beginning to die down as most of the audience managed to get out of the theatre. I tried to locate Davie, but couldn't make him out behind the solid line of bulldogs that had formed across the auditorium.

Raphael appeared, pushing people out of the way. She stood staring at Yamaguchi, her face impassive. Then she tapped Dawkley on the shoulder and gave him a stern look.

I turned to the other victim. He was lying spread-eagled over his seat, arms extended and chest blasted apart in the same way as his colleague's. This time I could see enough of the blood-spattered features to make an instant identification. It was Doctor Verzeni. I thought back to the visit we'd made to the Department of Metallurgy, and the advanced weapon and ammunition that he'd shown us. It looked very much like the Italian had been taken out by the products of his own research.

My mobile went off.

"Quint, come over to the entrance hall. I've got something."

The connection was cut. Davie really was excited – he'd forgotten to sign off.

I was let through the line of bulldogs by Trout. He was wearing the expression of a man whose girlfriend had just kicked him in the groin. I soon found out why.

"Jesus," I gasped, looking at the body on the floor of the hall. "What happened to him?"

"I'd say he took a single blow to the centre of the face."

Davie was standing over Perch's sprawled body, keeping his eyes off features that had been completely crushed. "He's dead." Then he grabbed my sleeve. "Look over here, Quint." He pointed to a low, clear plastic enclosure on the floor tiles a few feet away. "I saw the shooter heading this way. He—"

"You saw him?" I interrupted. "What did he look like?"

Davie's teeth closed over his lower lip. "Difficult to say. I saw the discharge flashes from his weapon first and then everything went crazy in there. He was big all right, like the—" He broke off and glanced around. "Like the specimens we're after," he said in a low voice. "He got out of the main chamber at speed. He was in a dark suit and I think he was wearing a wig – medium-length brown hair. But I didn't see his face."

"Bloody hell, Davie," I complained. "Did anyone else spot him?"

"None of the bulldogs at the door did. They were all too busy looking at the mayhem in front of them. The proctor's people are outside looking for witnesses; the crowd's probably halfway to the Poison Fields by now." Davie turned to the plastic surround again. "Anyway, I saw him heading in this direction. I reckon he went down in the lift."

I slapped my hand against my thigh. Of course; the plastic barrier was over a concealed lift shaft like the ones in the university departments. "Let's get after him," I said, stripping off my gown and bow tie.

Davie strode over. "How?" he said, waving his control card. "I don't seem to have the access code."

My card didn't do anything either. I looked around for a touch panel without success.

"Here, citizen." Raphael was standing behind me.

She'd removed the nostrum from round her neck and was holding it out to me. "I have the code programmed in."

I waved the device over the floor and a small square area was outlined in red light on the tiles. If the assassin had gone down here he must have known the code. I tossed the nostrum back to the chief administrator. "Thanks. There's only room for two. Davie and I are going after the shooter."

For a moment it looked like she was going to argue, then she nodded. "Very well. But you're on your own. There's no surveillance system in the mole runs."

"In the what?" I said, grabbing Davie's arm as the floor jerked downwards.

Raphael didn't answer. Her face was solemn, one cheek scratched from the enforced dive she'd taken to the floor.

Then she and her entourage disappeared from sight, replaced by a smooth metallic shaft. By the time the lift glided to a halt I'd already concluded that this strategic decision was on a par with that of Captain Scott not to take dogs to the South Pole.

Too late.

"Bugger me," Davie said, peering out of the reinforced plastic box we found ourselves in. "What is this?"

"I see what Raphael meant by mole runs," I said, taking in the horizontal shafts that led away in four directions, the roofs of the circular metal tunnels lit by strips of green light. This explained how she got to Queen so quickly yesterday. So much for utopian New Oxford. The subs lived in squalor while the administrators spent a fortune on high-speed private transport.

"Why didn't they tell us about this underground network?" Davie said, looking at the maze of different coloured lines that had appeared on a screen at waist height.

I was shaking my head. "There are a lot of things they haven't told us about, big man. The trick is to work out why." I turned to him. "But that's for later. Let's see if we can track this killing machine down."

Davie ran his fingers over the screen and brought up a menu.

"Try 'Last Car'," I said, pointing at one of the options.

He touched it and we watched as one of the lines on the network was highlighted.

"That's presumably the route the vehicle took," I said.

Davie zoomed in and what I took to be the names of stops came up.

"EX, JES, UN, PET, CAS, HOT, STAT," I read. "Shit." Not for the first time I regretted that I hadn't brought the old man's guidebook. "The line seems to be heading west. Yeah, STAT's probably the old railway station."

"Shall we get going?" Davie asked, a finger hovering over the screen

"Aye."

He touched "Call Car", his face splitting into a wide grin as a rush of air came into the plastic box through small ventilation slits. "This is magic," he said. "Almost as good as the helijet."

A low, unroofed two-seater vehicle whisked to a stop beside us. The lift shaft cover rose and we were able to step on to the car. As soon as we sat down – Davie making sure he got the driving seat – the cover came down again. Although the air was cool and there was a current of movement from the other tunnels, the atmosphere was sterile. I was glad I didn't suffer from claustrophobia.

"I'll go the way the last car went, shall I?" Davie said, his hands on the control panel.

"Well spotted, guardsman," I replied, settling my buttocks on the uncomfortable seat.

"Light blue touch paper," he said, "and ret—"

The word was lost in a blast of air as the car rocketed forwards. Fortunately a windscreen had risen up when we boarded, so I didn't lose my hair. I couldn't make out the speed monitor on Davie's panel, but we were going fast enough to make my eyes water. Almost immediately the speed was cut and we reached the first stop. It was an enclosed plastic box like the one we'd just been in and it was unoccupied. The letters EX were displayed on the outside.

"Stop?" Davie asked over his shoulder.

"No," I said. "This must be Exeter College. We can assume that bulldogs will be sitting on top of every exit shaft near the theatre. Go on."

So he did. We slowed down at every stop but saw no sign of the shooter. And then we came to the end of the line. What we found there wasn't a pretty sight.

"Fuck," Davie said, shaking his head. "We know where the bastard got off anyway."

The plastic shield that bore the letters STAT was hardly legible. It looked like the inside of a man-size version of the food processors I hadn't seen in Edinburgh since I was a kid – one that had been used to produce a barrel of tomato sauce.

We weren't able to activate the lift shaft's "Raise" function; no doubt the shooter had dealt with it. So we turned the car round in the circle dug out for that purpose and headed back to the previous stop. HOT turned out to be underneath a dilapidated hotel, the lift bringing us on to an enclosed section of the pavement outside it.

I got Connington on the nostrum and told him what we'd found at STAT.

"Bulldogs have already arrived there, citizen," he said. Even on the small screen I could see how grim his expression was. "The alarm at the top of the shaft was triggered three minutes ago."

"And?" I demanded.

"There was no sign of the target. The sentry had been shot and dropped down the lift. We think an Eagle One was used, with delayed detonation."

"Christ," I said, trying not to imagine what the last seconds of the bulldog's life must have been like; if he was lucky the impact of the projectile would have killed him instantly. "I don't suppose the shooter is showing up on your much-vaunted surveillance system?"

He shook his head. "Grendel Mark Twos are—"

"Yeah, yeah," I said. "Grendel Mark Twos are issued with cloaks of invisibility. I just wondered if he'd let his slip for a moment." I was thinking of what had happened in my bedroom when the Grendel's face briefly came into view. I broke the connection. "We've lost him," I said to Davie.

He was looking down the street towards the former railway station. There were two Chariots with flashing lights outside the low buildings. "What now?" he asked, looking at me. "Back to the theatre?"

I was peering down the road to my left, trying to get my bearings. A couple of hundred yards up there was the canal I'd walked down yesterday on Pete Pym's tail. What had happened to him? I wondered. Had he ever got out of the tunnel, or had the Grendel been waiting for him on the way to the House of Dust? Then I remembered where I'd been before that: the college called Worc.

"Raphael's people can handle the scene at the Sheldonian," I said. "Let's see how the chief toxicologist's getting on." I shook my head at him. "It might be our last chance."

There was a narrow wooden gate set into the high wall on the college's southern extremity. My control card made it swing open and we found ourselves only a few yards away from the brick building where Lister 25 had been lodged. Before we entered, I stepped over to Hel Hyslop's window. The curtains and blind were fully open. There was no one inside.

I ignored Davie's raised eyebrow and led him upstairs. It was dead quiet on the third floor and there was no sign of any interfering nurses. Lister 25's door clicked open when I waved my card at it. I stuck my head round cautiously.

"Hello? Ramsay? It's Quint."

No answer. I beckoned Davie in.

"Where is he?" Davie asked in a loud whisper.

"H-eeee-re," came a long-drawn-out croak from behind us.

We jumped and crashed into each other as we turned.

"Shit," Davie grunted. He leaned forward. "Is that you, Lister 25?"

The figure in the chair was bent and limp, the head facing the knees as if it were too heavy to be held upright.

"Hu-uuume . . . 2 . . . 5 . . .3?"

At least the old chemist's memory hadn't been affected. His brain must have been one of the few organs that was still intact, though. His hands were shrivelled and his breath rattled out of lungs that sounded like they were on the brink of terminal shutdown.

Davie kneeled down beside him and loosened the straps that attached his arms to the sides of the chair.

"The nurse . . . she . . . she said I might fall." Lister 25 made a cracked sound that I realised was a laugh. "I wish . . . I wish I would."

I joined Davie on the bare floor in front of the toxicologist. I was thinking again about the RED file that the visitor to my bedroom had put me on to. I wasn't only being pointed towards the Grendels. My attention had also been drawn to Lister 25's presence in New Oxford.

"Look, Ramsay," I said. "We haven't got much time. You remember you were telling me about the research facility at Sutt?"

The old man raised his head a couple of times, enough to signal that he was following me.

"Did you see anyone you recognised there?" I asked. "Anyone from back home?"

Now Lister 25 managed to lift his head and keep it up, one hand under his chin.

"Quint? Have . . . have you got . . . a blues cassette . . . with you?"

I stared at him then shook my head slowly.

His lips separated in a loose smile. "Pi . . . pity," he said with a gasp. "I'd . . . like to . . . to hear RJ once . . . once more . . ."

"You'll be hearing plenty of Robert Johnson songs when we get you back to Edinburgh, Ramsay," I said.

The toxicologist twitched his head. "Too . . . late." He focused his rheumy eyes on mine. "Did I see any . . . anyone . . . I knew?" His eyes narrowed and he seemed to nod his head.

For a few moments I thought I'd struck the mother lode. Then the old man's face slackened and his chin hit his upper chest.

"No, Qui . . . Quint," he drawled. "No." He looked up once more. "Now . . . get out of . . . here. I . . ."

We waited to hear the rest of Lister 25's sentence but he left it incomplete. I squeezed his fleshless arm once then left him to whatever thoughts were filling his mind.

And hoped that he was hearing sweet and melodious acoustic blues by the master.

Davie and I left the way we'd come. It was while we were on the corner under the spire of Nuff College as a posse of students on bicycles raced past that my mobile rang. Raising it to my ear, I saw that a message had also been left earlier, presumably when I was out of contact in the mole run. Shit, I hadn't checked it.

"Quint? Where are you?"

"Katharine," I said, relief breaking over me like a storm surge. "Where are *you*?"

"Don't interrupt me, Quint," she said, her voice taut. "Whatever you do, don't interrupt me." She paused and I had to bite my tongue to stop myself asking her what was going on. "I'm to tell you that he's waiting for you." Another pause. Who the hell was "he"? "He's waiting for you . . . and Davie." She stressed the last two words, which made me wonder. "He says you'll know where to find us." Again she left a space between sentences. "Us," she repeated. "You understand that? I'm . . . I'm at his mercy."

I felt my heart race even more, but I forced myself to keep quiet.

"And Quint? He says no nostrums, okay?"

I decided against answering.

"Come now, Quint," she said, her words suddenly rushed. "I know who he—"

Then the connection was cut.

"Fuck!" I shouted, pressing buttons to pick up the earlier message. I held the phone up for Davie to hear. Katharine's voice came again, this time the words interspersed with rapid breathing. The message was the same.

"Christ, he's got her," I said, kicking the kerb. "He's had her all morning. He must have had her stashed somewhere when he took the shots." An image flashed before me. "I hope she didn't see what he did to that poor sod at STAT."

"What does it mean?" Davie demanded. "Where are we supposed to go?"

I took off my nostrum and held my hand out for his. I put them in the pockets of my jacket and stuck it behind the nearest fence. Looking back towards the wall outside Worc, I nodded slowly.

"The tunnel," I said, starting to move. "The tunnel I was in yesterday."

"What?" Davie said, his eyes opening wide. "You mean the tunnel that leads—?"

"To the House of Dust? Aye, that's the one. Come on."

"What about Raphael and her crew?" he asked as he caught up with me.

"What about them?" I replied, thinking of Lister 25's wrecked body. "They can go to hell. Anyway, we haven't got our nostrums so how can we let them know where we're headed?"

Davie grinned.

Thinking of our destination and the Mark Two Grendel that was waiting for us down there with Katharine, I didn't.

We were standing on the towpath outside the tunnel entrance, the water of the canal stagnant and unrippled by bulldog punts or any other craft.

"In there?" Davie asked, inclining his head. "Do you think the surveillance teams in the Camera have picked up the Grendel and Katharine?"

I was looking at him thoughtfully. "I wonder. The shooter seems to be able to shield himself from the cameras and sensors, but Katharine would show up all right. But he told us not to bring our nostrums; presumably he's already dumped hers." I took my control card out of my pocket. "What about these? Do you think they have some kind of bug in them?"

"Maybe. Let's keep a hold of them all the same," Davie said, examining the brickwork of the arch. "We might need them later."

I nodded and stepped forward. "Right, big man. Let's do it." I went into the enclosed passage. My heart pounded as I thought of Katharine at the Grendel's mercy, but I managed to get a grip on myself. Walking into the lion's den in a state of panic wasn't a good idea.

We moved further inside and paused for our eyes to get accustomed to the ghostly light from the tunnel roof. Water was dripping on to the floor and the air had the stale, rank edge that I recalled from my last visit. I listened, but couldn't pick up the sound of anyone else in the vicinity. I started forward again as quietly as I could.

Underground, in a confined, brick-lined tube that bends all over the place, you quickly lose your sense of distance and direction. Keeping an eye on the time is the only way of maintaining perspective. After five minutes I reckoned we'd done about three hundred yards. I stopped before a left-hand kink in the tunnel and looked round it cautiously. I didn't get much joy. There was another bend about fifty yards on, this time to the right. In a patch of damp earth I saw a clear footprint among a series of scuffs. I recognised it immediately. It was a large Grendel-issue boot – size eleven, I was pretty sure.

"What do you think?" Davie asked in a whisper. "This must get somewhere soon."

I was trying to work out where we might be, but the tunnel's course had disoriented me. If Pete Pym was right about it leading to the House of Dust in what used to be Christ Church, we must have been pretty close.

"Where the hell is Katharine?" I said, swallowing hard. "The Grendel must—" I broke off as the unmistakable sound of booted feet moving at speed came from the canal end of the tunnel. "Shit. We've got company."

Davie grabbed my arm. "Come on. That sounds like a pack of bulldogs. I don't think the shooter's going to be happy."

We ran round the corner, then the next one. Now the tunnel was straight, a stretch of under a hundred yards leading to a heavy metal panel. There was more light around it.

"Jesus, there they are," I gasped. I broke into a sprint.

A pair of figures were standing at the tunnel end. Katharine was close to her captor and I could see a thin rope or wire joining her to him. They turned when they heard our footsteps and I saw the Grendel again. This time he was wearing a suit, as Davie had said, and his hair was brown and curly. But even at that distance, it was the eyes that got me. They were stark and inhuman, as black as a hole in the galaxy.

The Grendel pointed a device at the metal panel and it hissed upwards. He pulled Katharine through, then swivelled back to us. We were still pounding towards them, about twenty yards off.

"You led them to me, Citizen Dalrymple," Katharine's

captor said in a loud, steady voice. "Big mistake." He stared at me for a couple of seconds as I got nearer. "Now everybody dies."

The gate slid down an instant before we reached it.

"Bastard!" Davie roared, turning to look back down the tunnel. The stomp of bulldog feet was getting nearer.

I was waving my control card frantically around the solid barrier, trying to activate the sensor. Nothing. The shooter must have programmed in a delay.

In the seconds before the gate rose again I had a vision of Katharine's pale, lined face. Earlier, she'd thought I was the bait. Now it looked like she was.

The first body was a few paces beyond the gate. I heard Davie grunt as he bent over it.

"Bulldog," he said. "Head blown apart."

I was staring at a matt black box that had been attached to the wall inside the gate. Red numbers on a small panel were changing rapidly. "Fuck!" I yelled as I saw they were counting down towards zero. "Bomb! Move!"

We hurdled two more shattered bodies and ran down a much more high-tech passage, shining metal walls enclosing a cork-tiled floor. Access panels like those in the science faculty buildings were at regular intervals and the lights were bright. But not as bright as the explosion that boomed out and cascaded after us in waves of igniting gas. Fortunately my control card got us into an entry on the left, the door closing just before the blast reached us.

"That was a bit close for comfort," Davie said, squatting down.

We listened as another explosion rocked the underground complex, this one further down the passage.

"You could say that." I drew the blackened sleeve of my white shirt across my eyes, then stared as they focused on what was ahead. "Bloody hell, Davie. Look at this." I walked unsteadily down a narrow gantry that led out from the room.

He followed me into mid-air and, in silence, we took in the panorama of coercion that was all around. We'd moved into a small round area, some kind of viewing chamber. It was a glass-covered module suspended above a vast expanse of large chambers that must have been dug out of the ground at tremendous expense. There were retaining walls beneath us, separating the huge space into self-enclosed sections, all of them without roofs so that we could see down into every area. There were people all over the place, some of them in bulldog apparel but the overwhelming majority in tattered blue vests and trousers. They were mostly at work, those in the unit immediately below us bent over tables covered in the innards of large computers. I could see others further away packing books into cases and folding up clothes.

"What the . . .?" Davie's words trailed away as he pored over a screen at waist level. "Here, we can move this speed ball." He glanced at me. "Do you want to see more?"

I nodded slowly. "It's our best chance of spotting Katharine and the arsehole who tried to atomise us."

Davie ran his fingers over the keys and the viewing module glided smoothly away from the gantry, its suspension cables attached to a network of junction points on the roof.

"You know what this is, don't you?" I said, moving my eyes over the honeycombed complex below before pointing at the name on the screen. "It's a panopticon."

"Oh aye," Davie said, his head bent over the control panel. "What's that then?"

"The first modern prison was designed by Jeremy Bentham at the end of the eighteenth century. It was a circular building that grew out from a central observation tower. This is the New Oxford equivalent."

"Is that right?" he said, stopping the module's motion. "Well, take a look at this. According to the plan I've accessed, we're over the Interrogation Section now."

What we were actually over was a vision of hell. I stripped the skin from my lips with my teeth as I took in the naked bodies on racks, the women spread-eagled in front of bulldogs with leather aprons over their suits, the banks of machines with wires leading to the victims' tenderest parts. As we were hanging there, one of the torturers looked up and met my gaze. The Grendel's eyes were hard to live with, but this guy's were even worse. He gave me a twisted smile and went back to work with a knotted lash.

"Who are those poor souls?" Davie asked, his eyes wide.

I was thinking of the man I'd left in the tunnel yesterday. "Pete Pym told me there's a resistance movement in the suburbs. Those monsters are maybe trying to identify its members."

Davie shook his head. "Why are they using methods like that? This is Science City. Surely they've got truth drugs and the like."

I looked at him. "Truth drugs are no fun for the torturers, Davie. I bet these arseholes get a kick out of their work."

Davie was glancing around. "I want off this contraption. I'm going to rearrange those fuckers' faces."

"Hang on, guardsman," I said, touching his arm. "Katharine first." I caught his eye. "Please."

Davie scowled as he took a final look at the scene below. "All right, Quint. But I'm coming back here afterwards, I promise you."

"Okay," I said. "I'll come with you."

He nodded then turned his attention back to the control panel. "Where to then? This is a whole underground city. The Grendel and Katharine could be anywhere."

There was a blast of high explosive about a hundred yards to our right.

"There he goes," I said. "Follow the trail of destruction."

I just hoped that the bomber was keeping his hostage alive and in one piece.

The panopticon passed over more sweatshop enclosures and moved above heavy-duty incarceration units: people on treadmills, prisoners housed in coffin-shaped cells with no room to move, a group of at least twenty crammed in a small space. Jesus, the Black Hole of New Oxford. But the worst was yet to come.

"I don't believe this," Davie said, the skin above his beard pale. "I do not believe this."

I was having trouble on that front too. The module had stopped over an open area surrounded by higher walls than elsewhere in the excavated chamber. Great vertical pipes led up to the roof – I remembered the metallic columns we'd seen inside the former Christ Church – but they didn't distract me for long. What was going on below was a flashback to an older, more savage Oxford that was obviously still attractive to the city's contemporary rulers. A tall, pointed, pale stone tower stood in the centre of the space, a few bulldogs and observers in white coats keeping their distance. I recognised the monument at the foot of St Giles near the Faculty of Criminology. This was a detailed replica of the Martyrs' Memorial to Cranmer and his fellow clerics, who were burned at the stake for their Protestant beliefs by Queen Mary in the sixteenth century. Then I realised that the figures around the second stage of the tower weren't statues of the original victims – they were living human beings, shackled to the stonework.

"They're going to burn those people, Quint," Davie said, as men in fire protection suits moved forward and lit the heaped wood at the base of the memorial with torches. "This is fucking insane." He looked around the inside of the viewing unit. "I'm not standing for it."

"No, Davie!" I yelled, pointing at the pair of bulldogs carrying machine-pistols beneath us. "You haven't got a chance."

He pressed a button and a glass panel blew out of the module, an escape rope snaking towards the floor. "I don't care. This is murder." And he was gone.

Paralysed, I watched as he slid downwards, directing a loud stream of abuse at the executioners. "Jesus, Davie," I gasped, grabbing hold of the robe and leaning out into space. I got a lungful of acrid woodsmoke and started lowering myself incompetently, feeling my palms burn as I slipped.

I was halfway down when I realised that not all the smoke was coming from the pyre around the replica Martyrs' Memorial. My ears rang with the percussive effect of multiple explosions.

We weren't the only ones who objected to the cremation of live bodies: it seemed the Grendel did too.

* * *

By the time I got down, the armed bulldogs were sprawled motionless on the floor. The white-coated observers were cowering by the wall and the firemen were nodding dully as they were given instructions. Near them I made out the solid form of Katharine's captor, but I couldn't see her. Then there was a deafening noise as high-pressure hoses erupted all round the pyre. The fire was doused in seconds and fans sucked the smoke up the huge vent inlets.

Davie appeared by my side, knife in hand. The blade was stained with dark blood. I didn't ask.

"Get those people down!" came a loud command. The harsh tones belonged to the Grendel. "You two!" The voice was directed at us. "Drop your weapons and come over here."

I caught sight of Katharine as the smoke cleared. She was still attached to the Grendel by some kind of umbilical link. I turned to Davie and nodded at his knife. "Do as he says, big man," I said quietly. "He's holding all the cards."

Davie's jaw jutted forward. Then, with a show of extreme reluctance, he tossed his knife to one side.

"That's far enough," the man in the suit said, a sinister smile spreading over his smooth-skinned face. He opened the flaps of his jacket and I saw a waistcoat that was festooned with small black boxes like the one I'd seen on the gate. "I've got plenty more of these hyper-explosive devices on me, Citizen Dalrymple." He glanced at Katharine. "And your girlfriend's attached to one of them." He nodded at me slowly, the smile still there. "So if anything happens to me, the two of us, and anyone else within a radius of about a hundred yards, will go up. Clear?"

"Clear," I confirmed. I watched as the people – one

woman and two men – got down from the memorial. "Pete!" I shouted. "Pete Pym! Over here." It was only after I'd called him over that I realised I wasn't doing him any favours.

"Yes," said the Grendel. "Over here, Pete Pym. You others, get as far as you can from this area." The smile at last disappeared from his face as he looked back at us. "We're about to play the end game."

Davie and I looked at each other nervously. I tried to catch Katharine's eye, but she was staring at the wire leading from her midriff to the Grendel's waist. I could only hope that she wasn't going to do anything to it.

"Where are we going, Number Three?" I asked, trying to establish some kind of relationship with the assassin by using the number I was sure was his; something about the way he carried himself was familiar.

The Grendel narrowed his outer space eyes at me and ran his tongue along his lips. "Where are we going, Quint? We're going to find the people who designed this place."

"Let her go," I said, stepping forward. "Davie and I will come with you."

"Thanks a lot," Davie muttered.

Pete Pym was watching the scene in bewilderment, his face and clothes blackened.

The Grendel put a hand on Katharine's shoulder. "Oh no, I want all of you to meet these fuckers." He laughed harshly. "After all, they're responsible for me too."

My heart sank. The lunatic had already killed God knows how many people and now he was steaming at full speed towards what he himself had called the end game.

The problem was, I'd always been completely useless at chess.

CHAPTER TWENTY-ONE

The Grendel led us out of the fire chamber, Katharine keeping close to him to avoid stretching the wire that was attached to the explosive charge. Apart from one apologetic look, she concentrated on her captor rather than me. I didn't blame her.

Pete Pym drew up beside me. "How did you get in here?" he asked in a low voice.

"I was going to ask you the same question."

He shrugged. "I thought I was in the clear. After you left me in the tunnel, I went further in and lay low for an hour." He nodded at the Grendel's back. "God knows where the freak got to. I didn't see him again till he showed up now." He grinned loosely. "I'm bloody glad he did though."

"So the bulldogs caught you?"

"Yeah," he said, nodding. "Bastards. They must have managed to override my sub-machine. They were certain I had something to do with the resistance. Tried to get me to spill my guts about it." Pete Pym raised his hands. "They had fun with my fingernails first."

I fought to swallow the bile that shot into my mouth. His hands were blackened from the pyre and I hadn't noticed that the ragged fingertips were encrusted with dried blood.

"I didn't tell them anything," he went on, "so they

decided to smoke it out of me. They added a few innocent people they took off the street in Cowley to make me feel worse." He raised his shoulders again. "I don't know if they'd have put the fire out before we croaked. I wouldn't have talked."

The Grendel glanced round. "That's enough gabbing, Pym," he said, fixing unblinking eyes on the local. "I know exactly what you're in here for. If you behave yourself, you might see the light of day again." He turned to the front again, eyes now on a matt black device he was holding. It was similar to a nostrum but smaller. "Get a move on, all of you. The dogs will be here any second."

A panel in the heat-proofed wall slid open in front of us and we came out into a narrow passage.

"Where are we going, Number Three?" I asked.

This time the Grendel didn't look round. "Keep quiet. You'll see soon enough, Citizen Dalrymple."

At least he didn't seem so keen on blowing Davie and me to pieces now. But it puzzled me that he kept using my Edinburgh title. Perhaps he'd been eavesdropping on the conversations I'd had with Raphael and her colleagues.

There was a loud metallic bang ahead. The Grendel went into a half crouch, his limbs tensed like a big cat about to pounce. Then he glanced at the device in his hand and nodded slowly. "Interesting," he said. "They're leaving us on our own for the time being. That was the sound of a bulldog's steel toecap hitting the wall as he pulled out of the corridor ahead."

Davie leaned forward. "You can tell from that thing you're holding?"

The Grendel looked round at him and smiled vacantly. "Oh yes, guardsman. I know exactly what the dogs are doing." He started walking again, in a long, loping stride that forced Katharine to run in order to keep up. "Let's surprise them. Change of plan. There's a place you should see before we confront them."

Davie and I looked at each other helplessly; given Katharine's situation, there wasn't much we could do except go along with the assassin.

He led us down several passageways, all of them deserted. I could hear Pete Pym panting as he struggled to maintain the rapid pace. I looked up a couple of times but could see no sign of the viewing module we'd abandoned. I was pretty sure we were being tracked by other means though. As we went on, the rank smell that I'd noticed in the entry tunnel grew worse. The sound of heavy-duty extractor fans was also getting louder. I began to get a seriously bad feeling about our destination.

Finally, the Grendel stopped by an access panel and pointed the unit he was carrying at it. A door swung open and he led us in. But before I'd taken a single step, I gagged and put a hand to my face.

"Jesus, what is this place?" I gasped, breathing through my mouth.

The Grendel tossed us thick fibrous masks from a shelf on the inside wall. "This, citizen? This is the heart of darkness." His lips parted but he didn't smile. "This is the House of Dust itself."

I clamped a mask over my nose and mouth.

Then walked into the jaws of hell.

The authorities had managed to evacuate everyone who worked in the area. A long, wide chamber stretched ahead of us, the roof low. It looked like it had been tunnelled out of the bedrock. There was no matrix of cables for the viewing module here. On the right a series of glass-fronted rooms stretched away, each of them furnished with an operating table and banks of high-tech gear. In the first one there was a male body with the chest opened up.

I took a quick look. "The organs have been removed," I said, my voice muffled by the mask.

"Correct," the Grendel said. "What else do you see?"

Katharine's eyes were bulging above the white fibre. "My God, what have they been doing to those people?" she said in a weak voice, pointing at what looked like a perpendicular medieval torture frame. There was a pair of bodies hanging like St Andrew on his cross, the flesh and skin partially removed from the legs. In front of the rack were blood-drenched plastic boxes.

"Don't worry," the Grendel said gruffly. "They were dead before they got here. The bodies are being rendered. You've no idea how many uses New Oxford can find for human tissue."

"But these aren't scientific procedures," Davie said, staring at the scene of carnage.

The assassin glanced at him. "Not all the uses require scientific procedures," he said suggestively. "Remember the Four Horsemen of the Apocalypse? One of them was Famine."

I took a deep breath through my mouth and tried to shut out the obvious conclusion, but the Grendel wouldn't let me.

"Some of the senior employees of the transnationals that fund New Oxford have developed a taste for human flesh, it seems." He grunted. "Apparently they got bored with haute cuisine."

My attention was attracted by an insistent mechanical noise at the far end of the cavern, deeper and more grating than the fans.

"What's that noise?" I said, stepping forward. "It sounds like there's a mill down there."

The Grendel nodded, the skin around his eyes creasing. "Very good, citizen. Let's take a closer look, shall we?"

Davie and Katharine glared at me. It was obvious that we were about to be shown another facet of the underworld. I shrugged at them and tried to keep up with the Grendel. He was moving even faster now, eager to show us the pièce de résistance.

We passed a heap of skeletons and individual bones, some of them clean but others bearing remnants of tendons and other tissue. Despite the mask, the stench was overpowering. I was struggling to hold on to the contents of my stomach. Then the Grendel stopped and pointed up at a great grey, riveted machine that took up the whole of the end wall. There was an automated feeder system leading from the pile of bones to the top of the contraption.

"What is it?" Katharine asked, her voice raised above the noise of rotating metal.

The Grendel pointed to a stream of off-white dust that was being directed from a pipe on the left of the machine into a large plastic sack. "They grind the bones," he said, his eyes wide and bloodshot. I noticed that one of the irises was duller than the other. "They discovered that the residue is the ultimate in hyper-conductor material when it's combined with silicon."

I stared at the lettering on the sack. It read "NOX Computing Industries – Grade A+ + + Hyper-Conductor Base". I bowed my head. This was the bestial heart of Brave New Oxford. The administrators presided over a state where they stripped the citizens' flesh and ground their bones – having first done everything they could to crush their spirit.

Then, suddenly, the engine in the bone mill coughed and died with a long-drawn-out moan. The Grendel started nodding slowly; beneath the mask I was sure he was smiling again. But not for long. Soon afterwards there was a loud, sliding crash as a shining steel panel came down across the full width of the chamber a few yards behind us.

We were well and truly trapped, with only the dust of the dead for company. Then I heard a faint hissing noise and watched as a plume of white gas settled over us from a small outlet in the rock ceiling.

I was senseless before my body hit the floor.

I came round in a haze, the acrid reek of vomit in my nostrils. Gradually I managed to focus on my surroundings. Davie was next to me, sitting with his head in his hands, while Pete Pym was still comatose, stretched out with his hands on his chest like a decorous corpse.

"Where are we?" I said, the words running together as I struggled to raise myself. "Davie?"

He turned to me and blinked hard, his face ashen and drawn. "Fuck knows. A holding cell, I'd guess."

I looked around and saw the vertical bars that ran along one side of the confinement space. There was no furniture, no water supply, no nothing. All I could hear was the dull, continuous swoop of the fan in the ceiling.

"Shit," I choked, remembering the final scene in the House of Dust. "Where's Katharine?" I glanced behind me. "And where's the Grendel?"

Davie raised his shoulders and shook his head. "Search me."

I felt a wave of panic dash over me and tried to piece together what had happened. The cloud of gas. Maybe the Grendel hadn't been affected by it. But what about Katharine?

Then Pete Pym groaned and opened his eyes. "Where . . . where am I?" He sat up slowly. "Am I . . . dead or . . . alive?"

"The latter," came a dry voice from beyond the rails. "But very soon, the former."

The three of us looked to the front. I saw a figure that made my stomach clench. Jesus, how could I have been so stupid?

"Burton," I said, moving to the rails then jerking back as I got an electric shock that made every nerve in my body tingle. "Fuck!" I yelled, jumping about and rubbing my hands together. "Elias Burton," I said when the pain began to fade. "I should have guessed you were more than a drunken old don. Who are you in real life?"

The academic stared at me. "Appearances are deceptive, citizen. Any philosopher will tell you that. But I am no turncoat." He gave me a tight-lipped smile. "Besides, did I not tell you about the House of Dust?"

"You're a cold-blooded, murdering bastard," I said, glaring at him. "You were playing games all along, weren't you? Like all your bastard, lying colleagues."

He nodded. "Indeed." He smiled again. "Who am I? Frederick Wood-Lewis is my name. I am the senior proctor of this university."

Pete Pym groaned. "We're well and truly shafted now. This evil old vulture's behind all the worst things that have happened here."

Wood-Lewis gave Pym a look that managed at the same time to be both vacant and malevolent. I realised that the old don was wearing clothes that were a lot less ragged than his usual get-up. His tweed jacket and cavalry twill trousers must have come straight from

Nox Outfitters on the High Street. "The senior proctor?" I said. "What about Connington?"

"Doctor Connington is the junior proctor," Burton said. "He handled both roles while I was working undercover." That explained Haskins's use of Connington's correct title; unfortunately I'd been too distracted to follow it up.

"Where's Katharine?" I demanded. "Where's the Grendel?"

The bogus don's expression hardened. "They are still on the run. We thought we had the assassin, but he managed to fight his way out of the rendering chamber." He shook his head. "His immune system withstood the new gas compound, for all the assurances of Dawkley's people."

"What about Katharine?" I shouted. "Where is she?"

Wood-Lewis's eyes were locked on mine. "He carried her out of there. He killed seven bulldogs on the way."

"Good," Davie said.

"Where's he taken her?" I asked, standing as close to the bars as I dared. "For Christ's sake, Burton, Wood-Lewis, whatever your fucking name is – where are they?"

"Don't worry, citizen, we have them on the sensors." The senior proctor looked at me thoughtfully. "Perhaps you can help."

"How?"

Wood-Lewis glanced to his left and nodded to a bulldog in a stained leather apron. "The electrical charge is now off, citizen. If you agree to my proposal, I will open the barrier. If not, I will leave you in the capable hands of Jowett here."

I took a deep breath. I was about to be manipulated by the authorities of New Oxford again, but it was the only way I could help Katharine.

"What's your proposal?" I said in a low voice.

"Quint?" Davie was at my side. "You're not going to help this scumbag? He's responsible for—"

I put my hand on his forearm to silence him.

"My proposal," Wood-Lewis said when he was sure that Davie was under control, "is that we allow the Mark Two Grendel to exit through the escape tunnel where he and his prey are currently holed up."

"They're in the tunnel leading from the House of Dust to the canal?" I asked.

He nodded. "We have them under surveillance. Although the Grendel is beyond our systems, your companion is not." He gave me another tight smile. "She can lead us to him."

Davie stepped up and put his hands on the bars without a second's hesitation. "How do you know he hasn't just dumped Katharine there?"

"Until a few seconds ago she was showing in mid-air on our system," Wood-Lewis replied. "Obviously he was carrying her."

"I don't understand," I said. "Why don't you just block the ends of the tunnel and leave the Grendel and Katharine to rot? You don't care about her."

"True," he countered. "But the chief administrator and Dawkley want the Mark Two Grendel in one piece so that tests can be carried out and refinements made. We also want no more damage inflicted on the House of Dust. The only way to achieve those ends is to let him out of the tunnel unhindered and draw him to a location where we can snare him."

"Pretty risky strategy, isn't it?" I said, looking at him suspiciously. I knew there was more going on than he'd admitted, but this was Katharine's only chance. "All right," I said, glancing at Pete Pym. "But I want your assurance that you'll let this citizen go back to Cowley unharmed."

Wood-Lewis nodded after a credible amount of reluctance.

"And I want you to tell me what the hell's been going on," I said.

The senior proctor smiled. "Have no fear, citizen. You'll be told everything you need to know and more." He raised a finger to the bulldog and the bars slid aside. "That would be only fair," he continued, meeting my gaze. "In exchange for you giving us the Grendel."

I stared back at him and laughed. I stopped when I realised he was completely serious.

A lift took us up to the surface in a few seconds. The senior proctor's nostrum told him that the Grendel and Katharine were still in the tunnel, about fifty yards from the exit to the towpath. Presumably the assassin was waiting to see if any bulldogs approached. Wood-Lewis had ordered all his forces to keep their distance until we could see where the Grendel was headed.

"So you played me for a jackass and put me on to the House of Death," I said as we came up into a clear plastic box in the middle of a wide quadrangle. "Making sure that you didn't make it too obvious in case I felt the hook. Why bother?"

Wood-Lewis pressed a box on the screen and watched as the shaft cover rose up. "Surely that's obvious, citizen. We wanted you to lure the Grendel into our most secure area." He twitched his lips. "We imagined – mistakenly as it transpired – that we could neutralise him there."

I was staring at him in bewilderment. "You wanted *me* to lure him into the House of Dust? Why would he allow himself to be lured by me?" Then flashes of light began to appear in the deepest recesses of my mind. I stepped away from the others, my hand at my brow. I was only vaguely aware of the great tower that was lying horizontally on the ground, its top over what used to be a pond.

The Edinburgh connection – that's what this whole case revolved around. The mutilation of George Faulds and Lewis Hamilton's death had been the beginning of it and I'd allowed myself to overlook the significance of those events for too long. The Edinburgh connection: that had to be it. The Grendel had addressed me by my correct title several times. Not only that, he'd addressed Davie by his first name and his old rank. And he'd used yards as a measurement rather than metres. Christ, that was it.

"This Mark Two Grendel," I said, turning back towards Wood-Lewis. "Number Three, as he's been designated – he was originally from Edinburgh, wasn't he?"

The senior proctor nodded. "You've finally got it, citizen. From a recent review of the transcripts we made when he and his companions underwent the initial indoctrination sessions – we use powerful drugs to ascertain as much as we can – we discovered that you knew him." He glanced at Davie. "As did you, commander."

Davie and I were staring at each other. That explained the vague sense of familiarity I got from the photograph, as well as his use of our names and titles. But I still didn't recognise the solid features and empty black eyes.

"Quint," Davie said in an undertone. "Remember the wound on Dead Dod's finger? I always thought it was made by an auxiliary knife."

I watched as Wood-Lewis nodded, a smile spreading across his thin lips. "And remember the knowledge of guard procedures at Ramsay Garden," I said slowly. "As well as the location of the youth's body near the port in Leith." I moved closer to Wood-Lewis, causing the bulldog who was escorting him to step between us. "You said this guy had people with him when he became a Grendel?" I asked, looking round the bodyguard's solid frame.

The old academic nodded, the smile even broader.

"Jesus, Davie," I said, shaking my head. "You know who he is, don't you?"

Davie's mouth was open, his expression fraught. "Auxiliary, knowledge of the port area, tendency to extreme violence . . ." His eyes opened wide. "No, it can't be."

"Yes, it can," I said, biting my lip. "This Grendel is Jamieson 369." I watched as Wood-Lewis nodded triumphantly. "The former commander of the Fisheries Guard back home, known throughout the City Guard as Dirty Harry."

Davie's mouth was hanging open.

"Excellent," the senior proctor said.

"Oh no it isn't," I countered. Dirty Harry was the last person I wanted to be holding Katharine prisoner, especially if his innate ferocity had been chemically and psychologically enhanced by the lunatics in New Oxford.

"What do you think, citizen?" Wood-Lewis asked. "Can you trap him and talk him into surrendering? Can you terminate his career?"

I was watching a dodo flop across the grass of the quadrangle, its beady eyes regarding us haughtily as it picked its way around the base of the chimney. "The answer to both questions is no," I said, glancing back at him. "How did you produce that bloody bird, for Christ's sake? Genetic engineering?"

Wood-Lewis shook his head. "No, no. That's not one of Dawkley's interests. It's mechanically contrived."

"What?" Davie said, screwing his eyes up at the extinct creature.

"He means it's a robot," I said. "That's all we need."

Except it wasn't. What we really needed were a couple of Davie's crack guard units, but we were on our own in this city with its stinking honeycomb of underground passages and death chambers.

As we were led to the gate I remembered that Christ Church used to be referred to as the House. My old man had told me that was a translation of the Latin *Aedes Christi* – the House of Christ. Now it had been turned into the House of Dust. There was a lot more than Evelyn Waugh's handful of that substance beneath our feet; here Hamlet's precious quintessence of dust was heaped in great mounds and used as an industrial resource.

It was hell, an inferno, the end of the world.

And Katharine was still down there.

"He'll be waiting till it's completely dark," I said to Raphael. "Then he'll use his equipment to take out your street surveillance units so he can obscure Katharine from the Camera; like he did with Ted Pym on the way to Dead Man's Walk and Raskolnikov at the Botanic Garden."

She nodded, her eyes directed out of the window in the Hebdomadal Council chamber towards the lights that had just come on in Broad Street. "Very likely."

"Unless he's already killed her, of course."

She looked round at me. "Surely you don't want to take the risk of storming the tunnel? Your friend would not survive such a move."

I shook my head. "You know he'll be coming for you, don't you?"

She motioned agreement again. "I know," she said. "I don't know why he didn't fire at me during the Encaenia."

"He wanted Yamaguchi and Verzeni first." I was watching her face. It remained as impassive as ever. "They were involved in the Grendel project so they had to die like Raskolnikov. You're responsible for everything in this murderous state – that has to be why he's been gunning for you." I moved closer. "What happened to his friends? Dirty Harry deserted from Edinburgh back in 2025 with a full Fisheries Guard vessel crew."

"Didn't the senior proctor tell you?" the chief administrator asked. "They all died during the fitting-out process."

"The fitting-out process?" I repeated. Wood-Lewis had offered to brief me on the Grendels when we got to the building, but I refused; a blast of repulsion at what we'd seen in the House of Dust had made me tell him where to go. "What the hell is the fitting-out process?"

Before Raphael could answer, her nostrum chirruped and, at the same time, there was the noise of numerous feet at the far end of the room.

"He's moving, chief administrator," Wood-Lewis called from the front of a group that included Dawkley and Connington. For a change the junior proctor wasn't wearing his gown. Trout lurked at the rear.

"So I see," Raphael said coolly.

"You really must accompany us to the secure area beneath the Camera," Dawkley said, his eyes restless. "He may well look here first."

Wood-Lewis stepped forward. "We cannot stop him with conventional arms," he said in a low voice. "I suggest that Citizen Dalrymple tries to distract him while we surround the area with the supermax lasers Dawkley's people have been working on." The sardonic way he was looking at the science administrator showed how little faith he had in that weapon. "Let's hope they make the Grendel see sense and surrender."

"I thought you said *I* was supposed to terminate his career," I said. "How the fuck do you expect me to do that?" I glanced round. "Where's Davie?" He'd gone off with a pair of bulldogs an hour earlier to check the weaponry options, while Pete Pym had been sent back to Cowley.

"On his way," Dawkley said. "With a supermax."

"You've given him one of your precious lasers?" I said. "Why?"

"It's only a small one," the science administrator said. "Perhaps the Grendel's guard will drop and the commander will manage to train the beam on him."

I shrugged. "Perhaps." I gave them a pessimistic glare. "Or perhaps he'll use it on the fuckers who set up the House of Dust." I looked round their pallid faces. "Which means all of you."

That gave them pause for thought.

After a few minutes Wood-Lewis and Dawkley began to look even more concerned.

"The surveillance unit outside Worc has gone down," the senior proctor said, pointing to the large panel that had been lowered from the ceiling. "He's getting nearer."

"Patience," Raphael said, her expression unperturbed. "You've set up full blast protection on Crim Fac, I presume."

Wood-Lewis nodded. "His explosive charges can effect only limited damage. Of course, we don't yet know if the faculty's a target."

The administrators gathered round the screen with its network of coloured lines and building outlines.

"Another unit's gone down," Dawkley said. "On Beaumont Street. He's approaching the faculty. Should we not intercept him?"

Raphael shook her head. "Let him be." She glanced at me. "Remember that he has Citizen Dalrymple's female friend with him. We don't want any harm to befall her, do we?"

The science administrator's face suggested otherwise, but he didn't have the balls to stand up to his leader.

We waited for the Grendel's next move. I could feel the sweat running down my arms. Then I heard heavy footsteps behind me and turned to see Davie approaching.

"Armed and dangerous?" I asked.

"Oh aye." He patted his breast pocket gingerly. "This supermax thing looks like a pen, but apparently it can melt a man's heart at fifty yards."

"Did you give it a trial run?"

"Uh-uh," he said, his eyes locked on the Hebdomadal Council members and his jaw jutting. "But I will do soon. These bastards deserve—"

I raised a hand to stop him. "Save it till we've got Katharine back, eh?"

He nodded reluctantly.

There was a loud blast in the distance to the west.

"What was that?" Connington demanded.

"The Martyrs' Memorial, junior proctor," said Harriet Haskins from the large vertical display. "A charge at the base has brought the column down over St Giles."

"I wonder why he chose that?" Davie said.

"Showing this lot what he can do," I replied. "And making a statement about the replica in the House of Dust."

I looked back at the screen. Yellow crosses denoting surveillance cameras had been extinguished outside the former Balliol College.

"He's only a hundred and fifty metres away," Wood-Lewis said, his voice taut.

Raphael looked round at me and Davie. "It's time we cleared the Council building." She turned to Dawkley. "Everyone out except Citizen Dalrymple and the commander. Now!" Her voice was low but it didn't brook contradiction.

In a few seconds the three of us were on our own.

That was the way I wanted it.

"Why are you doing this?" I asked Raphael while we waited. "Why's the Mark Two Grendel so important?"

The chief administrator of New Oxford was standing by the screen, watching as the yellow crosses along the line marking the near end of Broad Street went out one by one. She glanced at me and I saw that her eyes were glinting and her cheeks were suffused. I'd never seen her so passionate.

"The Mark Two Grendel is our future, citizen. It has evolved since it was released into the world, it can survive the toxins from the Poison Fields. We must find out how that process occurred so that we can replicate it." She gave a single laugh. "Of course, the fruits of our labour will only benefit the intellectual élite. The subs are already doomed."

"See what I mean, Quint?" Davie said from the position he'd taken up by a window. "The lunatics in charge of this hell-hole aren't human."

Raphael laughed again, a dry, unpleasant sound. "Being human is greatly overrated, commander," she said, looking back at me. "I'm not afraid of the Grendel, citizen. It isn't the first time I've been his target. But your old colleague from the Edinburgh guard will find the tables turned when he enters this chamber."

Davie shot a glance at the screen. "He – I mean they – are within twenty-five yards." He turned away from the window and faced the door. "Stand by for fireworks."

There was a gap that couldn't have been more than half a minute, but which seemed to go on for several lifetimes. Then I heard a dull thump and the door burst open. A figure flew backwards and skidded across the varnished floorboards. From the dark suit I saw that it was a bulldog, though there was no sign of a bowler hat. The head had disappeared too, in a welter of crimson. If Trout had stayed on the door to protect his leader, he'd made the wrong career move.

Katharine appeared in the doorway, her expression neutral but her eyes moving from side to side. I watched as she turned her head and spoke quietly to her unseen captor. After a few seconds she moved forward slowly. An arm was clamped round her midriff. Dirty Harry had obscured as much as he could of his oversized body behind her slender frame.

Raphael gave the slaughtered bulldog a brief look then took in her visitors. "There is no need for caution, Number Three," she said. "We will not be disturbed."

The Grendel's head stayed behind Katharine's for a few more moments. "All right," he said, straightening up and pushing her aside as far as the umbilical link allowed. He looked up from his matt black device. "I can see that the nearest dogs are over by the Noxad building." He gave Raphael an unwavering look. "Let's hope for your sake that they stay there."

I stepped forward. "Well, well. If it isn't Jamieson 369." I gave him a smile to obscure the fear that was threatening to engulf me. "How are you doing, Harry? Sorry I didn't recognise you earlier."

The former guard commander grunted, one hand on the explosive charges on his chest. "The fucks in New Oxford fixed me up, didn't they? Off with the beard, in with the bodybuilding compounds. The plastic surgery took months."

"Aye, you're quite a piece of work, Harry," Davie said, staying by the window. "What happened to your eye?"

The first time I met the Fisheries Guard leader back in 2022 he was wearing a patch on his face; a smuggler with a death wish had put his eye out. Later Harry got a glass eye from the Medical Directorate that didn't match the colour of the surviving natural one.

"Oh, they fixed that too," he said, staring at Raphael again. "They fixed both of them. They can fix anything in this sewer." He shook his head. "Not that I like the colour very much. Black eyes, black heart, my granny used to say."

The chief administrator was nodding. "You're right, Number Three. We can fix anything. We can even fix your future." She returned his gaze. "But first, why don't you explain what you've been doing? Citizen Dalrymple is desperate to know." She stepped closer to Harry and Katharine. That made my heart pound even more. "Why did you follow me to Edinburgh? Why have you been picking off my colleagues?"

I glanced at Katharine. She seemed to have her breathing under control, but her eyes were still moving continuously. I could only hope that she would bide her time. Davie and I stood a better chance of helping her if I could show Harry that I was on his side rather than Raphael's.

"It's all to do with the Grendel project, isn't it, Harry?"

I said, risking another smile on him. "What happened to your crew?"

The assassin wasn't listening to me. He took another look at the device round his neck. He'd removed the brown wig he had on earlier and his scalp was now under a layer of unnaturally black, clippered hair. There was no sign of the dunt in his skull that used to pulse like a misplaced heart; presumably the Nox scientists had ironed that out too.

"It's a superb device, the Ghost," he said, raising the unit. "I could never have got away with what I did without its anti-surveillance functions. It even got me through the Poison Fields without being spotted. That much I'll tell you for free, Raphael." Then he dropped the device and his hand moved with bewildering speed to his belt.

There was a stomach-churning noise of honed blade entering flesh and the chief administrator collapsed to the ground clutching her left thigh. I could see the haft of an auxiliary knife protruding between her fingers.

"Everything else you want to know, you pay for," Dirty Harry said, his face showing no emotion. "The currency is pain."

Raphael was biting her lower lip, but she didn't cry out. Screwing up her eyes, she pulled out the knife and tossed it back towards Harry. Then she took out a white handkerchief and bound it round her leg. The fabric reddened but the flow of blood seemed to be staunched quickly.

"What happened to your men, Harry?" I said, watching as Raphael crawled to a chair and hauled herself into it. Davie didn't offer any help.

Harry stared at me then nodded slowly. "I did the right thing when I got you involved, Citizen Quint." He laughed humourlessly. "I used to think you were a right fucking smartarse back in the old city." He looked over at Raphael. "All right, bitch, you've put a down payment on the information you want so here it is – though I reckon you know most of it already. My guys and I deserted from Edinburgh in '25. There were sixteen of us when we sailed away. By the time we ran aground in the Wash five had gone; they were taken out when we stormed a container ship off Hull. Another couple were killed in skirmishes with headbangers on land. We found our way to the borders of this fucking state in the spring of '26. Then the nightmare really began." He broke off and glanced at the Ghost in his hand. "Looks like your people are staying put, chief administrator. Obviously they don't care that you've been hurt." He grinned vacantly.

"They have orders not to intervene," Raphael said, her voice surprisingly even. "Under any circumstances."

"That'll be right," Harry said. He looked at me. "With me so far, Citizen Quint?"

"With you, Harry." I could feel Katharine's eyes burning into me. She obviously wasn't with the former guard commander in spirit. "Go on."

He nodded slowly, looking at me as if he were trying to figure out where I stood. "Aye, well, the bulldogs on the outer perimeter saw that we had some potential in the violence stakes, so we were airlifted over the Poison Fields and put straight into the Grendel training programme." He glanced at Raphael. "Of course, back then it wasn't anything like as sophisticated" – he gave the word a heavily ironic emphasis – "as it is now. Afterwards we spent months patrolling the PFs." His voice lowered in intensity. "Four of my guys died towards the end of that time, their lungs eaten away by new toxic strains." He straightened his back. "That was when they started work on the Mark Two Grendels."

Raphael pulled herself up in the chair. "There is no need to share any more technical information with these outsiders, Number Three," she said in a firm voice. "Explain the murders."

The Grendel shook his head, the loose grin back on his face. "I'm not taking any more orders from you."

"I've got some thoughts about the murders, Harry," I said, opening my arms. I had the impression that when Harry got on to what happened to the rest of his crew, Katharine would be in the middle of a lethal crossfire. "The first one, Ted Pym, was an experiment. You'd discovered that he was involved in the Cowley resistance with his brother Pete, so he was expendable. You left him down at Dead Man's Walk because it's in sight of the House of Dust and you wanted to register your interest."

The former Fisheries Guard commander was nodding at me. "Not bad as far as it goes, citizen. I'm still listening."

There was more to be said about Ted Pym's murder, but I wasn't clear about the motive for the dismemberment so I moved on. "You followed Raphael and her entourage – all of them being involved one way or another in the Mark Two Grendel project – to Edinburgh." I shrugged. "I guess that the Ghost device enabled you to board the helijet unobserved."

"That's right," he confirmed. "I travelled both ways in the luggage hold."

I stared at him. "Christ. How did you? . . . doesn't matter. In Edinburgh, you severed a Leith Lancer's arm to bring me and my team on board the case. Then you took a shot at the chief administrator here during the prison inauguration, where you would cause maximum disruption to the incarceration policy and to New Oxford's involvement in Edinburgh."

"Fucking prisons," Harry said. "They've turned this place into a prison factory and look how much good it's done them." He paused and shook his head. "I didn't mean to kill the public order guardian. Even though the old bastard was never very keen on me and the Fisheries Guard. When I saw him move after I fired, I reduced the Eagle One's velocity and deactivated the explosive charge."

"Lewis Hamilton's heart gave out," I said.

Harry nodded slowly. "Aye. Another innocent victim of New Oxford."

Raphael was staring at him, her eyes wide. "What about Raskolnikov? What about Verzeni and Yamaguchi? Why did you kill them before me?"

Harry laughed again, his eyes meeting hers. "After Edinburgh I changed tactics, you heartless cow. I wanted to make you suffer as you waited for the shot." There was a high-pitched beep from the Ghost device. "What a surprise," he said in a level voice. "Your people have decided to intervene after all." He raised his right arm at her. "It's time for your suffering to end, chief administrator."

I stared at him, trying to make out what he was doing with his right hand. Then my ears were filled with the pounding of heavy feet on the stairs beyond the door and every window erupted into blinding light.

It looked like everyone except me was playing their end game at the same time.

CHAPTER TWENTY-TWO

I was stumbling around like a blind man, arms extended as I desperately tried to make contact with Katharine. Then, suddenly, the floodlights were doused and I managed to focus on the interior of the Council chamber. There was no sign of Dirty Harry or of Katharine.

"Are you all right, Quint?" Davie was at the window. There was a series of explosions, followed by screams and cries. "Bloody hell. Harry just took out a couple of bulldog Chariots. What kind of weaponry is he using?"

I was looking at an open window further down the room, its curtains moving in the breeze. Then my eyes fell on Raphael. She was lying back in the chair, completely motionless, her legs straight out and her upper body an overflowing crater of blood. She hadn't stood a chance against whatever Harry had fired.

I turned as a squad of bulldogs led by Harriet Haskins rushed in. Dawkley and Wood-Lewis were to the rear.

"Stay here!" I shouted to them. "The Grendel still has Katharine. Davie and I will find them."

The science administrator kneeled by his former leader. "Very well," he said in a defeated voice. "You have fifteen minutes. But I warn you: if the Grendel eludes you, we will hit him and his prisoner with everything we have."

Haskins came up and handed me a nostrum. "Here," she said. "You'll need this. It's programmed to monitor your female friend's location."

I thanked her and ran to the window. Davie was already halfway down the emergency rope.

"Where are they?" he asked as I got to the ground, my stomach hollow.

"Just up the road," I said, looking at the nostrum and pointing north. "They've gone into Wad."

We sprinted towards the college where the Encaenia procession had gathered.

"What the hell's he doing?" Davie said.

"Looking for a bolthole?" I suggested, my lungs already straining.

Davie grunted. "No way. Harry's got this all planned."

Maybe he was right. I followed him towards the gateway. There were a couple of blood-boltered bulldogs on the ground.

"Where now?" Davie said, peering at the nostrum in my hand.

I looked to the left. "Over there," I said. "The first staircase." There was another shattered body at the doorway.

We took the steps in threes, looking in each room that we came to. Those on the first floor were empty, the doors ajar. As we were halfway up the next flight, we heard a crack followed by a sharp cry.

Davie thundered into the room in front of me. "It's me, Harry," I heard him say. "Shit, what have you done?"

I made it to the landing and pushed him aside. "Where's Katharine? What's—?" I broke off as I took in the scene in front of me. Katharine was still hooked up to Dirty Harry, both of them standing dead still. Beyond them Billy Geddes was sitting in his wheelchair, an expression of sheer terror on his irregular features. He didn't seem to be hurt, which was more than could be said for the other occupant of the plush sitting room.

"Christ," I gasped. "Is that who I think it is?"

Billy nodded slowly. "Lachlan Lessels, also known as Slick." He was staring at the body that was lying in a scarlet pool in front of him. "Late senior guardian of Enlightenment Edinburgh." He turned and looked at the Grendel, the aggressive side of his nature reasserting itself. "Why the fuck did you kill him?"

"You're next, Heriot 07," Dirty Harry said, raising his right arm. There was no weapon in his hand. "You and he signed Edinburgh over to the bastards in New Oxford, didn't you? The toxins in the Poison Fields are going to make this golden sewer uninhabitable any day now, so you've let them move their operation to Edinburgh."

"Is that true, Billy?" I asked, moving between him and the former Fisheries Guard commander. I knew from the look on the occupant of the wheelchair's face that it was even before he nodded. "Harry," I said, turning to the Grendel and opening my arms. "Don't do it. Billy's just a fixer. The guardians would be the ones who took the decision."

Dirty Harry stared at me, his eyes cold glints, then lowered his arm slowly. He put his other hand to his waist and unfastened the umbilical link. "There you go, Katharine Kirkwood," he said. "You're free."

She stared at him and tugged off her end of the wire. "You aren't, though," she observed, her voice sharp. "What are you going to do? Kill every bulldog in the city?"

Harry took a deep breath and then shook his head. "No. I'm finished." He sank into an armchair and his head dropped to his chest. He looked like a man who'd run a double marathon. "I'm finished," he repeated, the words faint.

I squeezed Katharine's arm and got a frosty glare for my pains. She didn't seem too traumatised by her experience. I wanted to talk to her, I wanted to make sure that she really was okay, but I needed to question her captor first. It wouldn't be long before the bulldogs arrived.

"You're not finished, Harry," I said, kneeling in front of him. "You can come back to Edinburgh with us."

He was inhaling deeply, the breath catching in his throat. "Can I fuck, Citizen Quint." His eyes met mine and I felt the power of them again. "Don't you understand what I am?"

I was forced to look away. "I know what you've done, Harry. But there are mitigating factors."

He laughed until he choked. Perhaps his system was finally succumbing to toxic exposure. "You still don't get it, do you?" he said. "What kind of smartarse are you?"

I stood up, accepting the challenge. "All right, here's what I think, Harry. Your surviving crew – four of them, right? – were killed during the Mark Two fitting-out process, weren't they?" I repeated the term Raphael had used, not that I understood it.

"That's more like it," he said, giving me an approving nod. "And what was it that killed them, Mr Investigator?"

I was looking at his right arm. There had been something strange about it, something unnatural in the way he raised it at Billy. "Where's your ASAR, Harry?" I asked. "How did you shoot Hamilton and the academics in the theatre? How did you kill Raphael and Slick?" I glanced round the room. Katharine, Billy and Davie were staring at me in expectation. "You've got some kind of artificial arm, haven't you? An arm that contains an advanced long-range rifle."

"Bull's-eye," the Grendel said, flexing his fingers. "I hate the fucking thing but it has its uses."

"And your crewmen died when their arms were being fitted," I added.

He nodded. "Blood poisoning in the stumps. The fucking medics screwed the drugs up."

"That's why you've been going around amputating arms, isn't it?" Katharine said, shaking her head. "Jesus Christ Almighty. Why did you mutilate that poor kid in Edinburgh, you bastard? He didn't do anything to you."

Dirty Harry shrugged. "I made sure I picked a scumbag gang member and I made sure he didn't know anything about what happened to him." He put his hand in his pocket and came out with a small, matt black canister with a nozzle on the top. "At least I wasn't in full Grendel mode when I caught him – otherwise he'd be as dead as Raphael."

Katharine was standing over the former Fisheries Guard commander. "You left George Faulds in a coma on a stinking tenement floor!" she shouted.

"I tipped the guard off about his whereabouts," Harry said with a shrug.

Katharine turned away in disgust.

I peered at his arm. "You've got a laser in there too, haven't you?" I said, remembering the sound I'd heard on the way up the stairs as well as seeing Raphael's shattered chest. "That's what produced the cauterised wound on Dead Dod."

Harry nodded. "It's not a supermax, but it's lethal enough."

"And the drug you used on him is in there," I said, pointing at the canister. "Did it come from New Oxford?"

"Of course," he replied. "Not all their products are lethal. It was top secret, of course, developed for one of the transnationals. A combined anaesthetic and antiseptic for use during organ transplantation. I stole it from one of Dawkley's supposedly secure labs."

"You left a trail of people in deep coma," Davie said.

Dirty Harry raised his shoulders. "They should all have come round by now. The amnesia will begin to clear up after ten days."

It wasn't a surprise to discover that Haskins had lied to me in the Department of Forensic Chemistry, but I was still pissed off with her. And with myself for not giving the drug compound more attention. "They never admitted to us that it was a Nox product," I said.

The Grendel laughed. "They told you as little as possible – that's the Hebdomadal Council's way. That was why I slipped into your rooms in Brase and left you that clue about the Code Red file – it looked like you needed the help."

"That Ghost unit you've got obscured your appearance as well as keeping the surveillance at bay, didn't it?" I looked at him. "Christ, Harry, why didn't you just wake me up and come clean about everything?" Then I remembered the brief glimpse of him that I'd been given. "You almost showed yourself. Why didn't you go the whole way?"

"You're lucky I didn't, Citizen Quint," he said, drawing the fingers of both hands over his smooth face. "You have to watch me. I come and go. The psych regime they put us through was so severe that there are still times when I swing back into complete Grendel status, no matter how much I fight it. It's like a frenzy. That's how

Ted Pym ended up the way he did. You noticed that I used my auxiliary knife on him, like I did on the Leith Lancer's finger? I didn't mean to, but the conditioning leads to maximum savagery; Mark Two Grendels aren't just hitmen, we're propagandists of violence."

"All roads lead to Oxford," I said. "That was you, wasn't it?"

Harry nodded, his face sombre. "I knew where you lived. The message was a way of getting you down here. I had a feeling that you'd bugger up Raphael's plans." He looked round us all. "Whatever happens, none of you people are going to let New Oxford get its claws any further into Edinburgh, are you? No Nox, nowhere. That's the way it has to be."

Katharine nodded and Davie joined in. It looked like they'd finally found something they could agree on.

Dirty Harry smiled crookedly at me. "By the way, Katharine will confirm that I blew the bone mill in the House of Dust to pieces before we left."

"What the hell's the House of Dust?" demanded Billy. "What bone mill?"

"Never mind now," I said, raising a hand. "How did you lure Raskolnikov to the Botanic Garden? Was it a fake message from his lover boy?"

Harry nodded. "I found out about the male brothel." He held up the Ghost device. "This got me into restricted premises and gave me access to plenty of interesting databases." He ran his fingers over the miniature buttons. "Bad news," he said. "Lister 25's dead. I placed a pinhead monitor on him a couple of nights ago."

"Poor old sod," I said, hoping the toxicologist's last hours had at least been pain-free. "You pointed me in his direction by giving a file that contained a reference to him as well as to the toxins, didn't you?"

"I thought it would get you more involved," Harry said, his head moving up and down. "More outraged about the fuckers who run this place."

"You crushed Raskolnikov's nostrum with that robot hand, didn't you?" Davie said. He stepped forwards. "Bloody hell, Harry, how does it feel to have been turned into a killing machine?" Davie hadn't forgotten that the pair of them went through auxiliary training and served together in the guard. "Can you still remember what you were like before they . . . before they mindfucked you? How did you keep going?"

Dirty Harry kept his head down, then raised it slowly and smiled slackly at his former comrade. "I've had enough of this now. I've reached the end of the road now that Raphael and the bastards who helped her develop the Grendels are dealt with. But what kept me going was revenge, Davie. Revenge. It feeds the fire like nothing else."

There was a swift movement at the door.

"Indeed it does, Number Three," said a familiar voice.

The chief administrator stepped in through the open doorway, her right arm raised. There was no sign of a limp in her wounded leg, no visible trauma to her chest. Before anyone could move, there was an eye-shattering flash of light accompanied by a short, high-pitched report.

When I managed to focus on Harry, I realised that black smoke was emanating from his eyes and that the robotic arm was hanging stiff and motionless over the chair. There was no question about it: the ex-Fisheries Guard captain had set out on his last voyage. I hoped he would find his crew on the way.

I should have paid more attention during English literature classes. It had come to me far too late that

Beowulf didn't only have Grendel to contend with. After he'd pulled the monster's arm off, the hero had to face Grendel's mother.

As we'd just seen, she was even more lethal.

We were taken out of the room in Wad and moved under heavy guard to the Noxad building. Davie discovered the hard way that speaking was not allowed: a bulldog belted him over the back of the head with the butt of his rifle when he tried to address me. I watched him as he straightened his back. His limbs were loose but his eyes were steady enough. I reckoned someone would be paying for that blow.

They held us outside in the quadrangle of the former Bodleian, the bulldogs forming a ring around us with their weapons lowered. I glanced at the others. Katharine's lips were tight and she met my gaze with a questioning look. I shrugged. We didn't exactly have much room for manoeuvre. Billy's silk tie was loose and he was shivering in the chill night air – obviously his designer suit didn't have sufficient wool in the weave. His face was a picture of resentment. The way he stared at me suggested that he held me responsible for screwing up his latest big money deal. Tough. I had other things to worry about: such as how we were going to get out of this intact.

"Take them inside!" came a voice from outside the bulldog ring. I recognised it as Doctor Connington's.

They walked us inside the old library and through to the ornate Gothic hall where we'd been given dinner on our first night. It didn't look like a banquet was on the cards this time. There was a row of administrators at the long table on the platform, but no sign of any food or drink. Raphael had cleaned herself up and changed her blood-soaked clothes. I had a bad feeling about how she'd made such a rapid recovery. She was sitting between Dawkley and Wood-Lewis, Connington and some other individuals I didn't recognise filling the remaining seats on the side away from us. None of them had bothered with academic gowns. This was business, not cod scholasticism.

The bulldogs pushed us to the ground about five yards in front of the table and made us sit with our legs crossed like undergraduates in a matriculation photograph. They didn't have much luck with Billy on that count so they left him in his chair.

"Well, Citizen Dalrymple," the chief administrator began, her expression neutral. "I must congratulate you and your subordinates."

"Screw you," Davie said.

Raphael nodded to the nearest bulldog, who stepped up and jabbed the butt of his weapon down at Davie's head. He got it out of the way but took a heavy blow on the shoulder. Again, he didn't make a sound.

"Keep your observations to yourself, commander," Raphael said, her voice level, "if you want your head to remain on your shoulders." She turned back to me. "As I say, you have done what I hoped you would do. You brought the Mark Two Grendel to us by a combination of luck and ill judgement." She clapped her hands slowly. "Well done, Quint."

"Don't call me Quint," I said, staring at her. "How much of a machine are you, Raphael? Half? Three-quarters? Or have you no human characteristics at all? That would make sense. Only a robot could sanction what goes on in the House of Dust and what's done to the Grendel recruits."

The chief administrator gave a bitter laugh. "As in so many things, you are quite wrong, citizen." She glanced at her colleagues. "The House of Dust was developed by the senior proctor Frederick Wood-Lewis, while the Grendel programme was initiated by Administrator Dawkley. Both of them are one hundred per cent homo sapiens. Professor Yamaguchi was also deeply involved in the conditioning and fitting out of the Mark Two Grendels. He too was without mechanical enhancement."

"Unlike you," I said.

She nodded. "Quite so. I was one of the prototype Grendels, the only one to develop administrative as opposed to enforcement capabilities. As time has passed, I have received additional robotic implants." She stretched out her arms. "The upper part of my body is now substantially synthetic. It was a simple procedure to replace the components damaged by the laser Number Three used on me."

"Your head's full of wires and circuit boards as well as your heart, is it?" Katharine asked bitterly.

Raphael declined to answer.

"Here," Billy said, rolling his wheelchair forward. "Why am I with them?" He glanced back at us disparagingly. "I'm the senior representative of Edinburgh here now that Slick . . . now that the senior guardian is dead."

"Get back in line, Geddes," Raphael ordered, her eyes locked on him. "Our plans for Edinburgh no longer involve you."

Billy swallowed and put the wheelchair into reverse.

"What exactly are those plans?" I asked.

"I would have thought that was obvious, Dalrymple," Dawkley said, after glancing at his boss. "We will be transferring much of our operation to your city before the toxins from the Poison Fields overrun us. The remainder will be relocated to Glasgow." He gave a tight smile. "First Secretary Duart has been most accommodating."

"Is that right?" I said. "And do your plans to relocate include the people you refer to as subs?"

Raphael looked at me like a professor who'd mistakenly wandered into a primary school class. "Don't be ridiculous," she said. "As far as the university is concerned, the subs have reached the end of their useful life." She gave me a blank look. "By the way, your friend Pete Pym met with an accident on his way back to Cowley."

I felt my stomach freeze. "What?"

Her eyes, suddenly filled with pale fire and malice, burned into mine. "Yes, citizen. Regrettably he fell from a Chariot and cracked his skull on the parapet of Magd Bridge. He was dead before the medics reached him."

I felt the blood course through my veins like battery acid. I hardly needed anything more to demonstrate the callous depravity that lay beneath New Oxford, but this final heartless act was almost unbearable. I clenched my fists and somehow managed to get a grip on myself.

"Try to understand, citizen," the chief administrator said, her tone rational. "He was dead the second he entered the House of Dust. Subs who resist the Council cannot expect to survive."

I still didn't trust myself to speak. Fortunately Katharine took up the fight.

"He was a human being, for God's sake," she said, her hands at her forehead. "Maybe you can't understand what that means any more, Raphael, but surely the rest of you have some conception." She looked down the table then shook her head. "Jesus, you're all sick in the head. You oppress the people, you carry out experiments on them, you lock them up, you kill them—" She broke off and stifled a sob. "You burn them, you . . . you grind their bones . . . I can't believe you do all that and then gather to drink sherry in the evening . . ."

I nudged her with my elbow and looked into her eyes, not that I could do anything to assuage the pain. I turned to the front again. "Is it true that you use the bone residue in hyper-conductors?" I asked in a low voice.

Dawkley nodded. "Indeed. In certain combinations human bone meal has proved to be extremely effective. Not to mention extremely profitable."

Billy looked up when he heard the last word. "Haven't you got it, Quint? That's what New Oxford is all about," he said with a mocking smile. "The university, NOX industries – they're all businesses. The transnational corporations make a mint from this place."

Raphael glanced at her colleagues. "That is part of the story, yes."

"What do you mean part of the story?" Billy demanded. There was nothing but profit in his embittered take on the world.

The chief administrator laughed. "There's no harm in disclosing this information to you people now." Those words made sweat dampen my shirt. Christ knows what she was planning for us. "Although the global companies sponsor students and research programmes – for which they receive a handsome return – the bulk of the profits from New Oxford go to the offshore corporation which backed the re-establishment of the university." She ran her eyes over us and held them on Billy. "That corporation is based in Cyprus. It has a particular interest in the study of crime. Whence the significance of the Faculty of Criminology, whence the development of advanced security operatives like the Grendels, whence the extensive research into incarceration methods."

"Crime and punishment," I muttered, thinking of the concrete blocks in the former colleges, the tented city in the university parks and the torture chambers in the

House of Dust. The multinational element of the university also came to mind: senior academics from countries as far apart as Italy, Russia and Japan. Then I dredged something else from my memory of the years before Edinburgh's independence. "Billy," I said, turning to the wizened figure in the wheelchair, "wasn't Cyprus a hotbed of criminal activity at the beginning of the century? Weren't there stories about international crime syndicates setting up on the island after the Greeks and Turks massacred each other?"

"Fuck, aye," my former friend said, clapping his twisted hands. "That's right." He looked up at Raphael. "Don't tell me," he said, an avid smile spreading across his uneven face. "Don't tell me that this place is run by the Mob?" He let out a high-pitched laugh.

"It is many years since the corporation has been known by that appellation," the chief administrator said disapprovingly. "But yes, your assertion is broadly true. Our parent organisation did originally stem from high-ranking members of the major American, European and Asian crime groups." She was looking at Billy. "Of course, as you no doubt know, they had already started to diversify into legal activities such as banking, medical research, software development and so on."

I laughed, even though what I'd heard wasn't even vaguely amusing. "I suppose it was completely natural that they subsequently diversified into crime control, prison management and criminological research."

"Quite so, citizen," Dawkley said. "The states that managed to regroup after the drugs wars have major internal security needs." He looked at his leader, nostrum in his hand.

She checked her own device and nodded. "It is time," she said.

"Time for what?" Davie demanded.

I had the distinct impression that we were about to go for a one-way walk, so I tried to buy us more of what Raphael had called. "Hang on," I said. "You haven't let me explain everything that happened in the investigation."

The chief administrator laughed. "What is there to explain, citizen? We knew a Mark Two Grendel was on my tracks after Hamilton was shot. When he left the message on your bedroom wall in Edinburgh, I saw that you would be useful to us here and assumed, correctly, that the Grendel would contact you again. We kept you on a drip feed of information – some of it less than reliable – so that you would find your own way to the assassin. If we had told you his identity from the outset, would you have led us to him? I don't think so." She pursed her lips. "I have to admit you came too close to some of our most sensitive operations for comfort, but fortunately the Grendel aided us by kidnapping your woman friend." She gave Katharine a superior look.

"You didn't imagine that one of your precious semi-robots would rebel against you," I said, looking in disgust at the so-called enhanced human being who ran New Oxford. "You never thought that the urge for revenge could override all your programming and mind-altering drugs, did you?"

Raphael ran her tongue along her lips in a movement that almost looked natural. "No, we didn't, though I have just experienced that urge myself – a pity I succumbed to it. I'm glad to say that Mark Three Grendels will not be susceptible to unpredictable behaviour like that." She gave Katharine a tight smile. "They will all be female and much more reliable."

I thought of Hel Hyslop. What had she let herself in for?

Davie peered up at the chief administrator. "You said you wanted to see how Harry's systems had evolved, but all you really wanted was to terminate him." I could tell that he was affected by his old colleague's death, but I didn't think she could; his face was as impassive as an Edinburgh guard commander could make it.

She returned his gaze steadily. "I did want Administrator Dawkley's experts to examine Number Three," she said. "He attacked me before I could react, his combat conditioning being superior to mine, and I found myself more interested in trying out the new ultramax laser that was recently fitted in my arm."

Davie was still staring at her as she got to her feet.

"As I said, it is time." Raphael turned to Wood-Lewis. "Advise the House of Dust that the prisoners are on their way."

The senior proctor nodded, his lips forming into a slack smile. "Your friend may have destroyed the bone mill, but the rendering unit is still operational."

I saw Davie's arm come up. He was pointing to the area behind the dais where the administrators were sitting. "Look out!" he shouted. "Harry's still alive!"

Everyone craned to see, Raphael and her colleagues turning their heads. Almost immediately they – and I – saw that the space was unoccupied.

It was then that I realised Davie had grown an extra finger – one that was a dull silver colour. There was a sharp cracking noise and a line of blue light flashed from his extended arm towards the chief administrator. Her head exploded in a blast of sparks and liquid, lumpen red.

CHAPTER TWENTY-THREE

The acrid reek of charred tissue and melted circuits soon drove everybody from the former Divinity School. There was a tense period immediately after Raphael's enforced shutdown when we were at the mercy of the bulldogs. The way that Davie held the miniature laser on Wood-Lewis made them see sense. It soon became apparent that none of them, administrators included, had any stomach for a fight.

"She . . . it . . . I don't really know which applies, was becoming too autocratic," Wood-Lewis said in the quadrangle. He was keeping his eyes off me.

"I didn't see you doing much to get her hands off the controls," I said sarcastically. "What now?"

The senior proctor raised his shoulders. "That's up to you, Quintilian Dalrymple," he said, glancing at the weapon in Davie's hand. "You're calling the shots."

I glanced at Dawkley. "How long before Raphael acquires a new head?"

"You needn't worry, citizen," he said despondently. "As you saw earlier, replacing Grendel body components is straightforward. But it's different with the head. We retained the complex structure of the human brain, relying on drugs and psychological conditioning with only a minimum of implants to enhance capability." He ran a hand across his forehead. "You won't see the chief administrator again."

I believed him about as much as I believed in divine justice. We needed to move fast.

"We're going home," I said. "And Wood-Lewis? You're coming with us to make sure nothing happens on the way. Get a helijet warmed up."

The senior proctor's eyes opened wide then he nodded slowly. "Very well." He spoke into his nostrum.

"Next," I said, "get one of your minions to pick up our gear from Brase."

He dispatched Harriet Haskins.

"And next," I said, resisting the temptation to floor him, "I want Lister 25 on the plane with us." I glared at him. "And if you tell me that his body's already been sent to the House of Dust, you'll be taking his place in the coffin."

There was a hurried conversation on the nostrum, resulting in a look of desperate relief on the senior proctor's face. "It's all right," he said in a faint voice. "The body's still in Worc. It's being collected now."

"Just as well," I said, even though what I felt about the old blues freak's death was still threatening to break out.

"Quint?" Katharine was at my side.

"Aye." I smiled tentatively at her but didn't get a similar response.

"We need to tell the Council what's been going on down here." She looked at Frederick Wood-Lewis with open disgust. "We need to make sure they remove every piece of New Oxford shit from Edinburgh before anyone else is hurt."

She was right. There was also the matter of the ex-senior guardian. Someone had to tell his colleagues, not that I imagined they would declare a day of mourning. Slick wasn't anyone's favourite person.

I turned to Dawkley. "Can your people patch up a mobile phone link between here and Edinburgh?"

"Use my nostrum," he said, starting to remove the device from his neck.

"No, thanks," I replied. "I've had enough of Nox technology."

After a few moments my phone picked up the long-range connection. I walked to the other end of the old quad and rang Sophia's number. When she answered I heard the sound of a toddler burbling in the background.

"How's Maisie?" I asked.

"Quint? Is that you?" Sophia sounded both surprised and relieved. "The Mist . . . the public order guardian told the Council yesterday that you and your team had been reported missing by the New Oxford authorities."

"I wouldn't believe anything Hamilton's successor says. She's been following instructions from the bastards in New Oxford. Are you all right, Sophia?"

"On the mend, thank you. The dressing is off my eye." Sophia paused. "I'm not bothered that I'll have a scar on my cheek." Her attempt at indifference wasn't totally convincing.

I gave her a précis of what we'd been through. She listened in silence, the only noise at her end coming from the little girl.

"I'm appalled," she said when I finished. "I'll advise the Council immediately. I'll propose the severing of all links with New Oxford forthwith. In the light of what you've discovered, I don't think there will be many objections."

"What about the Mist?" I asked.

"Don't worry about her. Citizens have already been demonstrating against the prison. I'd hazard a guess that by this time tomorrow she'll be the only person occupying a cell."

"Very good." I was aware of Katharine at my side. She spoke to me in a low voice. "Oh, and Sophia? What's the status of Dead Dod?"

"The one-armed Leith Lancer? He's all right. Psychologically traumatised by the loss of his arm, but on the mend. The other victims have regained consciousness."

"At least they didn't end up in the House of Dust," I said.

There was a long silence. "Unbelievable," Sophia said finally. "To think I used to dream of studying medicine under the dreaming spires when I was a girl."

"You were well out of it," I said. "Out."

Katharine was staring at me. "Well?" she demanded.

"Don't worry," I said with a laugh, "Dead Dod isn't dead after all."

She turned on me. "This isn't a joke, Quint!" she yelled. "What's the matter with you? People are mutilated, people are killed, people are ground to dust and you go on in the same facetious way as if it's all some kind of game. I'm sick of it." She raised her fists as if to lay into me, then dropped them and strode away.

If I'd been quick enough, I'd have told her that being facetious was the only way to survive the horrors we'd witnessed – except I knew that was a cop-out.

My job is hell if you allow yourself to feel too much, but it's even worse if you don't feel enough.

We were standing inside the blast shields on the helijet apron at what used to be called Magdalen College. Harriet Haskins had arrived with our bags. She handed them over with an embarrassed expression on her shapely face. Maybe she was expecting me to give her a hard time for bullshitting about the drug compound, but I let her off; what she'd done was nothing compared with the crimes perpetrated by her leaders. A pair of bulldogs in orange overalls were loading Lister 25's steel coffin into the hold. Before that they'd rolled Billy Geddes up a ramp into the passenger compartment.

"At least the old chemist's remains will go up into the air back home," Davie said, the pencil-shaped laser still trained on Wood-Lewis.

I nodded. "Aye, I suppose that's some consolation." I turned to Dawkley, who was a few yards away. "In any other state you'd be tried as mass murderers, all of you." I glanced back at the senior proctor. "What gave you the right to destroy so many people's lives? What gave you the right to harvest their organs – Christ, and their flesh? You even made a profit on their bones."

The science administrator looked uneasy, but not for long. "You're wrong, Citizen Dalrymple. In most modern states we would never be brought to trial. People like us have the power to transform society. We are beyond laws, never mind your feeble ethics."

I felt my fists clench by my sides. "That's because your bastard parent corporation runs most modern states, isn't it?"

He nodded. "And more are being taken over every year. Even if Edinburgh won't take us, it will be easy enough to establish Nox in Glasgow."

"No, it won't." Andrew Duart had appeared behind Dawkley, briefcase in hand and suit carrier over his shoulder. Hel Hyslop was with him. "Earlier I heard from Katharine Kirkwood on my nostrum," he said. "She told me about the House of Dust, among other things." He put his hand in his pocket and took out a clear plastic bag, which he opened and tipped up. "This is all that remains of the contract I misguidedly signed with New Oxford. I burned it before I left Wad."

I watched as the stream of grey ash poured out into the still, floodlit air. It dissipated quickly in the breeze, flakes scattering over the science administrator's highly polished shoes.

Ashes to ashes, I thought. And boarded the aircraft.

The lights of central Oxford fell away beneath us as the helijet lifted up with a restrained scream. I looked beyond them and saw only the occasional streetlamp out in the suburbs. What would happen to the residents of Cowley and the outer areas? Maybe Dawkley and his experts would manage to develop an anti-toxin now they were being forced to stay in the city – if there was time. Maybe they would extend the benefits of their research to the so-called subs. I tried to make myself believe there was even a minimal chance of that.

Katharine was sitting across the aisle from me, her eyes closed. I could tell by the rise of her chest that her breathing was slow and regular, but I didn't think she was asleep.

"I'm sorry, Katharine," I said in a low voice, leaning towards her. "I know you think I wasn't serious enough about Dead— Shit . . . about George Faulds."

She opened one eye and fixed it on me. "And?"

"And I know you think I haven't been taking the things we saw back there seriously enough." I touched the hand that was on the armrest. It wasn't withdrawn. "But I was affected by them, I really was. I hate what they drove Dirty Harry to and I despise what the bastards have done to the ordinary people."

She turned full on to me. "I know you do, Quint. I just

think you need to show it more sometimes. After all, this case was all about human emotions. I always thought there was something unnatural about Raphael. If you'd picked that up then maybe we'd have caught on to what she was doing more quickly."

I nodded. I'd picked up something about the chief administrator all right but, to my shame, I'd allowed myself to be seduced by it. I always did have a thing for powerful women. Christ, I'd let myself be strung along by a middle-aged semi-robot.

I felt Katharine's other hand on top of mine. "Don't worry," she said. "I haven't given up on you." She smiled. "Student's end-of-term report: Much impressive progress. A particularly fine criminology project. More attention needs to be paid to interpersonal relations, especially those with the opposite sex."

"Very funny," I said ruefully. "One thing, Katharine. What was the long shot you were pursuing before the Encaenia?"

She laughed. "Long shot? What long shot? The Grendel got into my rooms and tied me up in a service shaft off the mole run beneath Brase. It was Dirty Harry who wrote that message."

"It wasn't the first time he took you prisoner," I said, thinking back to the case we'd worked in 2025.

"No, it wasn't," she said, shaking her head. "But it was the last."

I pulled my hand away gently and went forward. Davie was still watching over Wood-Lewis in case he or the pilots tried to pull a fast one.

"All right, big man?"

He looked up. "Oh aye." The laser was on his knee. "This thing will grill the old bastard's kidneys through the seat no problem."

The senior proctor shifted nervously in the seat to the front.

"We'll be over Edinburgh soon," I said.

"Thank Christ for that," Davie said. "I need a shower, a large meal and a selection of barracks malts."

I laughed and left him to it. He seemed to be getting over what we'd been through in New Oxford. I went back to my seat via Billy Geddes, who was still ignoring me, and stopped off at the Glaswegian contingent.

"So you decided against becoming a Mark Three Grendel, Hel?" I said.

She gave me a weak smile. "The first secretary put me off that idea." Her eyes flashed. "Not that the basic idea of enhanced human beings is a bad one. Maybe another time."

I glanced across the aisle at Andrew Duart. "Sending her back to Barlinnie, are you?"

He shook his head emphatically. "I've seen enough of prisons." He looked at Hel with blatant lust. "And I think I can find room for the inspector in my private office. Among other places."

I wasn't impressed. "Just keep her away from Edinburgh," I said. "Remember, she's got a criminal record the length of my arm."

That put a dampener on them, not that anything I said would stop them getting stuck into each other when the helijet took them home after Edinburgh.

I sat down and put my hand on Katharine's. This time she was definitely asleep, so I removed it and left her in peace. I looked out into the darkness and felt something hard in my ribs. I pulled out my father's guide to Oxford that was in the pocket of my donkey jacket – I'd discarded the remains of my formal suit in the toilet earlier – but I didn't open it. Although New Oxford bore only a passing resemblance to the city Hector knew, I'd still had enough of the crenellated colleges with their solid gates to keep out the masses.

Then I found myself considering Dirty Harry and Raphael. They were a new species, an amalgam of human being and machine, of biological and synthetic materials; but they'd turned out to be even more flawed than the real thing. Despite what he'd said, Dawkley had probably started working on rebuilding them, improving them the minute we left New Oxford. In that case mankind would be one step closer to immortality, the oldest, most seductive dream of all. I twitched my head. That was a bucket of shit. My long-lost lover Caro died back in 2015 and her face was clearer in my mind than those of the chief administrator and Dirty Harry. There are things you can't buy – or develop in a laboratory.

As the noise from the helijet's engines dropped and the fuselage sank into the final descent, I found myself thinking about Edinburgh. The Council's city was a lot less perfect than the guardians claimed, but it was where I was born, it was the place I understood best. I looked out over the darkened suburbs towards the blaze of light coming from the castle and the central tourist zone around it. The incarceration initiative had failed, but the youth gangs would still be giving us plenty of trouble. That thought didn't exactly fill me with joy.

Then, suddenly, the strains of an old master's guitar began to race through my head, strains that I'd first heard on a film when I was a kid before the Enlightenment's regulations banned all so-called subversive music. Alvin Lee was the performer and "Going Home" was the number – the epic performance at Woodstock when the world still retained a few reserves of innocence.

Going home. That would have to do.

For now.

Don't miss Paul Johnston's other highly-acclaimed thrillers: *Body Politic, The Bone Yard, Water of Death* and *The Blood Tree.*

BODY POLITIC

Winner of the Crime Writers' Association John Creasey Memorial Dagger for best first crime novel of the year

'Think of Plato's Republic with a body count'

The Sunday Times

'An intricate web . . . Johnston is a Fawkes among plotters'

Observer

'Fascinating and thought-provoking'

Val McDermid, *Manchester Evening News*

An independent city where television, private cars and popular music are banned, where the citizens are dedicated to the tourists attending the year-round Festival, and where crime is virtually non-existent, Edinburgh in the year 2020 has its drawbacks for blues-haunted private investigator Quintilian Dalrymple.

But the brutal killing of a guardswoman – the first murder in five years – is enough to scare the Council of City Guardians out of complacency. It looks like the Ear, Nose and Throat Man has returned. And they are forced to turn to the man they demoted to uncover a conspiracy of violence and sexual intrigue that reaches into a dark heart of corruption and threatens to dismember the body politic.

Read on for an extract . . .

In the last decade of the twentieth century people bought crime fiction like there was no tomorrow – which soon turned out to be the case for many of them. It isn't hard to see why detective stories were addictive. The indomitable heroes and heroines with their reassuring solutions prolonged the illusion that a stable society existed outside the readers' security windows and armoured doors.

Since the Enlightenment won power in Edinburgh, the popularity of crime novels has gradually declined, though not as much as the guardians think. They would prefer citizens to read philosophical investigations rather than those of Holmes and Poirot, Morse and Dalgliesh, but even in the "perfect city" people hanker for the old certainties.

I often have trouble deciding what to believe. All the same, the message that the Council sent on my birthday gave me even more of a shock than the first time I heard James Marshall Hendrix playing the "Catfish Blues".

I shouldn't have been so surprised. Sceptics and detectives have the same general principle: the only thing you can be sure of is that you can't be sure of anything at all.

CHAPTER ONE

Ghost-grey day in the city and seagulls screaming through the fog that had been smothering us for a week. Tourists started to head up George IVth Bridge for the Friday execution. I was the only local paying attention. If you want to survive in Edinburgh, you've got to keep reminding yourself this place is weirder than sweet-smelling sewage.

My shift with the squad of Parks Department labourers was due to finish at four but I'd made up my mind long before that. I had an hour before my meeting with the woman who signed herself Katharine K. It was 20 March 2020, I was thirty-six years old and I was going to break the rules.

"Are you coming for a pint, Quint?" one of the boys asked.

It was tempting, but I managed to shake my head. There would have been no escape if they had known what day it was. The Council describes birthday celebrations as "excessively self-indulgent" in the City Regulations, but the tradition of getting paralytic remains. It's one of the few that does. Anyway, I had a sex session later on and if you're pissed at one of those, you're in deep shit.

"Course he isn't." Roddy the Ox wiped sweat and snot away with the back of his arm. "He'll be away to the library like a model arse-licking citizen." Every squad's got a self-appointed spokesman and I never get on with any of them. So I go to the library a lot. Not just to broaden my mind. I spend most of my time in the archives checking up on the people my clients report missing.

"Actually," I said, looking the big man in the eye, "I'm going to watch the execution." Jaws dropped so quickly that I checked my flies. "Anybody else coming?"

They stood motionless in their fatigues, turned to stone. Not even the Ox seemed to fancy gate-crashing a party that's strictly tourists only.

The way things are, I usually try to stick out from the crowd. Not this time. As I was the only ordinary citizen pushing a bicycle towards the Royal Mile, I tried to make myself inconspicuous. The buses carrying groups to the gallows gave me a bit of cover. So did the clouds of diesel fumes, at the same time as choking me. Fifteen years since private cars were banned and still the place reeks.

The mass of humanity slowed as it approached the check-point above the library's grimy façade. Rousing folksongs came from loudspeakers, the notes echoing through the mist like the cries of sinners in the pit. Some of the tourists were glancing at adverts for events in the year-round Festival which is the Council's main source of income. Among them were posters of the front page of *Time*'s New Year edition proclaiming Edinburgh "Worldwide City of the Year". The words "Garden of Edin" were printed in maroon under a photo of the floodlit castle. I've worked in most of the city's gardens but I've yet to see a naked woman – or a snake.

I kept my head down and tried not to bump into too many people with my front wheel. The guards had raised the barrier as the time of the execution drew near. Fortunately they weren't bothering to examine the herd of people. I felt a stickiness in my armpits that would stay with me till my session next week at the communal baths. Why was I taking the chance? The fire in my veins a few seconds later answered the question – I'd managed to get into a forbidden part of the city. I felt like a real anarchist. Till I started calculating my chances of getting out so easily.

I let myself be swallowed up by the crowd that had gathered round the gallows in the Lawnmarket. Guides were struggling to make themselves heard, speaking Arabic, Chinese, Greek, Korean. There was a small group of elderly Americans in transparent rain-capes. They were among the first from across the Atlantic; until recently the Council refused entry to nationals of what it called in its diplomatic way "culturally bankrupt states". A bearded courier in a kilt was giving them the sales pitch.

"The Royal Mile runs from the castle to what remains of Holyrood Palace," he bellowed, pointing towards the mist-covered lower reaches. "The palace was reduced to ruins in the rioting that followed the last coronation in 2002. The crown prince's divorce and remarriage to a Colombian drugs heiress signed the old order's death warrant." He paused to catch his breath and gave me a suspicious look. "The already fragile United Kingdom quickly broke up into dozens of warring city-states. Thanks to the Council of City Guardians, Edinburgh has been the only one to achieve stability . . ."

The propaganda washed over me. I knew most of it by heart. I wondered again about the note I'd found under my door yesterday. "Can't wait any longer," it read. "Meet me at 3 Lennox Street Lane five p.m. tomorrow if you want work. Katharine K." The handwriting was spidery, very different from the copperplate required in the city's schools and colleges. The writer must have been hanging about on the landing outside my flat for quite a time. Despite the fumes from the nearby brewery, the place was filled with her scent. I knew exactly what it was: Moonflower, classified Grade 3 by the Supply Directorate and issued to lower level hotel and restaurant workers. Beneath the perfume lay the even stronger smell of a client desperate for my services.

It was coming up to four thirty and the guides took a break from their shouting competition. Looking around the crowd, I was struck by how many of the tourists were disabled in one way or another: some were in wheelchairs, some were clutching their companions' arms, a few even looked to be blind. The Council had probably been working on a braille version of the hanging.

Then there was a hush as the condemned man was led up to the scaffold by guards in period costume. The prisoner's hands were bound and a black velvet bag placed over his head.

The guides started speaking again. The bearded man was explaining to the Americans that this was Deacon William Brodie, the city's most notorious villain.

"Here, in the heart of the city where crime no longer exists" – at least according to the Public Order Directorate – "Brodie committed his outrages. He was a cabinet-maker by trade, rising to become Deacon of Wrights and Masons. But by night he was a master-burglar, robbing dozens of wealthy householders."

Encouraged by their guides' gestures, the tourists began to boo. The English-speaking guide moved nearer the gallows.

"Brodie was eventually caught, but not before his

reputation had gained a permanent place in the minds of his fellow citizens. A century later the Edinburgh writer Robert Louis Stevenson used him as the model for his famous study of evil in *Dr Jekyll and Mr Hyde*. The man in the kilt gave a fawning grin. "Don't forget to pick up a souvenir edition of the book in your hotel giftshop."

Under the gibbet final preparations were being made. I followed them closely, trying to work out how they faked it. There was no sign of a protective collar. It even looked like the victim was trembling involuntarily. I remembered summary executions I had seen, members of the drugs gangs that terrorised the city in the years after independence being put up against a wall. They had shaken in the same way, sworn at the guardsmen to get it over with. To my disgust I found that my heart was racing as it had done then.

The presiding officer, dressed in black tunic and lace collar, shouted across the crowd from the scaffold. "On 1 October 1788 Brodie mounted the set of gallows which he himself had designed – to be hanged by the neck until he was dead."

There were a few seconds of silence to let everyone's flesh creep, then a loud wooden thump as the trap jerked open and the body dropped behind a screen, leaving the rope twisting one way then the other from the tarred beam. The spectators went wild.

I pushed my way to the side, wheeling my bicycle past the tartan and whisky shops towards Bank Street. I felt a bit shaky. It had struck me that maybe the execution wasn't just a piece of theatre for the tourists. I mean, staging mock hangings in a city where capital punishment has been abolished and violence of any kind supposedly eradicated is cynical enough. Actually getting rid of the small number of murderers serving life with hard labour in the city's one remaining prison would be seriously hypocritical. But with the Council you never know. It's always boasting about the unique benefits it's given us: stability, work and housing for everyone, as much self-improvement as you can stomach. But what about freedom? Even suicide has been outlawed.

I turned the corner. By the Finance Directorate, a great, dilapidated palace that had once housed the Bank of Scotland, the barrier was down and the city guardswoman standing in front of it was definitely not friendly. She stuck her hand out for my ID.

"What are you doing up here, citizen?" She was in her mid-twenties, tall and fit-looking. Her red hair was in a neat ponytail beneath her beret and the maroon heart – emblem of the city – was prominent on the left breast pocket of her grey tunic. On the right was her barracks name and number. The heavy belt around her waist provided straps for her sheath knife and truncheon; since the gangs were dealt with, the City Guard no longer carry firearms. "Well?" she demanded. "I'm waiting."

I tried to look innocent. "I was working at the museum, Wilkie 418 . . ."

She didn't buy it. "Your flat's in the opposite direction." She had the neutral voice that all auxiliaries acquire during training. The Council has been trying to get rid of class distinctions by banning local accents. It's a nice theory. "You've no business to come this way."

She ran her eyes over my labourers' fatigues and checked the data on my ID card – height five feet ten inches, weight eleven stone in the imperial system: bringing that back was one of the Council's stranger decisions. Hair black, a bit over the one-inch maximum stipulated for male citizens. Eyes brown. Nose aquiline. Teeth complete and in good condition. Then she glanced at my right hand to check the distinguishing mark, showing no sign of emotion. Finally she gave me a stare that would have brought a tear to the eye of the Sphinx. She had registered the letters "DM" that told her I'd been demoted from the rank of auxiliary.

"I hope you don't think I'm going to do you any favours." The sudden hard edge to her voice rasped like a meat-saw biting bone. "You've no business in a tourist area. Report to your local barracks tomorrow morning, citizen." She handed me an offence notification. "You'll be assigned two Sundays' community service and your record will be endorsed accordingly." She glanced at my face. "You could do with a shave as well."

I stood at the checkpoint with the neatly written sheet in my hand for a few moments. Cheering from the race-track that had been laid over the disused railway lines in Princes Street Gardens came up through the fog. The seagulls had given up auditioning for the City Choir and now I could hear bagpipe music from the speakers beneath the streetlamps. It sounded more mournful than any blues song I ever played. My appetite for meeting the fragrant Katharine K. had gone completely.

"Oh, and citizen," the guardswoman called humourlessly from the sentry box. "Happy Birthday."

PAUL JOHNSTON

THE BONE YARD

'First-rate crime fiction with an original twist'

Sunday Telegraph

'Impressive follow-up to the award-winning *Body Politic* . . . Johnston's conceit with Edinburgh is brilliant and there's a mordant Scots wit . . . stylish'

Guardian

'A sly satire and gruesome thriller'

Daily Telegraph

'A powerful, fantastical thriller'

Mail on Sunday

New Year's Eve 2021. The one night of the year when the guards are less vigilant. The perfect time for murder.

Welcome to 21st century Edinburgh. An oppressive, crime-free independent city state, run by the Council of City Guardians. Subversive, blues-haunted private investigator Quintilian Dalrymple and his side-kick Davie are back on the case, trying to solve a series of murders in which music tapes are planted inside the victims. And the solution lies in the Bone Yard. If they can ever figure out what the Bone Yard is . . .

PAUL JOHNSTON

WATER OF DEATH

'An acclaimed crime series . . . Johnston brings an intelligent perspective to the dark excitement of the thriller'

Nicholas Blincoe, *Observer*

'Both prescient and illuminating'

Ian Rankin, *Daily Telegraph*

'Johnston's vision is shot through with the bleakest of black humour, never losing sight of the humanity of his characters. This series is getting better all the time'

Val McDermid, *Manchester Evening News*

'A thoroughly enjoyable tale'

Sunday Telegraph

Edinburgh 2025 – an independent, almost crime-free oasis surrounded by anarchic city-states. Except global warming has turned summer into the Big Heat and water, like everything else, is strictly rationed. Citizens live only for the weekly lottery draw while serving the tourists in the year-round festival. When a recent lottery winner goes missing, subversive investigator Quintilian Dalrymple is called in to deal with a minor case of the summertime blues.

Then a body is discovered face down in the Water of Leith – the only clue to the death, a bottle of contraband whisky. Quint thinks he sees the first traces of ruthless conspiracy to destabilise the city. And the body count, like the temperature, keeps on rising . . .

HODDER AND STOUGHTON PAPERBACKS

PAUL JOHNSTON

THE BLOOD TREE

'This futuristic series is still refreshingly original and entertaining'
Sunday Telegraph

'Quint Dalrymple [is] a testy, tenacious detective . . . a smart move to shift much of the novel to Glasgow'
The Sunday Times

'The platonic dystopia of Enlightenment Edinburgh is perfect for blending crime stories and satire . . . a pacy read and all the required elements are there: villains are unmasked, loose ends are tied up, and like revenge, justice is served cold'
The Scotsman

Independent Edinburgh – a tourist's paradise, a citizen's paradox. It's 2026. The birth-rate is down in the Council's 'perfect city' and gangs of disaffected kids roam the streets. A break-in at the former Scottish Parliament archive is rapidly followed by two gruesome murders, the victims mutilated and covered with blood-drenched branches.

Under the watchful eyes of the guardians, renegade investigator Quintilian Dalrymple is called in to establish a pattern and to stop the roots of violence spreading.

But Quint's investigation is driven in a different direction when Edinburgh's brightest teenagers are abducted to the much-feared democratic city-state of Glasgow.

What Quint finds there will change his life forever . . .

HODDER AND STOUGHTON PAPERBACKS